Mestizo

Master of the Wild, Book 2

J. Bradley Van Tighem

"There is no death, only a change of worlds."

—Chief Seattle

Dedication

To my wonderful sons, Jason and Aaron

"Work hard, act with compassion, and good things will happen…"

Acknowledgments

This story has been two-year endeavor made possible thanks to numerous contributions from friends and family. Any contribution, however large or small, was invaluable in helping me to complete this work. My heartfelt thanks goes out to everyone who contributed, but especially to these individuals:

A big thanks to the folks at NaNoWriMo, who provide a wonderful forum for creating early manuscripts and supporting authors. Most of "Mestizo" was written in two November sessions of NaNoWriMo.

My friend and co-worker, Will Mitchell, for being an early beta tester with the manuscript and offering much needed story validation.

My illustrator, Maxi Quy, for his excellent rendition of Thorn Bird, which became the cover.

My editor, David Gatewood, for many painstaking hours turning my creative chicken scratches into a readable manuscript, leaving no "t" uncrossed or "i" undotted.

My writing group: Amber-Rose Reed, Kerry Granshaw, Nathan Jackson, and Brandan Merrick. The story, the characters, the words are infinitely more interesting, believable, and entertaining thanks to your invaluable contributions.

My oldest son, Jason, for helping me with Spanish words.

And finally, special thanks to my wife, Lyn, and my sons, Jason and Aaron, for their unending love and support of my writing endeavors.

Contents

Glossary

Puha : spiritual power

Namunewapi : important person

Taiboo : white-skinned soldier or person

Paraibo : peace leader

Ahpu : Father

Noomah : Comanche (The People) (what they call themselves)

Navoonah : Apache (The Enemy) (what Comanches call Apaches)

Nokoni : A Comanche band ("The Wanderers")

Penateka : A Comanche band ("The Honey Eaters")

Lipan : an Apache band

Mescolero : an Apache band

"Aaa-Hey" : Comanche victory cry: "I claim it!"

Northerner : Comanche (from Apache or Mexican perspective)

Haa : Yes

Ura : Thank You

Shimaa : Mother

Nupetsu : Wife

Tekwuniwapi : young warrior, brave

Nami : little sister

Samohpu : brother

Waha-nanisu: two-spirit

Pole-Drag : Travois (wooden frame pulled by a horse or dog to carry supplies)

Wolf hawk : Harris' Hawk

Big-headed lizard : collared lizard or mountain boomer

Running bird : roadrunner

Bird-killer : short-winged hawk(accipiter) (Cooper's Hawk, Goshawk, Sharp-Shinned Hawk)

Old man-beast : grizzly bear

The late 1700s. Unsettled Texas.

Pack Hunters

With a wave of his arm, Many Wolves signaled his wolf to move farther to the left. He kept waving until Rojo was in position, then he held his palm up to wait. The wolf froze, looking at his leader.

Above Rojo, perched in a juniper tree, was Chiquito, Many Wolves's small brown wolf hawk. The bird was watching Rojo carefully. Many Wolves knew it was Rojo who would find and flush the morning's quarry—jackrabbit—and it was Chiquito's job to then chase it and bring it down. Many Wolves would arrive last, for the kill. This unique hunting partnership had allowed the three of them to survive in the barren foothills of the Rio Pecos.

Many Wolves looked at Rojo and signaled, touching his nose with his finger. The red wolf understood; he moved forward on padded feet, sniffing the ground for rabbit scents. He weaved left and right through the grassy meadow, pulled by the strings of many smells. Many Wolves followed, slightly behind the four-legged tracker. His hunting bag was slung over his shoulder and his bow was loaded with a blunt-tipped arrow, ready to stun a rabbit before it bolted, to give his aging bird a better chance at the capture. Due to Chiquito's small size and advancing age, it would be a challenge for him to grapple with a much bigger and stronger jackrabbit.

A light breeze tickled the pines and junipers that surrounded the meadow. Small birds chittered and flew from tree to tree looking for their morning meal. The sun had fully revealed itself, and the air was crisp and silent. The loose, dew-soaked grass clung to Many Wolves's moccasins as he walked.

As Rojo led them into a larger clearing, Many Wolves blew his antler horn whistle to call his bird to his "fist-perch": a rabbit-skin covering he wore over his hand to protect him from the bird's sharp claws. Chiquito responded instantly, flying from the tree to his master's raised fist. The hawk watched Rojo from here. The lower perch would not give him as much of a speed boost as a high tree branch would, but it was enough for the chase.

The big wolf froze, looking straight ahead. Many Wolves stopped as well and launched Chiquito up into the sky. The bird usually spotted prey before the man did, which left Many Wolves only a sliver of time to find the rabbit and shoot his arrow before it dashed. But this time, the man and bird spotted the jackrabbit at the same time, hunkered down in the brush. Many Wolves let loose his arrow; it thumped the rabbit's back leg, throwing it off balance for a moment and slowing it. Chiquito fought with the wind for more height to boost his dive, then crashed down toward the target.

The prey regained its balance, then bolted from its sanctuary in a flash in a series of quick leaps. "Go!" Many Wolves yelled.

Rojo took off at a sprint. He chased the quarry for a short time, tiring it, then slowed to a trot, watching carefully and panting.

Above, Chiquito matched every turn of the swift, leggy animal with shifting wings, cutting the distance between them rapidly, like an inverted shadow mimicking its movements. When the hawk's sharp claws grabbed their target, the rabbit screamed, and both hawk and prey rolled over in the grass. The quarry regained its feet, pulling the hawk along like a dog pulls a pole-drag, but Chiquito hung on, wings flapping madly.

Many Wolves raced to the spot. He grabbed the struggling rabbit's back legs and neck and pinned it down, then stretched the animal easily with his muscular hands, breaking its neck and ending its life.

Many Wolves thanked the Great Spirit for this gift, with the hope that new life would come from this death. *Life for life.*

Chiquito remained standing atop the corpse for several moments, as if to proclaim to the world that this was his kill, but hopped off when his leader turned the carcass over. Many Wolves sliced open the rabbit's chest with his hunting knife, so that he could remove the blood organs—the heart, lungs, and liver—for Chiquito.

"You caught the first one, old bird. Well done." He fed the bird its prize from his fist-perch hand.

When the hawk had gulped down this first part of the meal, Many Wolves severed the rear leg of the rabbit and tossed it to Rojo, who was lying patiently nearby. Then he cut off a front leg for Chiquito and sliced it open to reveal the moist, red meat. He tossed it a few steps away, and the bird hopped over to it and began eating. Many Wolves placed the remains of the rabbit in his hunting bag, then sat and watched the members of his pack enjoy their rewards.

Many Wolves had shared eight winters with Rojo and Chiquito since Laughing Crow's death. Their current home, and his favorite spot, was the Gray Face Camp, named after the giant grizzly he had killed and whose claws he still wore with great pride around his neck. In spring, summer, and fall, they would move around to smaller camps, but the Gray Face Camp was always at the center of the rotation, their base camp. It was a special place to Many Wolves; Laughing Crow and his Nokoni warriors had never found it, and Many Wolves hoped it would stay that way.

This had been a good hunting day. Rojo had found their prey quickly, and Chiquito had chased it down on the first try. It wasn't always so easy—some days they went without a fresh kill altogether. On those days, Many Wolves and Rojo ate dried meat. It was not to Chiquito's liking, but it always made the bird sharper for the next hunt.

Dreams of Dying

"Thorn Bird, follow us," said Laughing Crow. Walks on Feathers was by his side.

The three of them rode through the prairie, surrounded by low, rolling hills in every direction. The gigantic full moon rained light down on them like the sun, bathing them in a bleak, colorless world. There were no mountains or rocks or trees; just an endless spread of rolling grass, enveloped by the black sky above.

Thorn Bird's father, Laughing Crow, and his brother, Walks on Feathers, were riding ahead of him on painted horses, urging Thorn Bird to pick up the pace. With his legs and a whisper, he commanded his horse to move faster. The crisp world around him blurred as he built up speed, but his father and brother remained in focus.

Every muscle in Thorn Bird's legs was working at full strength to make his horse go faster, but still they pulled away from him effortlessly. His heart and lungs were pumping hard as he gasped, "Slow down! I can't keep up!"

"You have to keep up!" yelled his father, looking back.

"I thought you could ride faster," mocked his brother.

The sweat dripped down Thorn Bird's face and covered his eyes, though it felt thick and sticky, more like blood than sweat. As it trickled into his mouth, it carried the taste of blood, but he didn't feel any pain. *Where is it coming from?*

"Thorn Bird, your mixed blood slows you down!" Laughing Crow yelled from about fifteen horse lengths ahead. Walks on Feathers was just a few lengths behind his father.

"*Mestizo*! You're too slow, *mestizo*!" Walks on Feathers was a full-blooded *Noomah*, and often taunted his brother so.

"You have to cleanse your blood, Thorn Bird. Then maybe you can keep up with us," yelled his father, laughing.

"I don't know how, *Ahpu*," said Thorn Bird, panting.

"You know what you have to do. Follow us!"

Thorn Bird's face was completely smothered in blood now. He was already riding as fast as he could, and he couldn't push any harder, yet he didn't seem to be getting any closer. His father and brother were pulling away from him.

"Wait!"

Ahead of him, father and brother slowed their horses to a stop and turned to face him. Thorn Bird was hopeful he would catch them now. But suddenly he started to drop, as if he was riding off the edge of a cliff. He saw them floating away from him. Then he looked down, and he saw only an endless void below. He was falling into darkness, into nothingness.

When he looked back up again, they were gone.

Thorn Bird jerked awake in a cold sweat. He felt the ground with his hand. He wasn't falling anymore. He was in a familiar place: his tipi, with his wife lying beside him. Fragments of this same dream had repeated often in his sleep, though its ending varied among many different outcomes. Sometimes he was falling into an endless pit; other times he was trampled by buffalo; still others, he was pierced by arrows. But always, they were dreams of dying; and always, his father and brother were there taunting him.

The message of the dreams was always the same, too. *Cleanse your blood.*

Thorn Bird, unlike his father and brother, was of mixed descent, a half-blood—a *mestizo*. His mother, Rosa, had been a Mexican slave. That was why this dream haunted his sleep, relentlessly.

"Thorn Bird? Are you all right? Another bad dream?" His wife, Valencia, spoke in a hushed voice. She had once been the slave of his father; now she was his wife. The *Noomah* custom was to share or inherit wives from brothers, but since his father had no brothers and Valencia was close to his age, it had been deemed acceptable for them to couple without breaking any taboos. And like Thorn Bird, Valencia had Mexican blood.

"Tomorrow, when the sun rises, I must leave," Thorn Bird said quietly.

"Where are you going?" Valencia asked in Spanish, her voice groggy from sleep.

"I've had a vision, and I must follow it."

Thorn Bird rolled over on his side and closed his eyes. But he knew that sleep never followed these dreams.

Unwelcome Return

The large *Noomah* warrior, dressed only in a breechcloth, rode up to the edge of the Nokoni village—a village that had once been his home. He was surrounded by flat prairie grasslands, green from spring's beginning and speckled with horses as far as his eye could see. The pony-slaves—the young boys who watched and tended the horse herd—stared at him with scrutinizing eyes. However, they did not sound an alarm. Perhaps because the rider was alone.

The boys were too young to remember when he used to live in their village, but after a moment, a woman recognized the newcomer and instructed one of the boys, in a fearful tone, to ride back to the village with a message. The boy immediately ordered his mount to a full sprint. As he rode, he yelled, "It's Thorn Bird! Thorn Bird is here!"

To Thorn Bird's left, the bank of the Rio Brazos was spotted with at least a hundred tipis. It was a familiar landscape, but he expected he would find even more familiarity with the people. After all, it was the people who made a village. The young boys—and now the barking dogs—clearly regarded him as a stranger, but he hoped to still find some friends here. He did not know if he had come to make friends or enemies; that choice would be theirs. He was like a dancing blade of grass, always ready to react to the shifting winds.

The anxious dogs and the curious, chattering boys followed him to the edge of the camp. As he rode slowly forward, Thorn Bird observed that the bark of one small dog rose above all the others. He had long ago observed that every village seemed to have one such dog: one that was quick to raise the alarm, one that riled up all the others. Such dogs tended to be fearful of their own shadow.

Thorn Bird approached cautiously. After eight winters of exile from this village, he wasn't sure what to expect. He knew that the father would never be allowed back; but perhaps the son would be forgiven. *Every new moon brings new hope.*

Men on horses had gathered at the entrance to the lodges on this hot spring day. Gray Elk, the elder *paraibo*—the peace leader who had exiled Thorn Bird's father—and Stands Alone, Thorn Bird's childhood friend, were among the gathering, positioned as headmen on the front line. *So. The old buzzard Gray Elk is still alive.* Other villagers, mostly women and children on foot, were crowded behind the impassable wall of horsemen. The younger men wore breechcloths, while the older men, including Gray Elk, were dressed in deerskin leggings. All were bare-chested. The familiar scent of burning buffalo dung hung heavy in the air.

Thorn Bird continued to move toward them slowly and steadily. He reined his horse to a stop when he saw the whites of their eyes and teeth. He sensed that many of these people remembered him, or at least knew of him from stories. Recognition oozed through their eyes. He felt fear from the women, worship from the young boys, challenge from the warriors, and disdain from the elders. The bright teeth in Stands Alone's wide, sincere smile were easy to see against his dark red face, but the whites of Gray Elk's eyes were all the white to be seen there. His look was stern and serious.

It was the gray-haired leader who spoke first. "Thorn Bird, why have you come here?"

His cold tone was not a surprise. Thorn Bird knew how deeply the hate had bled between Gray Elk and his father. And Thorn Bird was too much like his father for that hate to not to bleed on him as well.

"I have come to see my friends here, Gray Elk. I was hoping our villages would be friends again, now that my father no longer leads us."

"Your father brought poison to this village. We cannot risk that again."

"I am not my father." Thorn Bird watched every crease of Gray Elk's wrinkled face for any indication of friendship or acceptance. The old man's body was withered, and his bones were easily counted, but Thorn Bird could see that his spirit still had fire. He wore two eagle feathers in his hair, one standing straight up and the other cocked to the right side.

"*Haa*," Gray Elk said in agreement. "You are not your father. But I sense the same hatred flowing through your body. I have seen it in you, ever since you were young."

Thorn Bird swept several strands of his long black hair away from his eyes and tucked them behind his right ear. "The world changes with the new moon, Gray Elk. People change, too. My village is not the same village my father led. We have fewer men."

"So, you have come here looking for protection? Your father would laugh at your weakness!" Gray Elk's eyes revealed a flash of satisfaction.

"No. I have come so that our children can play with your children and our men can share stories. I am not asking to live in your village or under your protection. We can take care of ourselves."

Gray Elk stroked the windblown hair away from his squinting eyes. He looked into Thorn Bird's face for several moments, as if trying to uncover a truth. At last he broke the silence. "The peace council will discuss your offer in our sweat lodge tonight. The smoke in our lungs will show us the truth. You are allowed to stay tonight, as Stands Alone's guest, if he welcomes you."

The conversation was over. Gray Elk and the other elders turned and walked away. The others dispersed more slowly, the village abuzz with muffled voices.

Childhood Friends

"Thorn Bird, it is good to see you again." Stands Alone rode over to Thorn Bird and offered him his forearm in friendship, his face lit with a smile.

If there was hate remaining in Stands Alone's heart, Thorn Bird could not see it. Long ago, Thorn Bird's father had killed Stands Alone's brother in a heated moment during a buffalo hunt. Soon after, Thorn Bird's entire family had been exiled from the Nokoni village. But apparently, Thorn Bird had been forgiven for his father's act—at least by his friend.

"You look well, Stands Alone. You look strong."

Stands Alone was average in height, his body lean and well conditioned, an athletic build. His hair was long, combed neatly, and parted in the middle like most *Noomah* men. Beads of many colors adorned his earrings and the side braids in his hair. He wore a single eagle feather, which drooped down the right side of his head. Like Thorn Bird, he was dressed in only a breechcloth.

"The Great Spirit has blessed us with many successful hunts, and the Earth Mother has provided much for our women to gather. You have grown, Thorn Bird, bigger than your father ever was. And he was a large man."

Thorn Bird *was* bigger than his father—most likely because his mother had loomed like a mountain over most of the *Noomah* women of their village. Laughing Crow had ceased to be the largest man in their Nokoni band when Thorn Bird reached his eighteenth summer.

Stands Alone whistled. "Badger, come here!"

In response, a boy of about eleven or twelve winters burst out of the group of watching children and ran toward them. Like most of the boys in the village, he was naked.

The warrior looked at Thorn Bird and asked, "Can he take your horse?"

Thorn Bird eyed the boy. "Your son?"

"*Haa*. Badger is my son."

"I remember him now. He was just learning to ride when I saw him last." Thorn Bird dismounted and handed the lead to Badger. The boy looked at him with wide, respectful eyes, and they followed Stands Alone as he led his horse deeper into the village.

"Is he a skilled rider?" said Thorn Bird.

Stands Alone looked back at his son. "He is a good rider, but seems to spend more time with the dogs than the horses. Sometimes I think we should name him 'Dog Leader.' He has taken it upon himself to be their keeper."

"A village needs people with special skills," Thorn Bird replied. "It is important to keep the dogs healthy, so they can protect the village." Thorn Bird thought back to the rainy night when the Pawnee had attacked his village and killed Malone's family. An earlier warning by the village dogs might have saved their lives.

Stands Alone led the way to his lodge, where Thorn Bird was greeted by Stands Alone's wife. She lowered her head reverently without looking at him. He could hear a crying baby inside the tipi.

"You have another child?" Thorn Bird set his shield and lance next to Stands Alone's weapons, then removed his quiver as well.

"*Haa*. After Badger, Sweet Words and I lost two children during pregnancy, and then we were blessed with a daughter."

"She has a strong voice. Someday she will lead the women in song!"

The two men shared a cheerful moment. Thorn Bird was happy to once again hear the boisterous laugh of his friend. *Some things never change.*

Stands Alone turned to his wife. "Sweet Words, bring us some water and boil some buffalo meat from yesterday's hunt. I'm sure my friend is thirsty and hungry from his journey." Then he motioned for Thorn Bird to sit down. "Eat first, and then we will find a tree to cool ourselves under."

Thorn Bird sat cross-legged next to the fire pit. The boys who had been watching him must have decided the excitement was over; they returned to their war games, leaving him alone with Stands Alone's family.

"Do you remember how we used to race our war ponies?" Stands Alone asked. then laughed loudly. "You were always faster in a straight line, but I beat you on the turns."

Thorn Bird smiled in recollection. "We were wild at heart, with nothing to worry about except when we would race again. The world is much different now." His smile faded as he thought about just how much life had changed for his village after his father died.

"How is your village?" said Stands Alone, looking at his friend with serious eyes.

"We survive. But we are always moving, staying hidden from the *Navoonah* and Utes and Pawnee. There is no time for leisure. There are hardly enough men to hunt. Our winter stores have been lean since my father died."

Stands Alone's face was grim. "You lost many good warriors in the fight with the *Navoonah*. Did you find the man who killed your father?"

"No. We made several search parties to look for Many Wolves, the white skin, but we did not find him. And after some time, we just couldn't spare the men anymore. But I have not given up. I will find him, and I will kill him." Thorn Bird paused to take several large gulps of water, then washed the dirt from his face and hands before speaking again. "This is one of the promises I have made to my father."

It will not be an easy death.

Crazy

The shadows grew longer around Stands Alone's lodge, but there was still plenty of heat and light left in the day. Thorn Bird and Stands Alone sat by the cooking fire while Sweet Words tended to the iron pot, which rested on heated rocks. Once the water had risen to a boil, she placed wooden skewers of buffalo meat into the cooking vessel. Meanwhile, the two men reminisced about their childhood.

"Thorn Bird, do you remember the time I bet you you couldn't lift Fat Dog onto your horse?"

Thorn Bird smiled remembering how big Fat Dog had been. He was easily the heaviest boy in their village. "No one else in the village could even lift him off the ground, but I knew I could do it."

Stands Alone laughed. "It took three tries, and you fell on your face the first two times! The rest of us were laughing so hard watching you two. Though I don't think Fat Dog was enjoying it too much."

"Lucky for me, he softened the fall both times. Even so, my shoulder hurt until the next moon after that. I learned my lesson. But at least I won the bet."

Stands Alone nodded, then offered Thorn Bird the first skewer of cooked buffalo meat, which was as long as a man's forearm and half as thick. The meat was still too hot to eat, but the smell made Thorn Bird's mouth tingle.

Badger returned from watering Thorn Bird's horse. He had left the animal grazing in a nearby field, where Thorn Bird could see it.

"Badger, join us," said Thorn Bird.

"Can I, *Ahpu*?" Badger looked at his father with pleading eyes.

"*Haa*, but don't bother our guest too much."

Badger sat a short distance away and, ignoring his father's instruction, immediately asked a question. "Thorn Bird, what was it like to ride with Laughing Crow and the Blood Riders?"

"Badger! Do not use the name of the dead—it is bad luck!" Stands Alone scolded.

"I'm sorry, *Ahpu*," said the boy, but he still looked to Thorn Bird for an answer.

"My father was a great warrior," Thorn Bird said. "He was strong and skilled, and his *puha* was powerful. We thought he could never die. For many years the Blood Riders were invincible. We could steal horses and kill men with few losses. Under my father's leadership, our village controlled the best buffalo lands and owned the largest horse herd."

The boy couldn't take his eyes off Thorn Bird, who was now furiously biting large chunks of meat off the skewer.

"Who was the toughest to fight? The Spaniards? The *Navoonah*? The Pawnee?"

Thorn Bird answered while chewing. "The ones who could fight us on horses were the toughest. Some of the *Navoonah* did this; the Pawnee, too. But none of them rode *and* shot a bow, like our people. That's why the *Noomah* are the most feared people on the plains."

Thorn Bird swallowed his mouthful, then opened his mouth and eyes wide and stalked toward Badger. He wrestled the youngster to the ground and held his half-eaten skewer to the boy's neck like a knife. The boy was giggling, enjoying the playful game; but then his smiling eyes turned fearful.

Thorn Bird put his own face directly in front of the boy's. "There is no greater moment for a warrior than when staring into face of your enemy, seeing the weakness and terror in his eyes, and feeling his body tremble against yours... and then, in one swift stroke, slashing his neck open."

Thorn Bird swept the skewer across Badger's neck.

"His body goes limp, and you watch the life drift from his eyes like a plume of smoke."

"Thorn Bird, enough!" yelled Stands Alone.

Thorn Bird released the boy, stood up, and began laughing. "I was just playing with him." He took another bite and walked back to his seat by the fire, still chuckling to himself.

With distance between them, Badger regained his nerve. His smile was gone now, replaced by anger. "Why is your hair all over your face? It's not like the men in our village. The way it hangs over your eyes, it makes you look crazy!"

"He is not crazy," said Stands Alone with a smile. "His heart is wild, but he's not crazy."

Thorn Bird chewed for a few moments, then wiped the juice from his face and again faced the boy. "Do you think I'm crazy?" he asked calmly.

"I heard stories that when you were young, you used to hang the animals you killed on sticks around your lodge so your father would see them, even though your family had plenty of other meat to eat. They say that's how you got your name. Just like the little black-faced bird who hangs his prey on thorns. Is that true?"

"It is. Let me tell you a little secret. Come closer." Thorn Bird gestured for the boy to approach, and Badger slowly, reluctantly, crawled on his knees over to the Nokoni warrior.

Thorn Bird leaned over and whispered in Badger's ear. "Don't tell your father, but I *am* a little crazy."

Thorn Bird laughed again and took another bite, his elbows resting on his legs. The boy glanced helplessly at his father, as if searching for comfort there, then backed away from the large warrior.

Poisoned

It wasn't the needle-prick pain of the deadly snake's fangs that roused Many Wolves's fear, but the realization that he had been bitten. *I am poisoned!* A lethal spirit was racing through his body like an unstoppable wildfire, and he was helpless to stop it.

He grabbed the squirming rattlesnake, which still clung to his left arm, and pinned it to the ground by its neck. Driven by anger and fear, he pulled his knife from its sheath and hacked off the creature's venomous head. Then he threw it into the sagebrush.

Chiquito, his wolf hawk, was perched on the ground next to him, wings spread and mouth gaping, staring at the still-writhing body of the decapitated reptile. Chiquito's kill, a small jackrabbit, lay dead in the brush a few steps away.

The struggling rabbit had dragged the hungry hawk close to the snake's hiding spot, and Many Wolves had not seen or heard the snake until after he had silenced the screaming rabbit. Chiquito must have spotted the snake at roughly that same moment, as the startled hawk had flown toward the snake, then veered at the last instant and landed right next to it—*protecting his kill,* Many Wolves thought. Many Wolves had sprinted over to pull his hawk away from the coiled snake, but a hissing strike had caught him sharply in the arm.

I have to get the poison out. Blood trickled from the two fang marks on his left arm. He felt the sharp, burning pain—and it suddenly dropped on him like a bolt of lightning. It was a strange trick, one that twisted his mind: *How could two small cuts cause so much pain?* But then he had never been poisoned before.

With his knife, he made two cuts around the swelling wound and then sucked the blood from it, just as his grandfather had taught him long ago. He tasted the bitter poison on his tongue before spitting it out, then repeated this over and over until he could no longer taste the bitterness. Blood was oozing from the wound, so he pulled his red bandanna off his head and wrapped it around his wounded arm.

"I have to get back to my camp," he said to himself. "It will be impossible to find in the dark." It was already late in the afternoon, and his search for more fruitful hunting grounds had brought him to an unfamiliar land. There were few landmarks rising from the endless mesquite and sage brush—no large rocks or trees to mark his path. He knew he had to head northeast, and then he would find his camp among the cottonwoods that lined the banks of the Rio Pecos.

"Chiquito, I need to get back to camp, but you should eat, Little One." Many Wolves returned to the rabbit carcass and cut open the chest of the rabbit, exposing the juicy organs for his hungry bird. Chiquito eagerly dug his head into the bloody cavity and began eating the rabbit's liver.

Many Wolves wiped his knife clean and returned it to his leg sheath, then drank from his water pouch, which was nearly depleted. Chiquito was gorging on his meal. "I can't stay with you, Chiquito. I have to go."

This would be the first time he had left his bird with a kill. As the pack leader, it was Many Wolves's job to protect the small hawk in these vulnerable moments, and it felt strange to leave him like this. "I wish Rojo were here to stay with you." Many Wolves had left the red wolf back at the camp because his paw was injured from stepping on a large thorn.

Many Wolves walked northeast. The pain was steeper now, and the swelling around the wound was increasing. He knew that resting would slow the poison, but he couldn't rest now. His water supply was low, and he needed to get back to the river. If he rested now, he was afraid he might never wake up. The poison was sapping his strength already.

I wish Rojo were here.

Unprotected

Fear was creeping into Many Wolves's mind. He wasn't sure how far he had to go to reach the river; Chiquito had chased at least four rabbits before finally capturing the last one, and each chase had led them farther from their camp, deeper into the ceaseless, unchanging landscape. At least he had discovered some of his own tracks, so he knew he was heading in the right direction.

He could feel the poison biting harder and harder at his insides. His arm had swelled to almost twice its normal size, and now it displayed various shades of blue, yellow, and purple. The pain, like the swelling, was also growing to nearly unbearable levels. His limbs and lungs seemed to be filled with sand. His forehead was sweaty and his mouth was dry, as if a fire was burning inside his body. He tried hard to save what little water he had left, but his thirst was overpowering, a temptation he couldn't resist. The venom of the snake had planted a jagged seed in his mind:

Am I going to die?

Many Wolves plodded on through the windy paths of sand that wove in and out of the mesquite and sage. *I have to keep going. I must be getting close.* His mind wanted to believe that he was almost home, almost to the life-giving water of the Rio Pecos. He saw the cottonwoods several times, only to then realize his eyes were tricking him. Dusk had begun to settle in, stealing the light. The poison was feasting on his vision, erasing the details of the landscape, and leaving a blurred path ahead of him. He fought to keep his weighted eyelids from pulling him completely into darkness.

He drank his last gulp of water and dropped the water pouch in the sand, then removed the quiver from his shoulder to lighten his load. As he stumbled along, each step was a concerted effort and each breath had to be wrested from his body. He thought of Ten Arrows. If only his friend were here. *He would take care of me.* He thought of Rojo, his protector, and cried out in a parched voice: "Rojo! Rojo!"

The poison was torturing him. He vomited several times, but the nausea only worsened with every heavy step and labored breath. Dizziness swallowed him like a dust storm, his head spinning in vicious circles. Spinning, spinning, spinning… until finally he collapsed.

Great Spirit, help me.

Many Wolves awoke to find himself on his hands and knees in a dark pit. Shards of light jutted downward from cracks above him, and a second pool of light poured down from a large cavity to the right of him, far out of reach. All was silent, still.

Until he started to move toward the outlet to his right, his only escape. As soon as he started to rise, a chorus of snake rattles, what seemed like hundreds of them, echoed in his mind. He froze—and the rattling stopped instantly. His eyes snapped to movements on the ground ahead of him, to his right, then to his left.

Rattlesnakes. I'm surrounded by rattlesnakes.

He was afraid to move his arms or his legs. *I can't move, or I will die.* He held his eyelids open, held his breath, and tried not to blink. *I have to stay like this, or I will die.*

Then a familiar voice spoke to him. "You will die here, Many Wolves. Are you ready?"

The voice was Laughing Crow's.

With his head still facing the ground, Many Wolves raised his eyes, but still didn't blink or breathe or move his head. The slivers of light revealed the shape of a large man, sitting on a rock. *Laughing Crow.*

Laughing Crow stood and approached. The snakes did not rattle. *Why aren't they rattling?* Snakes were wrapped around his muscular arms and legs, but they did not bite him. *Why don't they bite him?*

The Northerner laughed. "These snakes are my friends, Many Wolves, but not yours. One bite will poison you, and you will live an afterlife of pain and suffering. Forever." Then he laughed again. "Can you stay still so they don't bite you? Can you remain still forever?"

Laughing Crow walked all around him, but Many Wolves moved nothing but his eyes. The snakes surrounded him—he saw flashes of their movements—but strangely, they did not crawl on him as long as he didn't move. But one twitch of a muscle, he thought... *and I will be dead forever.*

"Your *puha* cannot save you, Many Wolves. Where is your red wolf now? Where is your Penateka friend?" Laughing Crow was clearly pleased with himself. "Maybe you can call your magic birds so they can bring a message to your friends. Go ahead and call them. Move your mouth so the snakes will find you!"

Laughing Crow stood over Many Wolves now, close enough to touch—but he did not reach for his prisoner. Nothing and no one could touch Many Wolves as long as he remained perfectly still.

Claws

A sudden bolt of pain shook Many Wolves out of his nightmare. Blood was oozing from what looked like claw marks in his shoulder, and he was curled up on the sandy desert floor with the morning sun beating down on him.

He spit the sand out of his mouth and tried brushing it off his face, but it clung like hungry leeches to his sweaty skin. *Where am I? Where is the cave? Why am I bleeding?*

Instantly, the nausea returned and the world around him began to swirl again. *Poison.* He felt encumbered by weakness, and a chill ran through his body like a northern wind. His mouth was dry; it hurt to swallow. It felt like all the moisture had been sucked from his body.

He heard footsteps behind him. He turned—and saw a cougar charging at him.

A blurred claw swiped at his back as the cat leaped past him, snarling. More pain; he screamed, his voice hoarse. His cracked lips could barely open.

The cat stopped and faced him, hissing and snarling, its obsidian eyes staring—and then it began to stalk slowly around him.

Is this another dream?

The predator darted in and out of focus. The cat snarled again, baring its fangs, then stopped several steps away from him, hunched on all fours, studying him.

Many Wolves slowly drew his knife from his leg sheath. It was heavy, and he struggled to grip it tightly in his sweaty, sand-covered hand. The life had been sapped from his body. *I have to find more strength.* The world blurred around him.

For several moments, the cat remained still, emitting a long, drawn-out snarl, appearing to size up its opponent.

I won't be easy prey for you, big cat. If I die, so will you.

Many Wolves raised the knife in front of him so the cat could clearly see it. It wasn't a full adult yet; perhaps only in its second summer of life. Its tawny fur was highlighted by snowy patches of white around the mouth and cheeks. Its labored breathing accentuated its protruding ribs. *This animal is hungry and desperate.*

The predator rose to its feet and again circled him, its tail thrashing like a menacing snake.

A familiar screech echoed from above—Chiquito, soaring overhead. The bird dove at the cat, pulled up at the last minute, then dove again. It captured the cat's attention only for a moment, though; the cougar soon returned its gaze to what it hoped would be a much greater prize.

Many Wolves wanted to stand, to look bigger to this predator, but his leg muscles would not respond. So he fixed a hard stare at the cat and yelled, "Go away!"

Or at least, he tried to yell; his voice was weak and muffled and his mouth only half-opened. The cat was unfazed; it continued to snarl and circle.

With one more burst of effort, Many Wolves yelled as loudly as he could, "Go away, big cat, go away!"

His stalker did not even flinch. Not at Many Wolves's shouts, and not at Chiquito, who continued to dive at it.

The cat leaped. Many Wolves held his right arm out in front of him to ward off the deadly jaws, and felt the pain as the animal's sharp claws dug into his flesh. The great cat's weight carried him backward, and the two of them wrestled, Many Wolves fighting to keep his distance from the snapping fangs. A single bite to his neck or head would be lethal. *That's how these animals kill.*

The knife was still in his right hand, but his arm bore the weight of his attacker and he couldn't free it long enough to swipe at the animal. His left arm was pinned to the ground, and besides, it was almost useless—still badly swollen from the snake's bite. The tingling in that arm now felt like a swarm of buzzing gnats, trapped and trying to get out.

The cat was heavy and Many Wolves weak. It took all of Many Wolves's concentration just to hold his ground and avoid a fatal error. But he knew his strength was already waning, and he wouldn't be able to hold out much longer.

In desperation, he dropped the knife to the ground where his left hand could reach it. He fumbled for it, the swelling making his movements clumsy; and as soon as he felt it firmly in his hand, he gathered all the strength he had left, like a rattlesnake coiling for one last strike. Yelling, he pushed the cat away from him with his right arm and awkwardly swung his puffy left arm forward.

He felt the knife drive deep into the predator's body.

The animal screamed and backed away. Many Wolves's heightened senses felt the relief, the momentary victory—and then he succumbed once again to the poison, the sickness that had invaded his body. His vision went blurry, and the world around him began to whirl out of control.

Then another growl came from his left, and a flash of reddish brown flew at the retreating cat, knocking it back.

Rojo.

Befriending the Dogs

"Now it's my turn to ask some questions, little man." Thorn Bird looked at the boy again. Badger was chewing on a skewer prepared for him by his mother.

"Remember, he's just a boy," said Stands Alone.

Thorn Bird nodded to his friend. He intended no threats. He'd already noted that the boy watched him warily and had lost much of his earlier lightheartedness.

"Your father says you are the keeper of the village dogs," he said to Badger. "That's an important job. Which one is your favorite?"

The boy's response was immediate. "My favorite is One Ear," he snarled. "If he had been here, he would have defended me."

Thorn Bird placed his half-eaten skewer on a rock and then grabbed a fresh one from the pot. "So where is this One Ear? I would like to meet him."

The boy clapped his hands several times and yelled, "One Ear!"

Thorn Bird heard the dog's footsteps before he saw it. The dog approached, but when he saw the stranger, he stopped and lowered his head, growling.

"Easy, One Ear. Easy," said the boy.

The dog stalked over to Badger, but it never took its eyes off of Thorn Bird. It was medium-sized—about knee-high in height—and its coloring was mostly a very light brown, almost white, interrupted by a few darker brown patches. One of its ears was pointed up to the sky, while the other was flopped over itself—that explained its name.

The boy stroked the dog's neck and back and tried to calm it with soft words, but still it growled at Thorn Bird, its hackles drawn.

Thorn Bird bit off a large hunk of meat and tossed it to the dog. One Ear lowered his nose to the ground to smell the offering, still keeping both eyes on the feeder. Then suddenly, he gulped the meat down in one big bite. The growling ceased. The dog still stared warily at Thorn Bird, but its hackles were now gone, as were the flashing teeth and the retracted ears.

Thorn Bird bit off another piece and threw it only half as far this time, so the dog would have to walk toward him. Cautiously, the dog approached, grabbed the meat, and returned to its safe spot next to the boy to eat it.

"See how the food cuts through his fear," said Thorn Bird. He bit off an even bigger piece, and this time he held it out with his hand. "Come and get it, One Ear. You know you want it."

The dog walked slowly toward Thorn Bird, who didn't move, other than to whisper encouragement. "Come on. Take it." To give the dog confidence, he avoided too much eye contact.

The dog looked from Thorn Bird to the meat and back again. Finally he snatched the food from Thorn Bird's hand, wolfing it down as he backed away.

"Badger, I bet you any arrow in my quiver that I can coax any of your dogs to my hand. There was a small reddish dog who barked wildly at me when I entered the village—bring that dog here and let's see if you can win that arrow from me."

Badger turned to his father. "Should I get Howler, *Ahpu?*"

"*Haa*, go get her. She will spoil my peace and quiet, but I want to see you win that arrow. It might be the easiest bet you'll ever win off Thorn Bird."

Badger jumped to his feet and ran off, leaving the two men alone.

Stands Alone grabbed a skewer and began to eat. "You were a little rough with him, Thorn Bird."

"It was a stick I held to his throat, not a knife."

"It wasn't the stick that bothered me, but the way you forced him down." Stands Alone scowled and pointed to the ground where Thorn Bird committed the mock attack.

One of the elders, dressed in a ceremonial deerskin shirt and leggings, approached. "Gray Elk wants you to join us in the council lodge, Stands Alone. The elders are meeting."

"Let me get dressed, and then I'll join you," replied Stands Alone.

The elder nodded and left. Stands Alone disappeared into his lodge, then returned moments later in his formal clothing.

Thorn Bird stood and put his right hand on his friend's shoulder to stop him from leaving. "What will you say about me when the truth smoke warms your lungs, Stands Alone? That I am a trusted friend? Or a danger to your village?"

"I will say you are a friend and not your father."

Thorn Bird believed his friend was truthful, but he also knew Gray Elk's hatred for him was rooted like the mountains. His fate rested on the shoulders of the other men in the council, many of whom he didn't know.

Deep down, he felt he already knew the elders' decision.

Some time after Stands Alone left, his son returned with a dog on a rope lead. The dog immediately started barking when it saw Thorn Bird. A few of the other dogs added to the cacophony and ran over to see what the commotion was.

Sunset was falling on the village and it was hard for Thorn Bird to see them clearly in the dim light, but as they got closer to the cooking pit where Thorn Bird was sitting, he recognized Badger's dog as the same fearful red one he had seen earlier.

"Where is my father?" asked the boy, looking a little uneasy.

"He went to the council lodge to join the elders." Thorn Bird pointed to his left.

"No, the council lodge is back there." The boy pointed to an area on Thorn Bird's right. "It's just on the other side of those trees."

"Then your father must have been going to Gray Elk's lodge first, because he went that way." Again Thorn Bird pointed to his left.

"No. Gray Elk's tipi is over by the trees, next to the council lodge."

"Well, regardless, he is not here." Thorn Bird directed his attention to the dog. "So this is the dog who will win you my arrow?"

"*Haa*, this is Howler. The loudest dog in the village, and the one who is scared of everything."

Badger kneeled a few steps away from Thorn Bird, keeping a firm grasp on Howler's lead. The dog was still barking wildly, unable to take its eyes off of the large Nokoni warrior for even a heartbeat.

Thorn Bird pulled a small chunk of buffalo meat out of his hunting bag; he'd saved it from their earlier meal. Then he faced the dog, whistled, and held the food out for the dog to see and smell. "Come on, Howler, take it. It's yours. Take it."

The animal didn't budge. It just kept barking, leading the chorus of dogs who were lingering around the lodge.

So Thorn Bird tossed the meat at the dog's feet. Howler kept barking, yet it was clear that the scent of the meat had drawn its attention. After a moment, the dog stopped barking just long enough to gulp down the meat. Its eyes never left Thorn Bird though. Then the barking started again.

Thorn Bird grabbed another piece of meat, bigger than the first, and tossed it a few steps away from Howler. The dog, hackles raised, stalked over to the food, grabbed it, then retraced its steps back to Badger. After a brief pause to swallow, the dog was barking again.

"So, here is the final test, Badger," Thorn Bird said. "This is the biggest piece. Howler has to touch my hand this time or I lose the bet."

Thorn Bird held out the third bribe to his target, but he did not throw it. "Come on, Howler. You can't resist this treat. You know you want it. Come on, Howler."

The dog looked at Thorn Bird, then at the treat, then back again at the *Noomah* warrior. But he did not budge, nor did he cease his barking.

For several more moments, Thorn Bird tried his best to entice the dog to come closer. But at last he gave up and threw the last piece of meat to the dog. "You win, Badger. Go grab whatever arrow you like from my quiver."

"Any arrow?"

"*Haa,* any arrow. I guess I'm not as good of a dog tamer as you." Thorn Bird smiled. Then he grabbed several more pieces of meat from his bag and tossed them to the pack of dogs lingering nearby, making sure each one got a piece.

"Let me take Howler back. Then I'll come back for my prize." The boy ran off with the dog, the big smile having returned to his face.

Thorn Bird grinned. *It was a good trade for me too.*

Peace Offering

The locusts sang the village to sleep, but Thorn Bird was not lulled by them. He lay awake in Stands Alone's tipi, envisioning how the rest of the night and the following day would unfold. His friend had returned to the lodge late in the night, but Thorn Bird had not waited up for him—instead he had pretended to sleep. He had already known what the council's decision would be. *It will not be different for the son than it was for the father.*

Quietly, he rolled up the buffalo robe he used for sleeping, grabbed his quiver and weapons, and went outside. The half-moon lit a path for him. He slung his quiver over his shoulder and walked out toward the pasture where he knew he would find his gelding. On the way, he stopped to relieve his bladder, like a war horse does before the first battle cry.

As Thorn Bird glided among the half-dazed horses, he whistled softly for his mount. A woman spotted him, probably a slave on night watch, but did not sound an alarm. He was not an enemy to her.

His war horse appeared like a ghost out of the darkness, nickering and grunting quietly as it approached. Thorn Bird stroked its nose and neck, whispering softly. He strapped his buffalo robe to the horse's back and led his horse to the council lodge.

As he grew closer to the pungent scent of burning buffalo dung, Thorn Bird heard an elder singing inside the glowing lodge. Threads of smoke rose from the top of the tipi and the shadows of at least two men were cast in firelight.

Thorn Bird left his horse by a large tree and walked to the lodge entrance. Two elder men were seated inside: Gray Elk, and the man singing. The old singer stopped when he saw the Nokoni warrior.

"Thorn Bird, why are you here?" asked Gray Elk, his voice hoarse from talking and singing. Thorn Bird remembered how the elders would often sit up all night smoking, singing, and talking, sometimes until sunrise.

"Gray Elk, I have come to say goodbye."

"You are leaving now?" Gray Elk's voice did not carry the same obsidian-sharp tone that had greeted Thorn Bird earlier. He struggled to his feet, using the tipi pole to brace himself from falling. "I have something to say to you before you go. We'll leave Wind Rush here to sing his song."

Thorn Bird could see that Gray Elk's eyes were glazed from his smoke and medicine. The elder held onto Thorn Bird's arm as they walked, at an old man's pace, over to the tree where Thorn Bird had left his horse. Behind them, the singer began his song again:

Great Spirit.
Give me the wisdom of the coyote
To find the moonlit path of light.
Give me the wings of the eagle.
To fly above the reins of darkness.

When they reached the tree, Gray Elk spoke again. "Thorn Bird, the council has decided that you and your village are welcome to return to us."

The news caught Thorn Bird by surprise. He was expecting the same fate as his father. In most villages, the *paraibo* had great influence over the rest of the council, and he knew that Gray Elk was set against him.

"You were against me, Gray Elk. Why would the elders not follow your lead?"

"The will of the council stands far above the will of one man." Gray Elk's voice was shaky and slurred.

Thorn Bird looked around the village, imagining what it would be like to live here again. This village would provide safety for him and his family, a more prosperous life. And he could spend time with his old friend, Stands Alone. Fall could be spent raiding the *Navoonah* and Navajos and Mexicans, as it had been when his father was still alive. Winter would be far easier with surplus buffalo meat.

Thorn Bird pondered all these things as the old man's song whisked through him like the wind.

Great Spirit.
Give me the wisdom of the coyote
To find the moonlit path of hope.
Give me the wings of the eagle.
To fly above the reins of despair.

"Gray Elk, I have a message from my father," Thorn Bird said at last.

"But your father is dead."

"He is not dead to me. He lives. In my thoughts and in my dreams. Especially in my dreams."

Gray Elk's voice and eyes grew fearful. "And what does he tell you in your dreams?"

"He says I will not have peace until he has peace. He wants his peace, Gray Elk. That is his message to you." Thorn Bird studied the old man's face, his wrinkled, dying skin and his feeble eyes. "Everyone has his day to die, old buzzard. And this is yours."

Thorn Bird grabbed Gray Elk by the neck and threw him against the tree. With one hand covering the elder's mouth, Thorn Bird pulled the knife from his leg sheath with his other hand and, in one clean swipe, sliced open the old man's throat. He forced the leader's chin up, allowing warm blood to spray all over both men.

Thorn Bird watched the proud leader's life bleed away. When the glint of life had vacated the old man's eyes, Thorn Bird let go and let the elder's lifeless body collapse to the ground. Then he bent down, sliced off the old man's scalp, and shoved it in his hunting bag.

The warrior looked around the camp. The other old man was still singing in the council lodge. Out of the corner of his eye, Thorn Bird spotted a flash of white. *One Ear.* The dog was watching him with a cockeyed, curious look.

Thorn Bird took from his pack another chunk of meat he had saved for the dogs, and he bent down on one knee and offered it to One Ear. The dog walked cautiously over to him, smelling the blood on the ground and the air, but the meat proved irresistible.

"That's it, One Ear, it's for you."

No other dogs were in sight. The mescal he had sprinkled in the scraps he'd fed them earlier had ensured their silence. Dogs were unpredictable, and Thorn Bird knew he had to control them.

One Ear took the meat from Thorn Bird's hand and swallowed it down; then he began licking Thorn Bird's bloodied hand as well.

The warrior flipped his hand over so the dog could clean both sides. "You like that." He laughed.

When the dog was finished, he backed away and sat down again, watching Thorn Bird with one ear up.

The old man's singing was all Thorn Bird heard. Looking around at the tipis nearby, he spotted a lance leaning against one of them. He walked over and picked it up, the dog watching him but not moving. Then he returned to the tree and the dead leader.

Thorn Bird picked up the old man's body and leaned it against the tree, facing him. Holding it in place with one hand, he drove the lance sharply through the old man's stomach with such force that the lance point dug deep into the trunk of the tree. The last of Gray Elk's blood ran down his body and soaked into the dry earth.

"This is my peace offering, father," Thorn Bird said to himself with great satisfaction. Then he looked up to the sky and paused to listen to the old man's song.

Great Spirit.
Give me the wisdom of the coyote
To find the moonlit path of life.

Give me the wings of the eagle.
To fly above the reins of death.

Thorn Bird mounted his horse, screamed "Aaa-hey!" and rode off into the dark night.

Blood is Water

The burning sun, a relentless master, beat down on Many Wolves. Dark brown specks of many sizes floated above him, circling in and out of the yellow haze. *Buzzards.* He lay on his back, unable to move. The birds continued to sway silently around him, growing bigger and closer.

Am I dead?

Crows joined the flock and shattered the silence with their raucous cries of hunger. The bird mass seemed endless. The screams of the crows were deafening now. Closer and closer they came.

Eventually, several landed on the ground around him. One jumped aggressively onto his leg, cawing madly, as if to claim Many Wolves as its kill. It hopped up to his chest, tilted its head, and stared at him with cold, black, shining eyes. Then the scavenger stepped closer still, staring directly at Many Wolves's face—at his eye.

Many Wolves was helpless. He couldn't yell or move his arms to rid himself of the feathered menace. The bird hopped onto his forehead and looked down on him, a cockeyed stare. Its attention was fixed entirely on his left eye.

It wants my eye. It's going to peck out my eye.

Many Wolves woke up. There were no birds in sight, not even Chiquito. Only Rojo was there, licking the blood off his right arm.

Blood had spilled all over the right side of Many Wolves's body. He felt weak, tired, and thirsty, and the pain from the claw wounds on his arm and shoulder was excruciating. Chills ran through his body, bringing shivers and sweat in the hot, late afternoon sun. His chest heaved up and down, every breath a struggle to overcome. The poison and the cat hadn't killed him, but he knew that the thirst would if he didn't find water soon.

He looked past Rojo. The big cat was there, lying dead on the ground. *Rojo must have killed it.*

"Thank you for saving me, again, my friend," Many Wolves wheezed, and he stroked the wolf's thick, coarse fur. Rojo stopped his licking and limped over to the shade of a mesquite bush to rest. The red wolf's leg was still not fully healed.

The knife was still sticking out of the cat's shoulder, but that wasn't its cause of death; its neck had been torn apart by Rojo's teeth. Many Wolves knew he was lucky to still be alive, lucky to have survived the attack.

The Great Spirit does not want me to die, to give up. Not yet.

I have to find water. He remembered a story Ten Arrows had once told him about how the Northerner warriors drank the blood of a freshly killed buffalo when there was no water to drink. *Does the life-giving spirit of water flow through blood as well?* He didn't know for sure, and he was finding it difficult to think clearly. The poison was clouding his mind, and the fever was trying to rip the life force from him, but he kept fighting. The flame inside him refused to burn out.

One thought kept floating through his mind. *Blood is water.*

Many Wolves tried to pull himself to his feet, but again the world started spinning around him, and he could not find any balance on his quivering legs.

I will have to crawl.

Propelled by his swollen left arm, he dragged his body over to the cougar carcass, doing his best to keep his bloodied right arm out of the clinging sand. His movement was slow—he had to stop every foot or so to rest—but it was movement. Finally, he made it to the dead animal.

He pulled his knife free and labored to cut open a cavity in the great cat's chest. The sweat and sand in his eyes, along with the dizzying effects of the poison, made it difficult to see, to concentrate. Many Wolves worked slowly, bursts of effort broken up by pauses to catch his breath, until he'd opened a cut in the carcass large enough to stick his hand through.

He reached into the bloody opening and felt around the cat's innards. Flies buzzed all around him. The animal's insides were moist and still lukewarm. He felt the liver, yanked it free, then carefully pulled it out of the cavity. Blood dripped down his arm as he lifted it to his lips. Slowly, he sucked small mouthfuls of the thick liquid into his dried mouth and swallowed them with labored difficulty. There was little taste—just the feeling of moisture in his mouth. His body welcomed it and yearned for more. He took his time and drank more of the cat's blood, but he did not eat any of the liver. He had no desire to eat anything.

Blood is water.

Many Wolves stayed a while at the carcass, drinking and resting, until he'd squeezed the liver dry. He thought he felt a little better, a little stronger, but he wasn't sure if that was true, or if his mind was simply choosing to believe that. Regardless, the sensation of renewed strength helped him as he crawled over to a lone juniper tree about twenty steps away. He knew he needed to get out of the sun.

When he reached the protective, cooling shade, he collapsed. Rojo padded over and lay down next to him.

I need to rest. And I need real water. Thirst still stung him. The blood had helped, but it wasn't enough; and besides, the carcass would dry out soon. *I have to get to water, but I can't walk. I can barely move.*

In the shade, the chills returned, and he began shaking again. He huddled on the ground, trying to stay warm.

Elk Dog could bring me to water. Yes, the horse. But how could he get to him? Was he still at the camp?

"Rojo, can you bring Elk Dog to me?"

The red wolf lifted its head in response, looking at Many Wolves with ears raised. But after a moment, Rojo once again rested his head back on the sandy ground. *He heard his name and Elk Dog's name, but he didn't understand.*

"Elk Dog," Many Wolves said again, and again the wolf raised his head, but did nothing.

It's just crazy talk to him.

Many Wolves rested again, this time closing his eyes. He tried to block the dizziness, the nausea, the pain from his mind. He tried to think of happy things: Ten Arrows's bubbling laughter, Chiquito soaring in the wind, beautiful sunsets stretching out to the horizon, Rojo begging him to play. It was good to take his mind away off of his sickness. It made him want to journey far away from his body and never come back.

A mind journey. Rojo can bring Elk Dog to me, if I lead him. If I lead his spirit.

Many Wolves opened his eyes and felt for his medicine bag. It was there, still attached to his belt. Usually he left it at his camp when he hunted. But this time, on this horrible trip, he had brought it with him. It was a gift from the Great Spirit, a ray of hope—or just plain luck.

His fingers felt inside the bag for the buttons of peyote. Finding one, he raised it to his mouth and cut it in half with his teeth, then returned the other half to his medicine bag. He chewed on the peyote, slowly, not concerned about the medicine's nausea-inducing effects. *I can't feel any worse than I do already.* He felt around in his medicine bag again, this time withdrawing the small sack that held the pieces of the white lion's paw flower; these would allow him to journey with his mind. He put the pieces of the flower in his mouth, mixing them with the softening peyote. Usually, he dissolved the mixture in hot water, but this time he had to make his own water in his mouth, which, in his dehydrated condition, took some time.

Eventually, he was able to swallow the medicine. He closed his eyes, placed his hand on Rojo's fur, and waited. The colors in his head spun faster and faster. He vomited once, and then again, but tried to stay focused, to keep his eyes closed.

Rojo, up! His mind kept whirling like a sandstorm. He couldn't stop it or even slow it down. He vomited again. *Rojo, up!*

Suddenly the storm in his mind passed, and from the calm he saw the world around him—through Rojo's eyes. He sensed the heightened smells and sounds.

Rojo, up! The wolf stood, and Many Wolves felt a surge of pain from Rojo's injured foot. *Rojo, run east to the camp, to the river!* The wolf began to trot. Every step snapped with pain, and Rojo cried out several times, but after a time the pain subsided. Many Wolves felt his breathing couple with the wolf's, like two birds entangled in a mating ritual. Rojo was running now, weaving around the sage and mesquite, toward the horizon where the sun would soon disappear and sleep for the night.

Rojo stopped for a brief rest at the top of a long hill. A valley was uncovered before them. *The cottonwoods! The river! Go to the river camp, Rojo!*

The wolf dashed again, but this time the downward slope aided his sprint. As he got closer to the camp, Rojo barked and shifted his direction to the left.

As the wolf ran, Many Wolves felt the calmness leaving him, the storm returning to his head. He would not be able to stay with the wolf much longer.

In a stand of cottonwoods, Many Wolves spotted Elk Dog. *Elk Dog! The camp!* The horse's shape was tumbling in and out of focus. He heard the rush of river water, but only in flashes.

Go to the fire pit. The pain was coming back to him. The world in his mind was spinning again. He was losing control, losing the vision. *Bring the water pouch, Rojo. Bring Elk Dog.*

Many Wolves opened his drooping eyes. He was back to his pain, back to his sickness. His journey was over.

The Sweetest Taste

Many Wolves was awoken by a tongue on his face. Rojo, licking away his sweat. The wolf yipped, but Many Wolves was confused and still in a poisoned stupor.

"What is it?" he muttered through cracked, blistering lips.

Rojo continued to bark.

Many Wolves lifted his head up and looked at the excited animal, who stopped momentarily, cocked his head with a curious look, then barked again. The wolf fell silent, then bent his head down and nudged an object on the ground in front of him.

"My water pouch!" blurted Many Wolves. He tried to move quickly toward it, but cried out from the pain. It wracked his body, held him back like a powerful headwind.

Slowly. He struggled to pull himself up on his knees, then crawled over to the water pouch. "Rojo, you brought it to me. You heard me. You understood!"

Carefully, he untied the top of the pouch, making sure not to spill a single drop of the precious liquid. He raised the pouch to his mouth and swallowed only a small sip. *Slowly,* he reminded himself. After resting for several moments, he took a slightly larger amount and swirled it around his mouth. His dry mouth absorbed so much of the water that there was hardly any left to swallow. And it had the sweetest taste—sweeter than any bee's honey or flower's nectar that he had ever tasted.

Again, he took a small mouthful and swallowed carefully. His hands were shaking from chills, so he set the pouch down, leaning it against his leg for stability, then tied the opening shut. *I have to drink sparingly.*

Many Wolves remembered a few of the details of his mind journey with Rojo. He wasn't far from his camp—it was just over that slope, he recalled, looking toward the east. The dusky sunset behind him painted an orange glow across the surrounding sky. Though he had drank little, the water invigorated his spirit and renewed his hope. *I have to make it over the hill. I have to walk.*

Despite the injury to his right arm, the grip from his right hand still felt stronger than his left, so he grasped the pouch tightly with it. He hoisted himself up on his shaky legs—and instantly, dizziness swarmed him like angry bees. *I have to fight it.* He steadied himself, then stumbled his way along an eastward path, fighting off the queasiness.

Occasionally he fell, clutching the life-aiding water with the grip of an eagle. But he always rose again. *Keep moving.*

Rojo followed closely by his side, still limping badly and whining. Somehow, the wolf had been able to suppress the injury during their mind-journey, but now it had returned like an annoying mosquito. "What a pair we make, big wolf," Many Wolves groaned to himself, coughing as he tried to chuckle.

Over and over, he pushed himself up and staggered forward on weakened legs as far as he could go, only to stumble once again. The small hill he had to climb felt like an enormously steep mountain, but knowing what was at the end of it, knowing that there *was* an end, gave him the strength to continue. After every fourth or fifth fall, he would rest for a moment, his chest heaving with every breath, and he would drink a small mouthful of the precious life-giving honey from his pouch. Then he would continue again.

One crooked step at a time, Many Wolves carved a path up the slope. His fever burned the water from his body almost as quickly as he drank it in. The pain was so intense that it was impossible to ignore, and every breath seemed like it would be his last, but he kept putting one foot in front of the other.

At last, he reached the summit. He collapsed, his lungs starving for air.

The light had been stolen by darkness, and he couldn't see the landscape around him anymore. But he knew he was close. His ears clearly separated the beautiful, rushing flow of the Rio Pecos from the stirring breeze. The river had always given him life in these suffocatingly hostile lands, and now he needed its water more than ever before. He drank several more gulps from his waning water supply. *The river is just down the hill.* A wave of relief washed over him at the thought, and finally his exhausted body gave in, allowing his mind to be dragged under a blanket of unconsciousness.

The next morning Many Wolves woke to familiar sounds. Snorting. Nickering. A blast of air hit his face. He opened his eyes and stared into two large nostrils.

A horse.

The animal nuzzled his face, trying to rouse him.

Elk Dog!

His horse's nickering was as distinct to him as Chiquito's screeching hunger cries.

"Elk Dog, you found me," he mumbled with his eyes half-open. "I'm not dead yet, my friend, but I need your help."

The water pouch was still in his hand, so he drank the last two mouthfuls of water and then tied the empty pouch to his belt.

The horse nickered again and nudged him. *Elk Dog must think I'm waking from a long sleep.* Many Wolves pulled his aching body up cautiously, battling the dizziness. He reached for Elk Dog's neck and shoulders to help maintain his balance. Leaning against the right side of his horse, he rested for several moments, trying to gather what little strength he had left.

Elk Dog wore no saddle, only his horse-hair lead. Many Wolves sensed his horse's nervous impatience. "Elk Dog, easy. I need to rest."

He knew it would be difficult to lift himself up with one swollen, snake-bitten arm, another badly clawed, bloodied arm, and a head still swirling from the snake's toxin. Even the simplest of tasks, like walking and mounting a horse, were now monumental challenges for his broken body.

Many Wolves prepared for a burst of effort. He counted to himself to help focus, the lead held in his left hand and his right hand resting on Elk Dog's shoulder. He struggled to calm his exerted breaths. *Five, four, three, two, one...*

Groaning loudly, the pain surging through his flexed arms like fire, he tried to lift his right leg, but it did not obey; there was no strength in either of his stiff legs. He rested again and caught his breath once more, holding onto Elk Dog to keep from falling.

Usually he mounted Elk Dog with the greatest of ease by kicking up his right leg from the side or jumping on the horse from behind. But without any leg strength, neither of these methods would work. *I will have to pull myself up with my arms.* He counted again, but this time he positioned his right hand farther from his left, resting on the horse's back. When his count was at zero, he tried to pull himself up with his arms. He screamed from the overbearing pain, but was unable to raise himself onto his mount. Many Wolves felt despair grip his mind like the fangs of a snake. *I am too weak to do this.*

Defeated, he let go of the horse and fell to the ground.

Perhaps I can use something to boost myself up? He staggered to his feet again and looked around him for a fallen tree or a large rock, but there was nothing—nothing but endless sand. Or at least, that was all his mind could identify in his dizziness. It felt like his body was slipping away from him, and his mind was following.

I'm not ready to die.

If only Elk Dog could drag me, that would be enough, he thought. But there was no pole-drag, no rope, nothing to tie himself to the horse.

I have no choice. I have to bury the pain and pull myself up. Either that, or I will die here.

One more time, he grabbed hold of Elk Dog like he had before. He tried to block out the thoughts of despair; in his mind, he pictured himself mounting the horse again and again. *I can do this.*

With one last burst of effort, every bit of strength he had left, he pulled. In his mind, he focused on what he had to do, saw himself doing it. He allowed no other thoughts.

And this time he did it—he pulled himself up. With his body slumped over the horse's back, he lifted his shaky right leg over to the other side, then rested his head on Elk Dog's shoulder. His mind reeled from the pain shooting through his arms, forcing a scream from his weakened lungs and tears from eyes. He was surprised there was any water left in his body. But he felt only joy.

I made it.

Using the lead, Many Wolves spun the horse around to face eastward, then directed him to walk.

"Take me to the river, Elk Dog."

Strangle the Poison

With the rising sun staring him in the face, Many Wolves rode chest-down on the back of his horse. He needed to find the Rio Pecos, the lifelong friend that could make him well again. Turning his head away from the brightness and the whirling landscape, he rested the side of his face on Elk Dog's shoulder. The bumping waves of movement from the horse's gait agitated the poison in his body, raising more and more convulsions in his stomach, though there was scarcely anything left for him to cast out. The contractions were more of a nuisance than anything. The jarring brought far more pain to his swollen and bloodied arms and his dizzied head. He persevered, however, knowing his friend was waiting at the end of his journey.

Elk Dog continued at a steady pace. Chiquito circled above them, his hunger screams cutting through the shy breeze and clopping hooves. Many Wolves occasionally caught glimpses of Rojo, still hobbling to keep up with them, aided by the downward slope. *It's good to be with my pack again.* For the first time in what seemed like several sleeps, Many Wolves felt this wouldn't be his last sunrise.

At last, the sound of rushing water caressed his ears— beautiful music to a thirsting man. Elk Dog stopped and whinnied. Many Wolves slipped off awkwardly and fell on the hard ground. Pushing himself up on all fours, he crawled to the riverbank.

With his cupped right hand, he splashed the cool water all over his parched, blistering face. Then he sipped the river water from his hand, savoring every drop. He coughed several times before his throat accepted the offering, but it grew easier with each swallow. Rojo, too, lapped up several gulps of river water before settling down in the shade of a nearby cottonwood.

With his thirst quenched at last, Many Wolves soaked his earth-stained feet in the river. Chills surged through him again, but he didn't care. His body needed the liquid medicine. Carefully, he rinsed the dried blood off his right arm and the right side of his body. The cuts on his arm from the cougar's claws stung when the water washed over them, but they were not nearly as deep as the bear claw wounds he had once suffered on his leg. They would heal quickly.

He lay back, his feet still soaking up life from the river, and stared up at the bright sun through squinted eyes, trying to settle his dizziness. Chiquito was chirping from a nearby cottonwood branch, urging him to look for food, as if nothing had happened. But the pack leader could not rise to his feet and lead the hunt. Not today. Many Wolves wondered how many more sleeps would pass before he could hunt again.

Now that the first and most important of his needs had been met, he needed rest to fight the poison spirit in his body. His grandfather had once said, "Rest will strangle poison." At the time, Many Wolves had imagined a snake strangling a rat, and he'd thought it strange that a snake could remove poison.

Comforted by the sunlight and the cooling water, Many Wolves drifted off to sleep.

The mid-afternoon heat roused him from his dream of wandering the desert alone, a familiar nightmare. Each path led him to another path, but never to water or shelter or a companion. There were no distinct landmarks either, just an endless desert panorama drenched in a blue, cloudless sky.

Many Wolves always woke from these dreams in a cold sweat, thirsting for water. So he sat up, untied the empty water pouch from his belt, and filled it with the river's gift. After several careful swallows, he stumbled to his feet and staggered over to his sleeping area and fire pit. Even that brief exertion brought back the chills and queasiness, so he found a spot that would be shaded by the cottonwoods for the rest of the day, wrapped his body in his buffalo robe, and rested.

Strangle the poison.

Pack Medicine

Many Wolves rested through two more sun-ups. He slept mostly, rising only to fetch more water from the river or to relieve his bladder. His body felt a little better with each new day. The dizziness and the chills were gone, and the swelling in his left arm had subsided, taking with it most of the pain. The claw marks in his other arm were beginning to scab, a sign of healing. Though his body hurt less, it was still weak—understandable, seeing as he hadn't eaten for days. As a result, standing up was an arduous task, and walking, even for a short distance, drained much of his energy.

Many Wolves surveyed the area around his small camp. Elk Dog was crunching on a patch of sage. *Horses bred by Northerners could survive in even the harshest lands.* Many Wolves was thankful his animals knew how to survive on their own; his ordeal had forced them to forage without him for several days. It was good for them; it sharpened their survival skills, should the day come when they were without a leader to walk the path ahead of them.

Suddenly, Chiquito flew into camp and landed in front of Many Wolves, squawking—his usual morning banter.

"I see your belly is full, Little One. Another successful hunt without me." Many Wolves felt the pangs of hunger gnaw at his own stomach. At least it was less of a discomfort than the nausea he had been feeling as a result of the snakebite.

The small hawk twisted his head at the words. The bird knew the words "Little One," recognized them as his own name.

"Did Rojo help you, or did you hunt alone?" Many Wolves had not seen his wolf, and figured Rojo was out searching for a morning meal. *His leg must be feeling better. Good.*

Although the three of them often hunted together, Many Wolves knew he was the glue holding the loose hunting group together; there was no real affection between the hawk and the wolf. They stayed out of each other's way mostly, performing their duties as cooperative hunting partners, but no more. They sought to please the leader and fulfill their own needs. Chiquito, for his part, was the lowest member of the pack—he had been so since the day Many Wolves had first found him hiding from a band of angry crows—and accepted that role without complaint.

Though his body had been resting for the past two sleeps, Many Wolves's mind had been restless, slipping in and out of dream worlds. And unlike the longer, deep dreams he had at night, these had been short, half-awake visions, almost like his peyote mind-journeys. Small pieces of his childhood faded in and out of focus, and each memory felt incomplete to him. He tried to wring more details from each scene, tried to remember something new, but he always fell short. In particular, moments spent with his grandfather and his mother preoccupied his mind; yet their memories seemed so distant to him now. They had changed worlds, and reaching into their world would be like reaching into the heart of the sun. Maybe someday he would see them again—when it was his time. But for now, the flame of survival—nearly squelched by the snake's poison—burned strong within him, bound him to this world.

Many Wolves's thoughts were interrupted by Rojo, who trotted into camp with a rabbit in his mouth. Many Wolves was relieved to see that the red wolf's limp was gone.

Rojo stopped and deposited the dead rabbit in front of Many Wolves, then lay down and stared at him, whining and panting, his tail swinging back and forth, brushing a pattern into the sandy earth.

"You brought that for me, big wolf?"

Rojo's tail flicked even faster as if to say, "Yes."

Many Wolves examined the carcass and noticed that parts of the head and chest had been eaten away. *Chiquito.* He laughed. "So, your little brother caught this and ate his share. I'm glad he left some for the scavengers. That's you and me, big wolf." Many Wolves laughed again, then grabbed his knife and sliced off one of the hind legs and tossed it to the wolf. "There's your share of the kill."

The red wolf jumped to his feet, grabbed the rabbit leg, and circled to a shady spot nearby to lie down and enjoy the meal.

Many Wolves had not taken food for many days. His mind had not allowed him to eat; it feared his body would reject it. It was a feeling he had never experienced before. Still, although even now he felt no urge to eat, he knew he had to if he was to regain his strength.

He gathered up dried grass and sage from around his camp and prepared a nest of kindling in a small fire pit. Even the simple task of rubbing his fire-sticks together was difficult for him in his current state, but he persevered, and eventually the flames appeared. Many Wolves welcomed the fire spirits back to his camp, feeding them with small mesquite branches, but kept them at a modest size to avoid drawing attention. Then he skinned the rabbit carcass, sawed off the head, mounted the body on two sticks, and placed it above the cooking flames. It was arduous work for a man at half strength.

Once the meat was cooked to his liking, he separated it from the fire and let it cool. He cut just a sliver of meat and placed it in his sore mouth. It was difficult to chew because his jaws ached, so he just sucked the juices out of it at first, then carefully swallowed it. It was as though his body needed to learn how to eat all over again. He did the same with several more small pieces, taking his time with each labored bite, forcing down the nutrients he knew his body needed.

When he felt he had eaten enough, he closed his eyes and thanked the Great Spirit for the meal. He tossed the uneaten head of the rabbit to Rojo, who grabbed it with his powerful jaws and carried it to a comfortable eating spot. Chiquito was perched above on a cottonwood branch, contently preening his feathers.

Thank you, my friends, for saving my life again.

Racing Thoughts

Thorn Bird plunged into the night in a swift gallop, his speed elevated by the darkness around him. He needed to get back to his village, and it would take him most of the new day to get there. Gray Elk's family, with Stands Alone's help, would gather a search party at first light. Half of a night was not much of a head start.

The endless prairie grass swarmed him from every side as he rode. Familiar landmarks— solitary trees and rock formations, rivers, hills— guided him home. His people, the *Noomah*, could map their way from one end of Comancheria to the other with only a working knowledge of landmarks. The half-moon shed enough light to spot these landmarks deep in the night.

Thoughts crashed through his head like the chilling wind in his face. What will they want for Gray Elk's death? To kill me? To wipe out my village? No. They would only attack the village to spill my blood. *This is my war.* My blood will spill and their blood will spill, but I will not allow them to spill the blood of my people. They must be led away from the village; and if they do find it, I won't be there.

Thorn Bird didn't bother to mask his tracks. He didn't want to lose more time trying to cover up what he knew they could uncover anyway. He also knew you could not hide a village from the *Noomah* in *Noomah* lands. That was like trying to hide a huge chunk of fresh meat from a pack of hungry dogs. They will always find it. *I must warn my village. Then I must leave.* It was settled.

Though his body was numb from the ice-cold air blowing across it, his blood was still hot from the killing. Thorn Bird would not soon forget the fear in the old man's eyes when the knife was drawn to his throat. It was hard to believe this was the same haughty man who had barked at him earlier that day; the same man who had insulted, and eventually banished, his father, so many winters ago. Thorn Bird had been the cause of his father's questionable act—the father had been protecting his son— so Thorn Bird had felt immensely responsible for his father's banishment. But now, he had healing. Gray Elk was silent. No more poisoned words would flow from his wrinkled lips ever again, and his bloodied gray scalp would soon adorn Thorn Bird's lodge forever.

Eventually, Thorn Bird came to a rushing river, an offshoot of the Rio Colorado. He commanded his horse to cross, and it entered the water reluctantly. The near-freezing water stunned both of their bodies and washed away their sweat and dust. The sensation was shocking at first, but then refreshing.

When they reached the far bank, Thorn Bird dismounted so the both of them could rest and drink. The cascading water drowned out all other sounds, even their heavy breathing—which, like an ongoing drumbeat, had paced their journey.

After a short time, the Nokoni warrior mounted his painted gelding once again and rode west. At his back, the lazy sun was just beginning to peek over the horizon, uncovering the landscape around him, but bullishly still holding back its warmth.

Though his body was fatigued, Thorn Bird's mind was still racing ahead. Now that Gray Elk was dead, it was time for Thorn Bird to revisit his greatest desire: finding his father's killer, Many Wolves. On several occasions, Thorn Bird had led exhaustive search parties to the deserts to the south and the plains and foothills to the west, but there had been no sign of the *taiboo*. So much time wasted. And with less than twenty useful warriors, he could no longer afford to send out more search parties; doing so would leave his village vulnerable to the dangers of an unexpected Pawnee, Ute, or

Tonkawa attack. In a village the size of Thorn Bird's, there could be no raiding or search parties; only hunting parties, to supply the village with fresh meat.

Then how do I find this Many Wolves?

It was a question it seemed he had asked himself hundreds of times before, with no good answer. But a new possibility had come to mind as he was conversing with his old friend—and now most certainly his new enemy—Stands Alone. Stands Alone had asked Thorn Bird about all the warriors of his father's band. Many had perished in the battle with Big Sky's *Navoonah*; others, like Mocking Bird, had survived. But there was one who had survived the battle only because he wasn't there to fight it. Someone with great hunting and tracking skill, perhaps the most talented of his father's men. Could this man find Many Wolves?

Thorn Bird felt certain of it.

He screamed a cry of victory as he raced across the dawn-drenched prairie.

I must find Malone.

The Old Buffalo

"Thorn Bird, you're back," said Half Weasel in a surprised and enthusiastic voice. He was one of the youngest warriors in Thorn Bird's band, and a close friend.

Thorn Bird was just stepping out of his lodge, where he had been packing arrows into his wolf-skin quiver. Many of them were unfinished, some without points and others missing feathers, but he wanted to make sure he had an ample supply. He had also packed away any spare arrow parts he could find around his lodge.

"Half Weasel, I need to leave again." Thorn Bird looked around at his small village; it was spotted with tipis in every direction. His was near the center, the largest, as his father's had been. The children were screaming and playing in the hot, late afternoon sun while the women were busy with their work: cooking, scraping buffalo skins, and tanning hides. Out beyond the lodges was the horse herd, grazing on the fresh prairie grass. Many of the boys and some of the men were riding the painted ponies, playing games of chase and tag with each other. Some of the village dogs joined in the games as well, barking at the heels of the running horses.

"Why? We need you here. We need you for the hunts. The men need their leader." Half Weasel looked at Thorn Bird with pleading eyes.

The Nokoni leader tied the quiver to his mount and began to fill another bag with dried meat and nuts. Then he stopped and looked into his friend's dark eyes. Half Weasel was the son of Silent Weasel, one of his father's best scouts. Silent Weasel had been killed in the war with the *Navoonah*—killed by the same *taiboo* who had killed Thorn Bird's father.

Half Weasel had barely lived seventeen winters, but he was brave, and he had already become one of the band's most talented warriors and scouts. He was stout and muscular like his father, and quick as lightning. Together, he and Thorn Bird made an odd pair: Half Weasel, the smallest warrior, and Thorn Bird, the largest. Half Weasel barely stood as high as Thorn Bird's shoulders.

"Last night, I slashed Gray Elk's throat."

Half Weasel's oversized eyes grew even larger in his stunned face.

"Stands Alone and Gray Elk's family will come for me with many men. They will want blood for blood. They will want my blood, and I do not want this to be a war between our villages. We cannot hide from them, so I must leave. I must be the old buffalo who leads the hunters away from the herd."

"But you will not die easily like the old buffalo."

Thorn Bird smiled. "You know me well, my good friend."

"Let me and Fire Eyes join you. We will fight with you," said Half Weasel, raising his hand to his leader's shoulder.

"No. This is my fight. You and Fire Eyes must stay here with the village. Keep up the hunts and protect our women and children. That is what I ask of you. The war party will not harm you because you are *Noomah*. Tell them I have left the village. My tracks will be easy to find."

"Where will you go, *namunewapi*?"

"I will head northwest toward the high country. I need to find Malone."

"Malone? He will help you fight them?"

"No. But he will find the *taiboo* who killed our fathers. He will not fail as we did; I am certain of it. Then I will barter with Gray Elk's war party."

"Your *puha* is strong, Thorn Bird. You will need every bit of its magic and power."

"When I return, it will be stronger, my friend." Thorn Bird raised his right arm toward his friend. The two men grasped each other's forearms, an act of deep friendship.

"This talk is making me hungry, Half Weasel. Did the hunting party bring in any fresh meat?"

"Just a few prairie dogs that some of the boys killed. The men are still out looking for buffalo signs."

"Good. There will be fewer holes to trip our horses," said Thorn Bird. Both men laughed. "Have Valencia cook them up for us, and have Fire Eyes and Long Claw join us so I can see them before I leave."

"Fire Eyes and Long Claw are out with the other men. I don't know when they'll be back," said the stocky warrior. "But I will tell Valencia."

Half Weasel left Thorn Bird alone to continue his preparations. Soon after, Valencia arrived with two dead prairie dogs, skinned and gutted, and began reviving the fire in front of their lodge. She added more dried buffalo dung to raise the heat of the fire, then began preparing the prairie dogs for roasting.

"Half Weasel says you will be leaving again," she said, a disappointed tone in her voice.

"Did he tell you why?"

"*Si*, he told me why." She switched to speaking Spanish. She always spoke Spanish when she was angry. "You killed Gray Elk, and now they will want to kill you! You never think what is best for your *villa* or best for your *familia*! You always do what's best for *you*. You are a selfish man, a selfish leader!" In her anger, she broke one of the roasting sticks, and she screamed in frustration.

"I did it for *mi padre* and for my peace," Thorn Bird said, fighting to remain calm.

Valencia stood so she could speak to him face to face. "Your father is not here anymore. *We* are here. You should do what's best for *us*! It's like you have this *deseo* to join him in the next world. Remember, I loved him too and doing this… killing… It will not bring him back from the *muerto*!"

Valencia was tall like him, the tallest woman in the village. Only Thorn Bird's mother, Rosa, was taller, but she had died two winters ago after a fall from a horse. Thorn Bird loved that Valencia could look at him at almost the same eye level.

"You don't understand!" he said. "It will bring his *espiritu* some peace." He combed the long black hair out of her flushed face so he could see her temper-stricken Mexican eyes, but she pulled away in anger. "Nothing will happen to me or the *villa*," he assured her. "You will see. If anything, it will make me stronger. It will make *us* stronger!"

Valencia returned to her work, but continued to mutter to herself. Once she had set up the forked cooking sticks, she skewered each of the gutted prairie dogs with other, sharpened sticks, and placed them over the modest fire.

"Do not let your shadow rest on my cooking fire, or you will cook the rest yourself," she said, closing the tipi door flap behind her.

In their village, it was considered bad luck to cast a shadow on the cooking fire. Luckily it was midday, so shadows did not wander far from the person who made them.

Thorn Bird preoccupied himself with cleaning Gray Elk's scalp. When he was done, he hung it with his other trophies on a scalp pole near his lodge. Most of the other scalps were *Navoonah* or Pawnee. Gray Elk's was the first scalp from one of his own people. He had saved a special place for it on his pole.

You see what I have done, Ahpu.

"You humble us all, Thorn Bird, with all your trophies," said Half Weasel with a grin, returning for a visit and a meal with his leader. He smiled often, like his father, and was almost always in a pleasant mood.

Thorn Bird invited his friend to sit near his fire pit, the dried grass beaten down by the enclave's inhabitants. The crackling flames were beginning to sear the meat, offering a new scent that mixed with the smells of burning mesquite and buffalo dung.

"How will you find Malone?" asked Half Weasel.

"I saw him last spring near Falling Turtle Rock. I am hoping he is there now, because it's a good place to hunt deer."

"*Haa*, I remember now," said the scout. "Why does he always ride away from us when he sees us?"

"Maybe he feels his spirit is not ready to return. Or maybe he just wants to be left alone. Our fathers were his closest friends, so now that they are gone, he has no reason to come back to us." Thorn Bird was drawing figures in the sand as he spoke. His mind was preoccupied with formulating war plans for the party of warriors who would inevitably come for his blood.

But now Thorn Bird turned to face his friend and spoke in earnest. "Listen carefully, Half Weasel. Gray Elk's party will come here looking for me, perhaps when the sun sets today. Do not provoke them. Tell them I have left the village and make sure all the men are here with you, mounted and ready with weapons. They will not risk their lives knowing their prize is not with you. Let them search the village so they know I am not here. Do you understand?"

"*Haa, namunewapi*. They will want to know where you are going. What do I say?"

"Tell them I am heading west on a medicine journey. That is all they need to know. They will eventually find me—because I want them to. But not before my war paint is ready."

Half Weasel nodded in understanding.

"Good. I have a favor to ask of you. After we eat, I want you to collect the best arrows you can find and bring them to me. Get as many from Talks Too Much as he can spare, since he makes the finest shafts and points."

"*Haa, namunewapi*."

The scout turned and began to walk away when Thorn Bird called to him. "One last thing, Half Weasel. I want arrows with war points, not hunting points."

I will be killing men, not deer or buffalo.

Dangerous Prey

"Chiquito!" Many Wolves yelled.

He searched around the camp on this chilly spring morning, calling the bird's name and whistling with his antler whistle, only to hear the dense, lonely forest of pine trees fling his cries back at him. A night had passed since Many Wolves had last seen Chiquito. It wasn't like his tame companion to wander far be away for long. Sometimes he roosted away from the camp at night, but he always returned the following morning.

Many Wolves had expelled the poison from his body and was finally feeling normal again. His pack had provided food for him when he'd needed it most. But now that his strength and appetite had returned, he had hoped to resume his normal routines. Those routines had been ripped apart by the snake's poison, and now they were again threatened by the absence of his friend.

"Rojo, where is he?" Many Wolves said, hoping he would his wolf would howl or bark to let him know he had found something—even if only a scent on the wind. But the wolf merely cast a bewildered look at him as if to ask, "What's wrong?"

As they continued their search for the bird, Many Wolves heard a sound springing from the forest shadows. It was the piercing cry of a bird, but it wasn't Chiquito's raspy cry, which was much lower in pitch. The sound was constant and repeating. He expected it would stop at any moment, but it didn't.

"Rojo, I think we should go see what it is."

He called for his wolf companion to follow him deeper into the forest. The foothills were silent except for the crunching of pine needles beneath his feet and the occasional rustle of a branch from a squirrel or chipmunk. He expected Chiquito would show up at any moment from out of nowhere, as if nothing had ever happened, giving him a look that said, "What are you waiting for? Let's go find something to eat!"

Rojo's nose and ears continued to sift the wind for sounds and smells. But the red wolf showed no sign of having found anything interesting. No Chiquito. No danger. Nothing but the strange bird-like sound, which grew louder with every step.

Then suddenly, Rojo bolted ahead, growling, disappearing into the brush. Many Wolves ran after him.

He found Rojo fighting with a bird of some kind. One of its grayish wings was flapping in the air as the wolf shook its body back and forth like a dog playing with a toy. When Many Wolves walked closer, Rojo stopped and looked up at him, blood dripping down his jowls. The bird was barely moving now.

"Rojo, easy," Many Wolves commanded, and he moved in closer to inspect the bird. It was nearly dead, and he snapped its neck with his hands to end the creature's suffering. It was a medium-sized bird of prey, a short-winged forest hawk with mostly blue coloration and blood-red eyes that had surely once been fierce, but which were now lifeless. Many Wolves had seen such birds darting through the forest many times; they were fast flyers who loved to hunt birds. Many Wolves called them "bird-killers."

While Many Wolves inspected the dead bird, Rojo's nose led him along the forest floor to another find about fifty yards away. The wolf sniffed his find, then looked up at his master and whined.

Many Wolves walked over to see what Rojo had found. His heart sank at the sight of a dark brown mass at Rojo's feet. His fear was confirmed when he spotted the reddish wings and the white patch on the tail.

It was Chiquito.

Many Wolves felt a rush of dizzying heat fill his body as he bent down to stroke the body of his dead companion. Tears welled up, and he fought them back. He closed his eyes and remembered the last time he had seen Chiquito. The small wolf hawk had been so full of life and energy, as always. It was hard to see him this way: cold, still.

Many Wolves tried to imagine how this had happened. The two hawks must have attacked each other; it was the only explanation. But he couldn't imagine Chiquito attacking another bird of prey. It had always seemed that there was a peace treaty among predators, an agreement to never attack one another. This bird-killer must have attacked Chiquito out of desperate hunger.

Yet Many Wolves's wolf hawk was not an easy kill. He had bravely fought back, crippling the bird-killer. Many Wolves did not know how much life had been left in the bluish hawk before Rojo got to it, but based on the bird-killers keening cries, it would not have lived for much longer.

Many Wolves opened his eyes and saw Rojo sitting quietly next to him. He softly stroked the wolf's head and back. "Big wolf. Our friend Chiquito is gone. He was brave, a warrior—a great hunter among birds. He deserves a warrior's burial. And so does the blue bird-killer."

Rojo licked his master's face, as if sensing his sorrow, or sharing it.

"Thanks, Rojo. Or are you just feasting on the salt from my tears?" Many Wolves forced a smile and scratched his companion behind the ears.

Many Wolves pulled the hunting knife from his leg sheath and began digging out a hole in the forest floor. The soil was moist from recent spring rains and easy to dig into. After a short time, he had a hole as wide and deep as his arm. But before placing Chiquito's body in the hole, he grabbed a sharpening stone from his bag. With it, he carefully sharpened the talons and beak of his favorite hawk, his tears spilling onto the soft, dark brown chest feathers.

"Your weapons will be sharp in the spirit world, Chiquito, just as a warrior takes his favorite horse and weapon with him when he dies."

When he was finished, he gently lowered the bird's body into the freshly dug grave and covered it with moist dirt. "Great Spirit, help him to find his sisters so they may hunt again together in the next world."

Then Many Wolves walked over to where the blue hawk lay. He dug a slightly bigger hole for the larger bird, then, as he had done with Chiquito, he meticulously sharpened the bird's talons and beak. "A great bird-hunting warrior you are to kill a proven warrior like Chiquito. I hope you have plenty of animals to hunt in the spirit world." He placed the bird-killer's body in the hole and covered it with dirt.

Finally, he lay down under a tree between the two graves and folded his arms behind his head. Rojo curled up next to him. He closed his eyes and imagined the two birds flying up to the sky together—as friends. Higher and higher they flew into the deep blue sky, spiraling and climbing. He saw Chiquito look down at him one last time, unleashing a loud, raspy farewell.

The emotions and tears rushed through Many Wolves like a waterfall.

Goodbye, Little One.

Spinning Circles

Many Wolves woke from his late-afternoon nap with Rojo lying by his side. Looking around, he spotted the loose mound of dirt—Chiquito's grave— and the overwhelming emotions from earlier in the day came crashing down on him again, like a violent rockslide. *Chiquito is dead.*

Many Wolves was tired to the bone and didn't feel like moving from the spot between the two birds' graves. Rojo licked his fingers, and Many Wolves stroked the wolf's back.

"Life will be different for us now, Rojo. There will be no more swift claws to catch our meals. Squirrels stop frequently, so they will be easy to kill, but to hit a moving rabbit with a bow will be difficult. I'll have to shoot them before they run. At least you can find them for me."

His thoughts were interrupted by a distant squawking. It was a mixture of two sounds, one at a slightly higher pitch than the other. It was probably just a couple of young hawks calling out to their mother. Or maybe they were ravens or owls.

Many Wolves remembered when his three wolf hawks were young; they used to squawk at him like that. He smiled at the memory. At the time, Chiquito had seemed like the weakest one, the one who wouldn't survive. *You proved us all wrong, Chiquito. You outlived them all.* Many Wolves had often felt that if Chiquito could survive all the pain in their lives, then he could live through it too. His smallest bird had lived a long, hearty life.

Dusk fell over the forest, bringing a chill to the air. But Many Wolves didn't want to return to his camp yet. He wanted to stay close to the spirit of his bird, at least for now. It would feel good to build a fire, but he didn't have his fire-sticks or hot embers to start one. And as he wasn't hungry— the emotions of the day had spoiled his appetite— he curled up next to his wolf. *Rojo will keep me warm.*

Still the two distant birds squawked and cried as Many Wolves lay staring into the blackening sky. Then suddenly, one of the young birds screeched loudly, panicked, as if screaming for its life. It was like the scream of a prey animal just before it dies. The cry lasted only for a moment. Neither bird squawked after that. The forest was silent.

As he lay on his back, Many Wolves stared up at the trees that reached to the dark sky with their long, pine-branch arms. He watched as stars began to appear, squeezing out what was left of the sky's light. He always thought of home when he looked at the stars. To him, they were the spirits of the people in his village, people whose lives had been lost long ago. The brightest stars were his family. There was one for his mother, Painted Wings, and his father, Red Arrow. And the one which burned the brightest was his grandfather, Yellow Feather. His memories of them were dimming like the faintest stars: his mother calming him when he had bad dreams; his father making weapons with him; his grandfather telling stories. These were the pleasant memories that lingered now. The horrific recollection of the last time he'd seen their remains also stayed with him. That memory was burnt into his mind like a tattoo.

Over and over the regret churned in his mind: *If only I had reached our village before Laughing Crow, I could have saved them.*

Many Wolves woke the next morning cold and immersed in the damp, musky smell of Rojo's coat. His world was covered in dew. The silence of the night before was broken by bird sounds, but not by the familiar cackling squawk of Chiquito, urging him to get up and begin the hunt. It sounded like one of the birds from the previous day, although its repeated call was less frequent than before, and now sounded more like contentment than a cry of hunger. His curiosity was piqued. *I have to find it.*

He grabbed his hunting bag and retrieved two pieces of dried rabbit meat, one for him and one for Rojo. The wolf gently took the offering from his hand, lay down, and began chewing it while Many Wolves ate his own piece. When they had finished, he said, "Big wolf, let's go."

They walked on wet pine needles in the direction of the bird's cries. Rays of morning sunlight sliced through the trees, and the chill of the morning nipped at Many Wolves's nose and ears. He kept looking back, expecting to see Chiquito following him. But the fresh graves had reminded him that his friend's death was not a dream.

He felt as though a poison was squeezing at his heart again.

The bird cried out again, pulling him back to the moment. In his mind, it was as if the familiar sound of Chiquito's raspy cry—the sound that had greeted his mornings for as long as he could remember—was being replaced by this persistent bird's squawking. *Would this bird replace Chiquito?*

Many Wolves felt they were near the source of the cries, and he spotted a large nest halfway up a pine tree. He walked closer and saw the snowy-white head of a young hawk peek over the side of the nest at him. Seeing a man and wolf approach, the young bird squawked again, louder—likely an alarm being sent out to a parent bird. But there was no adult bird to be seen.

Where are the adult birds?

Then, like a patch of clouds being burned away by the sun, Many Wolves's confusion lifted.

This bird's mother killed Chiquito.

If that was true, then Many Wolves knew exactly what kind of hawk was in that nest: a bird-killer. But where was the father? He knew these birds well. If either parent bird were alive, it would surely be diving on him right now, protecting its nest and its young. Bird-killers were fiercely protective of their offspring. Many Wolves remembered a time when he had climbed a tree next to one of their nests to retrieve an arrow, and had been attacked relentlessly by both nesting birds. They took turns diving at him as he came too close to their nest. One of them eventually cut his scalp with its sharp talons. He ultimately had to give up on the arrow and retreat down the tree.

So, there were no parent birds here. *I must help this bird. Otherwise, it will starve.*

He looked the tree over carefully. It looked climbable, if only he could get up to the lowest branch, which was beyond his reach. He would need something to boost him up.

Many Wolves surveyed the forest floor looking for a branch large enough to support his weight. He found just what he needed—a long but not-too-thin branch half-buried in the dirt and pine needles. He peeled it out of the ground and leaned it up against the trunk of the large pine, wedging it in tightly. But when he tried to stand on it, the rotting branch snapped in two.

Above, the young bird's voice still resonated through the forest.

Many Wolves searched for another branch. Scouring the forest floor, he finally spotted a log lying half-buried in pine needles. It was large enough and partly hollowed out. He squatted down and tried to lift it, but it barely budged. He tried again, grunting with the effort, and this time he did lift one end, but only slightly before he had to set it back down.

Many Wolves walked all around the log, kicking at it, trying to loosen it from the earth's grip. Then he walked to the middle of the log, crouched down low, and pushed hard with his legs and body. At last the log rolled over, freed from its soil casing.

He then pulled out his knife and dug gripping-holes into either side of the old trunk. Pulling the log by the holes, he managed to drag it a short distance before he had to stop to rest.

In this manner, he slowly hauled the heavy log over to the bird's tree. When he had dragged it right to the tree's base, he lifted one side of the log as high as he could and slanted it up against the big pine. Then he repositioned his body under the log and hoisted it again, at least another full arm's length higher.

This should be enough of a boost to reach the lowest limb.

Many Wolves rested for a moment before climbing the inclined log on all fours. At the top, he stood, using the pine's trunk to balance. He grabbed hold of the lowest limb with both hands and pulled himself up. The branches above him were spaced well for an easy climb, so he quickly moved higher, the bird's lonely cries driving him like the reins urging a horse onward.

As he ascended, his fear heightened as well. Each time he looked down, a surge of panic shook his body like a thunderstorm and his mind fell into a dizzying spin. And it only grew worse as he rose higher. The spinning circles now ran round and round in his head. *Don't look down. Don't look down.*

He stopped often, closing his eyes, trying to catch his breath and halt the whirling in his head. At last he reached the base of the nest. The bird looked down at him, its cries now silenced by its fear.

Many Wolves climbed a little higher until he was at eye level with the nest. He paused; it took a moment for his blurred vision to come back into focus. The snowy white bird backed away from him and lay back with its talons facing him, ready to strike. Its grayish blue eyes tracked every move of his hand.

Many Wolves peered into the nest. Beside the baby bird-killer were the bloody remains of another baby hawk. Little was left of it now, though— just its head and legs. That explained why Many Wolves had heard two birds, and then one had suddenly gone silent: the stronger fledgling had eaten the weaker one.

Many Wolves reached toward the hawk with his right hand, using his left to hold tightly to a branch. The bird struck out with his yellow talons, but he pulled his hand back in time. Knowing he would most likely die if he lost his grip added a mountain-sized amount of tension to his situation. *I have to do this quickly.* The pain of a few scratches from a bird's talons would pale in comparison to breaking most of his bones from a fall.

Many Wolves reached out again—and this time he let the bird sink its claws into his hand. He clenched his teeth from the pain, but he managed to grab the bird's body and pull it carefully across the nest. With the bird in hand, he leaned against the trunk of the tree so he could free his left hand to prepare the hunting bag, which was wrapped around his belt. He snapped open the bag with a flick of his wrist, then forced the bird closer to it.

After two failed attempts to put the squirming bird in the bag, Many Wolves realized the difficulty of his task. *Wild birds are not trained to go into strange bags.* Sweat was cascading down his face as he tried to focus. The initial shock of being clawed was long gone, but the fear of falling to a violent death still remained, and it was growing stronger by the moment. Three more times he tried to get the bird in the bag, but failed. He took a moment to rest, still holding on to the petrified bird's body with his right hand.

You're a wild one, aren't you?

The bird made no sound, but is mouth hung open in fear. Its frightened eyes burned into him, reminding him of the faces of Reina, Cazador, and Chiquito when he rescued them from the crows.

Then, with a deep breath, he slid the bird quickly into the bag. He sighed in relief. For whatever reason, the bird had not struggled that time. Perhaps it had given up the fight. *I'll never know.*

And once it was safely enclosed in the bag, the bird seemed much calmer, perhaps lulled by the darkness. Many Wolves remembered witnessing a similar behavior from his wolf hawks when he'd first caught them.

With the bird tucked safely away, Many Wolves climbed back down the tree, again reminding himself not to look down. The descent was less worrisome than the climb, however, because at least he knew the ground was getting closer, and there was great comfort in that.

When at last he reached the bottom, he felt a swell of relief. He rested for several moments and inspected his punctured hand. The wounds stung, but the pain wasn't bad. The bird's claws were not big enough to do much damage.

Rojo had been lying at the base of the tree waiting for him. The red wolf now stood up, walked over to the bag, and sniffed it. His ears perked when he saw the bag move.

"We have a new friend, Rojo."

The spinning circles had never come like this before, Many Wolves thought. He had climbed to high places many times when he was younger, and he had never endured such a battle within his mind. Was this higher than he had climbed before? Or was this a new kind of fear that came with age? Certainly, he had been at far greater heights when he flew with Chiquito, but somehow that had been different. He wondered if this new fear would prevent him from doing such mind-journeys again without panicking.

Without Chiquito, it would be some time before he could try again.

Now, he had a new friend to tame.

A Path With No Tracks

Thorn Bird drove his war horse westward into the vast, endless prairie. As he rode, the bright late afternoon sun narrowed his eyes, and the eastbound wind blew his long, straight black hair back from his face.

He called his black and white gelding "Snake," because it had once survived a rattlesnake bite that would have killed most horses. And from that day forward, Thorn Bird had believed that his brilliant mount was protected by the spirit of the snake. Trailing his war pony was a brown and white pinto on a lead; it was a spare, useful for carrying supplies and sharing the burden of a rider, so he wouldn't have to stop to rest his mounts.

Attached to the back of his riding pad were his war shield and his sheathed Spanish sword. Like his father, Thorn Bird had decorated his shield with the symbol of the Thunder Bird of War. The sword was one that he had acquired from killing a Spanish captain; it had the sharpest steel blade he had ever seen and it felt good in his hand, like it was part of him. Slung over his shoulder was a wolf-skin quiver, filled with over twenty arrows, and his black, Wichita-crafted bow made from the finest wood of the southern plains: Osage orange, or *bois d'arc* as the French traders called it.

Everything he needed for war was within reach.

He pushed his ponies at a frantic pace, avoiding the thick patches of prairie dog holes, which could easily shatter a horse's leg. He knew his horses' limits and knew they would ride to their death for him—but that would mean his own death as well. Without a horse in this unforgivably barren country, a man's life was an open sore to be picked at by thirst or hunger or a wandering enemy. To a Nokoni warrior, the horse was his lifeblood. *Dead horse, dead man.*

Thorn Bird arrived at a shallow, fast-moving stream and stopped to let his horses drink. He dismounted and drank the cold, muddy water, which rose only as far as his knees. The small, smooth rocks felt hard and slippery under his feet. *They will be good for covering my tracks.* He grabbed a small piece of pemmican from his food pouch and sucked the sweet berry flavor off of it before taking his first bite. Then he pulled himself back up on Snake and directed it north along the streambed at a much more deliberate pace. *They won't know if I'm going north or south.*

As his horse walked against the current, Thorn Bird scanned the western bank for a good place to exit the creek. He wanted a spot where it would be easy for him to hide his tracks. Trees and bushes, mostly cottonwoods, covered the banks on either side of him, but there were plenty of gaps between the foliage for a horse to walk through.

Thick clouds gathered above. He sensed it would rain soon—probably a brief thunder shower with hard, driving rain. Thunderstorms were common occurrences in the late afternoon. *The rain, too, will hide my tracks.*

Thorn Bird found a wide opening between two large bushes, and he steered his horses out of the stream. He walked them into the buffalo grass, stopping only once he was satisfied that he'd put sufficient distance between himself and the creek. Then he commanded Snake to stay, dismounted, and backtracked on foot back to the creek. There he brushed the horse tracks away with his hands, making sure to also erase his own footprints. The ground near the creek was gravelly soil with no grass, making it easy to eliminate their tracks, but as he moved backward toward the horses, it eventually gave way to thick buffalo grass. He covered up as much of the evidence as he could, then mounted his war horse again and looked back at his handiwork.

A good tracker will eventually find my signs, but the rain will make it difficult. It will give me more time for my journey.

With a whispered command, he launched back into a gallop. His bearing now was northwest, toward Falling Turtle Rock. There was at least one more creek ahead, as well as another river, and they would help to mask his route. The thunder rumbled around him and the sky darkened. He felt the rain tickling his skin. A downpour would soon bathe him and wash away traces of his passing.

Finding Malone

After two days, Thorn Bird spotted a familiar landmark, a giant rock formation that looked like a turtle lying on its back. *Falling Turtle Rock.* The rolling hills of green prairie grass surrounding it were covered in red and purple wildflowers. This was one of his people's favorite spots to hunt deer and antelope. Further north was Palo Duro Canyon, the largest canyon in the Llano Estacado, a clever place to find shelter and to hide from enemies. *For Malone, a great place for solitude.*

Long shadows reminded him the day would soon be coming to a close. As he rode, he felt the clear, blue sky enclose him. The cool breeze tickled his face and made the grass wave beneath him. Thorn Bird spotted a prairie dog village ahead, so he slowed his horses to a trot.

Many of the small burrowing animals watched him from an upright, sitting position, always ready to escape beneath the ground. Several of them scampered into their burrows as he approached, but many remained as protectors, to watch him, like the dogs of his village who looked out for strangers. And like dogs, several of them barked at him, a high-pitched call almost like that of a small bird, warning the wide-ranging underground village of his presence. Thorn Bird understood why the French traders called them prairie dogs, a name used by his people as well.

The visible prairie dogs were of different sizes and ages. Thorn Bird noticed a fat one, and it reminded him of his childhood friend, Fat Dog. He imagined the other animals chiding the heavier one: "Fat Dog! You eat too much of this grass! You won't be able to crawl back in your hole!" Thorn Bird laughed aloud at the thought.

He moved forward slowly, treading carefully as he guided his horse through the holes and mounds. The small animals scampered around him as he passed. He knew they were easy to hunt with a careful approach and an accurate bow, but there was no time for that now. *I will hunt them later, before the sun is lost. But first I must find a good place for my camp.*

He walked farther into the sun, then crossed over a small hill and spotted a line of trees in the distance. He remembered that a fork of the Rio Blanco flowed near Falling Turtle Rock. *A good place to rest.* Finally clear of the prairie dog hazard, he commanded Snake to gallop toward the river.

At the waterway, he found that the oak, juniper, and cedar trees that enclosed the river on either side provided plenty of cover. *This is a good spot.* He dismounted, unpacked his weapons and supplies from the two horses, then led them to water at a small clearing filled with knee-high buffalo grass.

Thorn Bird drank some water and filled his pouch, then returned to his camp, keeping his grazing mounts in clear view. He would bring them in closer when night arrived. Like the standing prairie dogs, they were his guardians. A nervous snort or twitch of their ears was as useful to him out here as the bark of a dog was in his village.

The Nokoni warrior spread his buffalo-skin robe out on the ground and sat down on top of it. His weapons and shield were at his side, within easy reach. He grabbed some dried buffalo meat from his food pouch and took a bite of the hardened jerky. A red-tailed hawk flew past him, landed high in a large oak tree, and disappeared among the branches and leaves. A night roost. *The trees will hide me, too.*

Thorn Bird thought for a moment to build a small fire; he had not built one since leaving his village, not wanting to attract attention. But it would be safer without one, he thought, and the tedious task of building fire from sticks was the last thing he wanted to do. Most times, Valencia made the fire for him. Besides, the air was warm and he had nothing to cook. And foremost on his mind was that he and his horses needed rest.

He watched the nearly cloudless blue sky turn to orange as the sun disappeared behind his back. The rushing sounds of water calmed his mind, and he sat looking out, past the trees, at the wide open prairie. Getting to this river and to Falling Turtle Rock had been the easy part. The hard part would be finding Malone. But whenever he hunted in this area, it was this river he used for drinking and watering his horses; so surely Malone would be using it too.

The grasslands were richer on this side of the river, which meant more deer and elk, and of course, prairie dogs too. And crossing this river would be a hard task for any horse.

I will ride north tomorrow along the east bank and find tracks that will lead me to him.

Surviving With Fear

Thorn Bird gutted and skinned the large prairie dog he had killed just after sunrise. He had awoken with a strong desire for fresh meat and a renewed energy to hunt and build a fire while the day was still new. The small fire, fueled by small branches and buffalo dung, crackled briskly in the cool, still air. He watched the small thread of smoke disappear quickly into the overcast sky. It was a safe fire, he thought.

He skewered the carcass on a stick and held it low over the flames. He rotated the stick often to allow the meat to cook evenly. The cold smell of raw flesh soon turned into the savory aroma of cooked meat, and the scent was invigorating. His body and his mind needed this meal.

When he was satisfied the meat was cooked to his liking, he leaned it up against a rock to cool off, then buried the flames carefully with dirt to smother the smoke.

After he had picked the choice morsels off the bony carcass, he threw the rest of it away in a clump of tall grass. *Nothing refreshes a man's mind like fresh meat.* He quickly packed his supplies and weapons, then led his horses to the river to drink. He didn't bother to cover his tracks, guessing he still had at least a two-day lead on the men hunting him—and if he left some trace, Malone would find it, and perhaps would find him, too.

Thorn Bird began his journey north to Palo Duro Canyon along the east bank of the Rio Blanco. His pace was deliberate as he searched for signs of Malone. The river was alive with life, the sun still squeezing the remaining coolness out of the morning air. Fish leaped from the water, chasing insects. A long-necked heron stood motionless on stick-like legs, waiting for a fish to dart past it. A fisher-bird flew by, breaking the silence with its rattling call. Thorn Bird enjoyed watching them dive headfirst into the water.

His mind drifted to thoughts of war. He knew Gray Elk's search party would eventually find him; it was simply a matter of time. He wondered how many men they would bring to kill him. Ten? Twenty? Whatever the number, he must be ready to fight them. Some of these men would be men he had grown up with, men he knew he could defeat in combat. Only the younger ones would be new to him. Stands Alone would be the smartest and bravest of their warriors, but even he did not have as many scalps on his lodge as Thorn Bird.

Thorn Bird knew he would not have to kill them all, only a few, so they could see his *puha* was too strong; then it would be over. *They will think they are fighting twenty warriors and not just one. They will lose many before I die, and it will be a good death.*

He found many deer tracks as he scoured the ground, and some wolf tracks as well, but no traces of horses or men. From time to time, he stopped and looked all around him for the most obvious of human signs— smoke—but found none. Smoke could lead him to Malone, but it could also lead him to men who were not his friends.

When dusk arrived, clouds gathered in the sky around him and a cool breeze cut through the heat. Smaller animals left their shady hiding places to feed on the grass and plant life. A small flock of birds soared above him, flying as one, as if trying to cool themselves from the day's heat. He spotted a hawk flying low over the grass looking for a final meal.

As his horses walked slowly through the tall grass, Thorn Bird noticed a rabbit sitting and eating peacefully, seemingly not fearful of either him or his horses. *An easy meal.* He stopped his horses, then slowly pulled his bow and an arrow from his quiver. He loaded the arrow, took careful aim, and released.

The arrow found its mark. The injured rabbit collapsed, screaming, then fell silent.

Thorn Bird returned his bow to his quiver, dismounted, and walked over to the dead rabbit. The force of the bow had pushed the arrow's point completely through the rabbit's body, so he grabbed it by the point and pulled the feathered tail of the arrow through the rabbit's flesh and out the opposite side. He cleaned the blood off the undamaged arrow and placed it back in his quiver. Then he picked up the carcass and tied it the back of his packhorse.

With darkness falling, Thorn Bird found a spot to camp: a small grove of cottonwoods on the river, overlooking open prairie to the east. On one side, the river afforded him its protection, and on the other side were the flat grasslands with their expansive visibility. Open spaces brought him familiarity and peace of mind. He felt too vulnerable with engulfing trees in every direction.

Sitting cross-legged in the grass, Thorn Bird faced the moon-glazed openness. The embers of his smoldering cooking fire glittered like stars, and the rabbit meat filled his stomach and lulled him into a relaxed frame of mind. He thought about the rabbit—how tame and unafraid it had been. Perhaps it had never seen a man or horse before, he thought, or maybe it had put too much trust in its ability to run from any predator that got close. *It had never had to outrun an arrow before.*

Thorn Bird laughed to himself. All creatures had an instinct to survive, and it was this instinct which bred fear. He needed this instinct also, but not too much of it—just enough to respect his enemies. And he possessed this fear, although for him it was not a fear of death; it was a fear only of dying too easily, killed by a weaker enemy.

Retribution

Stands Alone glared down at Thorn Bird, snarling. "This is how we treat a man who kills his own!"

Thorn Bird was buried up to his neck in dirt; he was unable to move his legs or arms. His torturers had hacked off his eyelids, so he could not stop the searing beams of sunlight from boring into his eyes. His hair offered no protection, because he had been scalped, and the mass of bloodied hair now lay before him, a meal for the swarming ants that also crawled up his neck. Wasps buzzed all around, attracted to the honey that had been poured over his head, oozing into his eyes and nostrils. The pain was so intense he could barely think.

How did I get here?

Women and children spat on him or poked his face and body with glowing-hot sticks. They shouted insults and taunted him.

"Murderer!"

"Coward!"

"Old Man Killer!"

Angry faces surrounded him, and it was hard to match the voices to them. None of them were familiar, except for Stands Alone.

Thorn Bird wanted to scream, but he wouldn't show weakness; wouldn't give the mob what they desired. Though it was impossible not to flinch when they hit him or burned his skin.

"This is how you will die, Thorn Bird," said Stands Alone, his familiar voice rising from the crowd. "Is this how you imagined it? To die at the hands of women and children because of your cowardly actions?"

Thorn Bird couldn't answer. No words came from his dry mouth because they had cut out his tongue.

"Where is your *puha* now? See how it protects you!" a woman's voice shouted from the crowd. "The crows will pick at your eyes in the next world, and the scavengers will feast on your flesh!"

"What will your father think of you when he sees what's left of your body, Thorn Bird?" jeered Stands Alone.

Then a horse snorted loudly as if knocking back all other sounds. Everything started to fade away: the faces, the voices, the pain.

A dream? Was it a dream? His world went black, and he opened his eyes to the dawn light.

A war scream jerked him out of his dream. He was lying on the ground wrapped in his buffalo robe. Sweat ran down his face, and his mind was foggy from sleep, but his eyes spotted movement. A man, running toward him, screaming, eyes bulging, a tomahawk in his right hand, his chest covered with tattoos. *Tonkawa!*

Thorn Bird pulled the knife from his leg sheath and braced himself. He was just in time: the Tonkawa warrior lunged, swinging his blunt weapon, but Thorn Bird stopped the blow with his left arm, whirled his right hand around, and plunged his knife into the side of the tattooed assailant. The younger man screamed and fell as Thorn Bird retracted his bloodied knife.

Immediately another war cry arose behind him. Thorn Bird leaped up, breathing hard, and spun around to face another approaching warrior, this one carrying one tomahawk in each hand. The man was running toward him at a full sprint, and when he was about four horse lengths away, he flung one of his tomahawks straight at Thorn Bird.

But Thorn Bird's reflexes were quick: he ducked to avoid the flying weapon, then ran straight at his attacker, ducking once again to avoid the swing of the second weapon. He collided into the warrior's midsection and knocked the smaller man to the ground without losing his own footing; then he drove his knife into the man's throat. When he removed the knife, blood spurted from the wound, spraying his face and body.

Another set of footsteps shuffled from the trees behind him; this time Thorn Bird heard the sound of a bowstring and felt an arrow *whoosh* past his ear. Thorn Bird quickly leapt to his feet, his heart pounding like a war drum. He ran back to grab his bow and quiver, then scrambled to a nearby tree, leaning his back against it to block his enemy's next shot. Pulling three arrows from his quiver, he set them in his hand, separated by his fingers, the tails clutched in his palm. He heard an arrow thunk into the tree behind him.

Then a second bowstring twanged, from in front of him this time. *Another one.* The arrow stuck in the ground less than a step from Thorn Bird's foot. He saw the attacker this time—the man stood in the trees, silhouetted in the early morning light. Thorn Bird had a clear shot, and he took it. The arrow cut through the warrior's chest and knocked him back among the brush. *One left now. That I know of.*

Thorn Bird peeked around the tree to find the other bowman, the one who had shot first. He caught the blurred movement of the Tonkawa, who was trying to get in position for another shot. *This one has skill with the bow.* Thorn Bird knew he would be dead if not for the protection of the tree. He rotated himself around it, keeping it between him and his attacker, and waited.

The Tonkawa shot at him again, and again the arrow lodged itself in the tree, kicking up bark. Thorn Bird sprang from his hiding place and sprinted at his enemy, loading one of the two arrows as he ran. He spotted the warrior in the forest, setting up for another shot. Thorn Bird weaved among the trees, using them as a shield. The Tonkawa shot anyway, but Thorn Bird's movement and the trees made the shot impossible; the arrow flew harmlessly past him.

The Nokoni scrambled to a spot where the path of his arrow would be unobstructed. He pulled back on his bowstring—the Tonkawa was in his sight and well within his range—then he released.

Thorn Bird's arrow lodged in the warrior's leg. The Tonkawa attacker cried out from the force of the impact.

Thorn Bird charged again, straight at his enemy this time, loading his last arrow as he ran. The Tonkawa warrior was clutching his wound and looking for cover. The Nokoni buried his final arrow deep in the man's chest before he could run away.

Then with gritted teeth and a grunt, Thorn Bird slashed the man's throat and left him to bleed into the earth.

Thorn Bird turned back to survey the scene. He saw no other attackers approaching; but even as he looked on, the third Tonkawa, the other bowman, stood and snapped the shaft off the arrow buried in his chest. He started to run away at half speed, holding one hand to his wound, leaving his bow behind.

Thorn Bird sprinted after him, invigorated, like a predator who smells the blood of injured prey. Barefoot and wearing only his breechcloth, the Nokoni warrior chased after his target with his knife gripped loosely in his hand.

The swift *Noomah* quickly caught up to the wounded man and tackled him in the knee-high grass. Thorn Bird pinned the man on his back, using his left hand and his right knee, his right hand holding the knife up to the Tonkawa's throat.

"How many?" Thorn Bird asked in the *Noomah* language.

The man looked at him, confused.

"*Cuantos?*"

The Tonkawa looked at Thorn Bird with frightened eyes. Then he opened his palm and extended his fingers to indicate "four."

Thorn Bird looked into the scared man's eyes. "You thought I would be easy to kill! This was your *caza grupo?*" Thorn Bird spit in the man's face. "You Tonks are like *buitros*. You eat anything—even human flesh. It sickens me!"

The Tonkawa said nothing. Thorn Bird wasn't sure if he'd even understood the Spanish words. But he felt his victim's body trembling and saw sweat dripping from his face. There was barely any fight left in the man.

"You make me sick!" Then, he slashed the man's throat.

The Wild One

Relieved that the ordeal of climbing the tree was over, Many Wolves retraced his steps to his camp, where he knew Elk Dog was waiting for him. On the way, he passed the spot where Chiquito and his killer lay buried in the ground. He tried to force thoughts of Chiquito's final moments from his mind. He chose instead to remember the dream of his companion circling away from this world, at peace with the bird that had killed him.

The sun was high above Many Wolves, but the pine tree canopy shaded him from the intense heat. Rojo followed behind him like a faithful dog, always on the alert for unexpected sights, smells, and sounds.

The young bird was tucked safely in his hunting bag, relaxed by the darkness, not squawking or struggling to escape its new surroundings. The moment reminded Many Wolves of the time he brought the three baby wolf hawks home after saving them from the crows. . The old fox den had worked out well for them, once he had cleared the rattlesnake from it.

He would now need to find a similar shelter for this bird, but he didn't know of any burrows. He hoped that since there was only one bird , and he didn't need to hide it from his family, a simpler shelter would suffice. The spot he had in mind was the rocky ledge above the camp where he had faced the great bear, Gray Face. With a few branches, twigs, and pine needles, the rocky floor of the ledge could easily be made into comfortable home for the fledgling, he thought.

This bird seemed wilder and more aggressive than his wolf hawks had been when he first found them. For one thing, the baby wolf hawks had never attacked him as aggressively as this bird had; they were much more restrained in their fear. And for another, this bird had killed its own sibling for food. The baby wolf hawks had never shown nearly so much violent aggression toward each other. Sure, there had been some initial squabbling between them while they established their ranks in the pack, but after that, they had all seemed to know their place. Although, perhaps if they, too, had been faced with the possibility of starvation, they might have killed each other to survive.

The Spanish word for "wild animal" popped into Many Wolves's head, and he liked the sound of it.

"Your name, little bird-killer, will be *Fiera*."

There were three types of bird-killers that Many Wolves was aware of. All of them were short-winged hawks with long tails, and they all lived in areas with lots of trees. They looked similar, but to one who had watched them as long as Many Wolves had, there were clearly three distinct sizes. Judging by the size of the bird's fully grown parent, Many Wolves guessed that Fiera was one of the middle-sized bird-killers, named the "blue darter" by his people.

He loved to watch these cunning predators hunt. They were rapid flyers that did not need height to gain speed, like falcons and eagles. They flew directly at their prey, at eye level, and ambushed them before they could fly or run away. They were persistent hunters, too, often chasing other birds on foot through bushes or on the ground, hoping to flush their victims back into the air where they could then easily overtake them on the wing. Other birds of prey, like falcons, gave up on their prey when it found a hiding place in a tree or bush—but not bird-killers. His wolf hawks had been just as persistent, especially when they hunted with the others in their pack.

When Many Wolves arrived back as his camp, Elk Dog shook his head and whinnied a greeting.

"Elk Dog, we need to head back to the Gray Face camp."

The camp was not far, an easy ride. Many Wolves set the hunting bag down in a safe place and packed his sleeping robe and supplies on Elk Dog. Then he tossed a piece of dried rabbit meat to Rojo. "We will hunt later, big wolf."

With his quiver slung over his shoulder, Many Wolves lifted the hunting bag and mounted. "Elk Dog, we will walk, so we don't frighten Fiera any more than is necessary. The poor bird is probably horrified by now." He made a cackling sound with his tongue to urge the horse forward.

"Let's go, Rojo." The red wolf had finished the rabbit meat and padded to his side.

Together, the pack headed out toward the Gray Face camp. Many Wolves grabbed another chunk of dried rabbit meat and sucked the salt off one end. Hunger bit at his insides. *Rojo and I will need a good fresh meal tonight.* With Chiquito no longer around to provide easy meals, he and Rojo would need to hunt often, especially now that they had Fiera to feed as well, and the bird-killer would require fresh meat each day.

It was strange how the Great Spirit worked, Many Wolves thought. Chiquito was gone, but Fiera was here. *I hope Chiquito's spirit is in this little blue darter.*

They walked out of the pine forest and into a meadow. A coyote watched them from a safe distance, nervously moved away, then stopped again to watch them. It repeated this ritual several times before it eventually ran off. Many Wolves wondered if the animal had not seen a man before. It most certainly had not seen a man, a horse, and a wolf all together in one pack.

It was late afternoon when they arrived at the Gray Face camp. Everything was as Many Wolves had left it: the huge bearskin rug, his winter clothing, his weapon-making tools, and the *libro* with the bird pictures, which was found with his dead white-skinned parents. He unpacked his horse and left the hunting bag in a cool, shaded spot.

He called Rojo, and together they ventured out to find small branches, twigs, and pine needles to use as nesting material for Fiera. Many Wolves packed what he found into a large hunting bag. When the bag was full, he returned to camp and climbed the tree up to the rocky ledge. He set up a nest away from the tree, in a small nook surrounded by rock on three sides. It would provide protection from ground predators, as well as some isolation from Rojo and Elk Dog. Overhanging trees provided plenty of shade from the hot afternoon sun and a blanket of safety from larger birds of prey.

Many Wolves carried the bag up to the nest. He gently reached in, pulled the fluffy bird out, and placed it carefully on the nest. The bird gawked at him, its beak wide open. Its flimsy legs collapsed below its body.

"I know you're frightened, Fiera. I'll leave you alone in your new home while Rojo and I hunt."

Many Wolves walked out toward the Rio Pecos with his red wolf at his side. Since Fiera was a bird-killer, he felt it should eat birds, and he knew that quail often flocked in the trees later in the day. It wasn't long before Rojo flushed out a flock of the stumpy, ground-dwelling birds. They flew a short distance away and landed in another bushy area along the river. Many Wolves knew they would be easy to approach and kill while they foraged on the ground.

Two arrows later, he had two birds in his hunting bag.

He wasn't as fortunate with larger game, however. It took several arrows before he finally killed a sitting jackrabbit. Without Chiquito to chase and harass the creatures, he had to kill them before they bolted. And Rojo was in the habit of flushing them out for Chiquito, so Many Wolves had to spot the creature before Rojo did or the meal would be lost.

Back at the camp, Many Wolves skinned one of the quail, cut the breast meat into small pieces for Fiera, then soaked them in a drinking-shell of water. He knew it would be important for Fiera to drink lots of water, and dipping food in it was the best way to make sure the bird got enough. The rest of the quail was cached safely in a bag buried in the ground.

For himself, he tore off the two hind legs of the rabbit, and he gave the rest of the carcass to Rojo.

Then he took the small chunks of quail meat up to Fiera. He spread the meat across a smooth piece of bark and placed the bark next to the young bird, then backed away to the other side of the ledge. *If you're like my other hawks, you're not going to eat it while I'm watching.*

He climbed back down the tree and made a small fire using his fire-sticks. Rojo had already devoured most of the rabbit carcass, and was now chewing on the skull and backbone.

"You think you are the leader of our pack, big wolf, eating before me like this." Many Wolves laughed. Rojo's tail wagged. He knew he was being spoken to.

After Many Wolves ate the two roasted rabbit legs, he climbed back up to the rock ledge. There was little light, but enough to see that the quail morsels were gone and Fiera was resting.

Many Wolves smiled. This was an excellent first step for his newest pack member.

Another Helpless Creature

Many Wolves rose with the sun the following morning; the wheezy shrills of the baby hawk had broken the silence. The bird's pleading calls were lower-pitched than his wolf hawk's and more deliberate: they repeated consistently, like heartbeats, sounding almost exactly the same each time.

Many Wolves climbed out of his sleeping robe and dug up his cache of quail meat from the previous night. He revived his fire and heated some water in his drinking-shell. The quail meat was cold, and he wanted to warm it up so it would seem more like a fresh kill. He preferred his meat a little warm and expected Fiera would too.

When the water was hot enough, he placed a chunk of quail meat in the drinking-shell. After a short time, he pulled it out of the water and cut it into bite-sized pieces for his bird.

Many Wolves found the baby blue darter still sitting in the middle of the nest. Seeing the man approach, the bird stopped its wheezy calls and fell into a fear pose, jerking its head back and staring with its beak spread open. Many Wolves placed the piece of bark with the food offering in the same place as before, then once again moved to the far side of the ledge, where he spoke to the bird.

"Fiera, I know you don't understand my sounds, but I want them to be part of your world, just as the sun and the trees are part of your world, and just as your parents' sounds were part of your world. I am your parent now, and Rojo and Elk Dog are your brothers." As he spoke Rojo's name, the wolf's ears perked up down below. From this vantage point, Many Wolves could see Rojo lying next to the fire pit and Elk Dog chewing on grass nearby.

The baby hawk seemed less afraid now that the strange human was farther away. Its beak was closed now, and it watched him, but still it did not eat.

"It's good that you watch me, because I am not only your parent, but your pack leader." Many Wolves alternated between Lipan and Northerner words. It was good to practice both languages. By now, both Elk Dog and Rojo were conditioned to his bilingual garble, though each of them only recognized specific words; they indicated their understanding by the turn of a head, the twitch of an ear, or a swishing tail.

Many Wolves watched the bird like a vigilant parent until finally Fiera stood up and snatched one of the morsels. *You must be starving, little bird.* The morsels were gobbled down hastily. Fiera seemed content for the moment, but he knew it wouldn't last long.

Many Wolves wondered if Fiera was male or female. He knew that the best way to tell was by their size: females were always bigger. He guessed that Fiera was female, but he wouldn't know for sure until the young bird was full size.

Several other questions popped into his mind. How good of a companion will this hawk be, compared to his wolf hawks? How good of a hunter will it be? Will it kill rabbits and squirrels, or just small birds? *Will it leave me the moment it learns to fly?*

Though he wanted to spend more time with the hawk, Many Wolves needed to hunt again. A parent hawk provided fresh meat to its young constantly throughout the day. And since Many Wolves was now the parent hawk, he needed to spend most of his daylight hours hunting and providing for this helpless creature.

The Thorn Bird

After a long rest, Thorn Bird cut the scalps off the two dead Tonkawas in his camp, then dragged their bodies away from his sleeping robe. The earth all around them was soaked in blood. The smell of death did not bother him as it did other men, but soon, the insects would come, and he didn't want to be annoyed by them.

He had already dragged the other two bodies from where he'd killed them near his camp. He'd scalped only one of them, leaving the other untouched for now. *I will save it for the end of my ritual.*

Thick storm clouds swallowed the moon and the stars, and a heavy darkness fell over Thorn Bird's camp. Thorn Bird sat next to a blazing bonfire, whittling the tip of a cottonwood branch. He had gathered four long, straight branches, tall and thick like tipi poles, to make into stakes. As he shaved off the end of a branch with his knife, he remembered the story of his spirit animal, the thorn bird. The old shaman, Snake Tooth, had first told him this story when he was a boy of six summers.

"Snake Tooth, why am I named after such a small bird? Am I not strong enough to be named after a bear or a coyote or a buffalo?"

The old shaman laughed and then spoke solemnly. "Those animals all have powerful spirits. The buffalo is strong and the coyote is clever, but the spirits give us what they think we need. You are a strong boy, but what you receive from the thorn bird, your spirit animal, is bravery, just as your father receives wisdom from the crow."

"How can a bird the size of a sparrow have bravery?"

Snake Tooth again laughed at the question. "Can the bear easily kill an animal its own size? How about the wolf or the eagle? No, they risk their lives in a fight like this. But animals like the shrew and weasel not only kill animals their own size, they take down creatures much larger than themselves. They are aggressive, sneaky, and extremely brave. The same is true of the thorn bird. The Great Spirit did not give it powerful talons like the eagle; the Great Spirit gave it the cleverness to use thorns to kill large prey. A thorn bird is so brave, it will kill more than it can eat just to show off to a mate, or to keep other thorn birds away. The spirits protect the thorn bird when it is near the dead animals it has hung on thorns."

Young Thorn Bird nodded. He was beginning to like this bird, his namesake.

Snake Tooth continued. "The thorn bird is gray and looks like a mockingbird, but the Great Spirit painted black war paint around its eyes so that other animals would fear it. Always remember, you must never harm the thorn bird—or it will bring terrible luck to you."

"And the thorn bird feather you gave me to keep in my medicine bag will bring me good luck?"

"Haa, Thorn Bird, it will bring you good luck and protection. You must never lose it."

Thorn Bird worked into the night making his four stakes—one for each of the dead Tonkawas. When he was done, he rode out into the dark prairie carrying with him one body, tied to his extra horse, and one stake. When he came to a hill that overlooked a large flat area of open grassland, he dug a hole for the stake, which was pointed at both ends, and planted it firmly into the earth. Then he lifted the corpse up and impaled it on the stake. Blood covered his hands, so he used it to mark handprints on his own body and on his war horse, and painted it on his face. *The blood of my enemies will protect me.* He remembered this from the Blood Rider ceremony long ago.

He repeated this ritual with the other three bodies, impaling them on stakes so that he'd left one in each of the four directions for good luck. *These bodies and the spirit of the thorn bird will protect me.*

He had just finished impaling the last body when he was startled by a familiar voice behind him.

"I see you are still trying to impress your father."

Out of the darkness came a single rider.

"Malone?"

"*Haa*, Thorn Bird. Don't be alarmed."

Thorn Bird breathed a sigh of relief. He was fatigued, and his quiver was back at his camp; he was foolishly unprepared for a visitor.

Malone seemed like a ghost this deep into the night, but as he rode closer, Thorn Bird recognized the man who was once his father's closest friend. "How did you find me?" Thorn Bird asked.

"When there is death, there are always scavenger birds." Malone climbed down off his mount.

"How long have you been watching me?"

"Since you started this ritual. But I don't like to interrupt a man when he is nurturing his spirit. I see that these men were Tonkawas." Malone pointed at the dead man.

"Why are there Wolf People so far to the north, Malone? I thought most of their villages were to the southeast." Thorn Bird was out of breath and tired from his work. As he spoke, he peeled his last victim's scalp off with one clean stroke of his knife.

"These are the first I've seen here in the canyon lands."

"They are young *tekwuniwapi*, not warriors," said Thorn Bird, placing the scalp in his hunting bag to clean later.

"*Tekwuniwapi* hoping to become warriors with your scalp on their lodge."

"It is *their* scalps that will decorate *my* lodge," said Thorn Bird, pleased with himself. He wiped the blood off his right hand and arm and cleaned his knife blade in the grass.

"I decorate my lodge with the skins of animals, not the skins of men," said Malone. "I've followed these Tonks for two sleeps. I lost them, but still, they led me to you. They would not have hesitated to roast my flesh in their fire pit. It's good they are dead."

Thorn Bird and Malone walked back to Thorn Bird's camp in the darkness, Malone leading his black and white pinto.

"Your horse has strong legs. I would not bet against his speed," said Thorn Bird.

"I captured him three summers ago from a wild herd. He was not easy to tame, but he is smart and as fast as any I have ridden. The wildest ones are always the smartest."

Malone looked almost the same as he had the last time Thorn Bird had seen him—when he'd left his father's village. There were a few more lines on his face and hands, but he looked strong and healthy; his long, straight black hair was neatly oiled, and his face cut like stone. A handsome man. He was taller and leaner than most Nokonis, but there was great strength in his sinewy body. Like Thorn Bird, he wore only a breechcloth.

"Why are you here, Thorn Bird? Why aren't you with your village?"

"I was looking for you. I should have known you would find me first," said Thorn Bird with a grin.

"The Tonks led me to you. Men do not stray far from the river in dry lands. That's how I found them, and how they found you." Malone led his horse over to Thorn Bird's horses, and they nickered greetings at each other.

Back at his camp, Thorn Bird headed to the river to drink and clean the blood off his hands and arms. He lowered his head to let his long black hair fall into the cool water, then stood, flipped his dripping hair back over his head, and groomed it with his hands. Then he returned to his fire pit, where Malone waited. Thorn Bird set to work reviving the flames to bring them warmth and light.

Malone waited for Thorn Bird to finish with the fire before speaking. "What do you want of me, Thorn Bird? Do you want me to go back to your village?"

"No," said Thorn Bird, pulling the hair out of his face and tucking it behind his ears. "You would have returned by now if you wanted to. Death has taken my father and most of your closest friends, so there is nothing left for you to go back to."

"I miss your father, but I know he rides with the wind at his back in the afterlife." Malone looked down, then back up at Thorn Bird. "I do not miss killing and seeing death in the eyes of women and children. I cannot return to that. It's the eyes of these innocent ones that haunt my dreams, even now, after many winters of solitude."

In the firelight, Thorn Bird saw that Malone's eyes were dodging his own. His father's close friend was uncomfortable talking about such things. The deaths of Malone's wife and daughter had changed the hallowed warrior forever. Like a piece of wood that has floated down a river, there was no way for this man to go back upstream, to be the warrior he had once been. Apart from his father, Thorn Bird believed that Malone was the greatest warrior he had ever known.

Thorn Bird caught Malone's shifting eyes and held them like a taut rope holds a restless pony. "I want you to find my father's killer, Malone. Many Wolves. I want you find him and bring him back to me with his heart still beating. My men and I have searched several summers for him, but our village needs us and we cannot protect our women and children if we are searching in faraway places. I know this *taiboo* is hiding in *Navoonah* lands, somewhere near the Rio Pecos. Like you said, men do not stray far from the river in dry lands."

Malone cut the eye-rope between them and walked away, toward the horses. He stroked his stallion's neck gently; it nuzzled him back affectionately. Without turning back to Thorn Bird, he spoke softly. "He will be as hard to find as the buried horned toad, and he has shown he can bite like the rattlesnake. But I will look for him. I will search until the last leaf has fallen and the winter nips at my ears. If I have not found him by then, I must return to my winter camp. His *puha* is strong, Thorn Bird. It may be too difficult to bring him back alive. That is all I can offer you, and all I can offer the spirit of your father, the spirit of my friend."

Thorn Bird was pleased. If any man could find Many Wolves, Malone could. His father had always said that Malone had "the gift of seeing invisible signs." And the *taiboo* would not be as wary of a single man as he would a search party, so Malone also had that in his favor. Dead or alive, Malone would bring him back.

Hopefully alive.

Thorn Bird believed torturing this *taiboo* would be the best medicine for his tormented dreams.

Preparations

Thorn Bird woke soon after the sun; Malone was already awake.

"Malone, let me hunt some fresh meat to fill our stomachs, then we can smoke and seal our agreement."

The sun rose to its peak as Malone and Thorn Bird shared a meal of roasted rabbit, the smoke of Thorn Bird's pipe, and talk of past times. Thorn Bird described in detail many of the events that had led up to his father's death: the parlay with the French traders, the death of his brother, the war with the *Navoonah*. He described everything he knew about Many Wolves and his "animal magic." Thorn Bird talked and Malone listened. His father had always said Malone's ears were like "spider webs that caught every word."

When Thorn Bird was finished, Malone climbed onto his horse. "Thorn Bird, I have enjoyed our talk, but I must go. I have a long ride west to the Rio Pecos." He looked down at Thorn Bird. "The new moon has brought many visitors to the canyon lands: the Tonks, the Nokonis, and you."

"The Nokonis?" asked Thorn Bird, trying to conceal his interest. Malone had not previously spoken of their presence.

"*Haa*. I thought they were with you. I saw the smoke of their fire yesterday. The only ones who were familiar were Stands Alone and Black Elk."

So, the search party is near. Thorn Bird did not want to tell Malone he had killed Gray Elk and that these Nokonis were hunting him, for revenge.

He was afraid Malone would not understand why he had killed the Nokoni *paraibo* and would turn against him.

"How many riders, Malone? And where are they? So I can meet up with them."

"Eleven or twelve men. They were a day's ride southeast of here."

It was good for Thorn Bird to know how many men were in the war party. Every scrap of knowledge was valuable for his preparation.

"This is not your war party?" There was a suspicious tone in Malone's voice.

"No, but I will meet up with my old friend, Stands Alone." Thorn Bird kept the truth buried in his mind.

Apparently satisfied with this response, Malone waved and rode out. "Thorn Bird, I will find you before the snow falls," he called back.

But Thorn Bird was already thinking about the approaching war party. *I must prepare.*

When dusk arrived, Thorn Bird revived the large fire. He painted blackberry war paint around his eyes and around Snake's eyes, to mix with the Tonkawa blood. Then he stroked his horse's nose gently, breathing in Snake's breath, and whispered, "The thorn bird will protect us. We cannot die."

His horse nickered back at him, as if understanding his rider's words and thoughts, and nudged Thorn Bird's hand for more affection.

As Thorn Bird sat by the blazing fire, his hands inspecting each of his arrows, making sure the shafts were strong and the barbed points tightly secured with sinew, his mind raced through possibilities. He knew that to survive against ten or more Nokoni warriors, he would have to ride faster and shoot farther than any of them. *That is my advantage.*

He remembered words his father had once said before a battle.

"Thorn Bird, you must always see the battle many times *before* you fight it. Once the arrow flies, the man who is still thinking will die. You must trust that the true spirit of war, the Thunder Bird, will raise you above your enemies, and that your animal spirit will protect you from harm. Use your strengths to expose their weaknesses, and always know that you are the strongest warrior on the field of war: you cannot be defeated. If you fail to believe this, even for a heartbeat, then that heartbeat will be your last."

While most men prepared for war with elaborate songs and dances, Thorn Bird prepared with visions, like his father had. He starved his body so his spirit would be hungry. His mind picked apart the details of battle, like a buzzard picks apart a rotting carcass, and he imagined each opponent's weakness and how his strength would overcome it. He wanted the carcass in his mind to be clean before the battle started, so there would be no surprises—and so that the war cry that ended the battle would be his.

Blood For Blood

A steady rumble broke the late afternoon calm. It was not the rumble of a violent thunderstorm; this sound came from below.

The rumble of horses.

Thorn Bird sat in his camp. Behind him, a crackling bonfire sent a message to the sky: *I am ready. Come for my blood.* A restless west wind curled around his back and shoulders. It was more than just a cooling breeze; its rushing air whipped his long, shiny hair across his blackened face. *This wind will slow horses—and arrows.*

The creek waters gushed behind him as he stood and looked out across the vast, empty prairie. Sleep had come and gone in the night, a feathered sleep without deep dreaming. He had fought the battle many times already.

The war paint on his skin had stiffened into a dry, protective coat. Thorn Bird slung his quiver of arrows over his left shoulder and his sheathed Spanish sword over his right. Snake greeted him with a nod and a grunt as he approached. The war horse's eyes were also decorated in black paint, and Thorn Bird could tell that it sensed the approaching danger. He inhaled a deep waft of Snake's spirit-giving breath and whispered: "One man, one horse, one warrior." Then he stroked the horse's nose.

Thorn Bird mounted, untied his war shield and strapped it to his left arm, then guided his horse in a trot toward the sound of the intruders.

Like spirits rising from shallow graves, the Nokoni horsemen appeared out of the distant rolling grassland, each separated from the next by the length of a horse. *Twelve riders.* They spotted him too and slowed to a trot. Thorn Bird angled his horse slightly to the left, searching for a spot that would direct the wind like a lance straight through his back and into his enemy's chest, giving his arrows the blessing of the Wind Spirit, and giving his enemies its curse. When he was satisfied with his position, he stopped, waited.

The Nokoni warriors rode closer, then stopped just outside of an arrow's reach. Thorn Bird recognized his friend, Stands Alone, and the dead *paraibo*'s son, Black Elk. They were positioned as leaders near the center of the line, and both wore buffalo headdresses. The other men were strangers to Thorn Bird, some of them thin with youth.

Thorn Bird glanced off to his distant right, to where the grisly remnants of his recent conquest were staked to the earth. What little hair was left on their rotting heads blew like a white man's banner at the mercy of the unrelenting wind. Though his heart raced at a fevered pitch, he felt calmed by the sight and smiled confidently knowing that his guardian spirit was with him.

"Thorn Bird!" Black Elk's shout broke the silence. "You are a coward and a murderer like your father. You have disgraced your people. My father's death can only be answered with your blood. Your death magic ends here!"

Thorn Bird knew there would be no bartering, only blood. He surveyed the row of warriors, most on painted mounts, some with lances, some with shields. All of them had bows. Their faces were painted black to bring death to their enemy—to him. He expected that all of them could ride and shoot well. These riders were not Mexicans or *Navoonah* or Tonkawas who had to dismount before using their weapons; these were not men on slow horses who would tire easily. They were Nokoni.

They have greater numbers, but I can shoot farther and ride faster.

The time for talk was over; Thorn Bird had nothing to say. His actions had been justified. Gray Elk had had to die to bring peace to his father's spirit. These men saw it as murder, but to Thorn Bird, it was culling a weakness and fulfilling a promise.

The lone warrior pulled five arrows from his quiver and placed one against his bowstring. His actions were immediately mimicked by his enemy. Snake snorted and stomped nervously, anticipating the conflict.

"You have betrayed us, Thorn Bird! Now you must die like a rabid dog!" yelled Stands Alone, waving his arm. The Nokoni men bellowed war cries and commanded their ponies to charge.

Thorn Bird barked a command, and Snake galloped straight toward their enemy. Within several heartbeats, his war horse was already in full stride. Thorn Bird drew his bow to a full bend and launched an arrow toward one of the Nokonis who lacked a shield. The arrow fell short of the target, but he knew his range now. The Nokonis whistled several arrows at him, but they fell to the earth far short of their target as well, dampened by the wind's curse. Only one arrow landed anywhere near him; he was sure it was Stands Alone's.

Now that he was within killing range, Thorn Bird launched his next four arrows quickly. Carried by the Wind Spirit, they brought down two of the unshielded riders. Then he reined in his horse and retreated, feeling the full force of the wind in his face. An arrow struck Snake's flank, but the wind had slowed it, and it lacked the power to cut through the horse's thick hide.

Snake's hooves tore through the grass, fighting the wind's curse. Thorn Bird rode hard, pulling out of his enemies' range as he grabbed five more arrows from his quiver. He glanced back to see his attackers in vigorous pursuit, still maintaining the same formation, though Stands Alone and Black Elk, the fastest riders, were now pulling away from the rest.

Thorn Bird turned left, his shield raised, to face the two leading attackers. He blocked Stands Alone's arrow with his shield and heard Black Elk's arrow hiss past his head. He gathered himself for his counterattack. His first arrow struck Black Elk's shield, but the second ripped into the Nokoni's shoulder, knocking him backward off his horse. Stands Alone dodged Thorn Bird's next attack and circled back to protect Black Elk.

Relieved to have a brief respite from Stands Alone's powerful attacks, Thorn Bird turned his attention to the other men, who still rode toward him. The battle fury pushed his body to greater speed and focus, slowing down everything around him. A quick shot from his bow unhorsed a rider before the warrior could loose his arrow. He dodged another arrow by leaning down to Snake's side, and then he shot his attacker in the back as he rode past.

The sweat dripped from his face and onto his now slippery horse. He sensed the battle tilting in his favor: only four of his opponents were still mounted; the others were injured or helping the fallen.

The remaining Nokoni attackers briefly turned back their pursuit to regroup around Stands Alone and Black Elk, both of whom had dismounted. Some shared their mounts with injured men, while others led horses carrying the burden of the badly wounded or dead.

"How much more blood must be spilled on these grassy fields, Black Elk?" Thorn Bird hollered, slowing his war horse to a trot. He could not see either Stands Alone or Black Elk, because they were shielded by Stands Alone's horse. "Your *puha* has failed you! The Great Spirit shows you on this field of war that your father's death was justified. How much more proof must be shown to you?"

An arrow whistled through the air and cut deep into Snake's flank. *Stands Alone's arrow.* The war horse screamed, catching Thorn Bird completely by surprise. The panicked horse bucked wildly, throwing Thorn Bird from its back, and ran from the danger, leaving its former rider alone and vulnerable.

Shaken only momentarily by the fall, Thorn Bird jumped to his feet and picked up the two arrows that had fallen from his hand, loading one instinctively.

Stands Alone leaped onto his horse and swapped his bow for a lance. His shield was tightly secured to his left arm. "Yee-ah!" he yelled, claiming Thorn Bird as his kill. Then he charged.

He smells my weakness. Thorn Bird stared into the face of his raging assailant, his boyhood friend, and cocked his bow, looking for exposed flesh behind Stands Alone's war shield. He fired at his attacker's shoulder, but the arrow flew past its target. Stands Alone was covering the distance quickly, his lance drawn, his horse grunting with bulging eyes, coming straight at Thorn Bird.

Roll away from the lance!

As Stands Alone bore down upon him, Thorn Bird dove to the shield side of his attacker, narrowly escaping the trampling hooves. Grass and dirt kicked into his eyes, but he regained his balance and launched an arrow into Stands Alone's exposed back shoulder. The warrior yelled in pain, then snapped the arrow shaft with his left hand. He turned his mount to face Thorn Bird again.

Thorn Bird pulled two more arrows from his quiver and loaded one quickly as his attacker once again rushed toward him. His first whistling arrow bored straight into the throat of Stands Alone's horse. *Dead horse, dead man.* The horse screamed and threw its rider forward into the air. Stands Alone landed hard on the earth; he lay still for several heartbeats. Then slowly, he staggered to his feet, struggling hard to breathe, trying to regain the wind he had lost. The screams of the dying horse sliced through the air.

Now it was Laughing Crow's murderous son who smelled blood. Thorn Bird drew his sword from his sheath and sprinted toward the fallen rider. His enemy's eyes were consumed by pain and confusion. Stands Alone was weaponless, his lance fallen to the ground, though his shield was still fastened to his left arm.

The larger Nokoni tackled his dazed victim and grabbed his neck with his left hand. Clarity returned to Stands Alone's eyes, though he still fought for each breath and seemed weakened by his fall. Thorn Bird looked directly into the face of the man who had once been his closest friend. The face of that friend—the boy who had wrestled with him, the boy with whom he had raced horses—was gone. The face that remained was that of a fearful enemy.

"I hope we will know each other again in the next life, my friend," said Thorn Bird.

He thrust his sword into his enemy's body.

Stands Alone convulsed; soon he was choking on blood. Thorn Bird watched the life trickle from the warrior's eyes. Only when they had gone dark did he close his friend's eyelids for the last time.

Stands Alone's horse still flailed helplessly in the grass, screaming in pain. The animal's breaths were labored, and Thorn Bird knew it did not have much life left. He walked over to the dying animal and whispered, "You must go now. You must stay with my brother."

Then he cut the horse's throat with his knife, ending its suffering.

Thorn Bird stood up to face the rest of the Nokoni war party. They were watching him in stunned silence. He knew they had not intervened out of respect for the two warriors. Thorn Bird wanted to return this favor. He wanted this bloodshed to be over.

"Black Elk, there has been too much killing today. It is over," Thorn Bird shouted. "Take my brother and bury him with honor and respect. He died bravely, and he will live bravely in the spirit world. I will not defile his body. He is my brother. He is my people."

Black Elk was hunched over on his horse, holding his injured arm. "Our war is not over, Thorn Bird!" he screamed. "Not until you have breathed your last breath!" Then he turned and commanded his men to prepare to ride home.

Thorn Bird looked up at the hill with the staked Tonkawas and thanked his guardian spirit for protecting his life.

I will be ready.

Paco

The setting sun painted an orange glaze around Thorn Bird's camp. The wind continued to massage the grass and trees, though it had lost much of its strength. The heat of the day had also passed. Thorn Bird had watched the Nokoni war party gather up Stands Alone's body. As far as he could tell, two of their men were dead and four were injured. It would be a long trip home for them.

Snake had made his way back to the camp by the creek, where he seemed to be comforted by the presence of the warrior's other horse. Snake was still jumpy and agitated when Thorn Bird first approached, but eventually the injured black and white pony calmed to its master's voice and touch. The horse's alertness was a good sign.

Thorn Bird inspected Snake's wound. The arrow point was too deep for an easy extraction, so he decided that Mocking Bird's medicine was needed. Mocking Bird was an expert at treating horse injuries, and Thorn Bird didn't want to butcher the horse needlessly trying to extract the point himself. But he would have to ride his other mount while Snake healed, and let Snake follow on a lead. It would be a slow trip home.

As he was rekindling his fire pit—with a much smaller fire than before—he noticed that both horses suddenly seemed agitated. Snake had been grunting and snorting frequently from pain, but now the other horse seemed bothered. Both horses' heads and ears were pointed eastward.

Thorn Bird looked out toward the prairie and spotted a group of riders approaching in the thin light. Their horses were walking toward him unhurriedly, and he could see the silhouettes of their hats as they came closer.

Mexicanos.

He grabbed his quiver, bow, and shield and mounted his brown and white pony. He loaded an arrow and readied a few spares. The men did not seem alarmed by his actions, and that relaxed him, but he was still prepared to bring the fight to them. There were fifteen or sixteen riders, plus some extra horses guided by a boy.

"*Señor* Alcaudón! Do not be alarmed. We are Comanche *amigos*!" called out a voice in Spanish. The shout came from one of the middle riders.

Most of the men wore the Mexican *sombrero*, and as they got closer, Thorn Bird saw that many of them had hairy faces. Their shirts and leggings were of many colors—blue, black, red, brown—and covered their skin from their necks to their feet. Some of them also wore shoulder-blankets, which Thorn Bird remembered were called *serapes*. Only *mexicanos* wore them. They also wore boots on their feet with shiny *espuelas* on the back for prodding their horses.

Alcaudón? Thorn Bird had never been called this name before. "Who are you?" he asked in Spanish.

"I am Francisco del Castilla y Salazar," said the *Mexicano*, the features of the man's face finally coming into view. His mouth was ringed with hair and his shiny white teeth revealed a smile.

"I do not know that name."

"Perhaps you know my common name—Paco." The man laughed.

"I have heard of that name," said Thorn Bird. "You are a well-known trader."

Paco smiled and looked over at the large man to his right. "You see, Rodrigo. I am known by the Comanches. Even out here in these desolate lands the name of Paco is known!" He laughed again.

It seemed to Thorn Bird that Paco's teeth were rarely hidden. His eyes were sharp and intelligent, and they were an unusually light shade of brown. The kind of eyes that a Nokoni expected to see on a white man, not a *mexicano*.

"Your Spanish is *muy excelente, señor* Alcaudón," Paco continued. "Especially for an *indio!* What do you think, Cardoza?"

"It is *muy bueno*, especially for a fighting *indio!*" replied another man, presumably Cardoza.

Paco and his men stopped only a horse length away from Thorn Bird. He inspected their weapons. Each man had one or two hand-sized *pistolas*—Thorn Bird knew this Spanish word for the weapons—and several had long guns, which looked like the French muskets that the *taiboo* LaFontaine had offered in trades.

"Señor Alcaudón, put the bow away. If we wanted to kill you, you would be a dead man. *Que pasa?* I live by one simple law in this land: dead Comanche, dead Paco." Paco grinned again. "You see, I do not want to die at the hands of Comanche torturers. No no no, that is not for me, *amigo*. I want to die an old man with a fine cigar and aged mescal on my dying breath with my lovely Rosarita at my bedside." He placed his hand dramatically over his heart as he said this. "That is how I will die, *señor* Alcaudón!"

Thorn Bird knew that Paco was right. One Nokoni had no chance against fifteen armed *mexicanos* at close range. If he fought, he would surely die. So he withdrew his bow and put it back in his quiver, along with the arrows. "I do not know this name, 'Alcaudón.' What does it mean, and why do you call me that?"

Paco laughed, as did most of the men. But it was Cardoza who spoke. "Alcaudón is the name that Mexicans and Spaniards know you by. It is the Spanish word for butcher bird."

Thorn Bird remembered the word now. His mother had once taught it to him, told him that it was his name in Spanish.

"My men and I watched you, *señor* Alcaudón. One man facing twelve Comanche warriors. *Muy magnifico!* I have not witnessed such bravery, such fighting skill, in all of my days, *amigo*. One man against a force of men who could easily wipe out fifty men. It was breathtaking! When I visit the trading posts of Taos and Santa Fe, it will be the gem of all stories."

Thorn Bird knew it was a great honor to be remembered in stories of bravery. But these were stories told by *mexicanos*, not his people. They did not carry the same power as the stories told of him at Gray Elk's village. It did not matter that he would forever be a hated enemy to his former village. Living to see another sunrise was what mattered, and even if he had died in this battle, he would have died bravely. That was of the greatest importance.

"*Mis amigos* and I would like to share a camp with the great Alcaudón. It would an honor for us," said Paco.

Thorn Bird considered this. He reasoned that since these men had not killed him already, they probably did not intend to. Besides, Paco's name was known throughout Comancheria, and his reputation as a valued trader was also widely known. The Nokoni felt he could trust this man; Paco's eyes had a spark that he liked.

"You and your *compañeros* can stay here, Paco, but only three of you can share my fire. *Que pasa?*"

"*Si, si amigo. Gracias!* I will have Rodrigo shoot some rabbits for us before the darkness comes, and my men will roast the *caballo* you killed for all to enjoy." Paco paused, thinking to himself and shaking his head. "I must say it again, *amigo*, your *espanol* is brilliant!"

"My *madre* was *mexicano*. I learned to speak Spanish words when I was very young, " said Thorn Bird.

"Ah, then you are *mestizo* like many of my men, *señor* Alcaudón!"

"*Si*," replied Thorn Bird. From Paco's tone it sounded like he believed that mixed blood was more of a blessing than a curse.

The Spanish words came easily to Thorn Bird, more than he would have expected. He had rarely spoken them after his mother's death, though he often got an earful of Spanish during Valencia's tirades. He despised the mixed blood that his mother gave him, but he was thankful to her for many things, and one was teaching him the Spanish words.

The Last Blood Riders

Thorn Bird walked to the creek and washed the blood off his hands and body, but left his black face paint on. *They may be friends, but I don't want to lose the protection of my guardian spirit.* After drinking some water from his cupped hands, he returned to the fire pit to talk to the *mexicanos.*

"So, why are you the leader, Shiny Teeth? You are certainly the leader of talk." Thorn Bird had come up with this new name for Paco because his teeth glowed in the flames. Paco, Cardoza, and Rodrigo—another of Paco's men—now sat around the fire with Thorn Bird, and the rest of the *mexicanos* had built a larger fire some distance away. Thorn Bird heard a distant hooting owl call in the darkness.

"*No sé.* You should ask Cardoza, *amigo,*" said Paco, looking at the man to his right.

"Paco is the one who likes to talk, so we let him be the leader," explained Cardoza. He was wearing a brown shirt made from the white man's cloth, while Paco's shirt was red and the larger man's was black. All of the men wore the thick leather *vaquero* riding pants. "And he has Rodrigo here as his guardian angel!"

Paco shook his head. "Come on, Cardoza! If there is a smarter man in our band, then bring him to me, *pronto!* Who is the one who makes the plans? It's Paco. Who gets the best deals for our trade goods? It's Paco. Who makes sure we don't get lost? Again, it's Paco. Who saves your *cuello* when you are in danger? Paco!"

Paco leaned toward Thorn Bird, who was across the fire from him, and said in a quieter voice, "I will admit there is some truth in Cardoza's words. Rodrigo is my protector, and believe me, *mi amigo*, there is no better protector than I have known. He is as strong as a *toro*, he is deadly with the knife, and there is no better man with the rifle in all of *México*. And he is a quiet man, as you can see. He does not wag his tongue like a silly woman—not like Paco!"

Paco leaned back and slapped the back of his hand against Rodrigo's muscular shoulder. The large, expressionless man nodded his approval. The shiny-toothed Mexican then reached into his shirt and pulled out what looked like small sticks.

"Cigar, *señor* Alcaudón?" asked Paco.

"What is a cigar?"

"Tobacco, rolled in leaves. *Indios* smoke pipes and *mexicanos* smoke cigars. *Que pasa*?"

"A smoking stick?"

"Ah. *Si, si*!" answered Paco. "You want to try it?"

"I am fine, Shiny Teeth, but I will have some more of that rabbit. I am still hungry."

"Cardoza, have Pedro bring more rabbit meat for our guest," said Paco. Then he offered a smoking stick to Rodrigo, who declined. "Rodrigo likes to chew his tobacco. That's why he spits all the time."

"A man who spits, but never talks," said Thorn Bird, looking at Rodrigo.

Rodrigo spat his response into the fire, sending sparks flying into the air.

Rodrigo is as big as I am, Thorn Bird thought, and he had met few men like that. He examined the large man. Rodrigo's black hair was shorter than the others'; it hardly covered his ears at all. The hair on his face was different, too: he only had hair above his upper lip, and it fell to the sides of his mouth like a weeping willow. The skin on his face was not smooth, but scarred like the skin of a horned toad, and his eyes were black like the night—perhaps he was *mestizo* also. Thorn Bird did not know what his voice was like, because Rodrigo had not yet spoken.

Paco grabbed a stick, dipped the tip of it into the fire, then used the tiny flame to light his smoking stick. He puffed on the cigar and blew the smoke out his nose and mouth, closing his eyes. "There is nothing like a good cigar to end a meal, *amigo*." He opened his eyes again and looked at Thorn Bird. "So, your father was *el Avispa Negra?*"

Thorn Bird nodded.

"When he was alive, I don't think there was a more feared man in all of *México!*" Paco took another puff on his stick. "They say that he killed men because the moon was full. No other reason than that. They say he called it a 'killing moon.' Is that true, *amigo?*"

"No. It is not true. He killed only when he had to, and when he knew the odds were in his favor. He was a great leader and a generous man."

"You were one of his Blood Riders, *señor* Alcaudón?"

Thorn Bird nodded. "And so was the man I killed today. He was my childhood friend."

"Why did you become enemies?" These were the first words Thorn Bird had heard Rodrigo speak. His voice deep and rich.

Thorn Bird looked at Rodrigo. "He turned against me." He did not want to offer any more details than that.

Cardoza returned with a rabbit leg and handed it to Thorn Bird, then sat down again.

It was Paco who broke the momentary silence. "Rodrigo, to think that we saw two Blood Riders fight against each other. My story is even grander now." He sucked in more smoke from his cigar. "How many Blood Riders are left?"

"Only two," said Thorn Bird as he bit into a juicy rabbit leg. "Malone and I are the last."

Fire-Water

Darkness settled on Thorn Bird's camp, though the heat did not relent. It was good to hear the sounds of a village again: crackling fires, men talking and laughing, the smells of roasting horse meat and tobacco. It almost felt like home. Though he had known these *mexicanos* for only a short while, he felt like they were friends, and he felt safe around them. The reputation of Paco and his men had been relayed to him in past seasons by warriors he knew and trusted. These *mexicanos* were friends of his people.

"So, Malone and you are the last of the Blood Riders, eh, *señor* Alcaudón? He is almost as *legendario* as your father. He was your father's second in command?" asked Paco.

"*Sí*. He was my father's closest friend. The man he trusted more than any other."

"And they say he is as deadly a man as you will find with a bow," added Paco.

"A brilliant rider, and he could pierce the rattle off a rattlesnake from over ten horse lengths away. But he no longer uses war points on his arrows, only hunting points," said Thorn Bird.

"We have seen him many times at the trading post in Santa Fe. He is always alone," said Cardoza, rubbing the smoldering tip of his smoking stick in the dirt to kill the embers.

"I saw Malone two mornings ago. After I killed the Tonkawas and staked their bodies on the hill," said Thorn Bird.

"A grisly altar, *señor* Alcaudón. That and your haunting black eye paint will feed your growing *celebridad*," said Paco. He was still holding his smoking stick in his mouth, but it was no longer lit.

"It reminded me of the Place of the Skull where Jesus died," added Cardoza.

Thorn Bird knew that Jesus was a god that these men worshipped, but he did not know of this skull place.

His thoughts returned to Malone. He smiled, knowing that Malone was looking for the white-skinned devil. Each sleep was one sleep closer to having the skin of Many Wolves under the blade of his knife.

"Shiny Teeth, have you seen this *gringo diablo* Many Wolves?"

"I have heard of this man, but I have never met him," said Paco. "They say he has strange magic with animals. I am not a believer in magic, *señor* Alcaudón, but he must be a great warrior to have killed your father."

"He's no warrior," said Thorn Bird with defiance in his voice. "He does not ride well or use a bow or knife with skill, not that I have seen. But I agree that he is a man of strange animal magic. It is my greatest wish to find this *gringo* and make him suffer for what he did to my father and my people." To think that men regarded this *taiboo* as a great warrior was laughable.

"*Gringos* are like cattle, Alcaudón: weak and defenseless, easily captured and auctioned back to the rich *gringo* who sent them," said Rodrigo in a hateful tone, spitting his tobacco when he was finished.

"*Señor* Alcaudón, I promise you, with my hand on the holy *livro*, that if I find this *gringo* Many Wolves, I will bring him to you."

"*Gracias*, Paco. Malone is looking for him now, even as we sit around this fire," said Thorn Bird. *Many Wolves cannot hide forever.*

There was silence around the camp. Shiny Teeth and Cardoza each lit another smoking stick, and Rodrigo continued to chew and spit his tobacco. These men seemed so relaxed, so carefree. What seemed like a dangerous place to Thorn Bird was like a familiar village to these men. Their numbers granted them safety, and as known friends of the *Noomah*, there was little for them to fear. If these men could ride and use their weapons as well they made him believe, then they would be powerful friends to have. Thorn Bird's Nokoni village needed more powerful friends.

"Ah, Chico! You are just the man I was hoping to see!" said Paco, grinning as a large-bellied man approached their campfire. This man was dressed in a matching blue shirt and pants. Fine metal beads lined the sides of his pants, and like most of the *mexicanos*, he wore thick leather *vaquero* boots that ran up to his knees, with those metal flowers on the heels for commanding their horses. The brim of his *sombrero* dipped low on his face, pitching a dark shadow over his eyes. He was holding a large water pouch in one hand and several metal cups in the other.

"Would Alcaudón like to try some of my mescal?" asked Chico. His voice had a low tone; it suited his large body.

"*Señor* Alcaudón, what do you think? I'm sure Chico would love to brag to his friends that a Blood Rider enjoyed his mescal." Paco laughed.

"Is it the same fire-water that the *Navoonah* drink?" asked Thorn Bird. He remembered tasting the *Navoonah* mescal long ago; it had been so bitter that he had spit it out.

"The *Navoonah*?" said Paco, confused.

"The *Navoonah* are the people you call *lipanos*. They are our greatest enemy," replied Thorn Bird.

"The *lipanos'* mescal tastes like the *orina* of a toad, *mi amigo*!" said Paco. "Chico's mescal is the good stuff, the best you will find on the Llano. Share a drink with us, *por favor*."

Thorn Bird nodded his consent. Chico poured a cup and handed it to him, then poured three more cups for Cardoza, Paco, and Rodrigo.

Thorn Bird took a small drink and swirled it around his mouth. The clear liquid felt warm and tingly, and it burned the sides of his mouth and throat when he finally swallowed it. The taste reminded him of one of the medicines Snake Tooth used to give him to chase the pain spirits away. He drank another mouthful, then another, until the cup was empty. The fire-water warmed his body in a good way. Thorn Bird could not stop the grin that reshaped his face.

Paco's men all laughed heartily when they saw Thorn Bird's reaction. Even the emotionless Rodrigo smiled. Chico flashed a proud look.

"Chico, you have made a powerful *amigo*! Pour him some more!" said Paco. "Let us make a *pacto* much like your leaders do, *señor* Alcaudón, when they smoke the truth pipe. The *indio* seals truth with smoke while the *mexicano* seals it with mescal!" His teeth flashed brightly in the light of the flames.

Chico poured another serving for Thorn Bird and some for himself, then Paco raised his cup above his head and urged Thorn Bird to do the same. The other three *mexicanos* raised their cups as well, so Thorn Bird followed along hesitantly, not understanding this strange *mexicano* ritual.

"Let us drink to our new friend, *señor* Alcaudón, and to a new, lasting friendship between *indio* and *mexicano*!" said Paco in a loud voice.

"To Alcaudón!" said the other men before draining their cups.

Thorn Bird drank his cup quickly. He enjoyed the warm, relaxing feeling seeping through him. He felt like his body was in a strange place, almost like a dream, except pleasant and peaceful—a stark contrast to the violence in his usual dreams.

"Alcaudón, there is a strange power within my mescal that you should know," said Chico.

"It will grow more hair on my face?" said Thorn Bird, smiling.

Chico laughed. "No, *señor*, but it will make the ugly girls look pretty, and the pretty ones even prettier!"

Thorn Bird laughed even though he was not sure what Chico meant. This mescal sounded like strong medicine.

"And it will make Pedro's *mulo* look much prettier too!" added Cardoza, who stood up and made a thrusting movement with his lower body.

The men erupted into laughter. Thorn Bird thought the humor was unusual—to joke about a man coupling with a mule?—but his mood was good, so he smiled along with the rest of them. He sat back and gazed at the *mexicanos*. They genuinely seemed to enjoy each other's friendship. He wondered how they had all come together.

"Shiny Teeth, are your men from the same village? Are they from the same *familia*?" he asked.

Paco chuckled. "It would be nice to know something about the men who are sharing your camp, *amigo*?" said Paco. "Some of the men are from the same village, and some worked at the same *hacienda*. A few of us, including Rodrigo, Cardoza, and me, were once soldiers at the garrison in San Antonio." Paco looked at each of his two companions. "One day, *capitan* Garcia sent our unit out to find the *lipanos* who were stealing our horses and our supplies. But the *lipanos* surprised us and killed most of our men. Only five of us rode away from that attack, and we survived only because we had faster horses. We decided on that day that it wasn't worth risking your life as a soldier for just a few *pesos*, only to be killed and tortured by *indios*. So we rode south past the Rio Bravo and found more men, most of them *mestizos* who labored on *haciendas* as *vaqueros* who took care of the cattle. The dream of every man here is to own his own *hacienda* someday." Paco paused briefly to smoke. "And to answer your second question, *señor* Alcaudón, a few of us are with our brothers. Like Rodrigo and I: we are *hermanos*."

"You are the elder *hermano*?"

"*Si*."

"Then that explains why you are the leader."

There was a break in the talk as a boy ran into the camp and whispered something in Rodrigo's ear.

"My son, Pablonito, wants to ask you something, Alcaudón," said Rodrigo.

Thorn Bird gestured for the boy to speak.

"I found this arrow on the dead *caballo*," said the boy, holding one of Thorn Bird's arrows in his hand. "I want to know if I can keep it."

Rodrigo nudged the boy as if to remind him to say more.

"*Por favor*," added the boy after a moment of thought.

Thorn Bird smiled at the boy. "You can keep it, but you have to trade me something."

"What, *señor*?"

"In the morning, I want you to go out and find all of my other war arrows and bring them to me. I will show you where they are. *Que pasa?*"

Pablonito's eyes widened and a big smile lit up his face. "*Si, señor.* I can do that. *Gracias! Gracias!*" He ran off with the arrow.

"He is a large boy for ten *años*, eh *señor* Alcaudón? Big like his father. And someday he will shoot the rifle as well as his father, too. You will see," said Paco.

"Already he's as tall as many of the men of my village," said Thorn Bird.

Paco smiled. "An arrow from Alcaudón. That is a nice treasure for any boy. You are a generous man, *señor* Alcaudón. *Gracias!*"

Chico's supply of mescal lasted only a short while longer, but Thorn Bird shared stories with his new friends deep into the night. With little sleep the previous night, his body finally gave in.

The fire-water had seemingly made it easier for him to sleep.

Eagle Eyes

Thorn Bird woke up with the mid-morning sun blazing in his face and a queasiness in his stomach. His mouth was so dry it almost felt like his parched lips were stuck together. He rolled out of his sleeping robe and reached for his water pouch, then gulped down the water as fast as it would go down. Still he was thirsty.

Cardoza and Rodrigo were already awake and sitting around the fire pit. They laughed when they saw Thorn Bird inhale the pouch of water. "That is the other magic of the mescal, Alcaudón. It gives you an unquenchable thirst the next morning," said Cardoza.

Apart from his thirst, Thorn Bird felt relaxed. He had fallen asleep easily without feeling tortured, and there had been no bad dreams to force him to wake in a pool of his own sweat. Perhaps this, too, was the magic of Chico's fire-water. And as far as he knew, he had not coupled with any mules, or even dreamt of mules, or horses, or any animals. But Valencia had been there in his dreams; that much he could remember.

After relieving his nearly bursting bladder and refilling his water pouch with creek water, Thorn Bird walked over to the fire pit. A strange aroma was floating in the air. "What's that smell?"

"It is *café, amigo.* Would you like some?

These mexicanos *have so many different things to drink.*

"I will try some. Will it make me feel good like the fire-water?"

"It is different, *amigo.* It will wake you up and make your heart beat very fast," said Cardoza, pouring him a cup from a steaming metal pot.

Thorn Bird took a small sip.

"You have to drink it slowly, *amigo*. It is very hot," said Cardoza. "It tastes better with a bit of sugar or honey to weaken the bitterness, but we do not have anything to sweeten it."

Thorn Bird took a couple more sips. The taste was bitter, almost unpleasant. He could see how a little honey or some sweet berries would help the taste. "Can I add salt or mesquite to it?"

"No, no, *amigo*. That would ruin it." Cardoza looked over at Rodrigo and grinned. "It is a new drink in *México*. We stole it from some Spanish soldiers who were traveling to San Antonio. I don't think many *indios* have ever tasted it. You may be one of the first, Alcaudón!"

Shiny Teeth joined them at the fire. His hair and face were dripping wet. "*Buenos dias, señor* Alcaudón. I hope you slept well." He combed his hair back with his hand and then put on his black *sombrero*.

"It was a good sleep, Shiny Teeth."

"*Muy bien*! No head pain from Chico's mescal?"

Thorn Bird shook his head.

"*Muy bien, mi amigo*! You feel no aching head with Chico's mescal like you would with the *lipano* mescal! I always sleep better with good mescal in my gut, *amigo*."

"You will have to ask Chico to make more of the fire-water sleeping medicine for me," said Thorn Bird. "I have many things I can trade you for this. Buffalo skins, deer skins, and pemmican."

"Ah. That would be a good trade for us too, *amigo*," said Paco. "We also have four *caballos* that we found yesterday. A young *indio* was leading them by himself, but he rode off when he saw us, leaving the *caballos* behind. As easy as taking a toy from a *niño*." Paco laughed, clearly pleased with himself.

Perhaps there had been another Tonkawa that got away.

"When I get back to my village, we will make these trades," said Thorn Bird.

Pablonito ran up to their fire pit, stopped next to his father, and stared at Thorn Bird. It seemed to Thorn Bird that the boy was ready to burst. "*Señor*, can I find the arrows now?" said Pablonito, excitedly.

"If you are ready," said Thorn Bird. "Get your *caballo*." Every arrow was valuable to Thorn Bird, and they were not easily replaced. Giving up one in exchange for the boy's help in finding his lost arrows was a trade he was willing to make. The Nokoni warrior did not expect the boy to retrieve them all, but he would need as many as he could get for the journey home.

Thorn Bird grabbed his quiver, sword, and shield and mounted his spare pony; Snake was still resting. Rodrigo and Shiny Teeth also mounted; apparently they intended to join them for the ride. Rodrigo carried a long, shiny gun and wore a belt of metal balls around his shoulder. Shiny Teeth carried a *mexicano escopeta*.

"Pablonito, lead us out to the altar of the four dead *hombres*," instructed Paco. "We will find the arrows near there."

The boy rode out ahead while the other three directed their horses to a trot. Thorn Bird retrieved some pemmican from his food pouch and offered it to the two *mexicanos,* one on either side of him.

"*Gracias,*" said Paco.

Rodrigo simply nodded as he took a piece of the dried meat, then spit out the tobacco that was in his mouth.

"*Muy delicioso,*" said Paco after biting a chewy mouthful, the juices running down his chin. "We will gladly trade you Chico's mescal for this, *señor* Alcaudón." His words were hard to understand with his mouth full.

Rodrigo seemed to enjoy it as well, though he did not admit it.

Thorn Bird was curious about the metal balls on Rodrigo's chest-belt. There were at least twenty of them. "What kind of *balas* are those, Rodrigo?"

"Special *balas* for my *rifle*."

"Rodrigo's *rifles* are very special guns," explained Paco. "My father gave them to us when we were young—one for each of us. But I gave mine to Rodrigo because he had the skill to shoot them. These rifles are made by a *gringo's* hands, and they are very rare and valuable. They can shoot three or four times farther than a normal *escopeta* like mine—and much more

119

accurately. My father always used to say that anyone can shoot a *pistola* or *escopeta* well enough, but few men have the skill to use a *rifle* the way it is meant to be used. Rodrigo has this skill, and I believe someday he will teach it to Pablonito."

"How is it that the *balas* go so far?" said Thorn Bird.

"There are special grooves that the rifle-maker carves into the barrel which makes the *bala de metal* spin when it is shot." Paco pointed to the barrel of his gun and simulated a metal ball leaving the barrel with a gesture of his hand. He used his fingers to show a spinning motion. "This gives the rifle greater range and accuracy over the French musket or the Spanish *escopeta*."

Thorn Bird didn't understand what grooves were, and he was skeptical that a weapon as powerful as this even existed. If the *mexicanos* and Spanish soldiers had these weapons and could shoot them as well as Paco described, then they would be extremely dangerous to his people.

"There are the dead *hombres*!" yelled Pablonito, pointing to a hill ahead of them.

Thorn Bird saw dark-colored birds near the bodies; he assumed they were buzzards, but he was too far away to tell for sure.

Thorn Bird spoke in a challenging tone. "Rodrigo, I want to see you kill one of those buzzards with your *rifle*, from this spot. Can you do this?" He estimated that they were still at least two arrow flights from the buzzards.

"From here, I can kill a *buitre* in three shots," said Rodrigo, loading his mouth with some fresh tobacco.

"Will you bet the *rifle* that you can do it?" offered Thorn Bird.

"This is a very rare weapon, Alcaudón. Almost impossible to replace. I will not wager it on a game of chance," said Rodrigo.

Thorn Bird laughed. "So you do not trust your skill? You have another *rifle*—so if you lose one, you still have another." He added a taunt: "I don't believe it's possible to kill a buzzard from here."

"And what will *you* wager, Alcaudón?"

"I will give you this horse and four others when I reach my village."

Rodrigo paused to evaluate the offer. "I have three shots to hit the bird?

Correcto?"

"*Si*," said Thorn Bird, growing excited about the wager.

"It is a bet," said Rodrigo, spitting out some tobacco. Then he yelled to his son. "Pablonito! *Ven aquí!*"

The boy quickly rode over. "What is it, *papa?*"

"Move the horses back and tether them," said Rodrigo, dismounting.

When the boy returned, Paco explained to him, "Your father has a bet with *señor* Alcaudón that he can kill one of those *buitres* in three shots."

"If I need more shots, I will need you to load the rifle, Pablonito," said Rodrigo.

"*Si, papa.*"

Rodrigo looked at Thorn Bird, his face determined. "The *buitre* on the left man's head will die."

Thorn Bird, Paco, and Pablonito moved away from Rodrigo as he raised the rifle to his shoulder. The large *mexicano* steadied the weapon for several heartbeats. He was as still as a large oak on a windless day.

Thorn Bird turned to watch the target; the buzzard was busily pecking at the man's head. Then he heard the loud blast from the rifle. It sounded quicker and sharper than a musket blast. He saw a puff of dirt kick up behind the bird. Thorn Bird was amazed that a metal ball could fly that far. He was not now thinking that he may be about to lose five horses; instead, he was thinking how easily he could kill a man with such a rifle.

"Pablonito, load it up," barked Rodrigo.

The boy ran over to his father, took the rifle and another metal ball from him, then loaded the weapon quickly and carefully.

"Rodrigo will not miss this time, *amigo*," said Paco with confidence. "The boy is his loader. His quick little hands can load a rifle faster than any man in our band. When Rodrigo fights, the boy loads one rifle while he fires the other, and then they trade. Rodrigo can fire off six shots before most men can load a second shot. The only man who is faster is the Comanche with his bow."

With the rifle loaded, Rodrigo aimed again. The buzzard had flinched with the first blast, but had quickly returned to its meal, seemingly unafraid of the distant predator that hunted it.

Again the rifle boomed, and again the bird flinched, but it was not hit. Thorn Bird did not see the metal ball kick up any dust this time.

The boy did not need to be asked. He sprinted over to his father, quickly reloaded the rifle, then handed it back to him.

"I will not miss this time, Alcaudón," said Rodrigo. He spit his tobacco and re-aimed his rifle. This time, he spent twice as long with his aim. The prairie was silent. It was not just Rodrigo holding his breath, but all of them. Thorn Bird had his eyes glued to the buzzard.

The rifle exploded, shattering the silence, and a heartbeat later the metal ball crashed into the bird, knocking it off of the dead man's head. The buzzard fell to the earth, flapped its wings twice, and then moved no more.

Pablonito ran over and hugged his father, who was now surrounded by a rising puff of smoke. "You did it, *papa!*"

Paco smiled from one ear to the next, but he was uncharacteristically silent.

Thorn Bird struggled to find his breath. He was engulfed in a thunder cloud of mixed emotions. He admitted to himself that he was disappointed to have lost his bet, but more importantly, he was astonished that a man could kill something as small as a bird from such a great distance. Rodrigo could kill with the eyes of an eagle.

Thorn Bird felt a new respect for Rodrigo and for these *mexicanos.*

My village needs men who can fight like this.

Paco at last broke his silence, but not his smile, "You see, *señor* Alcaudón, there is no man in *México* who can shoot like Rodrigo Salazar. Now you too are a believer. I hope you are not upset about losing the bet."

Thorn Bird was finding it difficult to find the right words. At last they came to him. "Rodrigo, I will not call you by that name anymore. My name for you is Eagle Eyes."

"*Gracias*, Alcaudón. I like the name." Rodrigo tipped the brim of his sombrero, respectfully, and did not spit. "You owe me five *caballos.*"

"This horse is yours; take it. I will bring you four more when you come to my village. That is my promise," said Thorn Bird, handing the reins of his horse over to Eagle Eyes.

"How will you return to your village without a healthy horse?" said Paco.

"Snake and I will find our way back."

"Snake is your war *caballo*? said Paco.

"*Si*. Good war horses do not breed like wildflowers. They are rare. As rare as the rifle in Eagle Eyes' hands." Thorn Bird paused, then turned to Paco. "Shiny Teeth, I would like to ask a favor of you."

"What is it, *mi amigo*?"

"Can you ride back to my village and tell them that I am alive and that I will be returning in four or five sleeps? Speak to Half Weasel. He is the leader while I am away. Tell him you are my *amigo* and to give you a fair trade for the four Tonkawa horses. When I return, I will let Eagle Eyes pick any four horses from my herd, except for Snake. Can you do this for me?"

"We will find your village, *señor* Alcaudón, and deliver your message and the *indio* horses. But then we must go to Santa Fe and Taos. We will return to your village after that, and Rodrigo will collect his horses."

"*Gracias*, Shiny Teeth. I will tell you how to get to my village, and then I must begin my long journey home. But first, Pablonito—let's find some arrows."

Beyond the Fear

The full moon passed, and with it, Fiera's fear. The once terrified little bird had blossomed into a tame companion. Many Wolves could now approach it without it flinching. He stroked the bird's downy white chest feathers and scaly yellow legs often, even while it ate, and Fiera would merely pull up one of its legs and puff up its body feathers. To Many Wolves, this was the purest sign of contentment.

"You are so big now. You must be a female," said Many Wolves.

The fledgling was growing each day. She was easily twice her original size. Dark feathers were growing on her wings and she flapped them constantly for exercise and strengthening. Her legs were longer and stronger too, providing excellent balance and mobility. Fiera did not hesitate to walk out of the nest and explore the rocky ledge, though she was not yet bold enough to jump off.

But Many Wolves felt that it was time to move the nest down to the ground, underneath the ledge. He feared that the bird would fall from the ledge and injure herself. And besides, it was time that Fiera met the pack, and they met Fiera.

"*Nami*, are you ready to meet my friends?" he said, using the Northerners' word for "little sister."

Many Wolves slipped his right hand gently under the nestling and placed her in his large hunting bag. She peeped and struggled a bit, but eventually succumbed. He climbed down the tree and set the bag aside,

124

then climbed back up to retrieve the nesting material, which was now covered in feathers and droppings. He carried it down a few pieces at a time and tried to set it up in exactly the same way below the ledge. Rojo's watched with curiosity, his head tilted.

Many Wolves then reached into the bag, pulled out the bird, and place her into the rebuilt nest.

Fiera looked around at her new surroundings with her beak open, panting like a dog, and then froze when she spotted the big, red wolf. Many Wolves quickly signaled the wolf to lie down where he was, about two horse lengths away. Rojo obeyed, but still watched the bird with pointed ears.

"Now you know where those strange sounds and smells are coming from, Rojo."

Many Wolves sat next to the nest with his back against the rocky wall and stroked Fiera's chest. The bird continued to act nervous, and she never took her eyes off the wolf.

"This is Rojo, Fiera. He's going to find birds and rabbits for you to chase, and he'll keep other predators away. I hope you two can be friends, like Rojo was with my other birds. When we eat now, we will eat together, as a pack."

The afternoon was passing and Many Wolves needed to hunt again, so he forced himself up. He was content to watch Fiera the rest of the day. He had killed a jackrabbit earlier for them to share, but this time he wanted to find Fiera's favorite: quail. The stumpy birds had become more scarce around his camp, perhaps because they were constantly hunted. Many Wolves had to walk farther and farther away now to find them. As he searched, he wondered what Fiera would do on her own now that there were no longer any limits to her exploration.

I hope you are there when we get back, little bird.

Neither Many Wolves nor Rojo could find quail this day, so he brought back a rattlesnake and a ground squirrel instead. Many Wolves was especially careful when killing rattlesnakes—knowing first-hand how potent their bites could be—but he couldn't refuse an easy meal. He savored the taste of cooked rattlesnake, though picking out the bones was tedious. Fiera would eat the ground squirrel, and Rojo would eat whatever was left over; he wasn't picky.

When they arrived back at the camp, Many Wolves heard Fiera's familiar hunger cry before he saw her. The young bird was standing outside the nest waiting for her next meal. Many Wolves was relieved to see that she hadn't wandered too far.

He sat a short distance away from her, keeping the meat hidden, and signaled for Rojo to lie beside him. He cut open the ground squirrel with his knife and gave Rojo half of it. The other half he saved for Fiera, including the blood organs, which she usually gulped down before anything else. In this, she was no different from his wolf hawks. Once Rojo was occupied, Many Wolves dipped Fiera's food in water, then placed it on the piece of bark in front of her nest. As expected, she gulped down the heart and liver.

Many Wolves then grabbed a piece of dried meat from his food pouch and chewed on that. He washed it down with water from his pouch. It was the first time the three of them had shared a meal together.

Yellow Eyes

Since moving down to the ground nest, Fiera had changed into a completely different bird. Most of the fuzzy, snowy white down on her legs, head, and body was gone, replaced now by mottled brown-on-white feathers, and her tail and wing feathers had grown out substantially. But the most impressive change was her eye color: the bluish-gray eyes of a helpless chick had turned to the bright yellow eyes of a nearly full-grown bird-killer.

And it was not just her appearance that had changed, but also her confidence and flying ability. She was no longer tethered to the earth, and would now fly from branch to branch around the Gray Face camp. Many Wolves worked with her each day, using a whistle to call her down from a branch to his fist-perch, always rewarding her with a small piece of meat. He also practiced calling her to the fist-perch by name, but this did not always reward her with food. The whistle always meant food.

"*Nami*," he said, "I think you are ready to follow me on a walk." The bird was perched on a low pine branch.

The few quail that remained around his Gray Face camp were extremely wary and had learned to quickly take flight when the wolf and man approached. There were plenty of them around, and their distinctive calls made them easy to track, but Many Wolves needed to change his tactics. So he had returned to using one of his oldest tricks: snares. He regretted not realizing their value sooner, because it would have saved him a lot of time and frustration compared to hunting quail with a bow. At least his time spent hunting had taught him where the best quail spots were.

On this late summer morning, he wanted to accomplish two things on his walk: he wanted to check his quail snares and see how well Fiera would follow him. He had not fed her since the previous night, so he hoped her hunger would motivate her to stay nearby.

"Rojo, this will be interesting. Let's go." He signaled to his wolf to follow and walked away from the camp, but he did not call Fiera's name or whistle for her, not just yet.

After about ten steps, he turned, held up his fist-perch, and called, "Fiera!"

She swooped down and landed on his covered hand. He revealed the hidden morsel, which she gobbled up eagerly. Then he raised his arm quickly, flinging her into the air, and yelled, "Up!" She flew to a nearby branch and watched them.

Many Wolves wanted to walk farther this time before calling her, but before he reached his target spot, she flew down and landed on the back of his head. Her claws dug into his scalp, painfully, so he held up his fist-perch, and she hopped onto it right away. No reward this time, so he tossed her back up into the air with the same voice command: "Up!"

The path he chose was perfect for this exercise: pine trees on his left and open grassland on his right. The Rio Pecos was even farther to his right.

It took several unrewarded attempts before she started to get it right. It was a game, and she was slowly figuring it out. He was amazed at how swiftly she flew; her wing beats were much faster than those of his wolf hawks. She was a lot more nervous and distracted than his other birds had been, and he wondered if she would ever settle down.

He passed the first area where he had snares set up, but they were all empty. So he continued farther along the tree line, prompting the bird to follow. She was responding well to his commands, so he decided to change the game: now when he called her in, she would get a reward one time but no reward another. She mostly took well to this change—she continued to respond to his call even after having received no reward—though sometimes he sensed that she was unhappy at receiving no reward, because she would dig her claws into the fist-perch. This was how he had taught his other birds, and he didn't want to abandon a training method that had worked well in the past.

"Fiera!" he called again, his fist-perch held high. He saw her approach from the corner of his eye, but this time she was coming in faster. She surged right past him, ignoring his offer completely, and flew in a straight line toward a clump of bushes near the river.

If she flew over the river, he would have to cross it to find her. The Rio Pecos was wide and turbulent here. *I can cross it, but how will I get back with Fiera?*

Many Wolves raced after her, Rojo running alongside. As he watched, she dove into the brush right at the edge of the river. It was a familiar quail area, and he'd planted several snares there. Many Wolves kept his eyes glued to the spot, being sure not to miss her if she flew off again. Even so, he knew she might sneak away without him seeing, since blue darters loved to run on the ground and she might take off from a completely different area of the riverbank.

Then he heard the commotion. It was a sound he had heard many times before: the cries of a dying quail. *She's caught something!*

Many Wolves was around twenty steps away, so he slowed to a walk and signaled Rojo to do the same. His eyes were peeled, looking for any kind of movement in the brush, but there was none—just the sound of the distressed quail.

Then he spotted them. Fiera had the head of the quail grasped firmly in her talons. One of the quail's legs was caught in his snare, preventing it from running away.

Many Wolves signaled for Rojo to lie down, then he got down on his knees and crawled slowly toward the birds. His heart was beating madly from the excitement, but he needed to remain calm. He needed Fiera to not feel threatened by his presence. "It's your kill, *Nami*." He whispered and moved closer. "It's your kill." Like it was all part of a strange wrestling match, the quail struggled to free itself, and Fiera responded with a tighter grip.

Many Wolves slowly reached into his food bag and pulled out a large piece of quail breast meat that he had been planning on giving her after the walk. He transferred the juicy, reddish meat to his fist-perch, then pulled his rabbit-skin headband off and set it on the ground.

He showed Fiera the enticing offering in his left hand and moved it closer to her. She looked at it and then at the quail, back and forth. Then she looked at him with yellow eyes that blazed like the sun. He slowly moved his hand closer, and when his fist-perch was underneath her, she took a bite from the raw offering. Many Wolves knew that his wolf hawks could not resist the sight of fresh, red meat, and he had hoped it would be the same for this hawk.

She took several more bites from the meat in his hand, and then finally she placed one foot on his fist-perch, claiming his offering as her kill. With his right hand, Many Wolves slowly dragged the headband over the quail to cover it up.

Once Fiera was firmly perched on his hand, he moved her away from the quail. With his other hand, he snapped the quail's neck to end its suffering, then stashed it in his hunting bag, the snare still attached to its leg. He would reset the snare later when he had two free hands.

He stayed with Fiera while she ate the rest of the meat. "Your first kill, *Nami.*"

He was overjoyed. This was a surprise; he had not expected this to happen so soon. The snare had made the kill easier for her. In fact, it was the perfect setup for a beginning hunter. *I will have to do this again to build up her confidence as a hunter.*

When Fiera was finished with her meal, she cleaned every little bit of flesh off her legs and off the fist-perch. Many Wolves stood up, with the bird still on his fist-perch, and started walking back toward the trees.

Suddenly, the bird-killer twisted her head sideways, looking upward. Many Wolves followed her gaze and saw what she had spotted: a red-tailed hawk circling above them. It screamed down at them, seemingly disturbed by their presence. *We must be in its territory.* He felt the smaller bird's grip tighten on his hand. *She must be terrified.*

"*Nami,* you are safe with us. Let's go home."

Tail Chaser

In search of more bountiful quail-hunting grounds, Many Wolves packed up his Gray Face camp and headed west, away from the Rio Pecos. He rode Elk Dog, with Rojo trailing faithfully and Fiera flying along from tree to tree. Occasionally, Many Wolves called the bird to his fist-perch for a small reward. But on this morning, he intentionally fed her less with the hope that it would keep her mind sharp, focused on staying with them. He had begun riding Elk Dog on their recent hunts, and Fiera had quickly become accustomed to the brown horse, accepting it as part of their hunting ritual.

Fiera had killed two more snared quail since her first kill. In Many Wolves's mind, she had mastered this game and was now ready to take the next step in her training: catching untethered quail. So he collected his snares, expecting that they would be useful again if their hunts were unsuccessful. On many days, their only meat came from his traps. He always found roots, berries, and nuts for himself to eat, but this would not suffice for the flesh-eating members of his pack.

Many Wolves was quickly realizing how spoiled he had become by having an experienced hunter like Chiquito in his pack. There was still a mountain-sized heap of training ahead before he could make Fiera into a steady, reliable provider.

Many Wolves directed his traveling group along the tree line. The foothills here were perfect for his hunting needs: scattered trees surrounded by scrub and grassland, plenty of hiding places for the plump game birds they sought.

They journeyed through the hottest part of the day, finally reaching a small creek in the late afternoon. Many Wolves remembered this creek from past explorations. He dismounted to rest and drink. Rojo and Elk Dog also drank. He was heading west now into land that was mostly strange to him, so he would have to be careful not to stray too far from water.

He reached into his food bag for a generous piece of quail meat, dipped it in the water, and called Fiera to his glove. "You need to have water too, *Nami*." Once she had eaten, he released her and filled his water pouch.

They crossed the creek, which was only halfway up his leg and about six steps wide, and continued west. The path sloped upward on the right, leading to a stand of pines and junipers, and leveled off to the left into a spread of patchy scrubland, small trees, and grassland.

By accident, they stumbled upon a covey of quail hidden in the brush. Instantly, the prey birds launched into the air and Fiera darted after them. The quail were fast flyers, much faster than Many Wolves had thought they would be.

The bird-killer singled one out from the flock and pursued it vigorously, but the game bird was equally as swift. The quail twisted and rolled, the tenacious blue darter staying on its tail, until both were nearly out of sight.

Many Wolves directed Elk Dog to a lope, keeping his eyes pinned on the spot where he had last seen the two birds. He at last found Fiera perched on a small tree looking into a patch of thick bushes.

Many Wolves dismounted and signaled for Rojo to come with him. He spread the branches apart looking for the quail—then heard a rustle and a whirring of wings as the quail bolted upward again. Fiera was on it in a heartbeat, and this time the bird-killer tackled the quail quickly to the ground before the chase could go too far.

Many Wolves ran over to the two struggling birds, pulled forward by the quail's labored screams. Fiera held the quail tightly, squeezing the bird repeatedly, until eventually its life was gone. Then she proceeded to pluck its feathers, one by one, to get at the fresh meat.

Many Wolves offered her some pre-plucked, pre-skinned meat as a trade, and she gladly took it. He stashed her fresh kill in his hunting bag while she was distracted. *Never steal from these birds.*

He looked at his bird on his fist-perch and spoke softly. "*Nami*, your first wild kill." He felt two emotions tugging at his heart: relief and fear. He felt relief that Fiera could kill on her own, but also fear that she would no longer need the pack. It was the same feeling he had felt with his wolf hawks, though less urgent.

I cannot worry about the future, he told himself. *The Great Spirit has a plan.*

Many Wolves shifted his thoughts back to the moment. He was amazed by the bird chase. It was like there had been a piece of sinew tied between the quail's tail and the bird-killer's head. And Fiera had flown a long way in a short time. His wolf hawks had never chased anything for even close to this distance.

Many Wolves marveled at the gift of speed that the Great Spirit had given these two birds. It seemed like every creature had its own special gift to allow it to survive. The bear was given strength; the rattlesnake its poison; the turtle its shell; and these birds, the ability to fly faster than almost any other creatures.

"Rojo, let's head back up to the trees by the creek and make our camp. We'll need to get some fresh meat for you too. I don't think this quail will be enough to fill a hungry wolf's stomach."

A Stronger Village

Thorn Bird knew his long journey back to his village was close to an end when he saw Half Weasel riding toward him. It had taken three sleeps to travel this far, but after the bloody fights with Black Elk's party and the Tonkawas and the friendly encounter with Shiny Teeth's band, he had welcomed the peace and solitude. And he had kept a close eye on his ailing war horse every moment. Snake's health had improved, but he was still too lame to be ridden. The arrow point embedded in his upper rear leg still needed to be removed, and Mocking Bird was the most skilled at this kind of medicine.

Half Weasel dismounted and approached Thorn Bird. "*Namunewapi*! It is good to see you."

"It is good to be home, Half Weasel." Thorn Bird offered his forearm as a greeting. "Many things have happened since I last saw you."

Half Weasel walked beside Thorn Bird, followed by the horses on leads. "The village was relieved to hear from Paco that you were well. Especially Valencia." Half Weasel gave Thorn Bird a smile.

"She is well?"

"*Haa, namunewapi.* I think she was worried that she would never see you again. It was good that she could speak the Spanish words with Paco."

"Shiny Teeth's visit went well?"

"Who is Shiny Teeth?"

Thorn Bird laughed. "He is Paco. I call him Shiny Teeth because he always shows his teeth when he talks and smiles."

"*Haa*, it went well, *namunewapi*. He has much respect for you and for our people."

"He and his men will be valuable friends to have. The one named Rodrigo can kill with the eyes of an eagle. His enemies will die before they even see him. I lost five horses in a bet against his skill with the long gun."

The two men walked through rolling hills of prairie grass on their way to the village. The summer sun blazed straight above them, heating their skin and causing their bodies to glisten with sweat. Both wore only breechcloths and moccasins.

"Your debt has been paid, *namunewapi*. Rodrigo was happy to take buffalo skins instead of horses. What did he offer in this bet?"

"One of his long guns. I respect a man who is willing to wager something of great value. After seeing what he could do with his long gun, I named him Eagle Eyes. These *mexicanos* are clever men to carve out a good life here on the Llano."

"Shiny Teeth, as you call him, also traded us the four horses of the Wolf People you killed."

"Good. Our village can never have too many horses, and it's good to make trades with our new friends."

More horses and more strong friends. In Thorn Bird's mind, that was what his village needed in order to prosper again. It would be time to hunt the buffalo again soon, to fill the winter stores. With a new trade partner, they would need lots of goods to trade, and killing the buffalo was the best way to get them. He hoped that Shiny Teeth's men could bring them security so that they could hunt in safety, without concerns for protecting the village while they were away.

"Did you find Malone, *namunewapi*?"

"*Haa*. He has agreed to find the white-skin."

Half Weasel nodded and smiled at his leader. "The *taiboo* will not escape him. I am sure of it."

Thorn Bird thought about Malone and how his hunt for the *taiboo* was going. It was good to see his father's friend again and for him to be connected to his village in even this small way. Thorn Bird had great faith in the revered Nokoni's tracking skills. He was fully confident that Malone would find this Many Wolves hiding under a rock somewhere near the Rio Pecos.

After some time, the two men dropped down into a valley. The smoke from the village fires trickled into the sky and the horse herd speckled the surrounding plush, green grassland. Thorn Bird heard the young voices of a few of the pony-slaves playing together.

I am home.

Home

As Thorn Bird and Half Weasel entered the bevy of lodges, the villagers greeted them with forearm shakes, hugs, and smiles. Shiny Teeth and Eagle Eyes were both there to welcome them as well, but Thorn Bird did not see any of the other *mexicanos*.

"Half Weasel, can you take Snake to Mocking Bird? He will know what to do to make him well."

"*Haa, namunewapi*. It is good to have you home."

Thorn Bird nodded thanks and farewell to his scout.

Valencia was waiting at the lodge. Thorn Bird's eyes met hers, and he felt that familiar tingling in his loins. Her gorgeous long legs and long, straight black hair made the sensation even stronger. Her eyes guided him into her arms. She was emotional and tearful, but happy to see him.

"When the Nokoni war party came here looking for you, I thought I would never see you again, *mi amor*," she said in Spanish as a tear rolled down her cheek.

Although she was one of the strongest and toughest women in the village because of her size and temper, she had a weakness for him. She showed this vulnerability only to him, and he loved it just as much as he loved the fire in her spirit.

"I made a promise to my father that I had to honor. It is over now, and we have new *amigos* to help and protect us." Thorn Bird tilted his head up to kiss her on the forehead. "Where are the *chicos*?"

"They are riding with the pony-slaves. Cold Raven is teaching Pablonito how to ride like the *Noomah*." She smiled. "You know it pleases me when you use the Spanish words, *mi amor.*" Her voice was playful.

Thorn Bird and Valencia had one son together: Esatai, who had lived through five winters. Valencia's other child was Esatai's half-brother, the son of Laughing Crow. His name was Cold Raven, and he had lived through eight winters.

Thorn Bird laughed. "I am surprised I didn't hear Cold Raven shouting commands when I walked past the herd."

"He will be a good leader someday, *mi amor.*"

The tingling was growing in him. He wanted to be with her.

"Is it the time when you go to the bleeding lodge?" Thorn Bird knew it was best not to couple with women when they were bleeding.

"No. That time has passed." Her eyes bored into him meaningfully.

"Then I think we should be together in my lodge, *muy bonita*, before they get back."

"You do not want to wait for the cool breeze to come, and the darkness?"

"No, I do not want to wait *otro momento.*"

She smiled at him, a timid yet welcoming smile, and led him into their lodge.

After he had enjoyed pleasure with his wife, Thorn Bird slept. When he woke up later in the afternoon and found Valencia scraping a deer hide outside their lodge, she had a glow on her face.

"Did you sleep well?" she asked.

"*Haa,* I needed the rest."

Paco and Rodrigo walked up to him.

"*Señor* Alcaudón, *buenos tardes,*" said Paco, smiling, "and *buenos tardes* to you too, *señora* Valencia." Paco tipped the brim of his *sombrero* at Valencia.

"*Hola*, Paco," said Valencia.

"You know, *señor* Alcaudón, it has been a great pleasure for me to watch the skilled women of your village work. I have seen no finer hides and robes, *mi amigo*. The *gringo* LaFontaine will pay generously for these goods."

Thorn Bird remembered LaFontaine as the French trader who used to trade with his father long ago. He had not seen him since those days.

"A prosperous village needs women who work hard, just as much as it needs strong men who can fight," said Thorn Bird with conviction.

"Women who work hard and who are as lovely as your wife, Valencia, are a rare thing, *mi amigo*," said Paco, tipping his hat once more toward Valencia.

Thorn Bird laughed. "You should see how lovely she is when she is angry, Shiny Teeth. It is best to stay away from her fire!"

Paco laughed, and even Rodrigo chuckled.

"So, where are the rest of your *hombres*?" said Thorn Bird.

"They have returned to Santa Fe to trade the *magnifico* buffalo hides from your village. And Chico has run out of his mescal and wants to make more. He knows it will please *señor* Alcaudón!"

"You and Eagle Eyes did not need to go?"

"No, no, *señor*. It is good to be the *capitan*, eh?" Paco laughed. "Cardoza will lead them well in my absence. Your village is feeling more and more like a *casa* to us. Your people have made us feel most welcome."

"You are welcome to stay with us, Shiny Teeth. We will be moving soon to follow the buffalo herds," said Thorn Bird, feeling relaxed and a little groggy from his nap.

Paco shifted his feet. "*Señor* Alcaudón, I have a matter to discuss with you. It is *muy delicado*."

"What is it?" said Thorn Bird.

"One of my men has taken an interest in one of the *señoritas* in your *pueblo*. I told him I would talk to you about it."

"What kind of interest? Does he want her as his wife?" Thorn Bird was surprised by this request, but as he thought about it, he realized that there could be benefits to relationships between his women and the *mexicanos*. Before he would allow a marriage, however, he wanted to know that he could fully trust these men. Time spent in the village and on the battlefield would tell him this.

"No, *señor*. Nothing that permanent."

"As long as she is not claimed by one of my men and can still do her work, then it is fine by me."

"*Gracias, señor* Alcaudón. I will let him know when he returns." Paco bowed and then walked away with Rodrigo.

"Valencia, is there anything to eat?" said Thorn Bird, feeling suddenly hungry.

"We have corn and pemmican."

"Nothing from the hunt?"

"Crying Dog and Clouds In His Eyes are hunting now. They should be back before the sun falls," said Valencia, not stopping her scraping.

"If they come back with nothing, we will kill a horse. I want some fresh meat, and I'm sure our *mexicano* guests will want some too."

The smell of roasting horse meat permeated the village. Thorn Bird looked forward to the meal, and he knew most of the people in the village did too. Most of their meals were lean, but on days like today, the people would feast. The return of their leader was cause for celebration.

Thorn Bird and several of his men, along with the two *mexicanos*, were sitting around the fire pit in front of his lodge. With dusk deepening into darkness, the flames lit the faces of the men gathered there.

"Talks Too Much, I need you to make more arrows for me," said Thorn Bird.

"*Haa, namunewapi.* How many would you like? I can make them from reed or dogwood? The dogwood shafts are heavier—"

"I would like ten," Thorn Bird interrupted. "Your dogwood arrows work well for me."

"Do you want me to use dogwood branches from the Rio Rojo or the Rio Brazos? If you want Rio Rojo dogwood branches, I will need to collect some more, and it will take more time. The Rio Brazos dogwood branches I have are a little older but they should—"

"Just use what you have, Talks Too Much," Thorn Bird interrupted again. Talks Too Much's biggest fault was that he didn't know when to stop talking, but Thorn Bird, and the other men of the village, could find no fault in the weapons he made or in his skills as a warrior.

"*Haa, namunewapi*. I understand. I will start making them now." Talks Too Much stood and walked away.

"*Señor* Alcaudón, may I inspect your sword?" Paco asked.

"*Si*, Shiny Teeth. Let me get it." Thorn Bird got up and retrieved the sword in its sheath from his lodge. When he returned, he handed it to Paco. If Paco had asked to see the sword when Thorn Bird was alone and away from the village, he would have refused, but now that the count of men was in the Nokoni's favor, things were different.

Paco slowly removed the sword from its sheath and inspected it carefully. "It is a *capitan*'s sword. Spanish-made, of the highest quality. The sword maker's name is etched on the blade: 'Fernando de la Cruz of Toledo, Spain.' This is a rare *espada*, *señor* Alcaudón. Where did you get it?"

Thorn Bird looked at Half Weasel and spoke with *Noomah* words. "Shiny Teeth is asking me where I got my sword."

"You should tell him the story of how you counted coup. I would tell him, but I don't speak the Spanish words," said Half Weasel.

Thorn Bird recalled the story well.

"My men had discovered Spanish soldiers in the desolate lands east of Rio Pecos and Horsehead Crossing. The soldiers did not look healthy. I spotted the leader of the Spanish men, as well as his sword, which gleamed in the sunlight amid the dirt and dust. I knew I had to have it. So I approached the soldiers with my thirteen warriors, and the man with the sword—the *capitan*—rode up to greet us, backed by many soldiers. I offered to show them to water in exchange for the sword, but the *capitan* just laughed. I was insulted by his response. Later that day, aided by darkness, I snuck into their camp, killed two of the *hombres* who were guarding the *capitan*'s lodge, and then traded weapons with the *capitan*."

"He had a sudden change of heart, *señor* Alcaudón?" said Paco with an inquisitive look.

"No," said Thorn Bird. "I took the sword from the sleeping *capitan* and left my lance in his chest."

Paco looked at Thorn Bird with a spark in his eye. "Another gem of a story, *señor* Alcaudón! Cardoza and my men will want to hear it!" He re-sheathed the sword and handed it back to Thorn Bird. "It truly is an impressive *espada*."

Against a backdrop of darkness, the people filled their stomachs with horse meat until they could eat no more. There was singing and dancing around the fire. Some of the men smoked, including the *mexicanos* with their smoking sticks. The women talked among themselves. The hunters had not returned, and many of the villagers were worried, including Thorn Bird.

"*Namunewapi*, do you want me to look for them?" asked Half Weasel.

"It's too dark, Half Weasel. If they have not returned by sunrise, then I will send you and Fire Eyes out to look for them."

"I'm sure they are just lost and need the sun to find their way back," said Half Weasel with a hopeful tone.

Thorn Bird nodded and stared into the black night.

A Taste for Man Flesh

In the mid-afternoon of the following day, Half Weasel and Fire Eyes rode up to Thorn Bird's lodge.

"*Namunewapi!* Clouds In His Eyes and Crying Dog have been captured by the Wolf People!" said Half Weasel in a loud, excited voice.

"Where are they?" said Thorn Bird.

"Near the Valley of the Wildflowers. They are heading west from there."

"How many men in their band?"

"I counted twelve."

"Then we will need at least ten warriors, and I will see if the *mexicanos* can offer their help. We cannot spare more without leaving the village unprotected. Have the men prepare for war." Then Thorn Bird added, "And ask Mocking Bird to come. He doesn't need to fight, but we might need his power with words."

"*Haa, namunewapi.*" Half Weasel and Fire Eyes rode off to gather a war party.

Thorn Bird collected his weapons, shield, and war paint. "Cold Raven?"

His son emerged from the tipi. "*Haa, Ahpu?*"

"Snake is injured. Get my brown and white war horse for me."

"The one you haven't named yet, *Ahpu?*"

"I've only had it for a short time." Thorn Bird had recently traded for the horse with one of his men. It had not yet been tested in battle, and he wanted to see how it would react.

"*Haa, Ahpu,* I will get it." The boy ran off toward the herd to find his father's mount.

Thorn Bird walked over to the lodge where the *mexicanos* were staying. "Shiny Teeth, we are going to war with the Tonkawas. They have captured two of *mis hombres*. We need your help." His voice was grave.

Paco looked over at Rodrigo, who nodded and smiled.

"*Señor* Alcaudón, the Salazar brothers will be honored to ride with you. Pablonito will also come to help Rodrigo kill twice as many men."

"*Gracias,* Shiny Teeth. Meet at my lodge when you are ready."

"*Sí.*"

Thorn Bird walked back to his lodge, where Cold Raven was now waiting with his horse.

"*Ahpu,* are you going to war?" asked the boy, holding the horse's lead in his right hand.

"*Haa,* my son. The Tonkawas have taken Clouds In His Eyes and Crying Dog. We need to help them."

"Will you bring back more scalps for our lodge, *Ahpu?*"

"If the Wolf People want to fight, then we will take their scalps."

"Aren't the Tonkawas those tattooed men that eat people? That is what I've heard in stories," said Cold Raven, a mix of curiosity and fear in his voice.

"*Haa,* my son. The stories are true. They eat man flesh."

"*Namunewapi,* the Wolf People are camped with the Rio Brazos at their back," said Half Weasel. The scout, along with Fire Eyes, had ridden out ahead of the rest of Thorn Bird's men to discover the enemy's location.

Thorn Bird's war party of fourteen, including the three Salazars and Mocking Bird, waited behind a hill not far from the Rio Brazos, hidden from the enemy.

"Did you see Clouds In His Eyes and Crying Dog?"

"*Haa, namunewapi.* Sadly, they are dead. Their bodies are lying in the

Wolf People's camp, but they have not yet been butchered."

Thorn Bird growled through gritted teeth, "We are too late." *Too late to save them in his world. But we can help them for the next.*

"They are digging a cooking pit, and I don't think it's for cooking buffalo or deer," said Fire Eyes.

"I know, Fire Eyes."

Thorn Bird turned his horse to face his men. "Paint your faces. Paint your horses. Check your weapons. We will ride in before they butcher our friends and before the darkness comes."

The Nokoni leader then turned to Paco and spoke in Spanish words. "Shiny Teeth, the Tonkawa camp is just over this hill. We will ride on them when my warriors are ready. *Que pasa?*"

"Si, *señor* Alcaudón. We are ready when you are," said Paco, checking his two *pistoles* and his *escopeta, which was shorter and thicker than a rifle.*

"Alcaudón, I will find a good spot to shoot from while your men are preparing," said Rodrigo.

"Good, Eagle Eyes."

Thorn Bird blackened his eyes and painted his horse. He missed Snake and hoped that this horse would ride well into its first battle. He painted more handprints and markings on this horse than he normally had with Snake. *We will need this protection.*

When his men were ready, he lined them up and rode past them, looking for fear in their black faces; he found none.

"No Tonkawa escapes alive!" shouted Thorn Bird, enraged by the thought of the Tonkawas butchering the bodies of his men for their cooking pits.

He spun his horse around and galloped up the hill.

As they crested the hill, the Nokoni warriors and Paco, who rode on Thorn Bird's left, spread out and charged upon the unsuspecting Tonkawa. The Nokoni warriors loaded their bows and screamed their war cries. Thorn Bird heard the blast of Rodrigo's long gun and saw one of the Tonkawa warriors fall ahead of him. The Tonkawas shouted to each other and scrambled for their weapons.

Thorn Bird released his arrow first, but it fell short. He quickly loaded another without slowing his mount. Another *rifle* shot rang from behind him, and another Tonkawa fell. Thorn Bird's second arrow whistled into an enemy's chest, knocking him down. The twangs of his men's bows sliced the air and two more Tonkawas fell. His shield caught an enemy arrow, and Thorn Bird quickly returned one of his own at the man who had shot it, cutting into his target's neck.

Thorn Bird saw a Tonkawa shoot his bow and a Nokoni fall to his right. Paco's *pistole* blasted smoke into the air, knocking this Tonkawa down. But Thorn Bird's horse screamed and bucked in response to the loud explosion, throwing him hard onto the ground. The frightened horse scurried away, leaving the bruised Nokoni leader to fight on foot.

The Nokoni horsemen and Paco charged into the camp and killed several more Tonkawas at close range. Thorn Bird sprinted after them, but by the time he arrived, the battle was over. Fire Eyes and Half Weasel were running through the enemy camp, separating the injured survivors from their weapons, while other Nokonis dealt finishing blows with their lances or tomahawks.

The dust and smoke were just beginning to settle when a flurry of hooves took off from Thorn Bird's left. A Tonkawa rider was trying to escape.

A blast from Rodrigo's rifle lifted the man from his horse.

Thorn Bird looked around. "Are any of our men hurt?"

"Talks Too Much was hit, but he will survive. Mocking Bird is taking care of him," said Half Weasel.

"Bring their survivors to me," said Thorn Bird.

Two of the Wolf People were still alive—both of them injured. The Nokonis dragged the men to Thorn Bird, their hands tied behind their backs, and forced them to their knees. Both of the captives were bare-chested, wearing only breechcloths, and their bodies were tattooed all over in black. Their hair was short with tufted scalp-locks.

The Nokoni leader looked each of them in the eyes. The older one—an experienced warrior, Thorn Bird guessed, judging by his elaborate tattoos—had one arm wounded by one of the *mexicanos'* weapons.

The younger Tonkawa was bleeding profusely from a chest wound and was barely able to stay up on his knees.

Thorn Bird stood in front of the younger man and reached for the knife in his leg sheath. "You died bravely," he said. Then he sliced the man's throat and kicked his body to the ground. "Take him away."

Thorn Bird called Mocking Bird over to speak the Tonkawa tongue for him. He wanted to be sure the surviving warrior understood his words.

The Nokoni headman looked at the older Tonkawa. "You filthy buzzard. Your appetite for human flesh makes me vomit! I do not understand how a man can do this to another man!" Thorn Bird pointed to his men's dead bodies, lying next to the Tonkawa cooking fire.

"Did you think we would lie down like tired dogs after you hung our brothers by stakes and left their eyes for the scavenger birds? Huh, Comanche dog?" barked the Tonkawa. He spat at Thorn Bird. "The flesh of a human makes us strong! It is the way of the Wolf People. We are not afraid to die, Comanche dog! We will feast on Comanche flesh in the next world. It is Comanche flesh that makes us stronger!" Mocking Bird translated the words as the man spoke. The Tonkawa's eyes were filled with hatred; he was unafraid.

The Nokoni leader bent down, lowered his knife to his captive's throat, and leaned in close to his face. "How much stronger will you be with Tonkawa flesh in your stomach?"

Thorn Bird retracted his knife and stood up, still glaring into the eyes of his defiant captive. "I have a special torture for you, filthy man-eater. I will cut off your fingers, one at a time, and feed them to you." Thorn Bird paused, then continued, "When you are hungry again, I'll cut off your leg, cook it in your fire, and cut pieces of it to shove in your mouth. Would you like the taste of your own flesh?"

The Tonkawa warrior was uncowed. "Do what you want, Comanche dog! You can't force me to eat anything! I will wait for you in the afterlife!"

"If you won't eat your fingers, man-eater, then I'll cut off your hand and feed it to you. If you refuse to eat that, then I'll offer you your arm or your leg. If you refuse to eat any of it, then I'll drop your limbless body on a blanket of burning coals and watch you roast to death!" Thorn Bird found it impossible to control his anger.

He turned to Half Weasel. "Untie his hands, I am ready to take the bravery from his eyes."

Mexicano Warriors

The victorious Nokonis rode away from the Tonkawa camp the following morning, leaving the stench of burning human flesh behind them, though it still lingered in the mind of their leader. Scalps were taken and stashed in pouches or tied to lances, to be displayed when they arrived in the village. The two dead Nokonis were wrapped in blankets and tied to two of the eight horses that were taken from the Wolf People.

"Talks Too Much, how is your arm doing?" asked Mocking Bird.

"It burns like fire," said the normally talkative warrior.

"If that's all you can say, then it must be painful!" said Half Weasel, laughing. He turned to the other men. "We have finally found a way to silence Talks Too Much. It's called pain!"

"I'll have to remember that," added Thorn Bird, laughing with the others.

Talks Too Much couldn't help but laugh along with them.

Thorn Bird was pleased with the outcome of the raid. Torturing the Tonkawa warrior had been good medicine for his mind. Now, however, he did not look forward to burying two of his men when they returned to the village. The victory was stained by this loss. At least, he reassured himself, the two bodies they were carrying back home had not been cut up by the Wolf People. There would be some peace in his mind, and in the minds of the men's families, to know that their afterlives had not been blemished.

The *mexicanos* rode up to meet them. They had departed earlier, not wanting to watch the torture, especially with Pablonito with them.

Thorn Bird and his men slowed their horses to a walk.

"The stench of death carries far on the *viento, señor* Alcaudón," said Paco with a disgusted look on his face. "I do not have the stomach for this kind of death, or for your torture."

"Is this true for most *mexicanos*, Shiny Teeth?" asked Thorn Bird. He had lived with death and torture his whole life. It was the way of his people.

"*Si.* Most *mexicanos* believe that torture will come to those who deserve the afterlife that we call hell. It is *el diablo* himself who is the torturer, and it lasts an *eternidad.*"

"But you trust this *diablo,* whom you never have seen, to do your torture? How do you know that this enemy won't be waiting to slit your throat when you reach the next world?" The strange beliefs of the *mexicanos* made no sense to Thorn Bird. He believed there were good and bad spirits, but that the bad spirits could not be depended on to punish his enemies.

Paco laughed. "I believe, *mi amigo,* that I will end up in a different place than my *enemigos.* A place where there is no killing." Then he made a motion with his right hand, the same motion that the Spanish men in the black robes always made.

"Your talk reminds me of a talk my father had with a Spanish man once. This man said the same thing about the afterlife." Thorn Bird smiled, remembering his father's talk with the man named Ferdinand. "I will say this, Shiny Teeth: if I am captured, I hope it will be by *mexicanos* and not *indios!*"

"Ah, *señor* Alcaudón, your death will surely be quick in *mexicano* hands—by a squad of *mosquetos* or hanged by a rope, would be my guess. The *mexicanos* will leave the torturing to *el diablo.*"

"If in the next world I have my arms, my legs, my weapons, and my horse, I will be ready to face this *diablo,*" said Thorn Bird, unafraid of any *mexicano* god.

"Your horse and weapons are useless, *señor* Alcaudón, against the fires of hell. But this is the afterlife we believe, and you can believe what you want. I am not like the Spanish *padres, señor,* who force their religion on others."

"That is good, Shiny Teeth. You have seen how many enemies the Spanish have made because they believe all people should worship their gods. A man's beliefs are his own, his family's, his village's. A stranger has no say in this."

"Though our religions are very different, *señor* Alcaudón, we both agree a man's religion is chosen by the man."

"I have enjoyed this talk, Shiny Teeth, but your gods and my spirits will not get us home any quicker unless we ride," said Thorn Bird with a smile. He urged his horse into a trot.

"*Si, señor* Alcaudón," replied Paco, flashing his big, shiny teeth.

The men rode over rolling plains of tall grass, marked by large spreads of purple, yellow, and orange wildflowers. A gathering of large thunderclouds floated above them, blocking out the sun. The rain would come soon, Thorn Bird thought.

"Are we going to kill the rest of their village?" said Half Weasel, riding at Thorn Bird's side.

"Tonkawas live in small bands, and they have lost most of their fighting men. Let them fester in their weakness," snarled Thorn Bird. "They are a bone to be picked by the first predator that finds them. It could be us, or one of the other *Noomah* bands. I am certain that the scavenger birds will soon feast on the eyes of their women and children."

After some time, the men stopped at a creek to rest their horses and drink. While Thorn Bird was drinking from his water pouch next to the flowing water, Rodrigo and Paco walked over to him.

"How is your *caballo*, Alcaudón?" asked Rodrigo.

"He is fine now, but the blast of Shiny Teeth's *pistole* caught him by surprise. That was the first time he had heard such a sound like that so close to him," said Thorn Bird. Fire Eyes had found his mount wandering far south along the Rio Brazos after the fight was over. "That is also the first time that I have fought with a boom stick on my side."

Mocking Bird translated the conversation for Half Weasel and Fire Eyes.

"I have never seen you thrown from a horse, *namunewapi*," said Half

Weasel. "No man or bear could do what this unnamed horse did." The scout smiled. "You should name him Throws Rider Like a Stone. Or perhaps Scared Rabbit."

Thorn Bird laughed, though inwardly he was a little embarrassed by the incident. "I like the name 'Scared Rabbit.' Trust me, Half Weasel, I will train the fear out of this horse so it won't happen again. I will need to borrow Shiny Teeth's weapon for this task."

"How many did you kill, Shiny Teeth?" said Thorn Bird, turning to Paco.

"*Dos.*"

"And you, Eagle Eyes?"

"*Quatro.*"

"It's good to have men like you to ride with us."

"I'm sure you would have killed more, *señor* Alcaudón, if your horse had not panicked," said Paco. "We have seen what you can do."

"Shiny Teeth and Eagle Eyes, you did not accept the scalps you earned, but I will make a scalp pole for each of you and hang it by your lodge when we return to the village. You can join us in the scalp dance and the people of the village will respect and honor you as warriors," said Thorn Bird graciously.

"*Gracias, señor* Alcaudón," said Paco. "We would be honored to have a scalp pole. But I don't think you want to see Paco dance!" He laughed.

"You can dance a *mexicano* dance, Shiny Teeth. We have plenty of *mexicano* blood in our village; it may be familiar to some of my people."

"It is this mixing of blood that makes us better friends," added Paco.

Thorn Bird could not help but agree with the *mexicano* leader.

Hooves in the Forest

Many Wolves continued to move west each day, following the call of Fiera's favorite prey, quail. As long as he found new water sources, there was no reason in his mind to stay at one camp. He wanted to find quail that had never before heard the footsteps of a man. He had grown to respect them as prey; these stumpy little ground-dwelling birds had many tricks. The more he hunted them, the smarter they became.

He had also discovered some tricks of his own. Many Wolves learned to imitate quail calls and used them to lure birds out of the hidden brush. When it worked, he always tried to get Rojo and Fiera into the best position for a kill. Each of the members of his pack had a role: Many Wolves found the quail, Rojo flushed them out, and Fiera chased and killed them.

Fiera's part was the hardest and most strenuous, because on most hunts, she ended up chasing the quail a long way before her swift quarry dove down into cover. Sometimes these little bluish birds escaped by running down a rabbit burrow or into thick, spiny brush full of stickers. Just two more tricks in their feathery medicine bag. At other times Fiera would be exhausted after a long pursuit, which ended the hunt for that morning or evening. It was always much too hot to hunt in the middle of the day.

Many Wolves rode back to camp on one of those days when the quail had won the game and his hunting bag was empty. Rojo and Fiera were following in their usual manner, when Rojo suddenly stopped and growled.

Many Wolves stopped his horse and looked to see what had alerted his companion.

The red wolf was focused on a distant stand of pine and juniper trees. He maintained a low growl as his ears searched for more sounds. His hackles raised, the wolf moved a little closer to the trees without straying too far from his pack, his protective instincts at play. *Was it a bear or a large cat?*

Rojo only reacted like this when it was a large predator. Many Wolves knew that the wolf's growl was a warning to find another path away from the danger.

The rider looked into the trees trying to find an animal, a movement, anything, but there was nothing. But now it wasn't just Rojo who was agitated: Elk Dog was snorting and stomping his hooves nervously, and Fiera flew to the safety of the trees. Seeking a feeling of security and comfort, Many Wolves reached back to touch the quiver that was strapped to his back.

Many Wolves urged Elk Dog to a walk in a path away from the potential danger, but still in the direction of their camp. The wolf's aggressive posture subsided, but he remained vigilant and continued to watch the same spot in the trees, keeping himself positioned between the danger and his pack.

Then the alerted wolf growled again, and this time Many Wolves heard a sound as well. It was the footsteps of a large animal. He saw a flash of white in the trees. The footsteps were those of hooves. *A horse. Ten Arrows?* The beating hooves disappeared deeper into the forest, away from them.

"Ten Arrows? Is that you, Ten Arrows?" Many Wolves called. He wasn't expecting to see his friend until the coming winter—after his people, the Penateka, had hunted enough buffalo to replenish their winter reserves. Though for some reason Ten Arrows hadn't visited last winter, as he had each of the previous seven. Many Wolves wondered if he would ever see his good friend again.

There was no response to his call, and Rojo's growling was once again quelled. Whatever it was—or whoever it was—was now gone. He was sure it wasn't Ten Arrows. His friend's arrival was never silent or secretive. Ten Arrows usually shouted a greeting from across the plains.

All Many Wolves knew was that he was being watched by a man on a horse. And it wasn't Ten Arrows.

Prey

Many Wolves shot a jackrabbit close to his camp just as the sun was fading away. Because of the stranger on the horse, he was nervous about wandering far from his fire pit. As he sat roasting a chunk of the rabbit carcass, he revisited everything he'd seen over and over in his mind, hoping to somehow extract more detail or something he had missed. He was convinced it had been a man on a horse, but now he questioned who, and why they were here. Perhaps they were simply traveling through and did not want to be seen by him, he thought. Was it truly a stranger? Or could it be someone who knew him? Was it a friend of Ten Arrows? *Was it a Nokoni scout?*

Rojo was calm now, feasting on a hunk of raw rabbit meat. Many Wolves knew that he could always trust his wolf to warn him if danger was near. To the red wolf it was as if nothing happened. Many Wolves wished he could be as calm as his companion.

Fiera seemed content as well. She sat with one foot up on a low branch near their camp, having eaten a healthy portion of the rabbit, enough to last her until the next morning. She usually slept on a branch in the middle of a large pine tree—often it was hard to find her because she blended so well with her surroundings—but tonight she was lower. She rarely even moved after darkness came, perhaps because of an innate fear of night predators. Some large hoot owls were common in this area.

But for now, there was peacefulness. After his meal, Many Wolves wrapped himself up in his buffalo robe and looked up at the star-filled sky. Rojo lay next to him and Many Wolves stroked his coarse fur, especially in Rojo's favorite spots: behind the ears, along the back, and on the top of his rump. When Many Wolves stopped the petting, Rojo nudged his hand for more. It was their nightly ritual.

He spoke to the Great Spirit and asked only that tomorrow could start like today: with just his family—his wolf, his horse, his bird—alone in the wilderness, alone with the wild things.

When Many Wolves awoke the next day at sunrise, the worries of the previous day thumped him in the head like a stone. As he sat in his sleeping robe, he thought to himself that if this stranger was following him or meant him harm, then why hadn't anything happened yet? This morning seemed as peaceful as the night before, and the day seemed ordinary: Rojo stretching his legs, Fiera preening her feathers, Elk Dog munching on grass and bark. These things were reassuring to Many Wolves.

He called Fiera down to his fist-perch and fed her a piece of soaked rabbit meat. Then he stroked her feet and breast and inspected her condition. Her breast was drawn in, which meant she was hungry—a good state of mind for hunting. "Today you will get a kill, *Nami*. I can feel it."

Many Wolves relieved his bladder, then drank some water from the creek. He put some extra arrows in his quiver and slung it over his shoulder. His bow was packed in the quiver as well. He didn't need it when he was hunting with Fiera, only when he was killing rabbits or squirrels with Rojo. *Just a normal day.*

He rode out on Elk Dog with Rojo and Fiera following. They would be hunting the same area where they had hunted yesterday, an area close to camp. There were plenty of quail here, but he knew they would just be a little smarter today. As they traveled, he began his mock quail calls to see if he could get a response, and thereby pinpoint the location of a covey.

The pack ventured deeper into the brushland and farther away from the tree line. Fiera followed, using any large bush or small tree as a perch. She was constantly on the lookout for her enemies: eagles and larger hawks mostly. Even a red-tailed hawk circling like a speck in the clouds caught her attention. From his flights with Chiquito, Many Wolves knew how powerful her vision was.

Many Wolves stopped Elk Dog to watch Fiera. She was bobbing her head up and down and staring into the brush ahead, excited about something she'd seen. He knew this was her signal that she had found something.

Then, like a tightly drawn arrow, Fiera blasted herself at a large clump of vegetation and disappeared inside. Many Wolves rode up slowly for a closer look. He watched as Fiera jumped in and out of the thick brush, trying to get at the quail inside. The distress call of the blue quail was by now as familiar to Many Wolves as the melodic call of a meadowlark or the cry of a red-tailed hawk.

The action brought a smile to Many Wolves's face—especially watching Fiera scramble on the ground more like a running bird or a prairie chicken than any bird of prey. It was not a game to her, though, as she was desperate to get her claws on one of those birds. The site of frightened prey got her blood flowing, thought Many Wolves.

At last, one of the quail dashed from cover and the aerial chase began.

Many Wolves broke Elk Dog into a trot and followed the rangy struggle. He hoped Fiera was up for the quail's tricks this time, because she needed the kill. The dodging and swerving of both birds was amazing. They commanded the air and mastered the winds.

Finally, Many Wolves saw both birds drop into the bushes and disappear. He was relieved to hear the quail's death call, a sound they only made when in a predator's grasp. He raced over to the spot and dismounted, then moved in slowly, low to the ground like a stalking cat, toward Fiera.

He found her in complete control; there seemed to be little fight left in the quail. Eventually, she squeezed the life out of it and began her plucking ritual. He reached his hand in and sliced open the dead quail's chest, exposing the juicy insides for her. She dug in voraciously, and soon her face was covered in blood.

The moment was stolen by Rojo's sudden growling.

Many Wolves stood, looked around—and saw his fears confirmed. Staring at him from a distance was a man sitting on a painted horse. It looked a bit like Ten Arrows, but it wasn't his friend. He was sure of that; Ten Arrows would have greeted him. By this man's straight long black hair and the way he wore his scalp-lock feathers, he looked like a Northerner. His horse was even decorated like a Northerner's horse, with feathers and war paint.

The Northerner made no move to approach; he just watched Thorn Bird from a distance. He had a bow in his hand, but his arrows remained in his quiver. His only clothing was a breechcloth. Man and horse stared at him like they were frozen in ice.

Many Wolves didn't like being watched. It made him feel like prey.

He pulled the bow from his quiver and mounted Elk Dog. Rojo was positioned protectively between him and the Northerner, his hackles fully exposed, and he was growling louder than yesterday. *I still don't know if he's a friend or enemy. But if he intended to kill me, would he not have attacked by now?*

His bow was not yet drawn, but it felt good in Many Wolves's hands. It was a source of comfort to him. He directed Elk Dog to move forward slowly toward the stranger, to see what the man would do. He wanted to get close enough to speak, or at least yell, to the man.

As he and Elk Dog moved forward, Rojo stayed ahead of them, never losing sight of the stranger. Many Wolves felt certain that this Northerner could not approach them without feeling the full force of Rojo's attack.

But as they moved toward the Northerner, he backed away. Like a wary coyote, the strange man knew what he wanted his safe distance to be.

Many Wolves continued moving slowly toward the retreating Northerner, feeling bolder and more confident with every step. "Who are you? What do you want?" he yelled in the Northerner language.

The Northerner didn't speak. He moved away, preserving that safe distance he seemed to want. His eyes just kept watching, burning into Many Wolves. And despite his blossoming confidence, Many Wolves couldn't escape one thought. *I am prey.*

Then suddenly, the silent stranger roused his horse into a full gallop— and was gone.

Burning Eyes

Rojo did not growl the rest of that day or into the night, but it was hard for Many Wolves to find sleep. He just stared at the sky and let his mind try to figure things out. It was like trying to tie sinew between the stars and make them into a familiar, pleasant picture. He wished that Ten Arrows was here, because his friend would know what to do.

This strange encounter had shed an even greater light on how valuable Rojo was as a friend and protector of their pack. Like the spines on a porcupine, Rojo was the barrier that kept enemies from gorging on the softer insides. This wolf had killed great warriors: Silent Weasel and Laughing Crow. For all that Many Wolves knew, Rojo's stories were as widely know on the Llano Estacado as Laughing Crow's were. It was for these reasons that Many Wolves's fears did not completely gnaw away his sanity.

He was not afraid of this one man, but he *was* fearful of the possibilities. *Are there more of them or is this man alone? Will he return to his village with a scout's report?* One thing that Many Wolves did know was that this Northerner was not looking for his friendship.

Many Wolves also wondered how much this man knew about him. *He knows my pack. He knows where I hunt. He knows where I sleep.* Many Wolves felt as though he was wrestling against a much bigger and stronger man, who knew all his moves. *I want to know where he sleeps.*

If Chiquito were still alive, his bird's powerful eyes would enable him to find anything. Fiera had powerful eyes too, but could he take a mind-journey with her? She was barely tamed. He remembered how Rojo had rejected him when he'd spirit-walked with the wolf the first time. He supposed that taking a mind-journey with Rojo was a possibility, but the wolf's senses were limited compared to those of a hawk, and more importantly, he could not travel nearly as quickly. Many Wolves did not have four or five sleeps to find this man's camp; he needed to know now. That made Fiera the clear choice.

He stared into the night sky and tried to draw a picture of a hawk using the stars and imaginary sinew, but before he finished it, he was asleep.

Many Wolves woke the next morning and immediately built a small fire. Then he mixed a small amount of peyote and some petal fragments from the white lion's paw flower into the water in his drinking-shell, and he placed the mixture on the fire.

Fiera was awake, watching him, waiting for that first meaty morsel.

"I know what you want, little beggar, but I want you to wait. Your hunger will help you to listen."

He had spirit-walked with Chiquito many times, and as a result he had figured out precisely how much peyote and lion's paw flower he needed to get the desired mind-journey. Some of their flights were longer than others, but they were always exhilarating. He believed these mind-journeys strengthened the already strong friendship he had with Chiquito; he hoped that seeing the world through Fiera's burning yellow eyes would strengthen their friendship as well.

When the mixture was ready, he called Fiera to his fist-perch for a small reward and then drank down the mind-journey tea, swallowing it as quickly as he could to avoid the bitter taste. He closed his eyes and let the unpleasant nauseating feeling creep into his stomach. Bright colors flashed in his mind.

Many Wolves stroked Fiera's breast until a blurred picture faded into his mind. The trees around his camp came into focus—and then he was seeing the world through the bird's eyes. Distant objects became incredibly clear; they looked almost touchable even from where he was. A part of him had wondered if the world would be yellow through the eyes of his bird-killer, but it wasn't.

He was ready to fly.

Up!

The command in his thoughts launched them both upward into the air. They quickly leveled off at a height that was roughly half as high as the tops of the trees. The bird's speed was impressive, and they dodged branches and tree trunks with frightening precision. It felt like they would crash at any moment, but always, at the last heartbeat, she would turn or dive or rise to avoid contact, to avoid death. It was dizzying. Many Wolves's mind could not react quickly enough to what he was seeing. He felt helplessly out of control.

Up! Up! Up! He pleaded for more height, for open air above the treetops.

They climbed up, still dodging branches, until at last they were free of the forest.

Flying in open sky was relaxing, familiar to him, from Chiquito's flights. He looked all around. *There! Go there!* He spotted a distinctive patch of bushes that was close to where he had seen the Northerner.

Like Chiquito, Fiera's eyes instinctively found movement: a running rabbit, a flying sparrow, a soaring hawk. And once her eyes were fixed on something, it was difficult to lure her attention away from it. "Leave it," he thought, over and over again, straining to get her to look forward into the distance where he wanted to look.

At last Many Wolves spotted a small plume of smoke in the distance, crawling out of the trees like some strange skyward snake. *The Northerner's camp! Go there!*

The bird steered them toward the new target. They weren't flying as high as he remembered going with Chiquito—just barely above the tallest trees.

Then Fiera's eyes spotted a red-tailed hawk above and ahead of them. She watched it only for a moment before diving down toward the trees, away from the predator.

Go to the smoke, Fiera!

She ignored his command. Again they were dodging branches at a horrific speed, and Many Wolves was feeling dizzy again.

Up, Fiera, up!

She did not fly up. She stayed level, dashing past one tree after another. Their minds—man's and bird's—were at war. She was fighting his thoughts, resisting his commands. The dizziness was making him light-headed, nauseated; the world was blurring around him. It moved faster and faster and faster—and then there was darkness.

Many Wolves opened his eyes at his camp and vomited. Not just once, but several times. The world was clear again, seen through his own human eyes. He still felt queasy, but at least the vomiting stopped, and his disoriented mind slowly came back into focus. Rojo and Elk Dog were there, but his wild little bird-killer was not.

A Missing Scent

Many Wolves waited until the middle of the morning for Fiera to return, but there was no sign of her. A part of him was worried that she was gone forever. She was not as dependent on him as his wolf hawks had been when they were young. Not only had the young bird-killer mastered hunting more quickly than his other birds had, she was strong-willed and lacked the same strength of desire to please him that the wolf hawks had displayed. When he was with Fiera on the mind-journey, it had felt like two minds, not one, and the desires of one were opposite those of the other—there was a conflict there that he had never felt with Chiquito.

Was I too reckless to try the mind-journey with her so soon?

The one positive that had come from their flight together was that now he knew where the Northerner's camp was. Not the exact location, but it was a place he knew he could find again easily. It wasn't safe to go there in the daylight, but he could scout it by night. *Or at least, Rojo can.* It was too dark to see at night with human eyes, especially with only a darkened sliver of a moon, but not Rojo's eyes—and the darkness had no effect on a wolf's nose and ears. Rojo could find out if the man was alone.

"Rojo, let's go scare up some rabbit." Many Wolves filled his water pouch and packed his quiver. He found a piece of rabbit skin from the previous day's kill and waved it in front of Rojo's nose. "Find me one of these, Rojo." This was his ritual when he needed Rojo to track for him: to wave anything with the desired prey's scent in front of the wolf's nose right before the hunt.

He looked around the area once more, but he saw no bird-killers, just a woodpecker pecking away at a rotting old pine. "I bet you feel safer now that Fiera is gone." He laughed to himself.

Usually, when he and Rojo hunted alone, he left Elk Dog at the camp, but Northerners were expert horse thieves, and from what Ten Arrows had once said, the first step in their plan of attack was often to steal the enemy's horses. So Elk Dog would need Rojo's protection too, every moment of the day.

Many Wolves rode out in a different direction this time, heading east. Rojo trotted out ahead, his nose sniffing the ground, looking for prey scents. The wolf was trained to stop when he spotted a rabbit, then wait for his master's signal to flush it. But without a pair of talented claws like Chiquito's around, there was no sense in flushing rabbits. Better to kill the rabbit before the flush.

While Rojo's nose hunted for scents, Many Wolves scoured the ground for fresh rabbit scat and tracks. Still, most times he relied on spotting rabbits outright. Scat and tracks told him that rabbits were in the area, but it was his eyes and Rojo's nose that usually found them.

Many Wolves watched the surrounding countryside with sharp, suspicious eyes. He wasn't afraid of seeing the Northerner; he just wanted to know if the stranger was still watching him.

Now that Fiera was gone, Many Wolves could ride away from this place if he wanted, get away from those prying eyes. There was no rope tying him here anymore. Then he thought to himself: *What if he follows me?* He had spent most of his life running and hiding, and he was tired of it.

A moment later, Rojo accidentally flushed a jackrabbit before he could stop himself. The rabbit sprinted away, weaving around bushes, and disappeared out of sight. This rabbit was one of the smart ones, the survivors who lived a long life and produced many babies. Many Wolves was looking for one that wasn't so clever.

The next time Rojo spotted a rabbit, he froze in time. Many Wolves searched the ground ahead of the wolf, and spotted it too. The jackrabbit sat just a few horse lengths farther on, its body hunkered up against a small bush.

Many Wolves dismounted as slowly and carefully as he could, then nocked an arrow. The twang of his bow and whistle of his arrow ended with the rabbit's scream. Many Wolves ran over to the suffering animal and snapped its neck, thanking the Great Spirit.

"Let's head back to camp, Rojo." He petted the wolf's forehead and ears.

When the dark night arrived, there was still no sign of Fiera. Only a piece of the moon floated in the starry sky, as if a large beast had taken a bite out of it.

Many Wolves lit a small fire for light and warmth. He wasn't afraid to signal his presence. *The Northerner knows I am here, and Rojo will protect me.* He kept his bow and arrows within reach.

Nighthawks buzzed around the sky, hunting for insects. Many Wolves knew what they were hunting because he had cut open a dead nighthawk once and had found plenty of the insects in its stomach. Nighthawks and bats made sure that no small, flying creatures felt safe at night.

Rojo's growl spoiled the rhythm of the crickets and the crackling fire. Many Wolves instantly reached for his bow. His knife was only a heartbeat away in his leg sheath. His heart pounded with the force of a war drum against his chest as he looked into the darkness; but he saw nothing and heard nothing. The wolf growled a little longer, then stopped. After a while, Many Wolves relaxed as well.

Some time later, Rojo walked out into the darkness. This was not uncommon for him. Sometimes the howl of a coyote or wolf stirred him up, or he went out to investigate a sound he heard, like a raccoon or a possum. *Don't roam too far, Rojo. I need your protection.*

To Many Wolves's relief, Rojo returned to camp soon after. The wolf lay down next to him, awaiting his master's nightly affection. He was licking his mouth clean.

"You must have found something to eat; probably a leftover kill," said Many Wolves.

Wolves, like dogs, would scavenge almost anything.

Only half of his sleep time had passed, but Many Wolves was wide awake. He balanced the drinking-shell with his mind-journey medicine against a couple of rocks in the low-burning flames and waited. Rojo was relaxing at his side, half asleep, except for those ears, which never rested.

"Rojo, we need to take a little journey to the Northerner's camp. I need to know more about him," Many Wolves said in a muted voice. He hadn't spirit-walked with Rojo in a long time, but when they did, the wolf was always responsive. The rope of trust that tied their spirits together was strong, unbreakable.

Yet he had never used the mind-journey medicine more than once between sleeps before.

Many Wolves gulped down the heated medicine and felt its discomforting magic settle in his stomach. He closed his eyes and stroked his wolf's thick fur. When his senses reawakened, it was with a heightened acuity. The smells and sounds were overwhelmingly potent. His vision cut away much of the darkness, and the world appeared to him with a greenish tint.

Rojo, let's go. We have a long journey. I need you to run.

The wolf sluggishly stood up and stretched his legs. He emptied his bladder on a nearby tree, and then they started to run. They moved quickly through the tall grass and bushes. Many Wolves guided the wolf to the correct heading. They captured the scents of animals they passed, as well as traces of other animals whose earlier passing still lingered in the air. The sounds of the night floated past them.

The big wolf ran on padded feet. The cool air blasted them in the face and the landscape blurred. The steady rustle of Rojo's footsteps was paced by his labored breathing. *Keep going straight on this path, Rojo. Stop if you need to rest.* The wolf did not stop. His breathing was heavy, but the speed of his steps did not diminish. They continued dashing through the glowing countryside.

Many Wolves spotted a lone juniper on a hill. It was a familiar landmark that he remembered from Fiera's flight. Beyond it was a clump of trees, the source of the smoke trail. *We are close. Rojo, stop at that tree on the hill.*

Rojo was tired when they stopped. The mist from his panting breath clouded their vision.

The Northerner's camp was hidden by the trees, but the smells of the camp floated into their senses: a horse, a smoldering fire, cooked meat, and the lingering smell of a man. Many Wolves heard the horse snorting and the popping sound of a fire, but nothing else from the camp.

Rojo, let's move closer to the trees. Slowly. The wolf stalked closer to the trees. The faint glow of a small fire was the first thing they saw.

Then the sure-footed wolf stumbled. *What happened?*

Rojo recovered and moved closer—and again, he stumbled. Now Many Wolves noticed other strange changes in the wolf: his eyes watered and closed slightly. His breathing was still heavy. *What's wrong Rojo? Are you tired?*

They stumbled closer and saw a brown and white horse nervously looking in their direction. Many Wolves saw the fire pit now; a sleeping robe and some cooking tools lay on the ground.

Rojo lay down in the grass. His eyes were half-closed now and his vision was blurred.

Rojo, what's wrong? What's happening to you?

Then a thought pierced his mind. There was a scent missing.

Where is the man? Why isn't the Northerner here?

He yelled, panicked, "Where is the Northerner?"

"I'm right here," came a strange voice from behind him.

Many Wolves opened his eyes and felt the blade of a knife at his throat.

Captured

"Who are you? What do you want?"

Many Wolves felt his heart racing in his chest. The knife blade was so close to his throat that he had to force himself to be still, though he felt his hands shaking and his body trembling despite his wishes. The human smell of the man washed over him, as offensive as the pungent aroma of a decaying animal.

"Stay still," the man said with Northerner words. "Slowly lay down on your stomach and put your hands behind your back. Any quick movements and this blade will cut you. No words, just listen."

Many Wolves obeyed. *He does not want to kill me.*

Once his hands were behind his back, he felt the leather straps rub against his hands and arms, coiling around his wrists like a snake suffocating its prey. He felt the man's breath, and felt the man's hair brush against his arms and back.

"Stand up," ordered the Northerner.

Many Wolves stood up slowly, the knife blade at his throat again.

"Call your horse."

Many Wolves whistled, and Elk Dog walked over to him hesitantly.

"Get on the horse."

"I can't with my hands tied."

"I'll push you up. Get up against the horse."

Many Wolves leaned against Elk Dog with his body, and the bare-chested Northerner pushed Many Wolves's right leg over to the other side. Then, using a long leather thong, his captor tied Many Wolves's ankles together. The strip of leather stretched underneath Elk Dog and dangled loosely between his feet. Many Wolves tested the strength of his bindings, but that only hurt him more.

The Northerner grabbed Elk Dog's lead and tied another piece of rope to it to make it longer. Then he led Elk Dog over to Many Wolves's supplies. He picked up his water pouch and all the small bags of food and medicine, and he placed them in one of the larger hunting bags. Then he gathered all the arrows from the ground and put them and Many Wolves's bow in the quiver. He slung it around his shoulder next to the quiver that was already there.

The warrior then led Many Wolves and Elk Dog into the darkness, heading east toward his camp. He whistled loudly into the quiet night air, and Many Wolves heard distant hooves. Soon, a gorgeous black and white pinto emerged from the darkness. The man stroked the horse gently on the nose and the side of the head, whispering words of affection. He tied Elk Dog's lead and the large hunting bag to the back of the horse, then he mounted.

"Are you taking me to your camp? Where the brown and white horse is?"

"*Haa*," said the man. Then he stopped his horse and looked back at Many Wolves. "How did you know I had a brown and white horse? Did you see me ride him?"

"*Haa*," Many Wolves lied. He did not want to explain how he knew about the man's other horse. It was best to leave some words unspoken.

The man urged his horse forward again. They walked for a long time toward the camp, toward Rojo.

"Who are you?" Many Wolves finally asked.

"Malone."

That name was familiar. "You're from Laughing Crow's village?"

"I was."

"Is that where you're taking me?"

"*Haa.*"

"But Laughing Crow is dead, and most of his men are, too."

"Not all of them." Malone's responses were curt and emotionless. "Thorn Bird is still alive."

Many Wolves remembered that Laughing Crow had had a son named Thorn Bird. Many Wolves had seen him once when Laughing Crow held him captive. He remembered that Thorn Bird had been just as frightening as his father.

A helpless feeling swelled in his stomach. He didn't want to think about what was going to happen to him now. He tried to think of something else, something pleasant, but it was difficult. He closed his eyes and tried to block it all out.

When they arrived at the Northerner's camp, Many Wolves spotted Rojo lying on his side. His chest heaved from strained breathing.

"Rojo!" he yelled.

The red wolf lifted his head briefly and wagged his tail for a moment before resting again. His eyes looked like they were glazed over with ice.

"What did you do to him? Did you poison him?" The stumbling, the watery half-closed eyes, and the fatigue—they could have been from poison. It was clear to Many Wolves now how it had happened.

"He will be fine some time after the sun rises," the Northerner said. "I would not kill a sacred animal like a wolf."

Many Wolves looked once more at the red wolf, realizing he might never see him again. But Rojo had always come back to him. Somehow, his faithful guardian had always managed to find him and protect him. This reflection brought a trace of a smile to Many Wolves's face.

Malone tied the painted horse to a tree and packed his supplies on the brown and white horse. He also packed Many Wolves's supplies and quiver on this horse, leaving only his own deerskin quiver hung around his shoulder.

The Northerner reminded Many Wolves of Ten Arrows. Malone was older, but there was a strong similarity between the lean, healthy bodies of the two men. His hair was straight and shiny and parted in the middle, and it was adorned with a single eagle feather, which dipped down on the right side of his head. His face was decorated with stripes of yellow and red, and his high cheekbones seemed to stretch the skin of his face. His nose was smaller than that of most Northerner men.

Many Wolves suspected that the black and white horse was the Northerner's favorite, because it was painted with stripes and handprints, and its mane had several eagle feathers dangling from it. The brown and white horse had no decorations.

When he was ready, Malone mounted his favorite horse and led the string of horses into the black of night.

Hopelessness sank into Many Wolves's white skin like a stinging sunburn. He looked back one last time at Rojo.

Goodbye, my friend.

Across the Prairie

The light of morning woke Many Wolves. He didn't remember falling asleep on Elk Dog, and he was amazed that he had not fallen off.

The wrist burns caused by his bindings immediately reminded him of his captivity. His dreams had blessed him with freedom and a brief respite from his unfortunate reality. Now he squinted his eyes at the glaring sun.

Malone looked back at him. "Are you ready to ride?"

Many Wolves didn't respond, because there was only one answer, and Malone knew what it was.

The Northerner commanded his horse to a trot, and they bounded off into the surrounding grassland, which swallowed them up like it was a giant spider web. With his hands tied behind him, it was difficult for Many Wolves to keep his balance, but he held tightly with his legs; he did not want to fall off the side of his horse.

They traveled most of the morning. At last Malone found a creek and stopped. The Northerner untied his captive's ankles and helped him dismount, then led him to a tree near the creek and retied his feet together. Malone served him as much water as he wanted, but he did not loosen or remove the bindings on his hands.

The three horses drank and ate the plentiful grass. Malone drank some water from the creek and then ate some dried meat from one of his food bags. He did not offer any food to his captive. This didn't matter to Many Wolves; the dried meat would probably just make him thirstier.

"You said you used to live in Laughing Crow's village. Why don't you live there now?" asked Many Wolves. He was tired of the silence, and he hoped that talking would somehow blot out the fear that permeated his mind.

Malone did not answer right away. Perhaps he was trying to be careful with his words, Many Wolves thought.

"Too much death. I didn't want to see death anymore." There was a glint of sadness in the warrior's eyes.

"Yet you will gladly hand me over to Thorn Bird? To *my* death?"

"My promise is to bring you to Thorn Bird, not to kill you or watch you die. I do this for Thorn Bird's father, my closest friend, and not for Thorn Bird himself." Malone looked his captive in the eye as he spoke.

It was difficult for Many Wolves to believe that this gentle man was Laughing Crow's friend. Their spirits were so different. Laughing Crow had had so much hate in his heart, yet this man claimed to hate death, and he seemed to hate the life that men like Laughing Crow and Thorn Bird lived.

"You speak our language with great skill," said Malone. "I have never heard a *taiboo* talk like you."

Many Wolves sensed some warmth in Malone's voice for the first time.

"My friend Ten Arrows of the Penateka taught me," Many Wolves blurted out, before realizing that he might somehow endanger Ten Arrows. But a strong feeling in his heart told him that this man would bring no harm to his friend.

Malone nodded. "I know Ten Arrows. He is a brave warrior, and his heart is warm like the sun. We are not friends, but I know of him from another friend."

Many Wolves noticed that Malone was looking at his captive's leg, at the scar from the bear that Ten Arrows had killed, but the Northerner did not ask him about it. Many Wolves was relieved to hear of Malone's high regards for Ten Arrows. *I did not endanger my friend. But I must choose my words carefully with this man.*

"How did you know about my brown and white horse?" Malone asked.

"I saw you riding him," Many Wolves replied, retelling his earlier lie.

He intended to protect his secrets.

"I have not ridden that horse in many sleeps. Your tongue is crooked, *taiboo*," said Malone. The chill had returned to his voice and his eyes.

"It is not the truth that I spoke, I admit it. But the truth will die with me."

"No more talk then. We must ride again. We have a long journey still."

Malone did not try to dig deeper for the truth; he posed no more questions and offered no threats. He was not like Laughing Crow; or perhaps he was just trying to remain distant. After all, it wasn't Malone's hate that drove his actions, but Thorn Bird's.

A Promise Fulfilled

Half Weasel galloped into the village and stopped at Thorn Bird's lodge.

"Thorn Bird! I have words that will please your ears, *namunewapi!*" he cried, his eyes and smile wide on his face.

Thorn Bird was sitting outside his tipi marking his special sign on some of the new arrows he had gotten from Talks Too Much.

"What is it, Half Weasel?"

"Malone is coming, and he has the white-skin with him."

Thorn Bird leapt to his feet with excitement. A rare smile shaped his face and he was powerless to fight it. An even rarer laugh exploded from his gut. "Those *are* pleasing words, my good friend! You could not have brought me words any more pleasing than these. Go tell Paco, then bring Malone to me."

For eight winters he had wished to capture this man, and now his wish was fulfilled. His search party had looked everywhere for the white-skin, but it had taken a clever tracker like Malone to find him. *I knew I could trust Malone.*

Thorn Bird couldn't stop smiling. He wanted to run out to see Malone and the *taiboo* for himself, but he held himself back. He was not a boy of ten summers, though at the moment, he felt like one inside.

As Malone rode in, a throng of villagers greeted him with cheers and great excitement. The white-skin was walking behind the third and last horse with his hands tied to a lead. The women and girls beat him repeatedly with their fists and any sticks they could find. The boys hit him with their bows and spat on him. Each man hit him once with his fist or with a stick that they shared.

Paco and his men rode up to the crowd, cheering and firing their weapons into the air in celebration.

It was a joyous moment for Thorn Bird as he watched them approach.

Malone dismounted and walked up to Thorn Bird. The crowd silenced, and the torturing villagers relented for the moment.

Thorn Bird put his hands on Malone's shoulders. "You have honored your promise, my friend. *Ura.*" Malone smiled back, but Thorn Bird sensed some reserve in his manner. "You will celebrate this moment with us?"

"*Haa*, Thorn Bird, I will celebrate tonight, but I must leave at sunrise. I am tired from my journey and from lost sleep. You must know that my promise was as much for your father as it was for you. I know this will please him." Malone looked tired, and he was covered in dust from his journey.

"Get some rest, my friend. The women will set up a lodge for you," said Thorn Bird, his hands still on Malone's shoulders. "The pony-slaves will take care of your horses."

Malone nodded with thanks. "*Ura.* I will go now."

"*Señor* Alcaudón, there will be plenty of us to celebrate tonight, even if *señor* Malone is too tired!" cried Paco from atop his horse. "Chico has reserved his finest mescal for such a celebration."

"Shiny Teeth, I am pleased you are here to share in this moment. When the sun is down, I will make trades for Chico's mescal," said Thorn Bird. It had been a while since he had drunk the mexicano fire-water.

"No, *mi amigo.* It is a gift from your *amigos.* There will be no trades tonight."

"*Gracias,*" said Thorn Bird, then shifting back to Northerner words he added, "Now bring me the *taiboo.* I want to see him."

Two of his men brought the captive to him. Many Wolves wore only his breechcloth and was dirty from travel. He was bleeding on his back and arms from the blows of the angry villagers. Blood was pouring from his nose and mouth as well. His thick brown hair was matted and uncombed and hung all over his face.

"We see each other again, *taiboo*," said Thorn Bird. He walked up to the captive and pulled his chin up with his right hand. "You thought you could hide forever."

Many Wolves looked away, seemingly trying to avoid Thorn Bird's eyes.

"You remember me, *taiboo*? We met when my father captured you. Look at me!" Thorn Bird demanded.

"You smell like your father," said Many Wolves, shifting his eyes to Thorn Bird. "I remember his sickening odor, and I remember the stench of his dead body."

Thorn Bird hit the captive across the face with the back of his hand. "You are brave now, magic man, but will you be brave when the torturing begins?" Thorn Bird laughed. "The Tonkawa was brave like you at first, but then the taste of his own flesh turned him into a wimpering coward! The filthy little man-eater deserved every bit of the pain I served to him."

Thorn Bird's eyes bored into his captive, looking for weakness, looking for fear. He found submissive eyes that avoided his gaze. *You are weak, taiboo.*

The Nokoni leader backed away from Many Wolves and continued speaking. "I have a great challenge, *taiboo*. How do I make your torture as enjoyable as the Tonkawa's? I will have to think about this. And while I do, the people of my village will soften your flesh so it is ripened when my turn comes." Thorn Bird again approached his captive and spoke in a soft voice. "I have one promise for you, *taiboo*. Your death will not be quick, and it will not be easy."

Thorn Bird turned to Half Weasel and Fire Eyes. "Tie him to a tree that is close enough to my lodge so I can hear his screams. Whoever wants to beat him is welcome to, but I want him alive when the suns comes up. No one touches him after that. Do you understand?"

"*Haa, namunewapi*," said Half Weasel.

"I want him guarded every moment," said Thorn Bird, "and make sure he has water to drink. I don't want him dying on me."

Half Weasel nodded his understanding, and he and Fire Eyes led Many Wolves away.

"Half Weasel. One more thing," said Thorn Bird, calling to his scout. "I need you to find me a large, straight branch, as long as a man is tall."

"Like a tipi pole?" asked the scout.

"Yes, but it needs to be thicker. Thick enough to support a man's weight."

"*Haa, namumewapi.* I'll try to find it before the sun is gone."

"Good," said the Nokoni leader. "And after you find it, I want you to sharpen both ends of it."

The scout nodded and smiled back at him.

Liar's *Dados*

The feast began at dusk. The hunters had brought back a large elk and a deer, and several roasting pits were set up around the village. There was also corn, squash, and other vegetables, along with several types of wild berries. The women were busy with the cooking—and with keeping the men and children away from their cooking fires.

The *mexicanos* had shown the men of Thorn Bird's village how to play a gambling game that used small stones with painted dots on them—they called it *dado*. The men were now split into different groups, each group a mixture of Nokonis and *mexicanos*, to play. There was laughing and shouting and excitement as the men cheered when someone predicted the outcome of the *dados* correctly or caught another man lying about what the outcome was.

This was not like gambling on horse races or shooting contests, because there was nothing to lose. But Thorn Bird enjoyed learning a new game all the same; and this idea of not telling the truth to fool another man in a game was strange to Thorn Bird.

However, Thorn Bird did not like the fact that the winners got to drink Chico's mescal. Because the winners were mostly the *mexicanos*, since the game was new to the Nokonis.

"Shiny Teeth, I have a new rule for this game," said Thorn Bird in a boisterous voice. "Whenever a man wins, then Thorn Bird gets to drink also." Thorn Bird hoped the game would be more enjoyable this way.

Paco and Rodrigo laughed, and then Paco spoke, with a smoking stick dangling from his mouth. "*Señor* Alcaudón, that is a great rule, and very fair since your village is hosting the game. Let us play by *señor* Alcaudón's rule!"

Half Weasel was in Thorn Bird's gambling group, along with the two Salazar brothers. The scout did not seem to enjoy the fire-water as much as Thorn Bird did, so winning the game did not seem as important to him.

"Everyone roll the *dados* in your cup and get ready to make your bid," called Paco. "I am first, and I bid *dos unos*."

No one else challenged Paco, so Half Weasel made his bid using sign language. He raised three fingers, then four, which meant "three fours."

Thorn Bird sat back and looked around. He could not recall a time in his life when he was happier. He had the love of a good wife, freshly cooked meat in his stomach, a village of strong warriors, the warmth of Chico's fire-water in his body, and most importantly, the *taiboo* who had killed his father was tethered to a tree nearby.

"*Señor* Alcaudón, it is your turn to bid," said Paco.

Thorn Bird noticed that both Eagle Eyes and Shiny Teeth watched his eyes closely when he made his bid—they hoped to catch him at a lie. He would need to try lying more so they would not assume he was telling the truth.

The Nokoni leader looked at his *dados*: three ones. He said, "*cuarto unos*." This was the truth if Paco had one too. Paco had told him that it was not always the best strategy to tell the truth in this game, but to add one or two more *dados* to the ones you have, and make that your bid. It was difficult for Thorn Bird to think that way, and it was difficult to accuse another man of lying, even though it was an important part of winning this game.

"*Señor* Alcaudón, I have to say, with your hair always covering your eyes, it makes it *muy difícil* to tell if you are lying about your *dados*."

Thorn Bird smiled and waited for the next man to play.

Rodrigo, who was next, spit his tobacco and said, "*cinco unos.*"

"A safe bid," said Paco. To Thorn Bird, he added, "It is difficult to know when my brother is lying, which makes him very good at this game." Paco peeked once more at his *dados.*

"I will stick with my *unos. Seis unos.*"

Rodrigo looked at his brother. "I think you are lying, *mis hermano.*"

"Let us see what we have then. Turn over your cups, *amigos,*" said Paco.

There were indeed six *dados* with one dot.

"Throw one of your bones in the middle, *hermano.* You lose." Paco smiled and puffed his smoking stick. "Which means, with the new rule, *señor* Alcaudón and I get to drink the mescal."

Chico poured some of his mescal in both Thorn Bird's and Paco's cups. Paco raised his cup into the air. "To the soon-to-be-dead *gringo*!" Then he tapped it against Thorn Bird's cup.

Thorn Bird drank the warming fire-water. "I like this new rule, Shiny Teeth!"

After several more games, Thorn Bird's body was relaxed, since he drank at the end of each one. He looked at Half Weasel and spoke in *Noomah*: "Half Weasel, my friend, you and I need to start our torture dance for the *taiboo* who killed our fathers, before Chico's fire-water weakens my legs. Have the men bring him to the big fire and we will dance."

"*Haa, namunewapi.*"

The Pain Sleep

The Nokoni men dragged Many Wolves to the fire. There were now cuts and bruises all over his face and body—so many that he had lost count. He was too weak to walk, and one of his legs had been hit so hard by a thick stick that he could no longer put weight on it. His left leg and his left arm hurt him the most, but there was pain everywhere.

He had only one thought left in his mind. *I want to die.*

The only faces that were familiar to him were Thorn Bird's and Malone's, and he had not seen Malone after he was delivered to Thorn Bird. Yet it seemed like all the people of the village—apart from Malone and a few of the Mexican men he saw—viewed themselves as his torturers. The faces were strange, and most of them were angry, though he heard laughing and celebration.

They are celebrating my death.

The Nokoni men forced him up against a large pole that stuck out of the ground in front of large, roaring fire, then retied his hands. The burning on his wrists from the rope was the least of his pains now. They had not tied his legs at all. *Perhaps it's easier to beat me this way,* Then they forced some water down his mouth. Many Wolves drank it willingly. A small flame deep inside of him still thirsted for life.

The people of the village began to gather and sit around the fire, forming a half-circle opposite him. Their faces were blurred, though whether that was due to the pain or the bruises around his eyes, he didn't know. Whatever the cause, the world was fading in and out of focus like a horrible dream.

Drummers appeared and sat near him, one on either side. They looked more like boys than men, and immediately they started to pound out a steady beat. Unlike the other sounds, the drumbeats did not fade in and out: they were loud and constant.

Many Wolves looked up at the embers flying from the bonfire, disappearing into the night sky like swift birds that had been flushed by the crackling and popping of the flames.

When he looked back down again, he saw that one of the men had started dancing around the fire. He was a small man with a muscular build, roughly the same age as Many Wolves. He wore a buffalo headdress, a breechcloth, leggings, and moccasins, his face was painted black, and his body was painted with pictures of men and animals in red and black. He carried a lance, which was dressed with eagle feathers near the tip.

The dancer stomped his feet, then raised his head and arms to the sky. He sang these words:

> *Rip out his teeth*
> *Tear off his claws*
> *Now he is ready*
> *For the shadow hunter.*

When he ended the verse, the dancer dipped the tip of his lance in the fire, throwing some kind of dust at the flames to rouse their embers.

Then he punctured Many Wolves's chest with the red-hot tip.

Many Wolves grunted and gritted his teeth. The people cheered, and the dancer yelled a victory chant. The captive needed to use all the power in his mind to keep himself from screaming. *They want me to scream, but I won't let my screaming spirit leave my body.*

After another verse, the lance tip again seared his skin with a burning pain, although it did not cut deeply. The pain forced water to his eyes, but he would not let the tears fall.

The buffalo dancer repeated this three more times, but none were as painful as the first—because Many Wolves knew how to prepare his mind.

Then a second man joined the dance. It was Thorn Bird. He danced in rhythm with the other dancer and was dressed the same, except that he did not wear a headdress of any kind. His long black hair swirled around his head like the swishing tail of a horse as he danced. On his face, only his eyes were painted black, but his body was elaborately painted in red, yellow, and black patterns. He did not carry a lance or other weapon, apart from the knife sheathed to his leg.

The two men danced for a short time together. Thorn Bird and the dancer sang these words and repeated them several times:

Father, we will bring him to the shadow lands.
Breath with your horse.
Breath with your bow.
We will bring him to the shadow lands.

Then the buffalo dancer left, leaving Thorn Bird to dance alone.

Thorn Bird motioned for the drummers to speed up, to match the beat of his stomping feet. To Many Wolves, the large Nokoni warrior looked like a demon, his hair flailing wildly around his head. The demon dancer threw dust into the flames and called on the spirits to join him: his father's spirit, and his brother's spirit.

See with your eyes
The soul that returns
Like a butterfly floating in a thundercloud
Feel with your hands
The soul that returns
To the shadows of the shadow lands
Father, brother
You will be whole again
And my blood will flow as red as yours

Thorn Bird stopped dancing, but he continued to sing as he stared into Many Wolves's eyes. Even through the haze of a thousand pains, the coldness of Thorn Bird's eyes still pierced Many Wolves. There was so much hate there, even more than in his father. *A hate that will end with my death.*

The Nokoni warrior unsheathed his knife and walked toward his captive. There was an unsteadiness to his walk, as if he was under the grasp of some powerful medicine. *Perhaps the Northerners use peyote in their torture rituals.*

Many Wolves saw that this was the end for him, and a wave of calm washed over him. He wanted this end. He wanted this end now.

"Take it!" Many Wolves yelled. "Your father's soul: take it! Your brother's soul: take it!" He looked through the disheveled black hair to find the demon eyes of his tormenter. "*My* soul, Thorn Bird. You have won. Take it."

Sweat and blood melted in Many Wolves's eyes, and the world became a blur. Thorn Bird's knife cut him. The pain was excruciating, mind-numbing. A cloud of warmth filled his body, and nausea, as if from too much peyote. Colors were falling from his world, replaced by gray, and his enemy, Thorn Bird, was fading. Many Wolves's spirit lifted above his body as if trying to escape, a mind-journey away from the pain.

Then nothing.

Nothing but the pain sleep.

Awaken

"Wake up. Many Wolves, wake up."

A voice called to him, from a deep cave, getting closer and louder.

"Wake up, Many Wolves."

His body shook, like a dog shakes to rid himself of water. But it was hands that were shaking him. Strong hands.

"Wake up, Many Wolves."

Ten Arrows?

The voice was close now, a whisper, a rush of air.

Many Wolves opened his eyes and found the eyes of a Northerner looking into his.

Malone.

"Am I dead? Are you here to torture me?" Many Wolves felt the pain crash over him like a lightning bolt.

"I am not here to hurt you," whispered Malone, the darkness of night surrounding his face. "We must go. Will Ten Arrows protect us? Will the Penateka protect us?"

Many Wolves was confused. "Ten Arrows?"

"Will his village protect us? Tell me!" insisted Malone in a soft, pleading voice.

"*Haa*," Many Wolves said. "Ten Arrows will protect us."

"Good. Then we must go. The first light of dawn is coming."

Malone cut Many Wolves's hands free, hefted the captive over his shoulder, and ran.

Then Many Wolves was riding on a horse, his arms tied around Malone's waist.

The pain sleep fell over him again.

Gone

"*Namunewapi*, wake up!" said Half Weasel, shaking the leader's shoulder.

Thorn Bird woke up, not happy that his sleep had been interrupted. His head was aching, and his mouth was dry from the previous night's fire-water.

"What is it, Half Weasel?" he grumbled.

"Many Wolves is gone!"

Thorn Bird sat up. "What? What are you saying? He's dead?"

"No, he's *gone*. Someone cut his hands free. He's not there where we left him!"

Thorn Bird boiled with anger. "How could he have escaped? Who was watching him?"

"He was there when it was my turn to watch him. Malone relieved me, *namumewapi*. There are footprints leading away from the pole. It looks like someone carried him. The footprints look like Malone's."

"Where is Malone?" snarled the leader.

"He's gone too. He said he would be leaving when the sun rose."

Suspicion crept into Thorn Bird's mind. *Malone helped him escape.* But that didn't make sense; Malone had been the one to bring the *taiboo* here. Why would he bring him here just to help him escape?

"Do you think Malone helped him escape?" Thorn Bird asked.

"*Haa, namenuwapi*, I think those were his footprints. To be sure, I will need to compare them to the ones around the lodge where he slept."

190

Thorn Bird reviewed other possibilities in his mind, but only this one made sense. *Malone has betrayed me.* Thorn Bird remembered how Malone had killed Ferdinand and his wife quickly to prevent their slow, painful death from snakebite. *Malone saved the taiboo's life because he knew my torture would be brutal. He was always the merciful one.*

"Half Weasel, I am certain that Malone helped him. Can you track him and find out where he is?"

"*Haa, namunewapi.*"

"Take Fire Eyes with you. But do not attack Malone; he is dangerous. I will gather a war party together to kill him and take the white devil back. Malone is bold to think he can escape us carrying a half-dead white-skin."

"*Haa*, we will leave now," said the scout.

It didn't matter to Thorn Bird that Malone was a Nokoni—nor that he had once been his father's best friend. His betrayal was unforgivable. The anger boiled inside him and he felt hatred rush through every muscle in his body. *How can he do this to me? To his people? If I capture Malone alive, he will suffer the same torture as the white-skinned coward.*

Fed by his burning temper, Thorn Bird clenched his fists and yelled at the skies, "Malone!"

Unturned Stones

Thorn Bird and his men, including the two *mexicanos*, approached the Penateka village after a half day's ride at a steady trot. Half Weasel had tracked Malone's horse to this village earlier in the morning and had led them here.

The village was huge. Tipis sprawled along the Rio Red extended beyond Thorn Bird's vision. The Penateka horse herd grazed in the vast grassland on the other side of the river. Thorn Bird estimated that this village must own over a thousand horses. It was as large and prosperous as the village his father had once led—before he was banished by Gray Elk. Even with all of Paco's men, the Penateka easily had ten warriors to his one.

It will be difficult to barter with them.

The elation of the previous night had now been replaced by hatred and anger. The warm, pleasant feeling of the fire-water was also gone, leaving a queasy discomfort that sat like a stone in the Nokoni leader's stomach. Malone's betrayal was just as hurtful to Thorn Bird as the *taiboo's* escape. He did not understand how an honorable warrior like Malone could turn his back on his own people. With the suddenness of a flash flood, Malone had turned from a trusted friend to a hated enemy in Thorn Bird's mind.

The Nokonis slowed their mounts to a walk as the boys and dogs of the village came out to greet them. The dogs barked, and the boys pointed at the strangers and whispered to each other. Then a wall of Penateka riders formed in front of the village, like a line of buffalo bulls protecting the cows and calves, and the boys called the dogs away—picking up the more stubborn ones who ignored their calls—and dispersed.

Thorn Bird recognized the gray-haired elder at the center of the line as Crooked Eagle, the undisputed leader of the Penateka, the *paraibo*. He wore an elaborately painted buffalo robe around his shoulders and two eagle feathers in his scalp-lock. The men to either side of him must be other elders from his peace council, Thorn Bird surmised. The only other man that Thorn Bird recognized was Ten Arrows, who was four riders to the right of the leader; this was the man who had brought the body of Thorn Bird's father home to the Nokoni village several summers ago. The warriors carried lances or bows, but the elders carried no weapons.

Crooked Eagle raised his arm, and the men stopped. Thorn Bird stopped his horse as well, and his men followed his lead.

"We expected that the winds of revenge would blow you to us, Thorn Bird," said Crooked Eagle in a gruff voice that whistled through his mouth. "I hope your father lives well in the shadow lands. He was a great warrior. I would liked to have known him better, to share stories of great victories for our people. But I know you are not here to talk about your father, so say what you have come here to say." His words were clear and deliberate, and he took deep breaths when he paused, which was frequently.

Thorn Bird knew that Crooked Eagle had once been a great warrior and leader of Penateka war parties. He wasn't like the elder buzzards of Gray Elk's village. This was a man who had done much to command his people, and now he commanded his words with the same power.

Though a wildcat was clawing at his insides, Thorn Bird tried to remain calm. "Crooked Eagle, are the *taiboo* Many Wolves and Malone here in your village?"

"*Haa*, Thorn Bird. Many Wolves is under the hands of our best healers, and Malone is our guest." The wrinkles on Crooked Eagle's face shifted back and forth as he spoke, but his unflinching black eyes remained fixed on Thorn Bird.

"These men are enemies of our people, Crooked Eagle. Many Wolves killed my father, my brother, and one of my father's best scouts. Malone has betrayed us by helping Many Wolves to escape from our village. I ask that you hand them over to us."

Crooked Eagle shifted his body on his horse before he spoke. "Enemies of Thorn Bird are not always enemies of our people. You choose to make enemies when a wiser man does not—the bee stings only when he is stung. Malone is an honorable warrior. The actions of his life speak loudly, far above the raging north winds, while the deeds of lesser men are carried away and forgotten. He has our protection as long as he stays with us."

The Penateka leader paused to look at Thorn Bird's men. "Many Wolves has the skin of our enemy, but he is not our enemy. He is a brother in spirit with one of our finest warriors, Ten Arrows, which makes him a brother of the Penateka. He has our protection as long as he stays with us."

Thorn Bird did not know that Many Wolves was friends with Ten Arrows—friends with the man who had found his father's body. A thought struck him. *Did Ten Arrows help to kill my father?* There was a stone that remained unturned.

The Nokoni leader looked at Ten Arrows and directed his horse closer to him. "You are friends with this *taiboo?*"

He saw that Ten Arrows's hair was cut short on one side. There must have been a death in his family, Thorn Bird thought.

There was some hesitation in Ten Arrows, then he said, "I am. We are life brothers. He once saved my life, and now I am forever in his debt."

Thorn Bird sensed that there was more to this friendship. More to uncover about his father's death. "When you brought my father's body to me, you did not say that you were friends with Many Wolves."

"It was not asked of me, so I did not offer it."

"What else did you not offer to me, Ten Arrows? What else are you hiding?"

Thorn Bird spun his horse in a circle, then again made eye contact with Ten Arrows, waiting for an answer.

But there was no answer, only silence. He moved his horse closer to Ten Arrows.

"Has a snake bit your tongue, Ten Arrows? Let me ask a question so there are no clouds around my words. Were the arrow points in my father's body from your arrows?"

Thorn Bird studied the man's eyes and face to see if an answer would bleed out.

"They were from me," Ten Arrows admitted at last. His voice was calm, not quivering. The muscles in his face did not twitch, and his hands were not shaking.

"Then you killed my father, Ten Arrows. You killed the blood of your own people to save the life of this white-skin?" He had always wondered who had shot those arrows. It all made sense to him now. *Many Wolves could not have killed my father alone.*

"It was an easy choice, Thorn Bird. I don't see the color of a man's skin; I see what is in his heart. Your father's heart was filled with hate. Is it the color of a man's skin that makes him your enemy, Thorn Bird?"

"I do not make friends with the white-skinned devils, like you do."

"And I don't murder men who share the color of my skin, like you do. You kill because it pleases you—just like your father," said Ten Arrows defiantly.

Thorn Bird smiled. "I will offer you that as the truth, Ten Arrows." Then he glared at the Penateka warrior. "It will please me to kill you and your white-skinned brother. You have protection now, but you will not always. I will wait for you to stray from the herd, Ten Arrows, like a weak buffalo, and then I will thrust my sword through your heart. And yes, it will please me!"

The Nokoni leader screamed and pulled the lead of his horse hard to the left to turn in a circle. He pulled the sword from his sheath and held it high in the air as he spun his horse around, yelling, "Many Wolves! Ten Arrows! Malone! There will be no peace for you until I suck the last breath from your writhing bodies!"

Then he spun his horse around once more and led his men away from the village.

A Strange Dream

"Where am I?"

Many Wolves awoke in a strange tipi, lying on his back on a sleeping robe. He was weak, barely able to move his arms or legs. His skin was stiff from all the cuts on his body, and he had bruises that dug pain deep into bone. His face had been cut badly as well. There was so much pain everywhere, it was hard to tell where his most painful wounds were. Trying to move an arm or a leg just magnified the pain, so he remained completely still.

"Where am I?" he said as loudly as his weakened voice would allow.

A figure walked closer and bent down over him; it was hard to see them clearly because his eyes were swollen nearly shut.

"Don't speak. Don't move. You don't want to spoil my hard work, do you?"

It was a woman's voice, speaking in Northerner words. It had been a long time since he had heard a woman's voice that wasn't angry. It wasn't the friendliest voice, but at least it wasn't mocking him.

"Who are you?" he said. It hurt even to speak. His mouth was swollen and it felt like some teeth were missing. "Are you here to torture me more?"

"I'm Ninakabaru. I help the medicine woman. Her name is Cooks Out The Marrow."

"Where am I?"

"This is a Penateka village. Your friend Ten Arrows lives here."

Many Wolves didn't say anything. He tried to smile, but it hurt too much. "Is he here?"

"I will tell him you are awake. Don't move. I worked hard closing your wounds. Don't spoil my work." She stroked his hair, moving it away from his eyes. "First, you need to drink this. Open your mouth."

She put her hand behind his head and helped prop his head up. Many Wolves opened his mouth and felt the cool water sting his lips and the inside of his mouth. It was difficult to swallow because his throat was dry and it hurt to move a single muscle.

He strained to lift his right arm to his stomach and chest to touch the sore areas. The rough sinew coiled around one of the cuts along his ribs, and there was an oily substance all over his body. He touched the gash that ran down the left side of his face and felt that same snake-like threading. It hurt him too much to move his left arm or his legs, because of cuts, bruises, and stiffness, and he didn't try; he didn't want to ruin any of the medicine woman's work.

"Wild Man! You're awake!" It was Ten Arrows. It was comforting to hear his familiar voice.

"Ten Arrows…"

"Don't talk, my friend. You need rest."

Ten Arrows lightly touched the cut on the left side of Many Wolves's face.

"Thorn Bird almost killed you, but you are safe now. He knows you are here, but he also knows that we will protect you. It would be foolish of him to try to take you from us. Many of his men would die."

Another person walked in and knelt down beside them.

"How is he, Ten Arrows?" It was the scratchy voice of an older woman.

"He's alive and breathing."

The woman put her hand on Many Wolves's face. "His skin is cooler. Many of the pain spirits are gone, and the death spirit no longer lingers here. He is strong; a weaker man would have died." She gently inspected his other wounds.

"His life flame burns strong, deep within him, and the spirits of wild animals protect him," said Ten Arrows. "I have seen these spirits before, the spirits of his birds and his wolf, but now they are much stronger in him. They keep him alive."

"He will need the strength of these spirits to be healthy again. Make sure he drinks water." The old medicine woman faced her patient. "Ninakabaru and I will visit you later, Many Wolves."

"*Ura…*" said Many Wolves, trying to remember her name.

"I am Cooks To The Marrow. I should have told you my name when I first spoke," she said, as if reading his mind. Then she left the tipi.

"Your spirits brought you much luck, Wild Man. When I saw Malone ride up to the village with a wounded man, I would never have guessed in a hundred winters that it was you. Laughing Crow's closest friend saved your life! Your *puha* continues to amaze me, *samohpu.*"

Ten Arrows poured water in a cup and raised it to Many Wolves's mouth. "Here, drink this. You have lost a lot of blood and your body needs water."

Many Wolves sipped the water from the cup slowly.

"It should be *your* turn to heal *me*, my friend, not the other way around," said Ten Arrows, laughing. Many Wolves wished he could see his friend's smiling face more clearly.

"What did Malone say?" asked Many Wolves, his voice cracking like an old, stiff tree branch. He still did not understand why the man who had captured him was also the man who had freed him.

"He said that his dreams would be haunted forever if he let Thorn Bird kill you. He said Thorn Bird is not *Noomah* anymore, but a bloodthirsty animal."

"But he's the one who captured me and brought me to Thorn Bird."

"Malone regrets that now," said Ten Arrows, reaching out to groom his injured friend's hair. "He will stay in my village. Thorn Bird has threatened to kill him too, but you two are safe here. Crooked Eagle, our *paraibo*, has promised this to me."

Many Wolves finished drinking the water in the cup. His world had changed, and his mind was struggling to understand why. It all felt like a strange dream—except for the pain. He knew that was real. But the rest had all happened so fast. He was free with his pack, then captured, then tortured near to death... and now he was with strangers in a strange place—except for his good friend Ten Arrows.

I am still alive. Ten Arrows will bring me back my strength and my health.

"You need to rest, Wild Man, so I will leave you, but first, I need to know—where are Chiquito and Rojo?"

"My little hawk is dead, Ten Arrows, and I don't know where Rojo is."

Ten Arrows looked solemn. "I am sorry for the loss of your beloved little friend, but I promise you, Wild Man, when you are strong again, we will find Rojo."

Mating Dragonflies

The heat in the air was hard to bear. The sweat gathered on Many Wolves's legs, under his arms, and in his face. Ninakabaru did all she could to try to keep him cool and comfortable. She dipped a small animal skin in tepid water and placed it on his forehead. Many Wolves, who was lying down, looked up at her and smiled.

"I hope this will help. I'll have to ask Cooks Out The Marrow if she has any medicine for the itching, and something to keep you dry," said Ninakabaru. "I don't want you—"

"I know, spoiling your work," Many Wolves said.

"Well, I was going to say, scratching apart my handiwork. Your mind is as quick as a whipsnake, *taiboo.*"

It was hard for Many Wolves to tell if she was joking with him.

The swelling in his eyes had subsided overnight, and he could see her face much better now. She did not have the roundish face of a Northerner. She had small, dark brown spots on her face and body. She was pleasing to his eyes, he thought, and he loved her smile, though she rarely shared it.

There was a sadness about her as well. A bruise on her face made him think that someone had beaten her. He wanted to ask questions, but it still hurt to speak, and often she snapped at him. He had noticed that her demeanor during the day was much different than at night: during the day, her mind was busy and her answers curt, but at night she was kinder, more relaxed. Though it was still hard to get her to speak many words at all, especially about herself.

"You had bad dreams again last night," she said.

"I don't remember." He did remember, but he didn't want to talk about them. Laughing Crow had been in his dreams again, asking him to do impossible things; and when he couldn't do them, he was beaten again and again. *Soon it will be Thorn Bird in my dreams.*

But although there had been suffering during the night, there had also been comfort. It was like his mother, Painted Wings, had been there with him. Perhaps it was Ninakabaru or Cooks Out The Marrow comforting him, but he didn't remember for sure. A soft voice, someone touching him—that was all he remembered, and it was hard to know if it had been part of a dream or if it was real.

"You were with me, Ninakabaru?"

"For some of it. Cooks Out The Marrow wanted me to stay with you," she said. "I've fallen behind on my other work. Proud Toad..." She started to say more, then stopped.

"Who is Proud Toad?"

"Never mind. It's not your worry."

She keeps me outside. I will ask Ten Arrows about Proud Toad.

"Ninakabaru, come outside," said a voice. It sounded like Cooks Out The Marrow.

As Ninakabaru left, and a man came inside. It was Malone.

"You look better," said Malone. He sat down next to Many Wolves. "We need you to heal so we can help you find your wolf." He cracked a wisp of a smile. "I put your things over there." Malone pointed to the other side of the tipi. "Your medicine bag, water pouch, weapons, and your bear claw necklace."

"Why did you help me, Malone?"

"Because Thorn Bird has a sickness in the head. Nobody deserves to die the kind of death that he brings. I have heard stories of his tortures. Stories that should never be told to you—or to anyone. It has taken my dreams many winters to heal from the brutality in my past. The guilt and the nightmares would never have ended for me if I had let Thorn Bird kill you the way he wanted to."

"What did you do that was so horrible?"

"When my wife and daughter were killed, I lost my mind, Many Wolves. I killed women and children who did not deserve to die. That night, I promised the Great Spirit that I would never hurt innocent people again and that I would protect those who needed my protection." Malone's voice was soft for a man his size, and his voice was laced with wisdom. It reminded Many Wolves of his grandfather's voice.

"But I'm not innocent," said Many Wolves. "I killed Laughing Crow, and Thorn Bird's brother, and Silent Weasel. They were your friends."

"I know now that you must have had a good reason to kill Thorn Bird's brother. Am I right?"

"I was protecting the wolves."

"Wolves are sacred animals." Malone grabbed the damp animal skin and wiped Many Wolves's face with it, then placed it back on his forehead. "You killed Laughing Crow and Silent Weasel because you were defending yourself and they slaughtered your family. Your heart is good, Many Wolves, and your actions are pure in the eyes of the Great Spirit."

"What will you do now, Malone? Thorn Bird wants to kill you too."

"I don't know, Many Wolves. I will think hard on this and ask Crooked Eagle to smoke with me. He will know what to do. You, me, and Ten Arrows are all targets now. Thorn Bird will not stop until either we are dead, or he is dead. The three of us are now bound like mating dragonflies. We will all live, or we will all die."

Buffalo Ravens

Thorn Bird rode his war horse, Snake, through the flat grassland on a clear summer afternoon, testing the horse's injury. He did not push the horse too hard because he did not want to aggravate the injury. Mocking Bird, the horse's healer, rode beside him.

"Snake is improving, Mocking Bird. He is almost ready to run," said Thorn Bird.

"With the arrow point extracted, he should recover to full strength soon, *namunewapi*. I wouldn't push him too quickly. Time and rest are his best healers now. I cannot do anything else for him."

Thorn Bird trusted his healer's advice. "Your healing magic is strong, Mocking Bird. I will rest him until after the buffalo hunt. I will need to train my second horse to not panic when the *mexicanos* fire their weapons." Thorn Bird knew that most horses could be taught to ignore the booming blast of a gun. "I think that first explosion from Shiny Teeth's weapon caught him by surprise."

"If the horse knows the blast won't harm him, then he won't panic," said the lean, aging warrior.

Thorn Bird nodded in agreement.

Half Weasel rode up and greeted them. "*Namunewapi*, my Penateka friend says that Malone, Ten Arrows, and Many Wolves are still there in the village. Many Wolves is still hurt badly and hasn't left the healer's lodge."

"Good, Half Weasel. I want you to talk with your friend before sundown each day. Many Wolves won't be leaving their village for many sleeps, but Malone might leave at any time, and if he does, he will be alone. I want to know the moment he leaves—not a heartbeat must pass. Do you understand?"

"*Haa, namunewapi,*" said the scout. "I also have good words about the buffalo."

"What's that?"

"The ravens that circle the buffalo herds are close—as close as they have been to us all summer. We should prepare for the hunt before the buffalo move farther north."

"Those words are sweet like honey for the ears, my friend. I will tell the men to ready their weapons and the women to prepare to move the camp."

"Will the *mexicanos* join us for the hunt?"

"I will talk to Shiny Teeth about it. They will want the skins from the animals they kill."

"It is the hard work of our women that makes the skin valuable. They can't take them all."

"You are right, my friend. I will need to barter with them."

With this idea still fresh in his mind, Thorn Bird rode Snake back to the village, with Mocking Bird and Half Weasel riding alongside. He left his horse with Mocking Bird, then walked over to Shiny Teeth's cooking fire, which was just outside of his village.

The *mexicanos* were roasting an elk carcass when Thorn Bird arrived.

"Eagle Eye's kill?" asked Thorn Bird. Most times it seemed that Rodrigo provided their fresh meat.

"*Si, señor.* He is a handy man to have around. Wouldn't you agree?"

"*Si,* Shiny Teeth. A man who is good with a *rifle* or a bow has many uses for a village."

Paco nodded his head in agreement. "Do you want to join us, *señor* Alcaudón? There is plenty for you too, *mi amigo.*"

"Did you save me the liver?"

"*Si.* We kept it in a cool place and covered it up so the flies couldn't feast on it."

Thorn Bird was pleased that the *mexicanos* knew how to take care of themselves. They did not depend on his village for anything, and they provided a useful service: protection. They were respectful of the village women as well. They only visited them at night when their work was done. So far, none of the women had become *mexicano* wives, but he knew it would happen eventually. He welcomed a lasting bond with these men.

One of Paco's men brought out a large piece of raw liver and handed it to Thorn Bird. Thorn Bird took a bite and let the moist meat roll around in his mouth before swallowing. The blood dripped down the sides of his mouth and his chin. "This is still fresh, Shiny Teeth," he said through a mouthful.

Paco laughed. "The fresher the better for an *indio*."

Thorn Bird devoured the liver in a hurry and then washed it down with water.

"Shiny Teeth, our village will be moving soon to hunt the buffalo. Do you want to hunt with us?"

"Si, *señor* Alcaudón. My men would like that. Many of us have herded *ganado* on *haciendas* south of the Rio Bravo, so we are used to riding this way. You will have to teach us the best way to kill the buffalo with our weapons."

"For me, it's like killing an elk or a deer," said Rodrigo, spitting out his tobacco.

"*Si*, Rodrigo. You do not need to mix with the herd, but the rest of us will need to get close to the buffalo to kill it. It is much more dangerous to ride with the buffalo than with the *ganado*, eh *señor* Alcaudón?"

Thorn Bird had killed cattle once before; it was much easier than killing buffalo. "*Si*, Shiny Teeth. The buffalo run much faster, and they will not hesitate to gore you with their horns or trample you if they get the chance."

"Do we keep the skins from the buffalo we kill?" asked Paco.

Thorn Bird had been expecting this question. "If you want to butcher them and tan the hides yourselves."

"The hides would not have much value if we prepared them ourselves.

They would have much higher trade value if your women prepared them."

Thorn Bird determined a fair barter in his mind. He knew the hides would be wasted if the *mexicanos* prepared them. "I will give you one finished hide for every five buffalo you kill, Shiny Teeth."

"But *señor* Alcaudón , killing the buffalo is the dangerous part!"

"My men can kill them just as easily," said Thorn Bird, though he knew having twice as many men to hunt would be better for the village.

"How about for three buffaloes we kill, you give us one hide."

Thorn Bird considered it a fair offer, but he wanted more value for the hard work of his women. They labored long and hard preparing a skin; it was not easy work. The men in his village were glad that they did not have to prepare the hides.

"My last barter for you, Shiny Teeth. One finished hide for every four buffalo you kill."

"You offer a very hard *pacto*, *señor* Alcaudón. I could use a tough *negociador* like you in Santa Fe." Paco smiled, then looked over at Rodrigo. "What do you think, *hermano*?"

Rodrigo spit his tobacco and nodded. "Take it."

"You have a deal, *señor* Alcaudón!"

"Good," said Thorn Bird. Unlike the *dado* game that the *mexicanos* had taught him, he knew how to play the bartering game, and he knew how to win what was best for his village.

Two-Spirit

The following morning, after another restless, sweaty night. Ten Arrows came to visit Many Wolves, who was still lying flat on his back.

"How are you feeling, Wild Man?" asked Ten Arrows.

"It still hurts all over, but at least my face isn't all puffed up. It's easier to talk and to see things." Many Wolves propped himself up carefully on his elbows.

"Is Ninakabaru taking good care of you?"

"*Haa*, but she's a strange bird, Ten Arrows. One moment she is pleasing to be with and the next she is sad with her head in the clouds."

"She is a woman, Many Wolves. You haven't spent much time with women," Ten Arrows said with a grin. "Here is some soup from the turtle for you to drink."

Ten Arrows offered Many Wolves a large cup of steaming liquid. With the soreness in his mouth, Many Wolves was still unable to eat solid food of any kind. Ninakabaru had brought him several other kinds of soups—buffalo, prairie dog—but never from the turtle.

Many Wolves took a sip. It had a bland flavor, but it was not unpleasant. "It's good. It would taste better with some salt added to it."

Ten Arrows laughed. "You and your salt, Wild Man. You would suck on those salted jerky sticks you make all day long, if you could."

"I miss them," said Many Wolves. A question haunted his mind. "Ninakabaru spoke of someone named Proud Toad. Is that her husband?"

"No. They are not husband and wife. She is his slave."

Many Wolves thought that she did not look like the other Northerner women.

Then Ten Arrows added, "She is *Navoonah* like your family. She was captured by our warriors after a *Navoonah* raid five or six summers ago, and Proud Toad claimed her."

"That bruise I saw on her face is from him?"

"*Haa*, Wild Man. He beats her often."

"Why don't you help her?"

"It is not the *Noomah* way to interfere with how a slave is treated."

"She is not a bad person, Ten Arrows. She comforts me when I have bad dreams; her touch is gentle and kind. It reminds me of how my mother used to comfort me. There is also a warm, tingly feeling in my loins that I don't remember as a child."

Ten Arrow laughed. "My friend, that is the feeling a man gets when a woman touches him, or even when he looks at a woman that pleases his eyes. It is this feeling that draws us to couple and make children."

"I remember my mother's sister, Desert Flower, telling me about these things. About men and women coupling to make children, but she never talked about these feelings."

Many Wolves sipped down the rest of the soup. It felt good to have warm food in his stomach and to feel his old appetite coming back to him. What he really wanted was to eat fresh meat, or even to suck on one of his salted dried meat sticks, but his mouth still hurt too much.

He noticed that Ten Arrows's hair was different—it was cut short on the left side. "Was there a death in your family, Ten Arrows?"

Ten Arrows's face grew serious. "Yes, my life partner died last winter."

"You never told me you had a wife."

"My partner wasn't a woman, Many Wolves, so I did not have a wife, but he fulfilled that role for me in my life. He was my friend and lover. My people call me *waha-nanisu*, two-spirit. I have both the spirit of a man and a woman in me, like my partner had. The white man's word for it is *berdache*."

"Can you tell me his name, or will that bring bad luck?"

"His name was Soft Cloud. But I cannot say it again. He was cherished by the village because he loved to do woman's work and did it as well as any woman. He loved to dress in woman's clothing too, not a habit that I shared. He was also a member of the peace council, because he was gifted at fixing disagreements between men and women, because he understood the spirits of both."

"What happened? How did he die?"

"Last winter, our warriors brought back a white-skinned captive, a young woman, who was sick with a fever. He tried to help heal her, but the evil spirit that was making her sick went into his body. He died of the white-man's fever."

"You never had children then?"

"No, Wild Man, and I probably never will. He was my life partner; there will never be another like him."

"Why didn't you tell me about him before? And about your two-spirited ways?"

"I did not want you to feel uncomfortable around me. There are some men in the village who do not understand my two-spirited way. I hear them talk when my back is turned, but most people in the village respect and honor my gift."

"How do I know if I am *waha-nanisu* like you?"

Ten Arrows smiled. "I can see it in your eyes, my brother. The way you look at me, at other men—and the way you look at Ninakabaru. One two-spirit will know another from just one look." He stood up with a big grin on his face. "I have a surprise for you, Wild Man, that will tell us if you are a two-spirit. But first I must speak with my brother."

A Saving Hand

The women of Thorn Bird's village had moved their camp's supplies to within striking distance of the buffalo herd. Thorn Bird had not seen the buffalo yet, only the buffalo ravens, the trampled grass, and the piles of dung littered across the path the animals had taken.

The Nokoni men had sharpened their lances and tightened their arrow points in preparation for the hunt. Protective red and yellow paint decorated their faces and the bodies of their ponies. Mocking Bird had decided that Snake was ready for the hunt; Thorn Bird had ridden him hard the previous day and the horse had responded well. It was good to have his war horse under him again.

The mounted Nokoni warriors and several of the *mexicanos* were gathered around the Nokoni leader. Thorn Bird remembered when his father used to talk to the men before a hunt. He also remembered what happened to the man who did not listen. His father's life, and his own, had changed dramatically after that moment when his father killed Stands Alone's brother during the hunt.

"Hunters, ready your weapons and your minds," said Thorn Bird, walking back and forth along the line of men on his prancing war horse. "Attack them from the right side, and pull your horse away from an injured animal, especially a bull. Their horns will gore your mount if you get too close, and you will be trampled. Do not be overconfident. Respect these beasts." Thorn Bird repeated the words in Spanish so the *mexicanos* would hear them too. Of course, he knew Eagle Eyes had a plan of his own for killing buffalo without a horse.

The hunters walked their horses in a line as they approached the valley of the buffalo. When they reached an overlooking vista, they looked down across the landscape. The great beasts were scattered across the plains as far as Thorn Bird could see, completely unaware of the threat that lay above them.

"Walk the horses as close as we can without startling them," commanded Thorn Bird from the center of the line. Paco was on one side of him and Half Weasel on the other. "Wait for my signal to charge."

The hunters approached the herd cautiously. Thorn Bird looked from one animal to the next, selecting the one he wanted to kill first. He was hoping to spear a large bull with his lance and then kill one or two more with arrows.

The pungent musk of the herd attacked his senses, but it was a smell that every buffalo hunter loved. The buffalo provided everything for them: food, tools, clothing, and many other things that they used in their daily life. They also provided food in great quantity and warm clothing to help his people survive the deadly cold of winter.

Thorn Bird heard the roars of the protective bulls and the yelps of the calves, but still he held his hand up, signaling his men to wait. Eagle Eyes had settled himself on a high position away from the men, with Pablonito at his side.

When the herd began to stir, Thorn Bird released the hunters.

The screams and cries of his men filled the air as their horses sprinted to full speed toward the buffalo herd. Below them, the thunder of hooves shook the ground as the herd stampeded, lifting dust into the air. Thorn Bird heard the blast of Eagle Eye's rifle and saw one of the huge animals fall.

He set his own eyes on the large bull he wanted. He rode closer and closer to it, pursuing it, his lance ready in his right hand. He willed his war horse to ride hard up along the right side of the bull. Snake did so, then steadied his speed, matching the pace of the thundering buffalo. Thorn

Bird felt and heard the labored breathing of both Snake and the buffalo; they seemed to be in perfect rhythm with the beating of his own heart.

Thorn Bird pulled his arm back, then thrust the lance into the side of the buffalo. The large animal roared and bucked his powerful horns at his attacker, but Snake quickly veered right, away from danger. Thorn Bird slowed a bit and looked back at the collapsing bull. He yelled, "Yee-ah!" to claim it, then directed Snake to gallop ahead for another kill.

The rumble of the herd was met with the sounds of blasting *mexicano* guns, twanging bowstrings, and the screams of injured animals and cheering men. Thorn Bird looked to his left and spotted Paco aiming his *pistole* in full stride. The weapon exploded, but the buffalo did not slow; instead it swung its powerful head at Paco's horse. Both horse and man disappeared in a cloud of rising soot.

Thorn Bird maneuvered his horse back against the flow of the herd and tried to find his fallen friend in the dust and chaos. He heard Paco's scream, and directed Snake toward the sound. Finding the injured *mexicano* on the ground, he quickly reached down and pulled him up on his horse. Then Thorn Bird guided Snake past the thinning herd, holding Paco, stopping only once he reached a clearing.

There the Nokoni leader set Shiny Teeth down on the ground. Paco was groaning and moving slowly; his breathing was heavy, and blood dripped from his mouth, but Thorn Bird did not see any other injuries. However, the ever-present smile on the *mexicano*'s face had been replaced by fear.

"Are you hurt badly, Shiny Teeth?" asked Thorn Bird. "Don't try to move."

"It's not too bad, *señor* Alcaudon. I got kicked on my back and my leg, and once in the head."

Thorn Bird was relieved to hear his friend speak clearly and to see that his eyes were still full of life.

"*Gracias, señor* Alcaudon, for saving my life."

"These buffalo are not like your *ganado*, eh, Shiny Teeth?"

"No, *señor*. They are not."

"You are lucky to be alive."

"You know what they say, *señor* Alcaudon. The lucky man outlives them all."

Thorn Bird could not disagree.

Covered in Blood

"You don't need a medicine man, Shiny Teeth?"

"No, *mi amigo*. I am very sore, but it is my pride that is hurt the most."

"And your horse?"

"He was shaken up, but he is a strong *caballo, señor*."

Thorn Bird brought Paco back to his lodge at the temporary camp the Nokoni women had set up near the buffalo. The day was nearly over, and the earlier excitement from the hunt had passed. It had been replaced by the sweat of men and women butchering the remains of the buffalo and hauling them back to the camp.

The hunt had been successful. Thorn Bird counted at least twenty buffalo carcasses as he surveyed the killing ground. He had claimed only a single buffalo himself, because of Paco's injury, but the Great Spirit had been good to his village, as only Paco had suffered an injury.

"*Señor* Alcaudon, you remember our *pacto*? How many buffalo were killed by the metal balls of *mexicano* guns?

"Eagle Eyes claimed three, and one we claimed for you. The rest of your men claimed four buffalo kills."

Paco was quick with numbers. "That is eight kills—which earns us two finished buffalo hides of the highest quality!"

"*Si*, Shiny Teeth. Your work is done. Now it is women's work."

"And we will feast like kings for the next few *noches,* eh, *amigo?*"

"*Si*, Shiny Teeth."

Paco laughed and smiled a big smile, though Thorn Bird could tell that he hurt inside.

Eight more buffalo was worth the price of two skins and some food, thought Thorn Bird. His own men could have killed even more buffalo, he thought, but he didn't want to overburden the women of the village. It was a hard time for them. Butchering buffalo meat and scraping skins was difficult work.

"You know, señor, it is a strange thing for a *mexicano* to see a woman covered in blood. At the *haciendas,* the men do the butchering."

Half Weasel joined Thorn Bird and Paco at his lodge.

"The *hombres* do their share, Shiny Teeth. We cut the big pieces for them, because the women aren't strong enough to do that," said Thorn Bird. "But the women know best how to do the finer cutting: how to cut out the liver and other organs, to strip off the sinew, and how to carve strips of meat for drying. We use everything on the *animal meurto.*"

"I know your men love to eat the liver, heart, and other organs fresh from the kill, but this is not a *mexicano* custom," said Paco.

"We do not eat the heart, Shiny Teeth. We bury it so that more buffalo will come."

"What are you and Shiny Teeth talking about?" asked Half Weasel, who did not understand the Spanish words well.

"We were talking about how the women do most of the butchering, and how we use everything from the dead carcass," said Thorn Bird, switching to Northerner words.

"The *mexicano* women do not work like our women, *namunewapi,*" said Half Weasel. Then he added, "I do not mean to insult Valencia."

Thorn Bird laughed. "Valencia is my wife; she does not have to get her hands as bloody." He put his hand on Half Weasel's shoulder and looked down at the shorter man. "I agree with you, my friend, though there are some hard-working *mexicano* women as well. It would make our village stronger to have more hard-working women. I would trade many horses for this. I know our men could kill many more buffalo than we did today, but if we did, the women would not be able to keep up."

Half Weasel nodded. "*Namunewapi*, if you are willing to give up horses, I will find good women for you."

Thorn Bird thought about this. He could get what he wanted in trade from the *mexicanos* as long as he had buffalo hides to trade, but for that he would need more women to scrape and tan the hides. Also, more buffalo would mean bountiful food reserves and security for his village during the lean, winter season. He wished he had more women covered in blood.

"Half Weasel, even one or two good women would strengthen our village. See what you can do."

"*Haa, namunewapi.* I will talk with my friend at the Penateka village.'

Enslaved

"Many Wolves."

Many Wolves heard a whispered voice as he lay on his back. The voice of a woman. He was half-awake now, deep into the middle of the night. *Am I still dreaming?*

"Many Wolves."

The same soft voice again.

"Ninakabaru?" he said, though he knew the voice was different than hers. He opened his eyes and saw the dark eyes of a woman looking at him. Her breath stroked his face and her hair brushed against his chest. The air was still except for the sound of their breathing.

"Don't be afraid. I am Topusana. I am the wife of Ten Arrows's brother, Stretches Like A Dog."

"Why are you here?"

"You are the brother of Ten Arrows, who is the brother of my husband. Brothers share wives."

"But I'm not a brother by blood." Many Wolves was confused. He didn't know what was happening and why she was here, but she was gentle, and what he saw and imagined was pleasing to his senses. Her white teeth glowed in the darkness when she spoke, as did her eyes. Her wildflower scent stimulated his sense of smell.

"You are his spiritual brother. That is a bond as strong as blood. Now don't speak, just listen." Topusana put her fingers to his lips and held them closed.

"I am your teacher. I want you to do everything I ask you to. I will not hurt you. If I hurt you, you will tell me. Do you understand?"

Her voice was sweet and breathy, and her words were easy to understand. He already felt safe with her. "I understand."

"I need you to roll over slowly onto your stomach," she said.

He rolled his stiff, sore body over and lay on his stomach. The cuts and bruises on his chest stung when they touched his sleeping robe.

"Rest your arms above your head," she said, and then helped move his arms. "Now relax. Breathe slowly and deeply, and close your eyes."

She put her lips to his ears and spoke in a hushed tone. "In this darkness, in my darkness, you will breathe only the air I breathe. You will feel only my skin and hear only my words. You will smell only my scent and taste only the salt of my body. I tell you when to stop and when to start up again. Do you understand?"

"*Haa*," said Many Wolves. And then he added, "So I am your slave?"

She laughed in his ear. "*Haa*, you are my slave. No more words."

Topusana touched his neck first, spreading some kind of oil on his skin. Her fingers dug deep into his skin and then relented, barely touching him, like lake water slamming against a rock and then pulling back. Her soft hair swept across his back as if it had fingers of its own. The pain that had crippled his mind for many sleeps melted under her powerful touch.

She caressed his shoulders and arms next. Even the bruises and cuts on his body obeyed her commanding touch. The pleasure in his body fought back the pain. It was overwhelmingly relaxing, but the tingling would not let him sleep.

"How does it feel?" she whispered, tickling his ear with the air from her voice.

His tongue struggled to find the right response. "It's good." He knew it was much more than that, but he did not know the right words.

She lowered her hands to his back, spreading more oil on him. She knew not to press hard on the most painful areas, but she covered them in oil and touched them with feathery-soft fingers. Then she moistened them with her lips and tongue. The warmth was satisfying to him. It was like a dream, but he knew it was real.

His teacher grabbed his breechcloth with her hands and whispered, "You won't be needing this." She slid it off his hips and down his legs, and he felt a surge of pleasure in his loins. She climbed on top of his back, with great care not to hurt him, until her warm, soft, naked body rested flush up against his. He adjusted his body to make it a little less painful, but she was not as heavy as he had thought she would be.

"Does this hurt?"

"A little," he said, but his mind was numbed by a cloud of warm feelings.

She tickled his ear with more arousing words. "Now, I want you to roll back over on your back. This is where the real pleasure, the real learning, begins."

Many Wolves didn't know how he could possibly feel any better than this, but she would teach him this, and teach him how to give this pleasure gift back to a woman.

A New Family

The pain crept back into his sleeping pad when Many Wolves awoke the next morning. Topusana had been with him most of the night, but now she was gone, though her scent still lingered. He lay back with his arms behind his head and replayed everything from the night over and over again in his mind. He wanted it to last forever. He wanted it to dig into his memory, like a tick burrows into skin, and not let go.

Ten Arrows pulled the flap of his tipi open. "Wild Man, can we come in?"

"*Haa,*" he said simply.

Ten Arrows walked in with another man and Topusana. She was as beautiful as he had imagined in the darkness.

"This is Stretches Like A Dog. He is my brother, and Topusana's husband."

"I have heard many amazing stories about you, Many Wolves. I am honored to meet you," said Ten Arrows's brother. He was taller and younger than Ten Arrows. *He must be a skilled warrior like Ten Arrows and a good provider to have a lovely wife like Topusana.*

"And I know you have met Topusana," said Ten Arrows.

Many Wolves felt a little embarrassed, but then all three of them laughed, and he felt better.

"Welcome to our family, my brother." Ten Arrows gestured toward the other two, then knelt down closer to Many Wolves. "How are you feeling today, Wild Man?" He laughed again, even louder this time. "Do I even need to ask?"

Many Wolves laughed too, even though the pain cut at his sore ribs. "No, you don't."

He was a little embarrassed that Topusana and her husband were there, but they seemed comfortable with the arrangement. The rules of a village were strange to a man who had lived most of his life in the wilderness. It would take time to get used to them.

"*Ura,* Ten Arrows, for your gift. And *ura,* Topusana." He smiled up at her and she smiled back. "And I am thankful to you as well, Stretches Like A Dog, for your generosity."

Stretches Like A Dog nodded back at him. "Nothing more than what one brother would do for another."

Then Topusana leaned down and whispered in Many Wolves's ear, "*Ura* for bringing Ten Arrows's smile back. That is a precious gift to us."

Ten Arrows laughed. "Look at them. They already have secrets!"

Topusana held her lips closed with her fingers, and Stretches Like A Dog laughed and said, "That is a secret you will never know, big brother!"

Then Stretches Like A Dog turned to Many Wolves. "We will leave to your peace and quiet, Many Wolves. When you are well enough, we hope you will spend time with us at our lodge. I am honored to be known by you."

"*Ura,* Stretches Like A Dog, and Topusana. I will visit soon."

The couple left Ten Arrows and Many Wolves alone.

"So, Wild Man, I think we know now that you are not a two-spirit."

"I am a one-spirit, Ten Arrows." Both men laughed together.

"I will have you meet some of the unmarried women in our village, if you like."

"Like I met Topusana?"

Ten Arrows grinned. "No, not as close up as that, my friend. When you are well enough to walk again, I will show you some of the women of the village, and you can tell me which ones are pleasing to your eyes."

Ninakabaru was pleasing to his eyes, but she belonged to Proud Toad.

Perhaps it would be better if he found someone he liked who did not belong to anybody. "I would like that, Ten Arrows."

"Good. Cooks Out The Marrow asked me to make a walking stick for you, so you can try walking with it. I should busy myself with this task. So long, one-spirit!" Ten Arrows left him alone.

Many Wolves didn't fully understand Topusana's words about Ten Arrows's smile coming back. His friend had always had that smile. That's what made him Ten Arrows.

The Penateka Village

The following day, Many Wolves woke up alone. It was the first night where he had had no visitor. He didn't expect there would be more teaching from his brother's wife; Ten Arrows had jokingly told him that he had mastered his lesson with her and that she would not be visiting again. However, he was surprised, and disappointed, that Ninakabaru did not at least stop by to check in on him. The pain lessened each day now, except for his leg, which he worried would not heal quickly.

In the middle of the morning, Ninakabaru at last dropped in to see him, carrying a stick with cooked meat on it and a cup of hot liquid. "Cooks Out The Marrow thinks you should be eating meat now, not soup."

"What do you think?" he said, trying to engage her in some kind of playful talk.

"I am not the medicine woman, just a lowly helper who does most of the work." She cut a small piece off the stick with her knife and placed it in his mouth with her fingers. "This is elk's liver that has been warmed on the fire. It should be tender and easy to chew."

"It must be hard to work for two masters," said Many Wolves. The meat melted in his mouth, though it still hurt to chew.

"Cooks Out The Marrow is kind. She does not make unreasonable demands like Proud Toad does." This was the first time that she had talked about Proud Toad.

"Does he hurt you when you don't do his work?"

"*Haa*. But I don't want to talk about that." A sadness fell over her face, and especially her eyes. It was a familiar melancholy.

"I'm sorry," Many Wolves said. "I won't talk about it again."

"You need to drink this tea. It will help with the pain." She gave him the cup of hot liquid, and he drank some while she cut more pieces of liver so he could eat them with his fingers.

"You smell nice today, Ninakabaru."

"You like the smell of a woman's sweat?" She flipped the reply quickly back at him.

He wasn't expecting that kind of response. Many of the words from her mouth were a surprise to him. He liked this about her; it kept him guessing what she would say next. He tried to come up with a playful response himself.

"I like it much better than the sweat of a man or a horse."

She did not respond with any more words, but he saw a small twitch in the corner of her mouth. To him, it was a half-smile, and a small reward for his playfulness.

There was not much more talk after that. Many Wolves ate and drank and watched Ninakabaru grind up medicinal herbs for Cooks Out The Marrow. It was her usual work for the medicine woman when she wasn't caring for Many Wolves. He imagined in his mind what it would be like to be with her in the way he had been with Topusana. Some of the pleasure feeling came back to his loins.

"Wild Man, I have your walking stick," said Ten Arrows, nodding to Ninakabaru and waving the stick in his hand.

Many Wolves shook himself out of his warm reverie. He was excited to finally get out of this sleeping robe and out of this tipi. "Can we walk now?"

"I was hoping you'd want to, my friend," said Ten Arrows, holding his arms out to help Many Wolves up.

It felt like all of the bones in his body cracked as he stood. Ten Arrows supported his left side, which was good, because Many Wolves was afraid to put any weight on his left leg. And when he finally did, a surging pain crashed through his body.

"Hold the leg up and use the walking stick," said Ten Arrows, still holding Many Wolves and helping him to balance.

Many Wolves hobbled on one leg over to the door of the lodge, then quickly turned around to catch Ninakabaru looking at him. She snapped her head back down as if embarrassed. "Goodbye, Ninakabaru."

"Goodbye," she said, staring into her bowl of ground medicine herbs.

The afternoon sun was bright, forcing a squint to his eyes, but the heat was welcome to his stiff body. Many Wolves watched the women work at their cooking pits or tanning racks and tried to match the faces with the voices he had heard. He also tried to identify the children he saw playing chasing and wrestling games around him.

Most of the women and children stopped what they were doing and stared at him as he hobbled by. In their whispered voices, he heard the words "animals," "hawks," "wolf," and "magic" most often. Though the word he heard the most, especially from the adults, was "*taiboo*," which meant "white man." With his white skin and his height—he was taller than all the villagers he saw—it was impossible to escape their attention.

A group of boys, all of them naked, ran up to him.

"Do you have a wolf that's trained like a dog?" said one of the boys, about ten winters old.

Many Wolves bent down slightly, looked at him, and smiled, "*Haa*, I do. The wolf's name is Rojo."

"What does that mean?" asked an even younger boy. He held a small bow in his hand.

"It's a Spanish word for the color red," responded one of the other boys before Many Wolves could answer.

"Where is the wolf? Can we see him?" asked the boy with bow.

"He is not here now. He doesn't like places where there are people. It makes him nervous," said Many Wolves, hiding some of the truth from them.

"You have hawks too?" asked a little girl who had just joined the group.

"I did," he said, "but they are in the shadow lands now."

"Oh," said the little girl.

Then another boy asked, "Where did you get those marks on your leg?"

"Those are claw marks from a giant bear."

The children's eyes lit up and they looked at each other.

The same boy spoke again; he was about twelve winters old. "Ten Arrows has the same marks on his back."

Many Wolves smiled. "*Haa*, he does."

"We are brothers of the bear!" Ten Arrows said, and then held his hands up to look like bear claws and snarled at the children.

The two men laughed, and the children smiled at them.

"We want to see your hawks and your wolf. We want to see magic," said the boy who had spoken first.

Many Wolves smiled and thought to himself, *So would I.* "I hope there will be a time when you can see them."

The children ran away and returned to their play, apparently satisfied with his answers.

"You see, Wild Man, they have heard your stories."

"I don't feel like the man in the stories, Ten Arrows. My body is broken."

"It will heal, Wild Man. You will be able to ride a horse before you can walk."

"How can I ride when I don't have the strength to get on a horse?"

"You have friends, my brother, who will help you, and friends who will protect you when you ride."

Many Wolves felt lucky to be alive—and even luckier to have friends like Ten Arrows and Malone. Two men with good hearts who were great warriors. The cloud of Thorn Bird still hung over his head, but he was sheltered from the lightning and heavy rain by his friends. *I hid from Thorn Bird, and I will do it again, but I need to get well, and I need to find Rojo.*

"Tell me if you see a woman who pleases your eyes, my friend, and I will tell you what I know about her," said Ten Arrows. He seemed to be enjoying this woman-finding task.

"Is it the role of the two-spirit to find wives for the men of the village?"

Ten Arrows laughed. "No, Wild Man. It is the role of a brother."

Trapped Eyes

Most of the cuts and bruises on Many Wolves's body had healed, and the constant, unyielding pain in his body was gone. It only came in lightning-like surges now, when he moved in certain ways or rolled over on a sore spot as he slept, and most of the remaining pain was in his left leg. The walking stick that Ten Arrows had made served as his replacement leg, bearing the weight of his body. He felt like Half Leg, the one-legged bird from his grandfather's story, hobbling around the village. Though he imagined that Half Leg had not moved at turtle speed.

Many Wolves thought often of his animals during this time, especially Rojo. He hoped that his red wolf was surviving well on his own. He occasionally thought of Fiera as well, but he knew that he would probably never see her again. Still, it was a warm thought knowing that she was alive because of him.

Ninakabaru's visits were less frequent now; she only came to bring him food, water, or medicine for his pain twice each day. And her visits were brief. She explained that there was much work to do now that the men of the village were bringing in more and more buffalo from the hunt. It was her job to scrape the hides, and she had to work hard from sunrise to sundown to meet Proud Toad's expectations.

"Wild Man, it's time for your walk," said Ten Arrows, urging him to get off of his sleeping robe on a warm, summer morning. His friend came by twice each day to help him walk around the village and also visited him each night, sometimes with Malone, who helped the Penateka men with the buffalo hunt during the day.

Ten Arrows held out his hand and pulled Many Wolves to his feet, then handed him his walking stick. "So, which lodges do you want to see?" Ten Arrows asked, smiling.

Many Wolves's friend was still intent on finding him a wife. Though there were over a hundred women in the village, the number of unmarried, not-too-young, not-too-old women who were somewhat pleasing to the eyes was not high. And in Many Wolves's mind, there were only three. Two of them were full-blooded Northerner women; the third was Ninakabaru. Ten Arrows had set up visits with each of these two Northerner women the previous day so that Many Wolves could talk with them. Their names were Squeaks Like A Mouse and Kuhiyai.

"What did you think of Squeaks Like A Mouse? Should we stop by her lodge?"

"She was nice. Her voice was high-pitched and she talks a lot. When I watch her at her lodge, she is always talking," said Many Wolves. He worried that she talked too much. Although she was pretty, she was small and seemed fragile to him.

There had been a change in the people of the village since his first walk. They didn't stare at him anymore or whisper behind his back. He was no longer the white buffalo sticking out in the herd, and he liked that. They were getting used to his presence, and he was getting used to them as well. There were many benefits to living in a village.

"Let's walk past her lodge again and see if she is talking, my brother," said Ten Arrows, helping him out of the lodge. "Some men like a woman who talks a lot, because they are quiet themselves, and they want their lodge to be filled with words. And how about Kuhiyai? Does she talk too much?"

"No. She is nice too. I like the way she looks and talks, but I don't think she is interested in me."

"Why do you think that?"

"When we talk, it is about unimportant things. I try to learn more about her, but she doesn't speak many words about herself. She doesn't seem interested in the things I like, because she doesn't ask me questions about them."

Ten Arrows laughed. "You are very wise, Wild Man, for one who hasn't talked with many women."

"It's not just that, Ten Arrows. With Ninakabaru, it is different. There is a feeling for her that I don't have with the other women. It's an exciting feeling. I think it is this same feeling which makes me think about her often. I think about being with her like I was with your brother's wife. But I don't feel these feelings or have these thoughts with Speaks Like A Mouse or Kuhiyai."

"Do you think Ninakabaru feels this way for you and thinks of you?"

"I don't know, Ten Arrows. But sometimes I catch her looking at me a certain way. I can't describe it. It's like our eyes are trapped in a snare together for several moments, and then they are free again. She doesn't reveal her feelings with her words."

"I know what you mean by that certain look. I saw that with my partner when we first met," said Ten Arrows as they walked together. He spent several moments in thought before speaking again. "I worry that Ninakabaru will be difficult to claim as your wife. She is very useful to Proud Toad. He will expect a trade of horses for her."

"I don't think that Ninakabaru wants to stay with him, because he beats her."

"It is not her choice to stay with him or not. It is his choice. She is his to own, like a horse or a weapon are for another man."

An idea sprouted in Many Wolves's head. "Can we ask Proud Toad what he wants for her?"

"*Haa*, Wild Man. That is a good idea. There is no harm in asking to barter," said Ten Arrows. "Let's go to his lodge now and speak with him. We can walk to Kuhiyai's lodge after that."

Many Wolves nodded. He was nervous about this visit. What if Proud Toad said he did not want to give her up? What if he asked for ten horses? *Where will I get ten horses?*

Proud Toad

When Many Wolves and Ten Arrows arrived at Proud Toad's lodge, they found Ninakabaru bent down on the ground scraping at a hide.

"Hello, Ninakabaru," said Many Wolves, hobbling on his walking stick.

"You have come to smell my sweat again, Many Wolves?" Ninakabaru's skin glowed from her hard work. She grunted as she cut out pieces of flesh from the skin, but she did not look up at him.

Before he could think of a response that he hoped would cheer her spirits, Proud Toad walked out of his lodge. "Why are you interrupting her? She is already behind in her work today."

Proud Toad was much older than Many Wolves—at least forty winters, Many Wolves guessed. His straight black hair was mixed with gray, and he wore braids on each side. He had many wrinkles around his eyes, and the skin at the top of his eyes ran like a straight line across his forehead, making him look like he had a permanent frown on his face. His voice was deep and cracked, and there was no friendliness in it.

Many Wolves was nervous; he felt a lump in his throat. "What would you trade for Ninakabaru?"

Proud Toad was so caught by surprise, he was for a moment without words. Ninakabaru stopped her work and looked up at them. Her face was expressionless, and Many Wolves could not read her reaction, good or bad.

"Get back to work," Proud Toad growled at her. "This does not concern you."

She did as she was told, but Many Wolves knew she would be listening to every word.

"I have never thought about trading her. She is a good worker, for a *Navoonah,* and does much of the work that my wife cannot do. My wife's hands are gnarled like an oak tree, and it hurts her to use them for heavy work." Some of the gruffness was gone from Proud Toad's voice, but still there was no smile on his face, only a frown.

"What can you trade, Animal Man?"

"My name is Many Wolves."

"Your name is Animal Man to me," he snapped. "You rode in on the back of Malone's horse. You have no horse, no weapons, no skins to trade."

"I'll find a way to get what you want. Just tell me what it is."

"I will need to think about it. A slave who works as hard as she does is worth at least two horses, but I will want more."

Many Wolves didn't know how he could get two horses. He didn't even have Elk Dog anymore. He would need Ten Arrows's help. He looked down at Ninakabaru and saw several bruises on her back that he hadn't noticed before. It made him angry to think that Proud Toad beat her like a yelping dog.

"Proud Toad, why do you beat her?"

"What?" asked Proud Toad. Either he hadn't heard the question or it was unexpected.

"Why do you beat her?" asked Many Wolves again, louder and as clearly as he could say it.

Ten Arrows whispered to him, "You shouldn't be asking this."

"She is my slave. She is *Navoonah* and less than a dog. I can beat her when it pleases me, Animal Man. "

Many Wolves persisted. "She works hard. She doesn't hurt you."

"Ten Arrows, what village does your friend come from? A *taiboo* village? A *Navoonah* village?" asked Proud Toad. "They don't beat their slaves in his village?"

"*Haa*, it was a *Navoonah* village, and they treated their women with respect and not like dogs!" said Many Wolves in a louder voice. Many

Wolves was feeling angry. He did not understand how a man could treat a woman like that.

Proud Toad approached him with anger in his eyes. He was close, almost touching. "You should learn to respect the warriors of this village, *taiboo*!" Then he pushed Many Wolves back and knocked him to the ground.

Ten Arrows quickly intervened and got between them. "Proud Toad, he does not mean to disrespect you. His village is different than ours and he hasn't yet learned our ways."

Many Wolves staggered to his feet, trying to balance himself. Ten Arrows turned around and helped him. Many Wolves was boiling with anger, but he knew he could not fight this man on a bad leg. He wished he could beat Proud Toad down so he would know how it feels to be beaten.

"Ten Arrows, get him out of here. I do not wish to see him anymore," said Proud Toad, gritting his teeth.

Ten Arrows held his hands up, hoping to calm Proud Toad down. "We will leave." Then he looked at Many Wolves and said, "Do not speak anymore!"

Many Wolves had never seen Ten Arrows mad like this.

As they were walking away, Proud Toad yelled, "Animal Man, if you came to me with a *hundred* horses for my *Navoonah* slave, I still wouldn't trade her to you!"

Outsider

Darkness fell on the Penateka village and settled in Many Wolves's heart. He knew now that he had made a grave mistake in accusing Proud Toad of beating Ninakabaru, but seeing the bruises on her back had thrown him into a frenzy. He could not remember any women in Walking Free's village suffering abuse like that. The Lipan men respected the women. Even the Mexican women, who were brought into the Lipan village as captives, were treated humanely. Worst of all, there was now a sinking feeling in his heart that he had lost Ninakabaru forever.

Ten Arrows invited him to join Stretches Like A Dog and Topusana at their family's lodge for a meal. Many Wolves had recently moved his belongings next to his friend's lodge, now that he was no longer under the watchful eye of the medicine woman, Cooks Out The Marrow. The three men sat around the cooking fire while Topusana prepared the food: boiled corn and strips of roasted buffalo meat—cut from the rump of the animal, she told them.

Many Wolves sat on the ground with his left leg outstretched, because it hurt to bend it. "What am I going to do about Ninakabaru? Is there no chance for me to barter for her, Ten Arrows?"

"You have disrespected Proud Toad, and he will not soon forget."

"Did you see the bruises on her back?"

"I did. But I have seen women beaten far worse than that, and no one spoke against it."

"It's not the right way to treat people," said Many Wolves.

"I agree with you, Wild Man, and so does Stretches Like A Dog, and Malone, and many of the men in the village."

"So why don't you stop it?"

"It is the tradition of our people not to interfere with the way a man treats his wife or his slave. I have told you this twice before, and still you question it."

"What am I going to do about Ninakabaru?" said Many Wolves again. It was third or fourth time he had asked this question, but he was unsatisfied with the advice he had been given.

"You may have to forget about Ninakabaru and look for someone else," said Topusana, serving the men boiled corn on the cob. For Many Wolves, she shaved it off the cob and served it in a cup.

"I am different, an outsider in this village. It will be difficult for me to find a woman who will accept that. And I have nothing to trade: no horses, no weapons, no animal hides. I should leave this place and go back to the wilderness!"

"You are not well enough to live away from the village, and Thorn Bird's men will hunt you down like a hungry pack of wolves!" said Ten Arrows. His voice was charged with emotion. Many Wolves noticed that since the confrontation with Proud Toad, Ten Arrows had not been smiling as much. His friend's voice was calmer when he spoke again. "We will find someone for you, Wild Man. You will see."

"I don't know how Ninakabaru feels about me. If I knew she felt the same as me, I would find a way to get the horses that Proud Toad wants. So many that he couldn't say no."

"If you know that she is the one for you, I would help you get those horses, Wild Man, and so would your other friends, like Malone."

"But I don't know, Ten Arrows. How would I know?"

Topusana, who was roasting the meat on the fire, stopped what she was doing and freed her hands. "When a woman loves you, Many Wolves, she will place her fist on her heart like this and look at you." She did as she described with her right hand. "It means that her heart beats for you."

The Barter

In the morning after two more sleeps, one of the boys of the village burst into the lodge where Many Wolves was staying.

"Thorn Bird is here!" the boy yelled and then ran out to tell other people.

The words sent a shiver down Many Wolves's spine. *Thorn Bird is here. What does he want?*

Ten Arrows and Malone met him in front of the lodge.

"Why is he here?"

"I don't know, Wild Man. He's at the edge of the village. Let's go see."

Ten Arrows walked beside Many Wolves. Many Wolves was still hampered by his leg injury, but at least he could move at a faster pace than before, with the aid of the walking stick. They fought through the throng of people, women and children on foot and men on horseback, to get a closer look. Malone, on horseback, cleared a spot for them in front of him so that they would have an unobstructed view of the scene.

Thorn Bird and another rider were a few horse lengths in front of the line of people, facing Crooked Eagle, who was at the center. Thorn Bird turned his head to his left and shot a hateful glance at Many Wolves.

"What are you here for, Thorn Bird?" said Crooked Eagle.

"I am here for trade... and for talk."

Many Wolves looked up at Malone and whispered, "Who is the other man?"

"It's Half Weasel. The son of Silent Weasel," he whispered back.

Half Weasel. Visions of that night of torture flashed in Many Wolves's mind. *He was the other dancer.*

Roughly ten horse lengths behind Thorn Bird and Half Weasel were several Nokoni men and a string of horses. Many Wolves was relieved. *This is not a war party.*

"Go ahead, Thorn Bird," said Crooked Eagle. "What is your trade? Who are you trading with?"

"I am trading with Walking Leaf," said Thorn Bird. Then he looked over at Many Wolves and smiled. "And Proud Toad."

Proud Toad? He's trading for Ninakabaru? How is that possible?

"The terms of your trade have been accepted by these men?" asked Crooked Eagle.

"*Haa*, I have the horses I promised. Three of them for Walking Leaf and five for Proud Toad."

Thorn Bird waved his arm, and one of the Nokonis led the string of horses forward. Proud Toad and another Penateka man walked out to examine the horses. Once they were satisfied, they each led a string of their horses back to the village.

"Where are my slaves?" demanded Thorn Bird.

Ninakabaru and another woman were led out from the crowd to Thorn Bird. Half Weasel pointed at Ninakabaru and spoke some words to Thorn Bird, then bound the hands of the other woman and led her to the Nokonis who had brought out the horses. They loaded her onto a spare horse, and then led Ninakabaru over to Thorn Bird.

"This one rides with me," said Thorn Bird. Half Weasel helped Ninakabaru up to Thorn Bird's horse, wrapped her arms around the leader's waist, and bound her wrists. "Tighter. I want to feel her body pressed up against me."

Satisfied, Thorn Bird rode over to where Many Wolves was standing. He looked at Many Wolves, Ten Arrows, and Malone with a sneer on his face. "My three favorite people. Lucky for you that Crooked Eagle doesn't accept my trades for *you*."

Then Thorn Bird looked at Many Wolves and laughed. "How do you like my trade, *taiboo*?"

Many Wolves refused to take the bait.

"That scar on your face makes you look tougher, *taiboo*," said Thorn Bird, still taunting.

Many Wolves saw flashes of himself ripping Thorn Bird's throat open with a knife, but he didn't have a knife, or any other weapon, with him, which reined him back to the moment. He looked at Ninakabaru. Tears rolled down her cheeks. He felt powerless. *There is nothing I can do for you now.*

Thorn Bird glared at Many Wolves. "When the leaves fall and the new moon comes, I will have no more use for her. Then she will die—unless one of you three surrenders to me. Those are my trade terms."

Then Thorn Bird whooped and rode off.

The Bee

"*Señor* Alcaudon, this will lure the bee out from the safety of the hive!" said Paco, who was waiting to greet Thorn Bird after the barter with the Penatekas. The smell of roasting buffalo meat permeated the early evening air.

"I want to lure *three* bees out, Shiny Teeth," said Thorn Bird. Fire Eyes untied the *indio* slave from his waist and helped her down from the leader's horse. She did not say a word. Her face and body were covered in dirt.

"Ah, *sí*! You know that the white-skinned bee is drawn to this honey?"

"That's what Half Weasel said. You should have seen the look in the *gringo*'s eyes." Thorn Bird had seen that Many Wolves could not take his eyes off of this woman.

"You are the *maestro* of the barter, *señor*. *Muy magnifico!*"

"It was Half Weasel's idea."

"How did he hatch this *huevo* of a plan, *señor*?"

"Half Weasel's Penateka friend saw the *gringo* arguing with the *indio* slave's owner, and he told Half Weasel about it. My scout knew that I wanted to find more working women for the village, so he worked the trade out through his friend. *Muy magnifico*, as you say, Shiny Teeth."

Thorn Bird dismounted and spoke to Valencia with Northerner words. "Here is our new slave. Clean her up and put her to work on the buffalo hides. I want her in my sight every moment. You don't need to be gentle with her—look at the bruises on her back. She is used to being mistreated."

238

Valencia led the slave away.

"Shiny Teeth, I don't know what the *gringo* sees in her. She is not a breeder," said Thorn Bird.

"What is a breeder, *señor*?"

"It is a woman who looks good to the eyes so you want to breed with her. This woman is *lipano*. Their men are weak and their women are ugly!"

Paco laughed and nodded his head in agreement.

"What is your plan for her, *señor* Alcaudon?"

"When we are finished with the buffalo hunt, she will die. I expect that the *gringo* and his two *amigos*, Ten Arrows and Malone, will come for her before this time. I need you and your men to stay with us through the hunt. I want to be ready for them."

Paco lifted his nose to smell the air. "A man can get used to fresh meat *cada noche, señor* Alcaudon! We will be here!"

"Good, Shiny Teeth. The trap has been set; now we wait for the prey."

Back to the Wild

"How does it feel today, Wild Man?" said Ten Arrows, riding alongside Many Wolves.

"It feels better each day, though it still hurts my leg to ride. I can't squeeze with it very well."

Many Wolves had begun to ride again three sleeps ago—after seeing Thorn Bird. That encounter had motivated him to get back on a horse again, and Ten Arrows had offered him a chestnut stallion to ride temporarily.

Many Wolves wanted to leave the village—there was nothing left for him here. Finding Rojo was foremost in his mind, and he hoped that being home in the wild would help him to forget about Ninakabaru.

"Ten Arrows, it is time for me to leave the village. I need to find Rojo."

"I expected that you would want to leave soon," said Ten Arrows. He did not look surprised.

"This village is not my home. These are not my people. You saw what happened with Proud Toad," said Many Wolves.

"I understand, Wild Man. You will need a horse for your journey."

"Do you know how I can get one?" He hadn't thought about how he would get a horse, but he knew he needed one.

"*Haa*, I have a trade for you. You can take the horse you are riding now," said Ten Arrows.

"What do I have to give you for it?"

"It's a simple trade, Wild Man. You get the horse, and I go with you," said Ten Arrows, with a satisfied grin on his face.

"You want to go, too? But it won't be safe for you outside the village."

"I'm not going to let you go alone, whether you take the horse deal or not. There is nothing here for me either, except for my brother and his wife, who can take care of themselves. The memories here are still painful for me; I feel alone even when I'm surrounded by a village of people."

It was the same with Many Wolves: feeling alone in a village of people. If he lingered, the memories of Ninakabaru would continue to burn him like the memories of Soft Cloud did to Ten Arrows. He fondly remembered his time living with Ten Arrows in the wilderness, and he would welcome such an arrangement again. Even if Thorn Bird found him, Many Wolves would have his friend, his life brother, there to fight at his side.

"I accept the trade. *Ura*, my brother," said Many Wolves. "When should we leave?"

"We can leave now, Wild Man, as soon as Topusana and I pack some supplies. Let's go to my brother's lodge, then we will say goodbye to Crooked Eagle and Malone."

"Your quiver is packed with twenty new arrows, Many Wolves. I made them myself," said Stretches Like A Dog.

"His arrows are the best quality, Wild Man," added Ten Arrows.

"*Ura*, Stretches Like A Dog, for being a good friend."

Stretches Like A Dog shook his head. "No, no, Many Wolves. I hope that you regard me as a brother. After all, if you weren't my brother, I'd have to kill you for coupling with my wife!"

The three men laughed and Topusana smiled.

"*Ura*... brother," said Many Wolves at last.

"That's better. Be safe in the wild. I know that it is your home."

Many Wolves offered Stretches Like A Dog a forehand shake, but his brother wanted a hug instead and pulled him in close to his body.

After the hug, he walked over to Topusana. "Goodbye, Topusana. *Ura* for…" Many Wolves paused, trying to capture the right words. "… For teaching me many things."

Ten Arrows and Stretches Like A Dog laughed as Topusana hugged him.

"Cooks Out The Marrow wanted you to have that sleeping robe," said Topusana, "since it is stained by your blood and sweat."

"Will you thank her for me?" The sleeping robe had many good memories for Many Wolves.

"*Haa*, I will." Then Topusana stood on her toes and leaned close to him, whispering, "I hope you find a woman who deserves your good heart, Many Wolves." It was a familiar, memorable whisper. Her eyes watered as she looked at Many Wolves, and a tear ran down her face like a tiny waterfall. "Take care of this one for me," she said in a half-crying voice. She grabbed Ten Arrows by the shoulder and smiled at him.

"I will," said Many Wolves. His eyes, too, welled up with moisture.

Ten Arrows and Many Wolves walked off, leading their horses, to find Malone and Crooked Eagle.

"Many Wolves, I hoped you would stay longer. At least until you threw that walking stick in the fire," said Crooked Eagle, standing out in front of his huge tipi. "I know the rivers and mountains are your home and give you strength, and it pleases my heart to see you return to them, but know that you are always welcome here where my warriors will protect you."

"*Ura*, Crooked Eagle. I hope to return here again, at least to visit my friends."

"May the Great Spirit guide you safely in your journey, Many Wolves," said Crooked Eagle, and he disappeared into his lodge.

Many Wolves packed away his walking stick and mounted his brown horse from the right side, because it was easier on his sore leg. Ten Arrows mounted also, and they walked to the edge of the village where Malone was staying. But his lodge was empty.

"He must be hunting or riding with the men," said Ten Arrows. "I think he has found a home here."

"I was hoping to say goodbye and thank him again," said Many Wolves. He had grown fond of the quiet man who had captured him, then saved him. *I will miss talking to Malone.*

"We will see him again, Wild Man. I am sure."

Three

"I missed this quiet, Ten Arrows," said Many Wolves, watching dusk slowly turn to darkness around their camp. "Loud voices, crying babies, and stomping footsteps… all these had silenced the chirping crickets and frogs, the screeching owls, and the whirring and booming of diving nighthawks—sounds that were part of my daily life."

"The animal sounds are the sounds of your home, Wild Man," said Ten Arrows, sipping a hot cup of tea. "I like this quiet too. My dreams are more vivid when I'm outside the village."

Many Wolves and Ten Arrows sat together under a large, twisted oak tree surrounded by rolling hills of endless grass. Ten Arrows built a small fire for making tea, and to add some light to the gathering darkness.

"Don't make the flames too big," said Many Wolves as Ten Arrows was about to add another branch to the fire. The survival instincts of a man who had lived most of his life hiding in the wilderness were hard to change.

Ten Arrows smiled and set the branch aside.

"Are you worried, Ten Arrows, that Thorn Bird will find us?"

"*Haa*, I worry. I don't think it is luck that he knew to trade with Proud Toad when he did. I believe that someone in my village was watching us—which means that Thorn Bird will soon know that we have left. The deeper we ride into the wilderness, the safer it will be for us."

"If we can find the Gray Face camp from here, then we have a good chance to find Rojo near there," said Many Wolves. "As far as I know, the only Nokoni who knows about that camp is Malone, and hopefully we can trust him to keep it secret." Many Wolves grabbed a piece of salted pemmican from his food pouch and started sucking on it. His body had healed well enough to ride a horse, and also well enough to once again chew on the foods he was used to eating. And that had led to the return of his appetite, along with much of the weight and strength he had lost.

"Do you think Rojo will still be there?" Ten Arrows asked.

"I think so. We have spent many sleeps around that camp. He knows it is our territory. I don't think Fiera will be there though."

"Fiera?"

"Fiera was the bird-killer hawk that I trained," said Many Wolves, biting off a small piece of the dried meat he had softened with his mouth.

"Now I remember. You said she flew off and didn't come back."

"She was fast, Ten Arrows. It was breathtaking to watch her hunt. But she didn't have the same tameness that my wolf hawks had. Those hawks were as tame as an old village dog."

Ten Arrows laughed. "That's what I remember about them. I also remember Chiquito digging his claws into the back of my hand!"

Many Wolves chuckled. "You didn't know how to handle him. You don't put a big piece of raw meat in front of a hungry predator and expect it to be gentle."

"That is your magic, my friend. I don't pretend to tame wild animals."

Then, from the quiet, came the distant sound of hooves.

"Did you hear that?" said Many Wolves.

"*Haa*. It's a horse. Load your bow!"

Many Wolves scrambled for his quiver, pulled out his bow, and quickly loaded it. Ten Arrows did the same.

The beating hooves were getting closer. Both men moved behind the large trunk of the oak tree, using it like a large shield. Many Wolves's heart was beating out of his chest. *Thorn Bird.*

Then the horse stopped and a voice rang out from the dark. "Many Wolves! Ten Arrows!"

It's Malone. Many Wolves was overcome with relief.

"Don't shoot. I'm Nokoni, but I'm not your enemy!" said Malone.

The horse galloped again toward them, and Malone emerged from the dark. "You were trying to sneak away without your friend Malone?"

Many Wolves and Ten Arrows laughed, then Many Wolves said, "You almost made my heart leap out of my chest!"

"You deserve as much, for trying to leave without me," said Malone with a grin. The Nokoni dismounted and led his horse to where the other two horses were.

"We didn't think you wanted to come with us," said Ten Arrows.

"You think I would let you fools die out here?"

"We thought you had found a new home in Ten Arrows's village," said Many Wolves. "You seemed so excited about hunting buffalo again."

"I did enjoy hunting the buffalo. It keeps my mind sharp and my horse in good health," said Malone. All three men sat down around the fire. "But my mind would never rest if Thorn Bird captured you again, Many Wolves."

"So you are coming with us?" said Many Wolves.

"You are a fool for leaving Crooked Eagle's protection, but I know your heart bleeds for wild places… as does mine. I should help you find the wolf I took away from you."

"So now there are three of us against Thorn Bird's men," said Ten Arrows.

"Three is better than two," said Malone.

A Storm is Coming

"This will be an easier winter, *mi amor,*" said Valencia to her husband.

"*Haa,*" said Thorn Bird in agreement, switching back to his native language. The Nokoni leader was sharpening a new lance point that Paco's men had acquired in Taos with the surplus of buffalo robes the women had prepared. His oldest son, Cold Raven, was sitting next to him watching him work. Thorn Bird was pleased that the *mexicanos* had relieved him and his men of this journey, which had become a chore for him in past seasons. "The women have worked hard preparing the skins and preserving the meat."

"Even the *Navoonah* women has done her share," Valencia said with a bone needle in her mouth. She was sewing some new moccasins for Cold Raven.

Thorn Bird laughed to himself. "I wasn't expecting that she would be so useful. She has proven her value in more than one way."

He still hoped that Many Wolves would come for the *Navoonah* slave with an offer of trade, but there was no word from him or the Penateka. It would be more difficult to kill her now that he knew how well she could work a buffalo hide, but this was the promise he had made to Many Wolves, and he had no intention of abandoning it.

It was approaching mid-afternoon and the heat had settled on Thorn Bird's village.

Esatai, their youngest son, ran up to his mother. "I'm hungry. What can

I eat?"

"You're always hungry," said Cold Raven.

Valencia started grooming the hair away from the youngest boy's eyes. Then she looked to her left and yelled, "*Navoonah*! Fix Esatai some buffalo ribs!"

Ninakabaru was cleaning a hide a short distance away from them. She stopped what she was doing and hurried over to attend to the boy, saying nothing. Thorn Bird had told her never to speak unless she had his or Valencia's permission. One time she had complained when they had asked her to do extra work on top of her normal routine of skinning and tanning; the beating she had received from Valencia had silenced her from that day on.

"It is good that he eats like a starved wolf. It will make him strong. He is already as strong as boys two or three winters older than him, and he is fearless on a horse. Many boys his age are afraid to ride," said Valencia.

Esatai walked over to his father and started hitting him hard on the arm. "What are you doing, *Ahpu*?"

"I am sharpening my lance."

"Talks Too Much can do it. He will make my weapons when I am a warrior."

The boy continued to hit Thorn Bird's arm, making it difficult for him to work. Esatai was the more physical of the two boys. He was always running or wrestling or throwing things, it seemed. He rarely stopped to do anything, it seemed.

"You need to stop hitting me, Esatai. Why don't you go hit *Navoonah* over there? She is used to people hitting her."

"But I want to be here, *Ahpu*."

"You need to stop hitting me then."

The boy finally relented, and instead he started throwing stones from around the lodge. It was a small wonder there were any left to throw, thought Thorn Bird, and he laughed to himself.

"Pemmican?" Ninakabaru asked the boy.

"No. I want you to cook me some meat!" he protested.

"He is like his grandfather," Thorn Bird chuckled. "Always demanding fresh meat. Get him what he wants, *Navoonah*! Talk to Fire Eyes. He can tell you if the hunters brought in a fresh kill this morning. You know that Esatai loves ribs, from any large animal. Get him some."

Ninakabaru nodded and ran off.

"I don't think she has eaten today," said Valencia, looking up from her sewing work.

"She has work to do, and there is only so much light in the day," said Thorn Bird in a cold voice.

"It's hard to work on an empty stomach," said Cold Raven. "Mocking Bird says that if you feed your slaves well, you will get more work out of them."

Thorn Bird knew that Cold Raven spent much of his time talking to Mocking Bird. There was much he could learn from the aging man who was the village translator, but learning how to be a warrior was not one of them. "Mocking Bird says this and says that and you repeat it like you are his mimic. Perhaps we should have named *you* Mocking Bird. A slave that fears its master is a slave that will work the hardest. This is what I have learned, and *I* am your father, not Mocking Bird."

"You are not my father. My father is in the next world. Mocking Bird has told me all about him, while you have said nothing. You are too busy killing and torturing and putting us all in danger!"

"Is this what Mocking Bird tells you? You sound more like your mother!" Thorn Bird was growing impatient with the boy. This wasn't the first time Cold Raven had challenged Thorn Bird's beliefs. "You would do well to learn the warrior ways, Cold Raven, and not from Mocking Bird. How many scalps are hung on his lodge?"

"It's not scalps that make a good leader or a good father!" Cold Raven said, then he stood up and ran off.

"He gets on my nerves!" shouted Thorn Bird. Sweat was dripping from his forehead and seeping out of his hands, making it more difficult to work.

"He is a smart boy, like his father," said Valencia. "One day you will be proud of the man he becomes."

Thorn Bird grunted, half-agreeing with her. But Cold Raven still had much to learn about being a warrior. *When Many Wolves is dead,* Thorn Bird thought, *and Ten Arrows and Malone with him, I will have more time to spend with my sons. Cold Raven's body and mind will be ready by then.*

Ninakabaru brought back some ribs and set a pot to boil on the fire pit.

"Antelope?" said Thorn Bird.

The *Navoonah* slave nodded.

"Good, and you brought enough for me too," said the Nokoni leader.

Moments later, Thorn Bird heard hoofbeats approaching his lodge. It was Half Weasel. The scout dismounted when he reached them. "*Namunewapi,* I have news for you. Good news." He was out of breath and sweating from the heat.

"Tell me." Thorn Bird stood to face him.

"Many Wolves and Ten Arrows have left the Penateka village. They are heading west."

"Just the two of them?"

"*Haa.*"

"That is good news. The best I've heard in quite a while!" Thorn Bird felt relief and joy fill him. "They think they can hide from us, Half Weasel. They are sorely mistaken."

"*Haa, namunewapi.* A storm is coming, and they are hoping it will keep them hidden."

A storm will not slow my vengeance.

More Protection

The three travelers awoke at sunrise the next day and started their long journey west to the Gray Face camp. Many Wolves's bad leg prevented them from riding as hard as Malone wanted, but he agreed with the medicine. Malone also agreed to cover their tracks as best he could, so he frequently dropped back on his own and then caught up to them again. Many Wolves trusted that a skilled Nokoni tracker like Malone could hide any tracks. The best trackers were the best at covering tracks, because they knew what a tracker would look for.

"Did it surprise you that Malone would follow us, Wild Man?" said Ten Arrows when Malone was not with them. Their horses were slowed to a walk. Ten Arrows rode a mostly white horse he had named Storm. Storm had been sired by Ten Arrows's white war horse, Cloud, who had grown too old for the rigors of daily riding.

"*Haa*, I was surprised. He seemed content to live in your village, and I felt he didn't owe anything else to me."

"Well, I suspected he would follow us. He seems a lot like us—he has our thirst for the 'wild places,' as he would say."

"Did you hunt buffalo with him?"

Ten Arrows nodded his head and widened his eyes as if he had just seen something amazing. "I did, Wild Man. He can handle a horse with the greatest skill. He was weaving in and out of the buffalo herd like a ghost. I have never seen such grace and speed. He was teaching the warriors of my village many tricks they did not know."

"So the Nokoni riders are more skilled than the Penateka?"

"I wouldn't agree to that. Malone is a special rider, Wild Man. I don't think many Nokonis can ride like that either."

"Then he can teach you things about riding a horse," said Many Wolves.

"*Haa*, he can, and he will!" Ten Arrows laughed.

Many Wolves heard a galloping horse, looked back, and saw Malone approaching. The Nokoni caught up to them quickly and then slowed his mount to a walk. His horse was breathing hard from the run.

"Many Wolves, I have a gift for you. It's a shield I made while you were healing at the village," said Malone, out of breath himself. He reached back on his horse, pulled a shield out from under his supplies, and handed it to Many Wolves. "It may save your life someday."

"He is right, Wild Man," said Ten Arrows. "I haven't had to use mine often, but the protective spirit it brings will ease your mind."

The thought of fighting Thorn Bird's men was frightening to Many Wolves, but he realized that Malone was right. *I have to be prepared.* Many Wolves strapped it onto his left arm, just like Malone always did with his own. "How did you make this shield, Malone?"

"Three layers of thick buffalo hide, just like mine," said Malone, pounding his right hand against the center of his own shield. "The most important part of the shield is the painting on it. I have the horse's spirit to protect me."

Many Wolves thought that a drawing of a wolf would be good for his shield.

"You could paint Rojo on your shield, Wild Man. Then the spirit of your wolf will always be with you," said Ten Arrows.

"I was thinking that also," said Malone.

"I'd rather have Rojo for protection," said Many Wolves, "but this shield will help too, especially if we don't find him. *Ura*, Malone."

War Plans

"Malone, how many men will Thorn Bird have?' said Many Wolves, sitting around the small cooking pit with his two friends, surrounded by darkness and moonlit plains. Malone had killed two prairie dogs at dusk for them to eat.

"If Paco's men are with him, then as many as thirty men."

"Are the Mexicans good fighters?" asked Ten Arrows.

"They have many handguns and long guns, at least two weapons for each of their men. They don't ride like the *Noomah*, but at short range, their weapons are dangerous," answered Malone. "If we can survive their first round of attacks, and force them to reload their black powder, then they are open to our strike."

"Our arrows will fly farther than their metal balls?" said Many Wolves. Ten Arrows cut a piece of prairie dog meat, impaled it on a stick, and handed the stick with the sizzling meat to Many Wolves.

"*Haa*, we have that edge. But there is one Mexican, his name is Rodrigo, who they say can kill from a great distance with a special long gun he uses. Thorn Bird calls him 'Eagle Eyes' and says he can hit a target at least as far as three arrows can fly."

"How do we kill a man if our arrows can't reach him?" said Many Wolves.

"We have to ride fast and weave like a sidewinder until we get in range," said Malone. "The other danger to us is that he has two of these long guns, and his son loads one while he uses the other, so there is very little time lost reloading." Malone stopped to take a bite of meat and then continued, "Then there are the Nokonis. Most of them shoot well with their bows and can ride fast while they shoot. Thorn Bird is the best of them, both on a horse and with a bow. "

"How do we fight them?" asked Many Wolves. He was too nervous to eat.

"We will have to knock them off their mounts or kill their horses. They are difficult to hit with an arrow."

"We should just run and hide from them," said Many Wolves, thinking aloud.

"Their horses would overtake us if we tried to run, especially with your bad leg, and Thorn Bird will never give up looking for us. He must know by now that we are on the run," said Malone.

"How is Thorn Bird as a leader?" asked Ten Arrows.

"He is not like his father," answered Malone. "His father was not reckless like him; he wouldn't jump into a fight if he knew it could not easily be won with little or no injuries to his men. He used his scouts to make certain he was prepared. Also, he was generous with the spoils of war, rarely keeping anything for himself, except for scalps. I don't see this kind of leader in Thorn Bird. He fights more for himself than his men. But as a warrior on the field of battle, it would be difficult to say which of the two is more skilled." Malone paused. "Laughing Crow was a great friend and leader. Thorn Bird is a killer and a torturer."

Many Wolves regarded Malone as a quiet man and had never expected to hear so many words from his mouth at once, but the quiet man was saying what needed to be said. Many Wolves wholeheartedly trusted Malone's vast experience with war, and he believed that Ten Arrows felt the same. With Malone as their leader, Many Wolves believed there was hope that somehow they could survive this, and that fighting, and not running, was the right thing to do.

"Malone, you are as cheerful as a screech owl," said Ten Arrows, seemingly trying to lighten the mood.

Ten Arrows and Many Wolves laughed, and the somber Malone smiled for a moment.

"Then I will change the mood of our talk," said Malone, taking a big gulp of water, then a gulp of air to catch up with his breathing. "Many Wolves, what kind of magic did you use to bring Topusana to your sleeping robe?"

Many Wolves and Ten Arrows looked at each other and grinned.

"That *is* a change!" said Ten Arrows.

"I have my brother here to thank for that," said Many Wolves with a big smile.

"How do *I* become your brother, Ten Arrows?" said Malone, lightheartedly. "So she will come to *my* sleeping robe!"

"You can save me from a rabid grizzly bear. That's what worked for Many Wolves."

"I'll have to keep my eyes open for bears then and then try to bait them into attacking you."

"Keep the bears to yourself, Malone. I already have enough bear marks on my back," said Ten Arrows with a serious tone, before breaking into laughter.

"How far west are we, Malone?" said Many Wolves, taking another bite of the succulent prairie dog meat.

"We will reach the Rio Pecos tomorrow at sundown."

A Familiar Voice

Many Wolves lay on his sleeping robe looking up at the stars. It was hard to fall asleep because of all the earlier talk of war. He tried to think of happier moments to distract his disturbed mind. Thoughts of his grandfather, his father, and his mother were just fleeting memories now for him. The memory of his night with Topusana was much easier to remember, and that one was calming. He also imagined what it would be like if Ninakabaru slipped into his sleeping robe at night, but it was hard to picture her without her sadness.

Malone was awake also, while Ten Arrows slept. It seemed like the Nokoni had been awake most of the previous night as well: whenever Many Wolves had woken up, there was Malone fixing his arrows or staring up at the night sky.

"You don't sleep much, Malone?"

"I take little sleeps here and there, but I like the quiet nights. Especially out here."

Then Many Wolves heard a faint, distant sound. Howling.

"Did you hear that?"

"Hear what?"

"That howling," said Many Wolves. "There, I heard it again."

"I heard some coyotes howling earlier, Many Wolves."

"Malone, it sounds like Rojo! I know that howl! It's Rojo!"

Ten Arrows woke up, groggy, "What is it?"

"Ten Arrows, I think I hear Rojo!"

"Are you sure it's him?" asked the sleepy Penateka.

"I think so."

"I think I hear it now too, Many Wolves," said Malone. "Walk toward it. Will he hear you from here?"

"*Haa*, I think so. His hearing is much stronger."

Many Wolves walked into the dark prairie grass, toward the sound, and yelled, "Rojo!" He kept walking and calling to his wolf. Then the howling stopped. *Is he gone? Did he hear me?*

There was nothing to see in the thick of the night, so Many Wolves waited and watched.

"I don't hear it anymore," yelled Malone.

"It stopped," said Many Wolves.

Then, after waiting for some time, Many Wolves turned back to camp. *The wolf is gone. It sounded like Rojo.* He was about to give up hope when the howling started up again, and this time it was much louder and closer. "Rojo!" *It* is *my wolf.*

From out of the blackened landscape, the red wolf appeared, running toward him and breathing hard with his tongue dangling from his mouth. The big predator was yipping like a puppy when he finally reached Many Wolves, his tail swinging back and forth wildly.

"Rojo, you're all right!" Many Wolves said as he hugged his companion. He was close to tears, but he held them back as best he could.

When the wolf looked toward the camp, his mood changed like a clap of thunder and a growl emanated from his belly. His wagging tail dropped and the hackles on his back stood up. He was looking at Malone.

"Rojo, easy, friend! Malone is a friend," commanded Many Wolves, but the wolf continued to growl.

"I don't think he likes you, Malone."

"He has good reasons not to," said Malone, from a distance.

"Ten Arrows, can you bring me my sleeping robe? I'll stay out here with him."

"Is he going to growl at me too?" Ten Arrows was now wide awake after all the excitement.

"We'll find out when you come near him."

Ten Arrows picked up Many Wolves's sleeping robe and walked slowly toward them.

Rojo did not growl at Ten Arrows; he was too busy watching Malone.

"Good. He still remembers me." Ten Arrows held out his hand to Rojo; the wolf sniffed it and then licked it briefly, still not taking his eyes off Malone.

Many Wolves grabbed the sleeping robe from Ten Arrows. "Come on, Rojo, we'll stay out here tonight. Away from Malone."

The wolf followed him out away from the camp. Many Wolves spread out his sleeping robe and lay down. Rojo lay next to him, his eyes facing the distant camp and Malone.

Many Wolves stroked his wolf's coarse fur and felt his ribs. "You have been eating well on your own, Rojo." The wolf licked his hands and continued to keep an eye on Malone. "I bet you missed the easy meals, the ear scratching, the belly petting, the back rubbing…"

It was good to have his protector back.

Surrounded

The late afternoon sun peeked in and out of the drifting clouds like a nervous prairie dog unwilling to leave the comfort of its burrow. A thick, black mass of thunderclouds surrounded the three riders heading westward. Flashes of lightning and loud, booming thunder awaited them farther west, as well as the thick tendrils of rain falling from the charcoal sky.

Ten Arrows and Many Wolves rode together, and Rojo ran a short distance behind them. Malone had backtracked to scout and cover their tracks and to keep his distance from the agitated wolf.

Many Wolves imagined that the familiar, salty waters of the Rio Pecos flowed ahead of them, fed by the storm like a large snake gorging on an oversized meal. He had seen the rain swell this river many times before. The Gray Face camp, which was still their destination, was farther north along the growing river.

Many Wolves heard a horse galloping. He looked back to see Malone sprinting toward them on Wind Chaser, his black and white painted stallion. Malone slowed his mount when he saw Rojo's posturing. Winded by the ride, Malone blurted, "Thorn Bird is tracking us! He and his men will be here at nightfall. Let's keep heading west and then veer north when we hit the Rio Pecos."

The thought of Thorn Bird drove a shiver through Many Wolves's body. *He is here.*

"It may be difficult for the horses to swim across the river in that storm," said Ten Arrows, pointing straight ahead.

"It depends on how strong the current is and whether there is a narrow gap to cross, Ten Arrows," said Malone, then he rode out ahead of them to search the river for a crossing.

The men galloped ahead with Rojo running behind them. Many Wolves still couldn't ride at full speed because the jolting movement hurt his leg. He hated being the slow buffalo that held back the herd.

As they got closer to the river, the wind and the rain pelted them from the north, and the cold air bit at their faces. The blinding flashes of light were less frequent now, but the thunder growled like an old bear warning them to stay away. They were in the heart of the storm, but they had no choice but to endure it, since a greater danger was behind them.

The landscape was rugged here. On their right was a massive plateau of solid rock, stretching westward toward the river and eventually turning sharply to the north. They bent their horses north to follow along the rocky wall, straight into the rush of air and rain. The plateau closed them in on the right, while the river, silhouetted by windswept trees along its bank, closed them in on the left.

Many Wolves and Ten Arrows lost sight of Malone in the fading visibility, but they headed north along the wall until eventually they saw that it took yet another turn west toward the river. The plateau was too steep for a horse to climb.

We are trapped unless there's a break in the wall or the river can be crossed up ahead, Many Wolves thought.

They rode deeper into the vicious storm and the binding rocky enclosure. At last they saw flashes of white from Malone's horse—he was still scouring the river. This wasn't a good sign. Ten Arrows rode beside Many Wolves, holding back his speed to stay alongside the injured rider, though the weather was now more of a deterrent to speed than Many Wolves was. Rojo followed, seemingly untouched by the violent weather.

Malone reached the wall ahead of them, then turned back. The three horses slowed when they reached a juncture. Rojo kept a safe distance away from Malone, but at least he didn't growl or bark.

"The river is too wild for the horses to swim across safely," Malone yelled to be heard above the howling wind, his body drenched and rain pummeling his face. "We could ride south and look for a calmer spot, but Thorn Bird's men will be gaining on us every moment, and the rain will only make the river harder and harder to cross."

"What other choice do we have?" said Ten Arrows.

"We can build our camp along that north wall. Just up ahead, the ground slopes uphill and is rocky. The wall will shelter us from the wind and rain, and the hill will drain the flood water. When the rain ends, we will be protected from Thorn Bird by rock and river on three sides."

"That's all we can do?" said Many Wolves.

"It is," said Malone, still slightly out of breath and wiping the water out of his eyes.

"Let's go then," said Ten Arrows.

When they arrived at the north wall, they dismounted and let the horses find their own cover. As the men scrambled over to the stony barrier, almost instantly the rain and wind seemed to abandon them.

Many Wolves looked out upon the raging water of the Pecos; he couldn't remember a time when it had risen higher than this. The flailing cottonwoods along the bank sat in what looked like knee-high water. The men were fortunately well uphill, protected from the advancing water.

The storm continued with great ferocity until dusk came, and then the lightning and thunder subsided, leaving only a steady rain and shivery air. Ten Arrows built a fire up against the base of the rising stone for warmth and put cups of water on for boiling tea.

The men walked all around the camp as the water heated. Much of the ground around the base of the wall was flat, but after about ten horse lengths, it sloped downward into terrain covered in rock and sediment.

"This hill will slow their horses if they try to charge up it," said Malone.

"Can they climb that plateau?" asked Many Wolves, pointing upward.

"Not from this side. But there may be a way for a man to climb up there from the back side," said Malone. "Still, that's in range of our arrows." Malone pointed to a crevasse on the northern wall that was barely visible in the faint moonlight. Many Wolves remembered that the eastern wall looked smooth and impassable.

"This is where we will fight. We will kill or be killed," said Ten Arrows in a grave voice.

"This place will be like a Spanish fortress for us," said Malone. "It will not be easy for Thorn Bird to attack us here. The Nokonis like flat, open spaces with soft, dry soil to maneuver their mounts. Here, they will have to attack us straight on from the south. There is no other way." Malone smiled after saying this, giving Many Wolves a shred of hope.

"Many Wolves, how much sinew do you have with you?" asked Malone.

"I have some, mostly rabbit sinew, but also some from a bear."

"I have some also. I'll get it for you," said Malone. "I want you to make snares and plant them all around that patch of ground right before the ground slopes upward." Malone pointed as he spoke. "If we can trip their horses, or even make them stumble, it will help us. Even if it works on just one horse, it will be worth the effort of setting the snares."

"You picked the right man for the task, Malone. Wild Man is the master of trapping with snares!" said Ten Arrows. "I will help tie them."

"Good. I will ride south and keep an eye out for Thorn Bird until it gets dark. I don't expect they will be here before then, so that gives us some time to prepare," said Malone. He mounted Wind Chaser, handed the sinew to Many Wolves, and said, "You should paint that shield when you are finished with the snares." Then he rode off.

Many Wolves thought about what Ten Arrows had said—that they would kill or be killed here—but in a strange way that thought made him less afraid. No matter what happened tonight or tomorrow or even after that, it would finally be over. It was all going to end here. There was a good life waiting for him in the next world if he died, and also a good life here if Thorn Bird was dead. That was comforting to him. His only fear was if Thorn Bird captured him—but he wouldn't allow himself to face that torture again. He would be ready to end his own life if it came to that.

When the dark crept in, Malone returned. "I didn't see them, but I didn't want to ride too far."

"They're probably using the rock as a shelter like we are," said Ten Arrows.

Malone agreed.

"The snares are set, Malone. Ten Arrows and I used two loops for the rabbit sinew snares to make them stronger. I hope they hold in the wet soil," said Many Wolves. He had made stakes, tied the snares to them, and then dug the stakes into the ground. He knew a trap like this could hold a rabbit, but a horse was much different. "I dug many holes about the size of prairie dog burrows. The wet soil made it easy."

Malone smiled. "Clever thinking, Many Wolves. The animals teach you many things."

"I also painted my shield," said Many Wolves.

"Let me see it," said Malone.

Many Wolves handed Malone the shield.

"You used Rojo's paws..." marveled Malone. "I've never seen a shield painted that way. I've seen many shields with handprints, but not pawprints. I can't think of stronger medicine for you, Many Wolves." He handed the shield back to Many Wolves and smiled.

"Now we must paint our faces and bodies," said Ten Arrows. "We must be ready for the thunder of horses when the sun comes."

Only Three

"There's three of them now," said Thorn Bird. "And the *lobo*."

He was gathered around a fire pit with the *mexicanos,* Paco and Rodrigo, and his scouts, Fire Eyes and Half Weasel. There wasn't much to eat besides the pemmican and nuts they had brought with them. The stormy weather had prevented his scouts and Rodrigo, who were the primary hunters for the band, from killing some fresh meat for the fire. But that was fine: Thorn Bird preferred not to eat, to prepare his mind for war, and his scouts felt the same. The *mexicanos,* for their part, seemed satisfied with the pemmican.

The wind continued to howl through the darkness, pouncing on them occasionally in gusts and bullying the modest fire that burned warmth into their bones. The rain had stopped, making it easier for the men to talk, to plan their attack.

"Was the *lobo* with them at the Penateka village, *señor* Alcaudon?" asked Paco, chewing off the end of one of his smoking sticks and spitting it into the fire.

Thorn Bird asked the same question to Half Weasel in the *Noomah* words, then translated his answer for the *mexicanos.* "The *lobo* was not with the *gringo*, but it's with them now. Half Weasel is certain of it."

"One *bala*, one dead *lobo*," said Rodrigo, spitting out pemmican juice with his mouth half full of the jerky.

Thorn Bird knew this was no ordinary wolf. One shot from Rodrigo's long gun would not be enough. "The *lobo* is your first target, Eagle Eyes, and your only target until it is motionless on the ground. *Comprendes*?" said Thorn Bird. *That wolf is much more dangerous than the taiboo.*

"*Si*, Alcaudon. It is done," said the serious *mexicano*.

"The three of them are trapped by the *rio* and the giant rock," said Thorn Bird, looking at Paco and Rodrigo, who were seated across the fire pit from him. "They won't risk crossing the *rio* at night, and the *mesa* is impassable. We must attack when the first light reveals them to us. They must die on this side of the *rio*. Their scalps will be in *mis manos* before I see the full circle of the rising sun. *Comprendes*, Shiny Teeth?"

"*Si, señor* Alcaudon. We will help you kill the *lobo,* the *gringo*, Many Wolves, and the Nokoni named Malone. But you must kill the Penateka yourself." Paco blew the smoke from his lungs and stared at Thorn Bird, his usual smile hidden.

"*Por que*, Shiny Teeth?"

"If the Penatekas find *mexicano balas* in the body of one of their dead warriors, it will be the end of our trade with them, *señor* Alcaudon, and perhaps the end of our lives. You remember what I once told you: dead Comanche, dead Paco. Please understand that we cannot kill this Ten Arrows." Paco pleaded with the Nokoni leader, letting his smoking stick burn itself out.

Thorn Bird was not pleased by this complication. To him, an enemy was an enemy, regardless of skin color or what band raised them. Malone was his family and his blood—but now he was his hated enemy. Enemies like Gray Elk needed to die, no matter how many men would be sent to avenge his death.

"Ten Arrows killed my father, Shiny Teeth. He is my enemy. If we are *amigos*, then my enemies are your enemies."

"I am sorry, *señor* Alcaudon. My men cannot shed Penateka *sangre*. It will bring bad luck. *Comprendes*? *Por favor!*"

Thorn Bird sighed and then relented. "I see this is *muy importante* to you and your men. I cannot make this war without you, without your men. I will have my men focus their attacks on the Penateka. I want your men to kill the *lobo* and kill Malone."

"*Gracias*! *Gracias*!" said Paco, the smile returned to his face and the smoking stick to his mouth. "And who will *you* attack, *señor* Alcaudon?"

"With your men killing Malone and the *lobo*, and my men killing the Penateka, I guess that leaves the *gringo* to me. But I will make sure that none of them ever breathes another breath again, if any of you should fail."

Paco laughed, smoke shooting out of his nose and mouth, and Rodrigo even cracked a smile.

"Shiny Teeth and Eagle Eyes, I must leave you now to paint myself for *guerra*," said Thorn Bird, standing. Then he looked over at Half Weasel and Fire Eyes and in *Noomah* words said, "Prepare yourselves for war. Tomorrow you will kill Ten Arrows."

With a plan worked out, Thorn Bird left the company of his men. He wanted to be alone to see the battle fought in his mind, not just once or twice, but many times.

A Pale Sun

The sun was pale like the moon, obscured by a thick layer of early morning clouds, but the rain and the wind had passed. The three men had been awake since the first light, painting their faces and horses, and there was still no sign of Thorn Bird and his men.

Many Wolves filled his water pouch with water from the swollen Pecos and drank some. It was full of salt and silt, but this was the water that he had drunk his whole life, and its taste was familiar to him. But the red and yellow painted face that reflected back at him from the surface of the river was not. Ten Arrows had painted it for him.

Malone and Ten Arrows had remained vigilant the whole night, making certain that one man stayed awake while the other slept, or at least tried to sleep. And they had kept the fire going the whole night—for warmth, light, and hot mint tea, Ten Arrows's favorite. The rain had poured throughout most of the night, but now it had finally stopped, as if commanded by the morning's pale sun.

Many Wolves trusted Rojo's keen senses for danger, even in the rain. The wolf was calm the whole night, and was seemingly feeling more and more comfortable with his pack leader's friend, Malone. As long as Rojo was calm, Many Wolves was calm, but there was still a tense feeling among them, knowing what was to come. Few words were spoken.

Visibility returned with the improved weather. The men saw the giant reddish-brown walls of the plateau clearly for the first time, and they confirmed among themselves that there was no way up to the top, at least not from this side.

"The currents are still too strong to cross easily," said Malone, sitting on the back of Wind Chaser and looking out at the big river, his face painted in yellow, red, and black. The Rio Pecos raged with watery muscle, puffing its chest like a male turkey in early spring. Its opposite bank was easily out of reach of any of their arrows. "Our best chance is to fight here. Even if we could cross safely, the Nokonis would only hunt us down. And a cornered animal is much more dangerous than a fleeing one."

Malone looked around the camp, then gazed back out to where Many Wolves expected the Nokonis and Mexicans would arrive. Wind Chaser was decorated with red and black handprints all over his body, and his eyes were ringed in black war paint. Several feathers were tied to the horse's mane. Malone's war shield was strapped to his left arm, and a quiver hugged his back, filled with his bow and about thirty arrows and covered by an animal fur to stay dry. In the silence, the Nokoni warrior studied the battlefield for several moments, then he rode back to talk to Many Wolves and Ten Arrows.

"When they come, you need to stay up here and fight on foot," he said to Many Wolves. "Ten Arrows and I will sweep back and forth along the edge here on our horses and bring the fight to them as best we can. Two things you must remember: keep your shield up and knock them off their horses."

There was no disagreeing with Malone. He was the war leader.

Many Wolves wore his shield on his left arm and his quiver on his back. Malone had shown him how to wear the shield, as well as how to shoot a bow while wearing it. At first it had been a little awkward for Many Wolves, but he had taken some practice shots with his bow and now he felt comfortable fighting with the shield.

Ten Arrows mounted his war horse as well. The Penateka warrior's face was painted mostly red, with yellow stripes going across. His mount, Storm, was decorated with handprints and eye rings, but the horse also had red arrows drawn on his body.

The way Ten Arrows looked now reminded Many Wolves of the day when Ten Arrows had killed the great bear that had left the marks on Many Wolves's leg. The only difference was that now Ten Arrows wore a shield. It was on his right arm, because he liked to shoot his bow with his left hand. Many Wolves had not seen another man in the Penateka village shoot a bow with his left hand.

The first sign of Thorn Bird's presence was Rojo's growl. Soon after, a single Nokoni rider appeared on the landscape. Many Wolves felt a tremor of fear surge through his body.

"That is Thorn Bird's scout, Half Weasel," said Malone.

When he saw the three men, the scout screamed a war whoop, which was barely audible in the soft breeze, and then he rode away, out of their view.

A little while later, they heard another sound: the booming pops of the Mexican guns. A celebration, Many Wolves thought, above the beats of his racing heart. Rojo was agitated, but this time, Many Wolves did not want to calm him.

These men were not their friends.

At last, the Nokoni and Mexican riders appeared.

"Eighteen men and one boy," said Malone. "Only eight Mexican men though. I expected more. I guess they don't all feel Thorn Bird's hate."

Eighteen is better than thirty, Many Wolves thought.

Thorn Bird's men held their mounts to a walk, the length of one or two horses separating each man from the next. The Nokoni leader himself was in the middle of the riders, with the black-faced Nokonis on his right and the hat-wearing Mexicans on his left. A Mexican boy followed the Mexican men, just a few horse lengths behind them.

Malone nodded to Ten Arrows and directed his mount to Many Wolves's left, while Ten Arrows moved to the right. Their horses grunted nervously, and they relieved their bladders of excess body weight. *They are preparing to run.*

One of the Mexican men barked a command that Many Wolves didn't understand, and the Mexicans moved their horses to Thorn Bird's right, swapping places with the Nokonis.

Malone spoke to his friends just loud enough for them to hear. "The one who spoke—that one is Paco," he said. "He leads the Mexicans. See the red colors on his shirt? The larger Mexican with the black shirt is his brother Rodrigo, the one with the eagle eyes, and the boy in the rear is his son and his weapon loader. They are positioning the Mexicans to fight me."

"Why?" said Many Wolves, watching their enemies approach, still out of range of their arrows.

"I suspect they are afraid to fight Ten Arrows, because they do not want to make war with their Penateka friends. Many Wolves and I do not belong to bands that they make peace with, so they will gladly fight us."

Thorn Bird signaled his men to stop, then said something to the black-shirted Rodrigo, who quickly rode toward the base of the plateau wall, his son close behind him.

"Rodrigo is setting up his long gun," said Malone. "When he is ready, we will be easy targets for him. I may have to ride straight for him—unless either of you has another plan."

"I will take care of him," said Many Wolves, "but I will need some time."

Dying Inside

Many Wolves limped back to where the fire pit was burning and found his drinking-shell full of hot water just as he had left it. He had needed it to kill Laughing Crow's scout long ago, and now he needed it for the Mexican with the eagle eyes. He unstrapped his shield and set it aside to free his hands.

He sprinkled the mixture of white lion's paw flower and peyote from his medicine bag into the hot water.

He heard Thorn Bird yelling as he stirred the mixture. "The three coyote pups have left the safety of the den!"

Many Wolves looked over his shoulder. He couldn't see any of Thorn Bird's men because of the incline, which meant that they could not see him either. *I will be safe here—for now.*

"This pleases me! Now I do not have to wait to see you die!" shouted Thorn Bird.

"Rojo, come!" Many Wolves beckoned to his wolf. His obedient friend came immediately and lay down at his side, still growling every time Thorn Bird spoke. Many Wolves stirred the mixture to dissolve most of the sediment in the cup, and then he threw his arms around his wolf and spoke softly. "I'm sorry to put you through this, Rojo. We must do this to help Malone and Ten Arrows, and to stay alive. There is no other way, big wolf."

He closed his eyes and drank down the mixture, still holding the wolf close.

"Malone, why did you betray my father?" Thorn Bird continued. "Why did you betray your people? My father sees your betrayal and waits to hunt you in the next world!"

The darkness and the flashing colors passed in Many Wolves's mind—and then the world came back to him through the eyes of his wolf. *Rojo! You need to run straight along the base of this wall. Go, now!*

If we run against the wall, Rojo will blend in with the reddish rock, and we will avoid the snares, Many Wolves thought.

The wolf bolted, following the wall as he was told. Through the wolf's ears, Many Wolves could hear Thorn Bird still talking, but Many Wolves didn't care about words. It was only his survival, and the survival of his friends, that mattered now. No words could change this.

Rojo was almost at the corner, at the meeting of the two walls. *Rojo! Turn right here. Follow the wall!* The red wolf turned and sprinted. The wind rushed past their face and the world blurred by them. *Rojo! Look for the black-shirted man. Find him!*

The black-shirted man came into Rojo's focused view. *That's him, Rojo!* A boy was with him. The man was down on one knee, aiming his long gun, and the boy stood behind him holding another long gun. *Rojo, bite at his eyes or his throat!*

The loud Mexican guns crashed all around them. Rojo shuddered from the sound, but quickly regained his footing. Dirt kicked up in front of them and rock pieces shattered off the wall above them, knocked free by the men's metal balls. Many Wolves heard men screaming now, and he knew the wolf was their target.

The war had begun.

Rojo! Go!

The wolf ran even faster now, aided by fear. The black-shirted man did not see him coming—and Rojo leaped on top of him.

For a moment, the crackle of gunfire stopped. The wolf snapped at the man's neck with his large fangs, but he could not reach the flesh, because the man held him off with his long weapon. The man looked at Rojo through terrified eyes, screaming.

Rojo! The eyes!

The wolf swung his muscular body around and dug his knife-sharp teeth into the man's face, puncturing the skin surrounding the right eye. Many Wolves tasted the blood in the wolf's mouth and on his tongue. The man screamed even louder. Then an arrow slammed into Rojo's chest, knocking the wolf sideways off his feet. Rojo yelped in pain, then looked to see where the arrow had come from.

Thorn Bird was staring at them from his horse, another arrow already loaded in his bow and aimed straight at them. He yelled with gritted teeth: "It's your time to die, magic wolf!"

He shot again, and the second arrow tore through the crippled wolf.

Rojo cried out and collapsed to the ground, choking for every breath. The taste of blood was overwhelming now. *Rojo's blood.* Rojo's eyes were closing slowly, letting in the darkness. His life was dimming. *Rojo! I'm sorry. Wait for me in the next world, my beautiful friend. Wait for me!*

Then there was only blackness.

Rojo was dead.

Screams of War

Many Wolves opened his eyes to a world filled with the screams of men and horses, the pounding of hooves, the thunder of Mexican guns, and the whirring of arrows; but he could see none of it, save for the rising smoke from the guns. He grabbed his shield and pulled his bow out of his quiver, stood, and limped into the horror of war.

Malone was to the left, riding hard along the wall where Rojo was, ducking behind his shield or falling to the side of his horse to avoid arrows and gunfire. He rode past the black-shirted man, who was writhing on the ground with his son screaming at his side, but did not fire on them. Instead he launched his arrows at the men who were attacking him, mostly Mexicans, but also including at least two of the Nokonis. Many Wolves saw that Malone had already sent at least four enemies to the ground; some were still moving, some were not.

On the other side of the battle, Ten Arrows was on his feet next to his screaming horse. The horse had two arrows protruding from his body, and several arrows stuck from Ten Arrows's shield as well. He was backing up toward the top of the small hill, shooting arrows as he retreated. Three injured Nokonis lay on the ground in front of him—one of them pinned down by a wailing horse. Then another one of the Nokoni horses tripped on something, and Ten Arrows shot an arrow through the rider's chest before the man could recover.

The snares!

Then Many Wolves spotted Thorn Bird. He was riding hard toward Ten Arrows, screaming. He rode straight through the patch of snares and holes, unleashing a swarm of hissing arrows at the unhorsed Penateka. Ten Arrows braced himself, too busy blocking the arrows with his shield to shoot back.

Many Wolves sized up the distance between himself and the Nokoni leader. Thorn Bird was within his range.

Many Wolves launched an arrow at the raging Nokoni, but the arrow sailed past harmlessly. He quickly loaded another arrow—and then heard Ten Arrows scream in pain. Many Wolves recoiled as he looked over to see Ten Arrows breaking the shaft off an arrow that was lodged deep in his chest.

Thorn Bird continued to race toward the reeling Penateka. Many Wolves took aim again … and released.

His arrow struck the rear leg of Thorn Bird's horse. The horse screamed and stumbled briefly, but did not stop; it continued sprinting toward Ten Arrows. The horse's hooves chewed through the loose rock easily, its leg muscles rippling, hungering for more speed. Thorn Bird grabbed onto the horse's reins and screamed as the rampaging beast reached Ten Arrows and trampled over him, crushing him with its hooves. The Nokoni leader then spun his mount around and drove another arrow into Ten Arrows's chest.

Many Wolves was stunned and horrified, but he forced his nerves to remain steady as he drew back his bow a third time.

Thorn Bird was looking down at his victim, preparing to launch another arrow into the Penateka's chest, when Many Wolves's whistling arrow ripped into the flesh of his left shoulder. The Nokoni yelled and turned his demonic gaze toward Many Wolves. His face was covered in long black hair, which stirred in Many Wolves the memory of the torture dance. The Nokoni crushed the shaft of the arrow with his hand and urged his war horse forward.

Thorn Bird loaded one of the two arrows in his right hand and buzzed it at Many Wolves, but the wolf shield stopped it, knocking Many Wolves backward. His ailing left leg was just barely able to hold him up. The

Nokoni leader swiftly unleashed the second arrow immediately after the first. This one, too, hit the shield, but with such force that it sliced right through it and dug partway into Many Wolves's shoulder.

Many Wolves felt a stinging surge of pain. But the tip of the arrow had not burrowed far into his skin, so he thrust the shield forward to extract it.

The Nokoni warrior continued to charge toward him. He was completely concealed by his large war shield, except for his eyes and the top of his head. With one smooth motion, Thorn Bird slid his bow into his quiver and unsheathed instead a large, shiny blade that had hung from his back.

Many Wolves loaded another arrow. There was time for one last shot, but only one, before the warrior was upon him. This arrow had to either knock down the rider or knock down the horse.

Many Wolves aimed at Thorn Bird, but he saw no opening in his defense—so he lowered his aim and cut loose with the arrow.

The horse bellowed in pain as the point of the arrow punctured its throat, and the giant animal slammed into the ground, spraying dirt and rocks all around. Thorn Bird was thrown off his mount, landing on his chest and rolling his body to cushion the fall. The blade flew out of his hand and landed several steps away from him. He looked at it as if to retrieve it, then pulled the knife out of his leg sheath instead. The Nokoni leader cast his gaze at Many Wolves. Only about fifteen steps now separated the two warriors. Thorn Bird cried out and sprinted toward Many Wolves, his knife in one hand, his shield on the opposite arm, and murder in his eyes.

But the Nokoni's fall had given Many Wolves enough time to load another arrow. Once again, he aimed low, away from his enemy's raised shield. *Cut down the legs, he thought, just like with a grizzly bear.* There was no time for Many Wolves to aim, no time to steady his panicked breathing, just load and shoot.

The arrow sailed from his hands, and the world slowed around him. He watched the arrow twist through the air, tear into Thorn Bird's leg. The Nokoni's leg buckled under him and he yelled as his body crashed to the ground just a few steps away from Many Wolves.

Many Wolves's first instinct was to run, but the moment he moved his leg, he felt a crushing pain. He had reinjured his wounded leg, and speed was out of the question. He stumbled, then slung the shield off his arm and ran toward the river as fast as his stiff, limp leg would let him.

He had expected to see his chestnut horse there, but it was gone. That left him only two options: swim or fight, and neither was much safer than the other.

He decided to swim.

He flung his bow and quiver to the ground; they would only hamper him, and the water would make the bow difficult to use. He didn't look back to see where Thorn Bird was or what he was doing. It didn't matter. He had to get away. But just as he was about to reach the river, he heard the twang of a bowstring and felt an arrow pierce his left shoulder. The force of it knocked him forward off his feet, tumbling into the cold, rushing waters of the Rio Pecos.

Swallowed

The frigid waters of the Rio Pecos stung Many Wolves's body and the salt bit at his wounds. The powerful current pulled him southward. He drifted, completely at the water's mercy. *If I can get to the other side, I will be safe*, he thought. *Thorn Bird won't find me there.*

With only one good leg and one good arm, he paddled and kicked his way across the river. For every arm length he swam westward, he drifted ten armlengths southward, but at least he was moving toward the other side. Yet his body was growing tired, and each time he tried to rest, the violent river pulled him under, trying to swallow him whole. Each time he fought his way back up and spit out the salty water from his mouth. The little fire that burned inside him refused to go out. There was something to live for, something to fight for.

Many Wolves tried to look back upriver to find his pursuer, but saw nothing. *What if Thorn Bird cannnot swim? Maybe the Pecos will pull him under?* It wasn't likely, not for a man of his strength. No, Many Wolves had to assume that Thorn Bird could swim well, even better than him, even though he knew that Thorn Bird's injuries would slow him down, too.

Then he heard Thorn Bird yell somewhere behind him. He couldn't tell what the Nokoni said, but the voice came from the river, not the bank. That quelled any doubts that his puruer could swim.

Many Wolves's body was slowing from fatigue and it was becoming more and more difficult to breathe. Still, his mind willed him on. He thought he must be at least halfway across now. *I have to keep going.*

Something bumped against his shoulder—a large piece of thick, rotting wood. He grabbed onto it and tucked it under his sore left arm while he continued to paddle with his right. *Here is a gift from the Great Spirit,* he thought. The river would not pull him under now. He knew that he could make it to the other side.

When he finally reached the west bank, he grabbed hold of a cottonwood branch. His body was so tired, he didn't know if he could pull himself out of the water, but the flame inside drove him up onto the bank. He lay there, gasping for each breath, but eventually his wind came back to him.

He inspected his throbbing left shoulder. The arrow had passed completely through so that most of the point stuck out from the front of his shoulder. The salt from the cold water made the wound sting even more.

Then an uplifting thought came to him. *Thorn Bird must be tired, too.* And the only weapon he had was a knife, if even that. The thought gave him renewed hope and strength.

Many Wolves was tired of running. He wanted to end this struggle, and that meant he wanted to end Thorn Bird's life. The big piece of wood in his hand would be a good weapon: a war club. *The Great Spirit brought me this for a reason. I must find Thorn Bird and kill him.*

He walked south along the river, dragging his bad leg, and scanned the water for any sign of the Nokoni. It would be hard for Thorn Bird to see him through the endless string of cottonwoods that lined the river, although there were enough gaps between them for Many Wolves to see through. *The Nokoni wasn't far behind me.*

At last he spotted Thorn Bird's head bobbing up and down in the rough water. His enemy was close to the shore, but still subdued by the powerful pull of the river. Many Wolves guessed the drifting man would reach the riverbank not too far up ahead. His body invigorated by the idea of killing his dreaded enemy, he raced to the spot where he expected his enemy to land, keeping his eyes pinned to the Nokoni.

When Thorn Bird finally reached the west bank, he pulled himself out of the water, crawling on his hands and knees. He coughed up water and struggled for each of his breaths.

Many Wolves knew there was no time to lose. He stepped out from behind the cottonwoods and staggered forward on numb legs before his opponent could rise to his feet.

Then he raised the war club high and, with all his strength, brought it down on the back of Thorn Bird's head. The thick wood knocked the Nokoni flat onto his stomach.

The Nokoni grumbled, gritting his teeth, and turned to look at his attacker, his long wet hair draped across his face and his lungs laboring for air. He had a dazed look in his eyes as he staggered to his feet.

"I offered you my life, Thorn Bird, but you did not take it. Now, I will take yours!" yelled Many Wolves. There were no more words to say. He swung the war club with both of his arms, crushing the left side of Thorn Bird's head and knocking the Nokoni leader's body into the water.

His enemy's head floated face-down in the killing water, his long black hair fanned out in every direction, the river's surface stained by a growing cloud of blood.

Thorn Bird's body didn't move.

It would never move again.

Many Wolves hunched over and breathed in deep. He savored the air that was of this world and of no other. It was not the air of the world that was reserved for the dead. Because he was alive. And it was over.

He fell to his hands and knees and cupped the life-giving water of the Rio Pecos, the same river that had been his friend for so long—the same river that had saved him from the snake's poison. He washed his face, scrubbing off the last remnants of war paint. He wanted to be cleansed of this hate forever.

Loneliness crept inside him, like the clouds that blocked the warmth of the sun on this dark, dreary day. Rojo was dead. Ten Arrows was dead. Malone was probably dead too. He felt alone again. Wet, cold, and alone. The pain had crept back too, in his arm and in his leg. His body and mind were overcome with exhaustion, and he was shivering uncontrollably. He just couldn't move anymore, so he closed his eyes and let the rippling waters of the Rio Pecos lull him to sleep, his mind calmed by a singular thought.

Thorn Bird is dead.

Luck

The warm sunlight filtered through the forest and a soft breeze caressed the leaves and branches. Chiquito and Cazador sat in the treetops, waiting for Many Wolves to shoot an arrow through a squirrel nest so they could start the chase. It was a forest that never ended, a forest that harbored a countless number of squirrels. Reina, his largest wolf hawk, sat on his fist-perch hoping that one of the furry-tails would try to escape to the ground. His birds had already caught many squirrels already, and each one had been devoured in a heartbeat. The crops of the three hawks never filled, it seemed. After finishing one meal, they were ready to hunt for the next.

"Many Wolves!" said a muffled voice from a different place. He couldn't see where in the forest it was coming from. It sounded like Ten Arrows's voice.

"Many Wolves! Wake up!"

"Ten Arrows?" said Many Wolves, feeling pain in his shoulder.

The forest, the birds, the sun, the wind, they all drifted away, and he opened his eyes to see a familiar face looking at him. "Malone?" He looked around him. He saw the roaring Pecos River and the body of Thorn Bird lying at the edge of the water. Emotion welled up inside him. "Malone! You're alive!"

"*Haa*, I'm alive. My ribs are sore and my head hurts, but I'm alive," Malone said, smiling down with a painted face. "It took me a while to find you. You drifted a long way."

"It all seems like a horrible dream now."

"But some of it ended well." Malone looked over at Thorn Bird's body.

"I was lucky, except for this shoulder."

"I was lucky too, Many Wolves, very lucky," said Malone. "Let me look at your shoulder."

Malone inspected the wound. "The point went straight through. I can pull it out for you now, if you want. It's going to be painful."

"Let's get it over with. I want this thing out of my body."

Malone motioned for Many Wolves to stand up. "Hold on to my shoulder with your right hand, and hold on tight."

Many Wolves braced himself against Malone's shoulder and closed his eyes, preparing himself for the pain.

"I'm going to pull the point out further so I can break it off from the shaft. The rest of the arrow should then slide out easily enough from the other side. Easy for me, but not for you."

"Do it before I change my mind," said Many Wolves, gritting his teeth.

The pain was indeed agonizing at first, and Many Wolves fought hard not to scream. His eyes watered and he became light-headed, but then he felt the shaft leaving his body, and soon after, the excruciating pain ebbed to a more tolerable level. He breathed a little easier as he opened his eyes. His shoulder was bleeding freely now, so Malone wrapped it with a thin strip of animal hide to slow the blood flow.

"Ten Arrows once told me that the good things you do in your life earn you luck. Do you believe that, Malone?" said Many Wolves, still wincing from the pain.

"With all of my mind," said Malone, grinning, as he finished wrapping the shoulder wound.

"I know that Rojo is dead. And I think that Ten Arrows is dead too."

"*Haa*," said Malone in a soft voice laced with sadness. "But I spoke with Ten Arrows before his spirit left him. He was smiling, Many Wolves. He saw Soft Cloud reaching his hand out to him. I told him the fight was over, but that you were gone, and..." Malone paused, a tear rolling down his face.

"And what?"

"And he made me promise that I would find you. He somehow knew you were still alive," Malone said at last, his voice quivering. "Those were his last words: 'Find Many Wolves.'"

Many Wolves grieved for his long-time friend, but he was uplifted by Malone's story. *Ten Arrows is in a good place now. And he will always be in my heart.*

"What happened in the fight, Malone? How many of their men died?"

"Four of the Mexicans were killed and seven Nokoni. After Rodrigo was hurt, Paco rushed to his aid and did not fire at me again. He and another Mexican helped carry Rodrigo away—he was still alive, and his son was with them. Then, after Thorn Bird attacked you, Half Weasel and Fire Eyes were the only Nokoni still alive, and they would not fight me. They rode away—but they will come back for their dead friends, I'm sure."

Malone paused for a moment before adding, "Ten Arrows was brave. He had to face most of the Nokoni himself. I was lucky that the Mexicans attacked me instead. Your wolf saved me, Many Wolves. Without his attack on Rodrigo, the Mexicans would have killed me. I also found your shield with arrows in it, so Rojo's spirit protected you, too."

"I will need to bury Rojo, Malone."

"And we need to bring our brother's body back to the Penateka," answered Malone. "I will also return Thorn Bird's body to his people, out of respect for his father and the Nokoni."

I would have left his body here for the scavengers, thought Many Wolves. But perhaps this kind of respect for your dead enemies was something learned in villages; Ten Arrows had returned Laughing Crow to the Nokoni in the same way. Many Wolves admired Malone and Ten Arrows for replacing their hatred for their enemies with kindness and respect. And it was this same kindness in Malone that had saved Many Wolves's life. A great warrior with a giving heart was a valuable friend to have.

A High Place

Many Wolves and Malone arrived at their camp near the plateau just before darkness. The return trip over the Rio Pecos had been much easier than the first crossing, as Malone's horse pulled Many Wolves across on a log that was tied to the mount like a pole-drag. Thorn Bird's body was tied to the back of Wind Chaser, so all told the horse had had to carry the weight of two riders while dragging a third on a log. But luckily the river had receded quite a bit during the day without fresh rain to replenish it.

Many Wolves looked over the deadly remains of the battle with Thorn Bird's men. Bloated, lifeless bodies—both men and horses—were scattered all around. The stench of death hovered in the air like a thick fog.

Many Wolves immediately found Rojo and stroked the stiff body of the dead wolf. Then he broke the shafts of the two arrows protruding from the wolf's body. *Thorn Bird's arrows.* It was extremely difficult to see his companion this way. He could almost believe that the wolf would wake up at any moment and greet him with a wet, warm tongue and a wagging tail. "I will bury you in a good place, big wolf," he said. Then he covered the wolf with a sleeping robe he found on a dead horse and walked back to the camp.

Malone found Many Wolves's chestnut mount, along with three other horses, wandering near the big river. He wrapped up Ten Arrows's body in a Mexican blanket and packed it on one of the horses; then he did the same with Thorn Bird's body.

Many Wolves built a fire as the chill of night fell upon them. He offered a piece of dried meat to Malone and took a piece for himself. The Nokoni thanked him. Many Wolves couldn't remember when his dried meat had ever tasted this good, and he sucked the salty juice out of it.

"I would like to find a high place to bury Rojo. I want him to be close to the moon and the sun and the stars," said Many Wolves. "I want it to be a place so high that when he howls the whole world will hear him."

Malone nodded and smiled.

Many Wolves had lost so much, and he was exhausted after all that had happened, but the relief from Thorn Bird's death put his mind at ease. He hoped that the lingering memory of Thorn Bird's last moments would not give him nightmares; it was the first time he had killed a man face to face. True, he had witnessed Silent Weasel's death through Rojo's eyes, but this was somehow different. Back then, he had not taken life with his own hands.

"What do we do now, Malone?"

"We bury Rojo and we return these men to their villages," said Malone. He looked into the fire and then stared into Many Wolves's eyes. "And one more thing."

"What?"

"Ninakabaru."

"What about her?"

"I think she would be happier in your lodge than any Nokoni's lodge. Is that what you want?"

"*Haa*," said Many Wolves, without hesitation. "But I don't know if she wants to live in my lodge."

"When we return Thorn Bird's body, we will see what she says," said Malone. A calm smile fell over his face. "You should get some sleep, my friend."

Many Wolves nodded and then yawned. He was tired. He lay back on his sleeping robe and stared at the cloudy sky, thinking of Ninakabaru, imagining what she would say and hoping that these thoughts would blot out the flashing memories of Thorn Bird's killing. It was a warm feeling on a cold night.

The next day, the sun woke Many Wolves later in the morning than usual. Malone was already packing the horses.

"You slept a long time, Many Wolves. Finally, the sun burnt through the clouds and woke you up." Malone had attached pole-drags to three of the horses and was tying one of the wrapped bodies to one of them.

"You made those?" said Many Wolves, pointing to one of the pole-drags. He crawled out of his sleeping robe and slowly stood up on his bad leg. Both his leg and his shoulder were sore and stiff. The left side of his body was in bad shape.

Malone laughed and nodded. "Unlike you, I was up with the sun. We have a long journey, and these will make it easier to carry the bodies. I wrapped the men's weapons with their bodies. The *Noomah* will want them for the burial ceremonies. I also collected all the Nokoni arrows I could find. I kept some and left the rest for you." Malone pointed to ground where the arrows were. "If you want any of the Mexican weapons, you should take them off the bodies."

"I don't want any of their weapons, but I will take those arrows," said Many Wolves. He walked over to pick up the arrows Malone left for him. After depositing the better ones in his quiver, he relieved his bladder, then limped over to the river and drank some water.

"We should go. These bodies aren't getting any fresher," said Malone.

Many Wolves packed his supplies onto his chestnut pony. Malone had tied two of the other horses to his own horse, and he'd tied the other to Many Wolves's horse.

"We can carry Rojo with that last pole-drag, and then we can use it for extra supplies after we bury him," said Malone.

Many Wolves gingerly got his stiff body onto his horse, with Malone's help, and then his friend mounted Wind Chaser.

They rode over to where Rojo lay, and Malone tied the wolf to the last pole-drag, insisting that Many Wolves not get down from his horse. Then they walked the horses south along the wall of the plateau. Many Wolves was happy to be leaving this death-place.

There was no easy way up to the top of the plateau as Many Wolves had hoped there would be, so they kept traveling east. At last they found a good spot: a mesa with a scenic overlook of the vast prairie. *This is perfect*, thought Many Wolves.

"Let's go up there," he said to Malone.

Once at the peak, Many Wolves carefully dismounted and walked to the edge of the mesa. The cool breeze brushed his sun-warmed face as he looked out over the distant panorama. The ground was like rock here, but there were plenty of stones he could gather.

"This is a good spot, Malone."

Malone untied the wolf's stiffened body, carried it over to where Many Wolves was, and gently laid it down. "He will enjoy many sunsets here," said Malone, and Many Wolves agreed.

As Many Wolves bent down to look at what was left of his companion, he knew that his friend's soul just wasn't there anymore. He stroked the wolf's coarse fur for the last time. "I would have died long ago if it wasn't for this wolf. When I think about all the times he was there to protect me... He must have saved my life a hundred times. When he was with me, no bears or mountain lions would approach. He could see and hear things I never knew were there. I will miss him dearly."

Malone knelt beside him and squeezed his shoulder, but said nothing. His presence was enough.

"I am glad you are with me, Malone," Many Wolves said at last, tears shining in his eyes. "Let's cover him with stones."

The two men gathered large stones and covered the red wolf's body. Because of Many Wolves's injuries, Malone did most of the work, but he insisted that Many Wolves place the final stone on the grave.

"His spirit will always protect you, Many Wolves. Always."

A New Sunrise

Two long days of travel through the prairie finally brought Malone and Many Wolves to the edge of Thorn Bird's village, which was much smaller than Crooked Eagle's. The horse herd and tipis were now in plain sight. As they approached, they strapped their shields to their left arms and held their bows in their left hands, though Many Wolves could barely even lift his shoulder. Riding a horse was also extremely painful on his leg. He knew he needed rest for it to fully heal.

The village dogs sounded the alarm as they approached cautiously, and some of the boys ran back to the village. Many Wolves wasn't sure what to expect. They would be outnumbered, but not by many warriors. Malone had assured him that Half Weasel and Fire Eyes would not fight them, and they were the leaders now. Malone didn't know if Paco and the remaining Mexicans would be here.

The villagers, mostly women and children, walked out to meet them. Only a few of the boys and two older men, around forty winters of age, were mounted. Some of the women wailed when they saw them. There weren't any men who looked like warriors or Mexicans.

"The tall Mexican woman in the middle is Thorn Bird's wife, Valencia," said Malone. "Her two sons are on her left."

Many Wolves examined the faces of the people. These were not the angry, hostile faces that had once tormented him, but somber faces of people in mourning. The people were quietly watching, except for the two or three women who were crying, covering their faces. He wasn't sure if the village yet knew of Thorn Bird's death.

They stopped their horses, and it was Valencia who spoke first using mostly Northerner words. "You have come to kill us now, *diablos,* while our men are away!" Her voice was loud and angry. "Where is my husband?"

"Your husband is dead. We have his body for you," said Many Wolves, calmly.

"You are lying, *diablo!* You are too weak to kill my husband! This is a trick!"

Malone dismounted and untied the two horses behind him.

"That is not his horse!" she yelled.

Malone handed the horse's lead to one of the boys and then remounted.

"See for yourself," said Many Wolves.

"It is a trick!" she yelled again.

One of the Nokoni men got off his horse and walked over to the pole-drag with the covered body. He was tall for a Northerner and thin, and his face was familiar to Many Wolves. He unwrapped the top part of the body, and then he turned and nodded slowly to Valencia.

She screamed. Then she walked over to see for herself. She looked at her husband's lifeless body and buried her face in the blanket. Distraught with sadness, she stayed there sobbing for some time. Finally she raised her head up, the tears streaming down her face, and yelled something in Spanish. Then she charged Many Wolves's horse, beating her fists on his leg and yelling. The thin Nokoni man ran over and pulled her away and held her, trying to calm her. Her youngest son was also crying, but the oldest did not show any emotion.

"If this is what you have come for, then you can leave," said the older man.

"We are not finished, Mocking Bird," said Malone. That name was familiar to Many Wolves from long ago. Malone continued, "We will take the *Navoonah* slave with us."

"Ninakabaru," added Many Wolves.

"She belongs to us!" yelled Valencia. "My husband gave five good horses for her. Are you willing to give your horses for her?"

"We have given these two horses to you and your husband's body. That is all we can give. I am not willing to barter right now," said Many Wolves.

"Go get the slave, Cold Raven," barked Valencia.

The oldest of her sons ran back to the tipis and returned shortly with Ninakabaru.

Many Wolves's heart was sad when he saw her. She was thin, dirty, and unkempt, and her body was cut and full of bruises. She had been beaten severely. She wore a ragged deerskin dress that was torn in many places. She seemed spiritless.

Valencia grabbed her son's knife and seized Ninakabaru's hair, holding the knife to her throat. "This is the woman you love, *taiboo?* She is less than a dog! Perhaps I should spill her blood now and end her miserable *Navoonah* life! Give me a reason not to, *taiboo!*" Tears were falling down Ninakabaru's face as Valencia held her head up.

Many Wolves did not answer. He felt the anger of a hundred suns burning in his chest. He dismounted, hung his shield on his horse, and pulled an arrow from his quiver, fighting the pain with every bit of his will. Then he walked closer toward her, dragging his stiff left leg. He drew his bow and aimed it at Valencia's oldest son. "If she dies, I will put an arrow through your son's chest. That is your reason!"

The youngest son ran behind his mother.

Valencia called out to Cold Raven and motioned for him to get behind her as well, but he did not move. He just stared at Many Wolves, frozen in the moment. His eyes were familiar to Many Wolves. *Laughing Crow's eyes.*

Many Wolves held his aim and then spoke in a loud, angry voice, "If she dies, Valencia, then Cold Raven will die. And then you, and your other son, and anyone else who stands in my way. There is no mercy in my heart for the people of this village! None of you showed me any kindness. You cut me. You beat me with sticks. You spit on me with the hatred in your hearts. You bled me and then left me for the horse flies. I have no mercy for you. I will cut down every one of you until I breathe my last breath! That is my promise to you, Valencia, and your village of hate!"

"Malone, do you stand with this *taiboo*, or is there still some Nokoni in your heart?" Valencia stared at Malone when she spoke.

Malone did not answer her, his bow at the ready.

"Why did you betray us, Malone?" bellowed Valencia, flushed with anger. "You turned your back on your people! I promise you this. My husbands will hunt you down in the next world, and they will kill you and peel the skin from your body!"

"This does not involve Malone!" blurted Many Wolves. "It is between you and me and your village, Valencia. Release her now or I will free this arrow!"

Valencia retracted the knife and pushed Ninakabaru to the ground in front of her, yelling, "You belong in the dirt with things that crawl, *Navoonah*!" Then she looked at Many Wolves and said, "Take her and get out of here. You would not be so bold if our men were here!"

With the few men you have left, Valencia, your village will be like an old, toothless mountain line surviving only until a pack of hungry wolves finds you and rips you apart.

Many Wolves walked over to Ninakabaru and loosened his bow, then helped her to her feet. He walked backward with his eye on Valencia. She instructed Cold Raven to lead the two horses with her husband's body to the village, and the villagers followed them.

"Can you ride, Ninakabaru?" asked Many Wolves, looking at her tearful face, her eyes cast down to the ground.

"You tell me what to do and I will do it," she said in a soft, quivering voice, just louder than a whisper.

He pulled her chin up gently. "Look at me. No one will be telling you what to do. You choose what to do. You can take this horse and ride away from here if you want. You are nobody's slave! Do you understand?"

She looked into his eyes, and he felt her warm spirit melting his heart. A tear rolled down her cheek and she said, "*Haa*. I choose to ride with you." Her eyes were dark, like a crow's eyes, and then he caught the tear with his fingertip before it rolled off her face.

Many Wolves smiled and captured her eyes with his. "Ninakabaru, I promise you that no one will ever hit you again."

"You are the only one who has ever protected this slave," she said, and then she looked down again.

Many Wolves returned his bow and the arrow to his quiver, then he mounted his chestnut pony, a horse which had no name. Malone got off his horse and helped Ninakabaru up onto Many Wolves's horse.

"We have a long ride to the Penateka village," said Malone, and he smiled as if reading his white-skinned friend's thoughts. Many Wolves grinned back, and then together they turned their horses and rode away from the gathered people.

But as they rode past the Nokoni horse herd, Many Wolves stopped his horse. He grabbed his antler horn whistle from the bag around his waist and blew loudly. Most of the horses turned their heads momentarily, ears raised, but one galloped from the middle of the herd toward him. *Elk Dog.*

The brown horse stopped next to Many Wolves and nuzzled him, nickering playfully. "It's good to see you, old friend." He stroked the horse's nose and mane. Elk Dog appeared to be in good health. *The Northerners know how to care for horses.*

Malone rode over to Elk Dog and tied him to a lead behind his own horse. "We are ready to go now, my friends," said Malone, laughing.

Ninakabaru wrapped her arms around Many Wolves's waist, and he felt her hair and body against his back. It was like basking in the warm morning sun after a frigid night. A single tear from her eyes trickled down his back and Many Wolves knew that saving her was worth offering his life. He hoped that tomorrow would feel like a new sunrise for Ninakabaru.

Return to Penateka Village

Many Wolves, Malone, and Ninakabaru rode their walking ponies into the Penateka village. Behind them, the rider-less horse pulled the pole-drag with Ten Arrows's body. It was late afternoon and the clouds blocked the sun, darkening the world around them.

Topusana seemed to know instantly that it was her husband's dead brother wrapped in the blanket. "No!" she cried as she ran over to them. She fell to her knees, sobbing. Stretches Like A Dog followed her and tried to comfort her.

Other women in the village cried when they saw Topusana. Some walked over to comfort her and her husband. The people of the village stopped what they were doing and surrounded the three horses that had stopped in front of Topusana. A hum of whispers fell over the crowd.

Many Wolves dismounted and helped Ninakabaru off the horse. He walked over to Topusana and helped her to her feet, then hugged both her and Stretches Like A Dog. "I'm sorry for this," he said, and then added, "He died bravely."

Many Wolves didn't know what else to say at the moment. He just wanted to be with them for as long as they needed him to be. He was trying to be strong, but it felt like an avalanche of grief was tumbling down on his heart.

He tried to think of something they wanted to hear. "No scalping knives or scavengers have touched him."

Topusana buried her head in Many Wolves's chest, still crying, and said nothing.

"*Ura* for bringing him back to us, "Stretches Like A Dog said at last. "I know it was a good death. I know he is not alone in the shadow land and he is happy."

Malone dismounted and greeted Stretches Like A Dog with a hug. "I'm sorry for you loss, my friend."

"*Ura* for returning him to us, Many Wolves," said Topusuna, looking up at Many Wolves, her voice nasal from crying. Then she turned and hugged two of the other women in the village, her two closest friends. She hugged Ninakabaru also and Many Wolves overheard her say, "I am pleased that you are back with us, Ninakabaru. Come with us to my lodge. Cooks Out The Marrow will take care of your wounds."

Ninakabaru looked at Many Wolves as if asking his approval. He smiled and motioned for her to go with them.

"How did it happen?" said Stretches Like A Dog, in a soft, emotionless voice.

"Thorn Bird killed him," said Many Wolves. "But Thorn Bird is dead now. My war with the Nokoni is over."

"That is comforting to hear. And I am grateful to the Great Spirit for returning you and Malone to us," said Stretches Like A Dog in a solemn, stoic voice. "I must go now and prepare my brother for the burial ceremony."

Many Wolves grabbed the forearm of Ten Arrows's brother and squeezed it affectionately. Then Stretches Like A Dog led away the horse that hauled his brother's body.

The somber crowd dispersed. Only the youngest children were laughing and talking now, oblivious to the sadness.

Crooked Eagle emerged from the retreating throng and approached them. "Many Wolves and Malone, please follow me to my lodge. I wish to speak with you."

The elder led them down the beaten dirt path to his lodge. Many Wolves saw that Ninakabaru was still visiting with Topusana and the other women. It pleased him to know that she could visit them when she wanted and for as long as she wanted, without fear of angering anyone.

Crooked Eagle asked them to sit down in his lodge around the small fire. Then he grabbed his pipe from a blanket next to him, filled it with tobacco, and lit it. He took a few small puffs to ensure the tobacco was lit, and then he closed his eyes, pulling the pipe away from his mouth. After a long moment of deep thought, he placed the pipe to his lips again and slowly inhaled deeply. He held the smoke in his lungs for several moments before letting it escape out of his mouth and nose. Then he passed the pipe to Many Wolves.

"Let the smoke fill your body, Many Wolves, so you will speak the truth from your heart."

Many Wolves took the pipe to his lips, slowly breathed in the smoke, and held it in his body, like Crooked Eagle. The smoke tickled his throat as it went down. He exhaled and coughed from the tickling smoke, then passed the pipe to Malone, who sucked the smoke in and out of his body much more gracefully than Many Wolves did.

"Thorn Bird's blood war is over?" asked Crooked Eagle, holding the pipe but not smoking it.

"*Haa*, it's over. His body has been returned to the Nokoni," said Many Wolves.

"Though he is my *Noomah* brother, I do not feel sadness in my heart for his death. It is good that his mindless killing is over, though we have lost a dear brother because of it. Thorn Bird's path was not the true *Noomah* path, and not all of his people followed it. We will help them if they ask for it and hope that the next leader follows a path of wisdom, not war; of life, and not death. I will ask the Great Spirit to show them this vision."

Many Wolves did not share Crooked Eagle's vision. The Nokoni were Northerners, his enemy, and the hatred he felt for those people choked him to the bone. They were not Penateka in his eyes. If they were, then why would a man like Malone turn against them?

"Many Wolves, what will you do now? Stay with us?" asked Crooked Eagle, looking at Many Wolves with his large, saggy eyes.

"This is not my village, Crooked Eagle. It will never be my village," said Many Wolves, remembering the time he was chastised for standing up to Proud Toad for beating Ninakabaru. "I do not wish to live in a village where women are beaten down like dogs and nothing is done to stop it. A village that judges a man's worth by the number of horses he owns or one that whispers behind a man's back because his skin is white. My village protects those who cannot protect themselves. My village shares the horses, and my village does not care what color a man's skin is. I have lived in my own village most of my life, a village of one, and I will return to that village after I help bury my brother. I mean no disrespect to you or your people, Crooked Eagle."

"There is no disrespect shown here, only our differences, Many Wolves. A village of hundreds has different needs than a village of one, and different ways of meeting those needs. When you lead a village of many, you will see this. When my skin was less withered, I saw the world through your eyes, with a vision much like yours. Age hardens the skin and clouds the eyes to small injustices—as long as the village grows and prospers."

Crooked Eagle drew in more smoke from the pipe and then offered it again to Many Wolves and Malone. Many Wolves declined, but Malone accepted his offer.

The revered elder asked the same question of Malone. "What will you do now, Malone? You have earned the respect of my village. I see you as a great leader for Thorn Bird's Nokoni."

Malone filled his lungs with smoke before answering, then handed the pipe back to Crooked Eagle. Once the smoke was exhaled, he spoke. "I do not wish to lead, Crooked Eagle, and I do not wish to live in that village. The mixed blood clouds their vision. Like mosquitos, they are drawn to the blood of their enemies, and when the blood runs dry, they find more enemies. I was once like them, but not anymore. My village is in the wild places, much like Many Wolves. I only wish to draw blood from the animals I kill for my survival."

The lodge was silent for a time. The only sounds were the crackle of the flames and Crooked Eagle's puffs on his pipe.

"Crooked Eagle, tell me about Ten Arrows's life," said Many Wolves at last. "I feel there is much that I still don't know about him, though he was my closest friend. My only friend for so long."

"Men like Ten Arrows are a rare thing, Many Wolves, like the white buffalo that roams the plains only once in a lifetime. You know that he had the gift of two spirits?"

"*Haa*, he told me that."

"Some of the men in the village did not understand his gift, but most of the women cherished it. They could share many things with him that they would not share with other men; in many ways, he was like a sister to them. He was as gifted on the back of a horse as any man in our village and his skill with the bow was unsurpassed. He always preferred hunting alone, for elk or deer or for the great grizzly bear, and rarely went on buffalo hunts or war parties with the other warriors of the village. He valued your friendship, Many Wolves, and spoke of you often."

Many Wolves was pleased with Crooked Eagle's kind words. "I will miss him. He saved my life more than once. I loved watching him ride at full speed and hit targets with his bow. He rarely let a sun set without practicing his riding and shooting."

"What the village loved most about him, Many Wolves, was his warm heart and his steadfast smile," said Crooked Eagle, smiling, and then returning to the comfort of his smoke. After another puff and a moment of thought, Crooked Eagle spoke again, "Many Wolves, will the *Navoonah* women, Ninakabaru, stay in our village?"

The question caught Many Wolves by surprise. He hadn't thought of what she would do. Deep in his heart, he hoped that she would go with him to his village in the wilderness, but it was her decision.

"I don't know, Crooked Eagle," said Many Wolves. "It is her choice. I'm hoping that Stretches Like A Dog will welcome her to his lodge if I ask him. Unlike Proud Toad, he will treat her with kindness, like he treats Topusana."

After some silence, Crooked Eagle spoke again. "She is a hard worker and will help Cooks Out The Marrow with her medicine. She is welcome in our village."

"You have risked your life to save her, Many Wolves. She should be in your lodge," said Malone, with an earnest look on his face.

"She will not have the protection and the friendships that she has here. This is her home, and it will be a happier place for her without fear of Proud Toad's beatings. She is no one's slave and will choose her own village," said Many Wolves.

"I'm sure her heart will choose the right village, Many Wolves," said Crooked Eagle, with a smile and a glimmer in his eye.

Two Bears

Dusk, and an unusual silence, fell on the Penateka village as the people prepared for Ten Arrows's burial. Many Wolves was standing outside the lodge where Ten Arrows's body was. Several men from the village had painted his friend's body in black, red, and yellow, and his eyes were covered with red clay. The bear claw necklace that he always wore around his neck was still with him. It was hard for Many Wolves to see him this way—with no breath in his lungs or life in his face.

"What will you do with his body?" asked Many Wolves, unfamiliar with the Northerner burial customs.

"We must prepare him for the afterlife," said Stretches Like A Dog in a voice that was deliberate and somber. He was standing next to Many Wolves and Malone. "If his body is not presented well to the spirits who guard the afterlife, then he will not make it to the next world and will float forever around us as a bad spirit. We must make sure that he is well equipped with everything he needs to live well in the shadow land, especially his weapons and one of his best horses. His friends and family will give him what he needs to pass on to the next world."

Many Wolves had never seen a burial like this before. He was too young to remember the death ceremonies from his Lipan village. "Will they bury him here in the village?"

"No, the burial ceremony will be in a place west of here. I will take his body, with the gifts the people have given him, to its final resting place when it is over. I have chosen a spot at the base of a mesa for this, where he will face east to see the rising sun, and I will cover his body with rocks. You and Malone are welcome to come with me."

"I will come," said Many Wolves, and Malone nodded in agreement.

Once the body was ready, Stretches Like A Dog lifted it up on a horse, with the help of two other men, and then he led the horse to where two bonfires were burning. Many Wolves, Malone, and Topusana followed the horse, walking with the beat of the two drummers, and seated themselves close to the fires, in front of the rest of the people who gathered. Crooked Eagle sat next to them as well.

Two men in painted buffalo robes wearing animal headdresses began dancing and chanting around the fires. Many Wolves assumed they were the village medicine men. They threw antler dust into the flames to stir up embers, and cedar to make the fire crackle. The two men imitated men riding horses and shooting bows as they danced, including yelling a victory cry after an imaginary arrow was shot. The drummers maintained a loud, steady beat throughout the ceremony.

Many Wolves looked behind him, and his eyes quickly captured Ninakabaru's face from the crowd of people gathered there. She was sitting with Cooks Out The Marrow and several other women. She glanced back at him and shot him a hint of a smile before turning away. He wondered what she would do now that she was free. *Will she follow me to the wilderness?*

The medicine men continued to dance to the music of the drums. Many Wolves's thoughts drifted back to Ten Arrows. It was hard for him to imagine a life without his friend. The loneliness—which bit at him like frost even with Ten Arrows's presence in his life—would have consumed him whole without him. He was thankful now to have a friend still in Malone. Otherwise, without Ten Arrows, without Rojo, and without any birds, he would be completely alone. It would be difficult, perhaps impossible, to replace friends like Ten Arrows and Rojo, and his friendships with Malone, and with Ninakabaru, were still as new as freshly dropped snow—snow that could easily melt and disappear forever.

The drumming stopped, and Stretches Like A Dog stood up and addressed Many Wolves. "Do you wish to give anything to my brother for his journey?"

"*Haa.*"

Many Wolves stood up and followed Stretches Like A Dog and Topusana, who was weeping. Some women handed Stretches Like A Dog a quiver filled with a bow and some arrows: Ten Arrows's quiver. Then they handed Topusana a sleeping robe. The three of them, Ten Arrows's family, led the procession to where the body was laid. Malone, Crooked Eagle, and others followed them.

When Topusana reached the body, she was crying. She bent down and placed the sleeping robe next to it. Then she whispered some garbled, sobbing words, and left. Stretches Like A Dog was next. He took the bow from the quiver, broke it, and left it next to the body. Then he did the same with each of the arrows.

"I hope you find friendship and good hunting in the next world, my brother," said Stretches Like A Dog, then he, too, walked away.

Many Wolves approached the body. He bent down and slipped the bear claw necklace around his friend's neck. "Now, you will have both of these great bears to protect you, my life brother." Many Wolves kissed his lifeless friend on the forehead, and then he followed Stretches Like A Dog and Topusana, who were waiting for him, back to their lodge.

The Resting Place

With only a sliver of light left in the day, the three riders arrived at Ten Arrows's final resting place. Stretches Like A Dog led them, with Many Wolves and Malone following. The body was strapped to a fourth horse that was tied to Stretches Like A Dog's mount. This horse also carried the gifts from the people who had said their final goodbyes.

"The burial place I have chosen is there on the other side," said Stretches Like A Dog, pointing to a large reddish mesa in the distance. The falling sun cast a bright yellow shine on the western face of the large rock formation and onto the golden plains of flowing grass that enveloped them. Soon the brilliant bright colors would be swallowed by the inevitable darkness.

The men rode around the northern tip of the protruding landmark and into its shadowy eastern side. Up close, Many Wolves saw that the base of the mesa was covered by loose rocks and gravel. Stretches Like A Dog rode over to a spot where a pile of large rocks had been arranged earlier in the day as part of the burial preparation.

They halted their mounts, and Stretches Like A Dog motioned for Many Wolves and Malone to bring the body to him. They carried the stiffened corpse, the remains of their friend and brother, to the spot where Stretches Like A Dog was pointing and lowered it carefully down to the rocky substrate. Then Stretches Like A Dog unpacked the bundle that held the people's gifts—weapons, medicine and food bags, some extra clothing, and a sleeping robe—and carefully arranged them around the body.

While Malone comforted the horse, Stretches Like A Dog removed the bridle, reins, and riding pad from it and placed them on the ground. He pulled a knife from his sheath and then looked over at Malone, who nodded back to him while caressing the horse. Keeping the knife hidden from the horse's view, Stretches Like A Dog quickly raised it as he approached the animal and cut its throat in one swift motion. The animal screamed and collapsed at Malone's feet, breathing hard, choking on its blood.

It was difficult for Many Wolves to watch this brutal act against a harmless creature, so he quickly turned away, but he understood why the men had to do it.

When the snorting breaths stopped, Many Wolves looked back at the dying animal, but it was silent and the life had left its eyes.

Stretches Like A Dog cleaned the blood off his knife. Then he pulled the hair on the left side of his head taut, and he cut it off with his knife. He sprinkled the loose hair over the body and said, "Let's cover the bodies."

The wavering in his voice told Many Wolves that this burial ritual was extremely difficult for him.

Many Wolves helped the other two men cover the bodies with the stones from the pile. Stretches Like A Dog made sure that his brother's body was completely covered, and the rest of the stones were used to conceal most of the dead horse. Once all the stones were stacked on the bodies, Stretches Like A Dog rearranged a few of them to his liking until finally he was satisfied with the grave. Then he looked up to the sky and sang a song for his brother.

Many Wolves closed his eyes for a few moments and imagined it was daylight.

From the rings of the sun appeared a great bird, the Cloud Eagle, falling down from the sky, its talons dangling below it as it twisted and turned with the wind. It fell, circling, getting closer and bigger until finally it swept past the body of his friend and snatched his soul with its powerful yellow talons. It pumped its wings and screamed, as if to announce to the next world that a new life was coming, then carried the soul upward in a growing spiral. Eventually, the screams faded into the blue sky and the great bird flew into the dazzling sun.

When Stretches Like A Dog finished his song, Many Wolves opened his eyes to the impending darkness and heard the screeching nighthawks darting around him like strange spirits of the night. Perhaps, like the Cloud Eagle, they played some part in bringing his friend to the next world. Many Wolves felt connected to them, and their lively spirits brought him warmth in this cold moment of death.

"My brother is journeying to the shadow lands now. His name must never be spoken again until our mourning has passed," said Stretches Like A Dog.

Malone approached Stretches Like A Dog and put his hand on the grieving man's shoulder, then looked into his eyes. "Your brother was a skilled and brave warrior. He earned the respect of men in this world as he will in the next. Many Wolves and I would not be alive if not for his courage."

"Our village did not honor him as you do, Malone. He did not join the war parties like most of the other men, though he had the skill to be one of our village's strongest warriors," said Stretches Like A Dog with eyes that glistened. "He did not feel he had to prove himself this way. He followed his own vision. His two spirits led him down a path that most men did not walk. Topusana and I will miss him dearly."

Many Wolves walked over to Stretches Like A Dog and embraced him, whispering softly into his ear, "I will miss him too, and his memory will shine like a bright star in my heart forever."

After several quiet moments, Stretches Like A Dog spoke again. "I am deeply honored that two great men are here to share this final farewell. I feel certain a spacious lodge and welcoming friends await my brother's spirit when the sun rises again. Let us return to the village."

Wildflowers from Ash

After a restful night in a lodge next to Stretches Like A Dog and Topusana, Many Wolves enjoyed a late morning meal of wild berries and pemmican with them and Malone. "Where is Ninakabaru?"

"She is staying in the medicine lodge where you were healed," said Topusana. She glanced over at her husband and smiled. "You should visit her. I'm sure she would enjoy seeing you. She hasn't spoken much since her return to the village. Her wounds have cut deep into her spirit."

"What will I say to her?"

"You don't need to say anything, Many Wolves, just be with her," said Topusana in a reassuring voice. "The wounds to her spirit will take a long time to heal. From the ash of a prairie fire, the wildflowers eventually grow. So will her spirit."

"Your visit will lift her spirits, Many Wolves," said Malone, pushing him to his feet in a playful way.

"Malone is right. She doesn't have many friends," added Topusana.

Many Wolves rose to his feet, and a nervous chill ran through his body. *What if she doesn't want to see me? What if I don't know what to say?* Facing an enemy village with his bow drawn seemed much less stressful on his nerves than this. He took a deep breath and then said, "I feel nervous, like a hunter stalking dangerous prey."

The three of them laughed.

"Your teasing is not helping to calm my fragile nerves!" said Many

Wolves, feeling flushed and a little light-headed.

"Just go, Red Face! And don't trip on that rock!" said Malone.

Just as Malone said that, Many Wolves stumbled, but caught himself from falling. Then he laughed with them and limped away.

Many Wolves met Cooks Out The Marrow standing at the entrance to the healing lodge.

"Can I see her?" Many Wolves said, his voice trembling.

The old medicine woman's head barely reached his chest; her height was lessened by her hunch. She looked up at him and smiled. "*Haa*, you can see her. She is awake now."

He entered the lodge and found Ninakabaru resting on a sleeping robe on her side. She sat up when she saw him, squinting from pain. She was dressed in a deerskin top, tied with leather in the back, and a plain deerskin skirt. Her hair was well groomed, combed, and oiled. The dirt on her body and face was gone, so now the bruises and cuts were more prevalent. Many Wolves hadn't realized that her wounds were this bad.

"Hello," she said in a subdued voice.

The sound of her voice calmed his nervousness some. He crouched down. "Hello, Ninakabaru. How are you feeling?"

"I'm tired. It's not so bad."

"I didn't realize they did all this to you. The dirt covered most of it."

"My skin is thick and tough like a buffalo."

Many Wolves thought to himself how true this must be, knowing that Proud Toad had shown her no kindness for so long, only the back of his hand or the end of a stick. It was hard for him to imagine a life of this kind of cruelty from people in her village who were not her enemies. His torture at the hands of the Nokoni had lasted only a short time; hers had lasted a lifetime.

"Cooks Out The Marrow is taking good care of me."

Many Wolves nodded without speaking. He was still feeling nervous and was unsure what to say as the silence fell upon them like a thick fog. Her eyes were fleeting, like a butterfly avoiding capture, but when they met his, he felt a tingling warmth, like a sunbeam burning into his heart. Only her eyes burned him like this.

Ninakabaru broke the silence at last. "Many Wolves, I misjudged you because I did not see your heart, only your skin."

He heard a quiver in her voice, and she brushed the hair out her eyes with her hand more frequently than he remembered before. *She is as nervous as I am.*

"When I was growing up, my family taught me not to trust the white-skinned people. They said that white-skinned people were cruel and greedy and only wanted to take our land from us. They said the white-skinned men were lazy, too lazy to clean the hair from their faces, and that they smelled like dirty dogs. Proud Toad also shared these beliefs. He didn't understand why Crooked Eagle let you live with us."

"Why did Proud Toad let you heal me?"

"He bartered my work for food and other things he wanted from Cooks Out The Marrow's family. He wanted me to poison your wounds, but I would not do it, so he beat me and he poisoned my thoughts about white-skinned people."

"It's his heart that is poisoned. There is no kindness in it," said Many Wolves, anger in his voice.

Ninakabaru looked at him, and tears welled up in her eyes. "I had never met a *taiboo* before, so I covered my heart with the thickest of hides to protect myself from you because I did not see your heart, only your skin."

"Ninakabaru, I am white, but I am not from the white man's world. I don't know the white man's tongue. A part of me is *Noomah* and I speak the *Noomah* words." Many Wolves shifted to speaking to Lipan words. "And a part of me is *Navoonah*. I speak their words as well. There are no white man's words on my tongue and no white man's thoughts in my head."

"I know that now, Many Wolves, but I misjudged you, and I am sorry." Tears streamed down her face as she blurted out her words. "No one has ever stood up for me like you did with Proud Toad, and no one protected me like you did at the Nokoni village. I thought to myself, why is he doing this? Why does he protect me? My skin is blistered and scarred and I have had hate in my heart for you. Your name is spoken in stories, and mine is spoken only in disrespect. I can only think that your heart is so kind that it pities my ugly life."

Many Wolves was shaken by what she said, but he knew these words came from her heart. It was the first time he could remember her speaking this way. He wanted to touch her, to hold her, to comfort her, but he was afraid. Her body and her spirit were wounded, and he wanted to tread carefully, remembering what Topusana had said. He did not want to bring her any more pain.

"You have been kind to me, Ninakabaru. Don't forget that you cared for me when I was bloodied and helpless, though you despised my white skin. I have been abused and cast out in my life, too; perhaps I felt a shared spirit with you. It's hard for me to watch the strong prey on the weak just to show strength or to bring fear. With animals, there is always a purpose for aggression— hunger, protecting offspring, guarding a territory. It is hard for me to understand sometimes why people are different."

Many Wolves took a deep breath. It felt good to talk this way. It was relaxing for him, and his words seemed to calm her. He wanted to say more. He wanted to tell her that she was different from the other women in the village. How her touch melted his skin and her eyes burned his heart like sunbeams. Her voice was like a whispering wind soothing him on a blistering hot day. He *wanted* to tell her these things, but he couldn't— because he was afraid she would not understand and would think less of him.

She was sniffling now, her eyes cast down, but she was not crying. She appeared lost in her own thoughts until finally she said, "Will you be leaving the village?"

"*Haa.* I don't know when, but soon. This is not my village."

"Where will you go?"

"Back to my home in the wilderness, where I have lived most of my life. Malone is going with me, though I don't know if he will want to stay in my village in the foothills for long. What about you?"

"Stretches Like A Dog says I can live with him and Topusana. Cooks

Out The Marrow has also offered a place in her lodge for me. She can teach me to make medicines."

Many Wolves was pleased that she had good choices. Stretches Like A Dog and Cooks Out The Marrow would not beat her, he was sure of that. As Crooked Eagle had said, she was a good worker who would earn her keep.

Many Wolves was pleased, but also scared. He wanted to be with her, and he knew that he could not stay here. Would she consider going with him to the wilderness? His village did not have as much to offer as this one. It would be a big change for her, like going from winter to summer, without spring between them. Though he could not reveal his feelings to her, he had to at least offer his village to her—although in a manner such that she could easily refuse.

He looked at her, hoping she would raise her eyes to his. "Ninakabaru, I am pleased that you are welcome here. You will be happy with either Stretches Like A Dog or Cooks Out The Marrow. They will treat you as family and not as a slave. I know this in my heart."

She looked up at him again with eyes that cut through his skin. Then he continued, "I am offering you a third choice. You are welcome to come with Malone and me to my village in the wilderness. I know it seems like a strange offer, but part of me believes that you might want a new village, a fresh start. I can always bring you back here if you don't like it. I don't want an answer now; just think about it, please, and let me know before we leave, which will be before the next new moon."

She nodded her head and smiled at him, but did not say anything.

"I will go now, so you can rest and get well. I would like to come back again tomorrow, if I am welcome."

"I would like that, Many Wolves," she said, smiling again. "*Ura* for your visit. I have much to think about."

He stood up and walked out of the medicine lodge.

Nina

Many Wolves visited Ninakabaru every day, and sometimes more than once, for several straight days. Her wounds were healing and her moods grew more cheerful after every sleep. They talked a lot about their past lives in their Lipan villages, because it was a comfortable, common ground.

And when there was no talk, the silence was pleasant, too—at least to Many Wolves. He made sure to bring an unfinished arrow or two to work on during his visit, while Ninakabaru helped Cooks Out The Marrow by mixing medicines or sewing. He enjoyed her company and he hoped that she enjoyed his.

"I think you should call me 'Nina' from now on," she said during one of these quiet moments, looking up from the beads she was sewing onto a moccasin. "That's what Cooks Out The Marrow calls me, and I like it now."

"I am in your close circle of friends?" said Many Wolves in a half-joking tone, smiling at her from across Cooks Out The Marrow's tipi. The wind was blowing steadily outside on this late fall afternoon.

"I guess so. Any mistakes in your behavior though, and I'm casting you back out with the dogs." She looked at him with a quick glance and a wry smile.

"The dogs aren't so bad. Remember, I've lived with a wolf for many winters."

Many Wolves enjoyed the banter. He sensed that she was fond of him, but still she hadn't said one way or the other if she was going to leave with him. The new moon was quickly arriving, and Malone wanted to leave before the frost began to bite. Many Wolves hoped that she would bring the subject up again, because he didn't want it to sound like he was forcing her decision. For now, however, he wanted to enjoy simple talk.

"I know, and that brown dog follows you around like a second shadow," said Ninakabaru in a muffled voice, holding a piece of sinew in place with her mouth.

She was right. Many Wolves had befriended one of the dogs in the village, and now they had become friends. He had felt sorry for the dog because it was weak and thin and did not win battles for scraps with the stronger dogs.

"I think you should spend more time with dogs," Many Wolves said. "They make excellent friends. They are loyal and protective and will never turn their back on you. Your inner circle of friends can grow even larger with a few dogs in it."

Ninakabaru laughed. "Well, I'm sure they make good friends, but most of them smell bad and their fur is full of ticks and other bugs that will eat you alive."

Many Wolves believed that many of the villagers felt the same way as Nina about dogs—that they were dirty, insect-ridden nuisances. And it was true that most of the dogs in the village were untamed scavengers. But that was only because the villagers hadn't taken the time to tame them properly. Their time was spent with the horse herd instead. He doubted than any of the villagers had ever had a companion like Rojo.

"Your silence says that you agree with me," she said, dropping another glance his way.

"I can see why you feel the way you do, looking at the dogs in this village," Many Wolves said, conceding. "But if you knew my wolf, Rojo, then you would be more accepting of dogs. I am certain of this."

"Well, it depends on his smell... and the bugs on him."

Many Wolves laughed. Ninakabaru was stubborn and held firm to her beliefs like an old oak in a violent windstorm. He understood why she had been given the name Ninakabaru, which meant "one who refuses" in the *Noomah* language.

Just then, Cooks Out The Marrow walked in through the door flap.

Ninakabaru reacted in a panic, trying to hide the moccasin she was making from the old medicine woman. She grabbed a piece of deerskin and pretended to be working on that instead.

"I can boil some buffalo flank for you two if you're hungry," said Cooks Out The Marrow. "Malone keeps bringing fresh meat to my lodge from his hunts, so there is plenty to eat."

"That sounds good," said Ninakabaru.

"With your secret spices added, I hope," said Many Wolves. He loved Cooks Out The Marrow's cooking. She liked to experiment with different spices and flavors, and all of it tasted good to him.

"Of course, Many Wolves," Cooks Out The Marrow chuckled.

He also loved to watch her eyes squint when she laughed.

"Then I'll have a little bit please." He felt his mouth watering already.

"So I guess I should make enough for five, even though there's only three of us," said Cooks Out The Marrow, who had figured out quickly that Many Wolves had a bear-sized appetite. "There is rarely any meat left over when you're eating with us, Many Wolves. Just keep your shadow away from my cooking fire."

"I know; I keep forgetting that it's bad luck," said Many Wolves.

"Typical white-skin, always roaming where you shouldn't," mumbled Ninakabaru, teasing him.

Cooks Out The Marrow left the tipi and began preparing her meal.

"Why did you hide that moccasin from her?" said Many Wolves.

"It's a surprise gift I'm making for her," said Ninakabaru. "I need to finish it before you leave."

"Why does it matter when I leave?"

"Because I'm going with you."

"You are?" Many Wolves's heart skipped a beat.

"*Haa*, you said I could go with you. Are you taking your words back?"

"No. I just didn't know you had decided. You never told me."

"I won't be a burden to you, right?"

Many Wolves laughed. "No, I want you to come. I am happy you are coming." He was so elated that he was stumbling over his words.

She looked at him with a serious look. "I can't stay here, Many Wolves. Every day that I see Proud Toad, it brings back all the painful memories that I want to forget. I need to leave here. I'll try not to be a burden to you."

"I am happy you are coming with us, Nina. I want you to wash those memories away forever," said Many Wolves. "We can leave after two sleeps?"

"*Haa*. I will be ready then."

Many Wolves couldn't have stopped smiling even if he'd wanted to. "Malone has been ready to leave for a while now, and we need to get my camp ready for winter. There is a lot to do. I need to go tell him."

Many Wolves floated like a feather as he stepped out of Cooks Out The Marrow's lodge.

Going Home

The day had finally arrived to leave the Penateka village. Many Wolves, Malone, and Ninakabaru had packed four horses with supplies for their trip and had just finished a light early morning meal at Stretches Like A Dog's lodge. A few of the villagers gathered around them to say goodbye, including Cooks Out The Marrow and Crooked Eagle.

"May the journey to your wilderness village be safe," said Crooked Eagle to the three travelers, who were standing next to him with horse leads in their hands. "You are always welcome here if you need protection or help of any kind, my friends."

The venerable old leader hugged each of them.

"*Ura*, Crooked Eagle, for welcoming us and letting us stay here," said Many Wolves, looking into his craggy face. The Penatekas were blessed to have a wise and generous leader like Crooked Eagle, Many Wolves thought. In many ways, he reminded Many Wolves of Walking Free.

"I must go now. My duties on the peace council call to me," said Crooked Eagle, smiling at them one last time before walking away.

Cooks Out The Marrow approached them and hugged Ninakabaru. "*Ura* for these moccasins, Nina. They will keep my feet warm for many winters." Looking over Ninakabaru's shoulder at Many Wolves, she said, "You take good care of her, Many Wolves."

Many Wolves nodded and smiled back at her.

When she was finished hugging Ninakabaru, the old medicine woman turned to Malone. "*Ura* for the buffalo meat and skins. I am ready for the winter now."

"Hunting is the easy part," said Malone. "The work you and Ninakabaru do—scraping the skins and drying the meat—is much more difficult. *Ura* for the pemmican. It should last us through most of the winter."

"It was the least I could do," said Cooks Out The Marrow in her old, crackly voice. She looked at Many Wolves and Malone with her wizened eyes. "You are kind men with good hearts. I would not let Nina go with you if this were not so. Come back and visit us when you can. Nina is like a daughter to me, and I don't want her to be a stranger."

"If she does not like life in the wild, we will be back sooner than you think," said Many Wolves, grinning and glancing at Ninakabaru. "We will visit when the grass is green again and you have returned from your winter camp."

Cooks Out The Marrow laughed, straining her breathing a bit. "With the attention of two handsome warriors, she is the envy of many of the village women. I'm sure she will not have too many complaints."

"*Ura* for healing her, Cooks Out The Marrow."

"It is my work, Many Wolves. Work that I love."

The medicine woman left, leaving the travelers alone with Stretches Like A Dog and Topusana.

Stretches Like A Dog clasped forearms with Many Wolves and drew him into an embrace. "Be safe, my brother, and *ura* for bringing my brother back to us." Then he pulled away and looked into Many Wolves's eyes. "Don't be a stranger. Visit us when you can. I don't want the village dogs barking at my brother as if he was a stranger."

"*Ura* for treating us like family," said Many Wolves, "and thank you for the extra horses."

Stretches Like A Dog looked over at Malone and shook his forearm. "You should thank Malone for the horses; he traded us the spoils of his buffalo hunts for them. Our winter stores are secure because of this man."

Malone smiled back at Stretches Like A Dog. "It was a better trade for us because your heart is generous."

Topusana hugged Malone and Ninakabaru and said her goodbyes, and then she approached Many Wolves. Tears were falling from her eyes. She hugged him for several moments without saying anything, and then she whispered softly into his ear, "Remember what I taught you and what I said about the wildflower."

"I will," he whispered back to her.

She walked back and put her arm around her husband.

"You better go now before she floods the village with her tears," said Stretches Like A Dog, smiling at his wife. "I think that little brown dog wants to go with you too, Many Wolves."

The small brown dog who had been following Many Wolves around the village was lying next to the lodge. He had been watching them the whole time, his tongue dangling from his mouth.

The three of them mounted their horses and Many Wolves said, "The wilderness is no place for a small dog." He remembered too well what had happened to Amarillo when he was a boy. "Let's go, Elk Dog."

They waved goodbye to their Penateka family and together the three of them rode off westward. The little brown dog followed them out of the village, but Many Wolves instructed one of the village boys to hold him so he couldn't follow them any farther.

If he had been leaving alone, Many Wolves might have thought differently about taking on a new animal companion. But he was not alone. He had a loyal friend in Malone, and he had a woman he loved.

The Cleansing Rain

The rain clouds crept up on them with the silence of a snake. Many Wolves felt the droplets quickly turn to hard rain, pelting his face and body, forcing him to brush away the drops that swarmed his eyes. Ninakabaru was gathering hickory nuts and acorns with him for their winter store. Several days had passed since he had felt the first chill in the air. *Winter will be here soon.*

"We'd better get back to the camp." he said, shouting to be heard above the pounding rain.

Ninakabaru nodded and then handed him one of the two bags full of nuts. The Gray Face camp was still a good distance away, and they would be racing against the darkness without their horses to carry them swiftly.

"I felt the rain in my bones, so I brought my robe," she said, raising her voice as well.

"My bones didn't feel anything," he shouted back, smiling.

"Here, we can share this. Wrap it around your head. It will keep the rain out of our face." She unwrapped the buffalo robe from around her shoulders and offered half of it.

Many Wolves didn't mind the rain. He enjoyed its cleansing powers, but he took the robe anyway and wrapped it over his head. He did not object because he knew that sharing the robe would bring him closer to her.

They plodded back to camp along a path that was quickly turning from dirt to mud. Time had healed the pain in his leg and his shoulder, leaving only a little stiffness. He felt oblivious to the wet world around him. He was alone with Ninakabaru in their cozy little cave under her robe.

A moon had passed since they had arrived at the Gray Face camp with Malone, and with each sleep Many Wolves felt his friendship with Ninakabaru growing. There was little physical touching between them because he did not want to force it, but he felt her touch through her warm words and her blazing eyes. The bruises on her body, now mostly healed, still left a stain on her mind, a mistrust for men that he sensed from the subtle physical space she maintained between them. But despite this discomfort, there was also a comfort between them, just from being together, and they were drawn to each other's company like a hawk is drawn to the sanctuary of a clear blue sky.

"I love the rain," said Many Wolves. "It washes the dirt and dust from everything. It brings life-giving water to all the rivers and lakes." He stayed as close as he could to Ninakabaru without forcing her retreat.

"But it also brings thunder and lightning and floods."

"It's just the Great Spirit's way of getting our attention, like a crying child or dog that nudges a hand for petting. The Great Spirit reminds us that we live in his world."

"Proud Toad hated the rain. It always put him in a bad mood and made lots more work for me," she said, briefly looking up at him.

"He made you work harder in the rain?"

"*Haa*. He wanted a clean lodge all the time. The rain and the wind just made it dirtier."

"And he never helped you to clean it?"

"No. It was woman's work."

Many Wolves sensed her deep-rooted anger, so he remained silent for the moment, not wishing for the thought to linger. *Some memories will be hard to forget, for both of us.*

Most of the dirt had turned to mud and the light to darkness as the rain continued to pour. Their feet clopped in puddles as they walked, and then they began to play a game to see who could make the biggest splash. The game lasted until they reached the camp, and Ninakabaru seemed to enjoy it. Perhaps it took her mind away from her sadness, for a time. Many Wolves wanted it to last longer. Her sweet laughter was nectar to his ears.

Malone was waiting for them at the camp, his face glowing in the light of a flickering campfire and his attention drawn to the arrow point he was sharpening. The rain did not seem to deter him. He briefly looked up at them, smiled, and then continued with his work.

"You can do that in your tipi and stay a little dryer," said Many Wolves from under the robe canopy.

"I'm almost done with this one. A little rain won't hurt me," he muttered.

To Many Wolves, it seemed nothing ever bothered Malone. Sitting out in the pouring rain was just another small example of his calm. Even staring into the face of death, there was a quiet confidence, a grace under pressure, in his friend. Many Wolves had witnessed this when they had fought Thorn Bird and his men. Malone was like a great oak tree: freezing winds or flash floods could not shake his calm or make his mood unpleasant. And he seemed happier now that he was away from people, away in his wilderness home. Like Many Wolves and Ten Arrows, Malone enjoyed the solitude of nature. The wilderness was his village.

"We are going to leave you to your rain then, Malone," said Ninakabaru. "Many Wolves and I prefer a dry shelter. There is a bag of hickory nuts if you want some. Help yourself."

"*Ura*, Nina," he said, looking up at them, smiling, and then looking back down at his work, the rain drenching his face and body.

Many Wolves and Ninakabaru entered the tipi they shared to escape the storm.

Soaked, Many Wolves dried himself off with his sleeping robe. He then laid it back down on the right side of the lodge and sat cross-legged on top of it. Ninakabaru had brought a bag of blackberries inside, and she set it next to Many Wolves's sleeping robe before arranging her sleeping robe right next to his and sitting down on it.

Many Wolves felt a flash of heat rush to his face. Her sleeping robe had never been this close to his before. He remained silent and curious.

"You better eat some berries or your stomach is going to rumble like thunder while I'm trying to sleep," she said, cracking a smile. She grabbed a handful of berries from the bag and set them down on the ground. "Here, lay down and open your mouth."

Many Wolves did as he was commanded. She held one of the berries in her right hand, aimed it, and then tried to throw it in his mouth. The berry hit him in the chin, coaxing a smile from her.

"Nice throw," he said, picking the berry up off his robe and tossing it into his mouth. "Try it again."

She picked another berry from the pile and threw it at him, and again she missed, hitting him in the eye this time. They both laughed.

"You better leave the hunting to me," he said, enjoying every moment.

"Who says I'm trying to hit your mouth?" she giggled. "Let me try again."

This time, she leaned in closer. Her long, wet, black hair dripped water on his chest and then brushed lightly against him as she aimed the berry. She flung the berry at him, and again she missed, hitting him on the cheek. She burst into laughter.

She picked up the loose berry this time. "Open your mouth. I promise I won't miss this time."

She brushed the hair out of her face and bent down even closer to him, placing the berry gently into his mouth, letting her fingers caress the side of his mouth as she slowly retracted them. She didn't giggle this time, but smiled and stared into his eyes.

The heavy rain pounded against the walls of their shelter, masking the silence, masking the storm in his head.

Then she placed her hand on her heart. "Do you know what this means?" she said, gripping his eyes with hers.

"*Haa*. Topusana taught me what it means."

"I think I am ready now," she said with a tremor in her voice.

"Ready for what?" said Many Wolves. His heart was racing wildly, a trapped hummingbird inside it.

"Ready for you, Many Wolves." She leaned down on top of him and gently kissed his lips. She lingered there for several moments and then leaned even closer and whispered in his ear, "You must show me *everything* that Topusana taught you."

He felt her rain-soaked cheek rub against his and felt his body flood with warmth.

The rain cleanses everything.